# Frank and Stan's Bucket List #3 Isle 'Le Mans' TT

J C Williams

You can subscribe to J C Williams' mailing list and view all his other books at:
www.authorjcwilliams.com

Copyright © 2019 J C Williams

All rights reserved. No part of this book may be reproduced in any manner without written permission except in the case of brief quotations included in critical articles and reviews. For information, please contact the author.

All characters appearing in this work are fictitious. Any resemblance to real persons, living or dead, is purely coincidental.

ISBN: 9781794098138

Second printing June 2022

Cover artwork by Paul Nugent

Proofreading, editing, and interior formatting & design provided by Dave Scott and Cupboardy Wordsmithing

# Contents

Chapter One ............................................................. 1
Chapter Two ............................................................ 17
Chapter Three ......................................................... 33
Chapter Four ........................................................... 49
Chapter Five ............................................................ 69
Chapter Six .............................................................. 85
Chapter Seven ......................................................... 97
Chapter Eight ......................................................... 111
Chapter Nine ......................................................... 127
Chapter Ten ........................................................... 149
Chapter Eleven ...................................................... 167
Chapter Twelve ..................................................... 173
Chapter Thirteen ................................................... 183
Chapter Fourteen .................................................. 207
Chapter Fifteen ..................................................... 219
Chapter Sixteen ..................................................... 227
Chapter Seventeen ................................................ 241
Chapter Eighteen .................................................. 249
Chapter Nineteen .................................................. 261
Chapter Twenty ..................................................... 271
Chapter Twenty-One ............................................. 285
Chapter Twenty-Two ............................................. 295
Chapter Twenty-Three ........................................... 307

## Chapter
# ONE

"Frank-and-Stan's Cabs," announced Susie with a polished perfection. "Sure," she continued, bobbing her head as her fingernails rattled against the keys of the nicotine-stained keyboard. "That'll be five to ten minutes," she offered, with a generous smile down the receiver of her phone. Of course, customers couldn't see the smile. But it came through in her tone, regardless.

Susie's practised smile evaporated, however, now replaced by an apprehensive curling of her top lip. "Are you okay, Stella?" she asked, bravely... eventually... pushing her heels into the lino flooring, propelling her chair to a less-than-discreet distance of safety away.

Susie tilted her head in a moment of empathy, but the only response she received was the gentle caress of Stella's exhaled smoke across her cheek. "Only..." continued Susie with an admirable, stoic determination... "Only, you seem somewhat on edge, Stella. If, you know, you don't mind me saying so," she ventured. "Oh, and you should be careful with that knife, Stella. You really could hurt yourself. And what with you making me the official Health and Safety Officer and all... well... you know."

Stella removed the tip of a butter knife from under the nail of her index finger, examined it for detritus, and flicked away the small globule of unidentified matter thereon that she'd smartly liberated from her person. Then, addressing Susie, she lolled her head back, relaxing her lower jaw and her lips parting in the process — with her cigarette remaining steadfast, adhered to her lower lip as it was.

"Don't let it go to your head," Stella put forth to Susie, who was busying herself pushing her seat back to its original position.

"What's that?" enquired Susie.

"The responsibility of being a health and safety officer, Susie. Don't let the power go to your head— I can take it away just as quickly as I granted it."

Susie gave a half-smile, casting a glance to Stella's side of the desk at the smouldering ashtray festooned with the many remnants of cigarettes past, and stationed millimetres from a pile of paper invoices on the one side and several Kit Kat wrappers on the other. "I'll be sure not to," she replied. "Let it go to my head, that is." She nevertheless made a mental note of the office fire extinguisher's proximity, lest the need arise to employ its use.

"Is everything okay, though, Stella? You know, with you and Lee, I mean? I don't mean to pry, of course, but you just seem tense, like maybe..."

Susie's soliloquy continued on, but Stella paid her no attention, instead pushing herself into a standing position, and throwing a suspicious glance towards the portal window into the office next door. She tugged down on her leather skirt, which had ridden up since her previous toilet break, stubbing out her cigarette into the palm of her hand.

Susie winced as Stella twisted what remained of the filtered end into her skin without consideration to the red-hot ash, in what appeared to be a practised, fluid motion. The ashtray on Stella's desk overflowed, waging a battle to contain its contents with dignity — rather like Stella's leather skirt — and its contents increased further as the snubbed-out butt was dispatched with precision, coming to a rest on a quivering stack. If the contents had not been toxic and foul-smelling, this whole procedure may have made for a fairly enjoyable game, like Jenga. As it was, Susie was only concerned with edging the fire extinguisher ever closer.

"It's those two tossers," announced Stella, pressing her nose up against the cold glass of the aforementioned porthole as she stared — eyes narrowed — into the adjacent room. It was unclear if this was in response to the question Susie had posed to Stella or if, rather, it was simply a declaratory observation.

"... And one of them has just crawled back into the office."

From Susie's vantage point it was unclear at first if those in the other room could see their over-attentive observer, but as Stella slowly unfurled and extended her middle finger as if it were operated by a mechanical wind-up key, Susie made the assumption that eye contact had indeed been made.

Stella held her extended digit aloft for several more seconds, both for maximum effect and to make her intentions clear, before turning back to Susie. "What are they doing back here?" Stella asked rhetorically, not really requiring nor desiring a response. "They were supposed to have buggered off to the Isle of Man," she stated grimly.

Susie offered a conciliatory smile, for anything else could conceivably be considered dangerous in the response it might potentially provoke. She cleared her throat before responding.

"Well they do own the place, Stella."

"*PART*-own!" barked Stella, lowering her arm and pointing to her very own mug emblazoned with the words 'Co-Owner.'

"Maybe they just missed you, Stella?" Susie suggested. "After all, it's been a couple of months since you came back from the TT. Maybe they longed for your company. Longed for your company, as we all do..."

"Are you taking the piss?" Stella replied, eying Susie coolly.

"I would never," Susie assured her.

"Did they not tell you they were coming back, Stella?" Susie asked. "Stella?" Susie repeated, after no response was offered. "Anyway, I don't know why you're so anxious?"

"Private appointment, they told me," Stella offered up. "What's that even mean, anyway, *private appointment?*" she continued, but not directed at Susie, necessarily, but rather a rant in general. "It's rubbish, is what it is."

Stella picked up the butter knife, once again, and resumed the mining operation formerly underway beneath her fingernails, pacing back-and-forth like a caged bear as she did so. She stopped, mid-excavation, and used the blunt edge of the steel in a familiar manner to caress the shadow — or the stubble, as it were — under her chin.

"Maybe they're selling the business?" Stella advanced, coming to a sudden halt, and punching the wall for good measure with her ham-shaped fist. "Those two wet blankets are selling the business and trying to cut me out— That's it, I'm sure of it!"

"What? Stella, of course they wouldn't sell the… Would they?" replied Susie, apprehension drawn across her face. The apprehension was both at the thought of this prospect, as well as it was from the sight of the freshly damaged wall. Stella's might was indeed terrible to behold.

"The business has never been busier," Susie continued. "It's thriving, surely?" she said, struggling for breath. "Oh god, Stella. What would I do if they sold the business—?"

Stella, not normally one for overt acts of compassion, lowered her knife and marched towards Susie's desk. She gripped Susie's head and thrust it into her own ample, heaving bosom. Once nestled in place there, Stella stroked the back of Susie's head, making comforting — or that was the intention, at least — grunting-type noises.

Stella continued to stroke Susie's hair with one hand, and with impressive dexterity managed to expertly retrieve and light a cigarette, and all while retaining a grip on her knife as well. Stella could always sort out a fag no matter the circumstance, no matter the challenge presented.

"I've got your back, Susie," Stella commiserated, adding, in solidarity, "Not like those two traitors!"

… Over the years, Stan had become desensitised to Stella's peculiar ways. Positioned at the portal window, he nonetheless gave a bit of a start when he found himself caught in Susie's — imploring? begging for help? — eyeline, an eyeline which was at present partially obscured by a rather large breast flopped over the side of Susie's face. He shrugged his shoulders. No. Business-as-usual, he decided. No cause for alarm...

"I can't breathe," gasped Susie, now fixed into a headlock-slash-chokehold of the most compassionate nature.

"I know, I know, dear," agreed Stella soothingly, the grunting noises now turning to clucking noises. Stella was, by this point, now caressing the side of Susie's face. "But I'm not going without a fight. I can tell you that!"

"No. Stella. I mean I really cannot breathe. Please let me go."

Once released, Susie took in a lungful of air, but being in proximity to Stella meant that this air was contaminated — or Stella might say reassuringly and therapeutically infused — with second-hand smoke, and Susie burst into a coughing fit.

"Here, hang on!" shouted Stella, impressing her ham-hock fist squarely down between Susie's shoulder blades like a pile-driver.

The shock and pain alone caused the coughing to abate.

"You're welcome," said Stella, puffing her chest out with pride as Susie clutched at her back to locate any vertebrae possibly knocked out of place by the assault. Susie was in too much distress to have witnessed it, of course, though Stan, looking on through the porthole, remarked to himself that he hadn't thought it possible for Stella's chest to puff out more than it usually was already.

"Come here," continued Stella, walking towards the partition door.

Stan, oblivious to what was being said in the other room but terror-stricken regardless at the sight of an advancing Stella, instinctively leapt towards the door and gripped the handle, clenching it tightly.

"Open up!" demanded Stella, her thunderous voice easily permeating the closed door, and all but tearing the handle from Stan's delicate grip. "I just want to have a little chat with you is all!"

With no response, Stella placed her lit cigarette behind her ear. How her hair was not ignited was a mystery undiscernible even to Science. Stella used her two hands to exert more force upon the handle, which elicited, in response, a desperate plea from the other side of the door.

"Thhtella!" came a panicked voice. "Pwease dwop the weapon!"

Stella released her grip and looked back towards Susie, who yet retained a bluish *I've-been-choked-and-assaulted* tinge to her cheeks. "Is he having me on?" Stella asked of Susie. "He sounds like Daffy Bloody Duck!"

"Thhtella!" shouted Stan once more, in a manner which should certainly have left a trail of expectorated saliva on the other side of the door. "Whathhh thup?"

Stella moved to regain her grip. "If you're taking the piss, Stanley, you're going to need to have your plastic surgeon on speed-dial. I'll tell you that for nothing!"

Stan took a step back, allowing the door to open with a portentous creak. Stella took a step forward, her prodigious frame now filling the doorway.

"What the hell have you done?" she asked. "Just what the hell have you gone and done??"

Though Susie's scrutiny was obscured by Stella's bulk and she therefore couldn't see what was going on nor make out what was being said, she readied herself, certain that her Health & Safety duties would soon be deployed in Stan's aid. To Susie's surprise, however, Stella remained unnervingly calm. In fact she took the carefully placed cigarette from behind her ear and, after a turn, began to cackle. Her cackling became a belly laugh and progressed to the point where she could no longer stand up straight. At this point, she bowed down, her hands placed on her knees for support, her body silently quivering like a giant blancmange, finally offering, in the process, Susie a glimpse of a cowering Stan.

"Everything okay?" called Susie from her position of relative safety.

When Stella brought herself back up to normal height, she turned with tears of laughter running down her face. "Come and look at this bloody plonker," she insisted, pointing to Stan, panting and trying to catch her breath. "This is fucking priceless."

Susie lowered her first aid kit and moved, as instructed, to come look at the plonker — with Stella actually moving over to one side accommodatingly to afford Susie an optimum view.

"Oh, my," giggled Susie, placing three fingers over her mouth to stifle the less-than-polite snigger. "Are you okay, Stan?" she asked without removing her hand from her mouth, her voice slightly muffled. "I mean... *oh, my.*"

"*Ah-ha-ha!*" screamed Stella, struggling for breath. "Look at the state of it! The bloody state of it!"

It was unclear if, by *it*, Stella were referring to the particulars of the spectacle before her, or by Stan — the plonker — in general.

Stan raised his hands to offer a reply. "I thold you I couldn't thee you, Thhtella. I *thold* you you couldund come in," he offered, slowly, and with dribble running out the side of his mouth and down his chin.

Stella wiped her cheek of its excess moisture. "Oh, Stan," she told him. "You look like one of those... one of those..." she said, trailing off, and waving her arms up like she were throwing confetti as the word she searched for escaped her. She looked towards Susie for help.

"Like a trout?" suggested Susie, using her fingers, once more, to stifle a further fit of laughter.

"*Ha-ha-ha!* That's it... Stan, you look like a trout, is what you look like. What the hell have you done to your lips? You look like a right baboon's arse! Even more than usual, I mean. And in addition to looking like a trout," she told him, so full of mirth she was fit to burst. Truly, she thought, it was moments such as these that made life worth living.

Susie stepped in, sensing Stan's turmoil. "Have you had collagen in your lips, Stan? Is that what's... gone wrong?"

Stan took one pace back, likely to feign a denial, but his face was that full of product that his expression barely altered. In defeat, he shrugged his shoulders and lowered his head.

"Yeth," Stan replied, nodding. He lifted his head to reply further, but it didn't come up all the way. He rather looked like a bull that'd had its neck muscles lanced by a picador.

It was difficult to watch, if one had any heart at all.

"Yeth... yeth I did," Stan confirmed, showering them both with a fanfare of spit in the process.

"Is that..." asked Stella, pointing at the bloated remains of what once must have been a pair of lips... "a result of the private appointment you were wittering on about?"

"Yeth!" affirmed Stan, resulting in a further spray of spittle to decorate — or desecrate — Stella's polo shirt yet again.

Stella reached out and grabbed Stan's jacket — the one Stan was presently *wearing* — and used it to mop up the saliva on her shirt.

"And Frank?" Stella enquired, dabbing at her shirt without breaking her stride. "Has he been off getting cosmetic alterations as well?" Stella said, now letting Stan and his jacket go.

"No," Stan said, his head moving side-to-side, and now covering his mouth when he spoke. "He had an apointtthment of hith own — I was suppotthed to meet him back here. Hethe not been back?"

Susie shook her head 'No' as Stan grabbed his phone from his pocket, but there were evidently no messages to be had on the device.

"You look concerned... I think...?" suggested Susie, her eyes running over Stan's face, scanning it for any sign of movement and expression through the immobilised collagen-induced mask.

Stella's face — considerably more elastic, despite her several-pack-a-day cigarette habit — exhibited a flicker of enlightenment. "Wait. Is he at the doctor's?"

Stan went to speak but thought better of it this time given the condition of his lips — and their current spittle-projecting mechanism — opting for a nod of the head, instead, as an indication of the affirmative.

"And you didn't go *with* him?" chided Stella with a disappointed tut-tut. "You're like his *wife*, forfucksake— you should have *been* there."

"He thed he wanted to go on this thone," replied Stan, eventually. But as soon as the words came from his mouth, he knew exactly where he ought to be, regardless, and he fastened his jacket and legged it.

"You should have him up for that, Susie," suggested Stella to her, after a bit.

"What's that?"

"Sexual harassment, Susie. I'm sure that saucy bugger was blowing kisses at you," she chuckled, setting herself off once more. "Face like a baboon's arse!" she said, once again. "What an absolute plonker."

Stan pulled his vibrantly coloured scarf tight across his face as defence against the wind whipping in from the Irish Sea. It not only served to protect his expensively preserved skin against the corrosive salty wash, but also obscured the scale of his lips — which had fortunately, at least, by this time begun to deflate — protecting him from the eyes of the casual observer as well.

"Two coffees, please," asked Stan of the hardy vendor plying his trade in spite of the less-than-ideal weather. *Oh, bollocks*, said Stan to himself a moment later, an unhappy memory washing over him in a wave of regret, recalling the cup he procured the last time he'd stood at this very spot — a cup of coffee managing, somehow, to be at once both disappointingly weak and yet surprisingly strong in its unpleasantness of flavour.

The gruff fellow behind the mobile cart's small countertop produced said order a little too quickly for the coffee to conceivably have been made fresh-to-order, or even poured-to-order. "Four pounds," the man said with a clap of the hands for either warmth or emphasis, or perhaps both.

"Thanks," replied Stan, lowering his scarf, once he had coffee in hand, to take a cautious sip.

"Are you, eh, okay there, mate?" the vendor asked, in a curious dance of motion, simultaneously taking a step back but at the same time craning his neck forward in order to focus in on what was on view before him. "Only," he said, squinting his eyes. "Only, are you allergic to peanuts, or similar?"

"What?" asked Stan, coffee dribbling down his chin for lack of required muscle control. "No," he continued, wiping the overflow on his sleeve. He found, as he said this, that his cosmetically induced lisp had subsided, however. *Thank goodness for small favours*, he thought to himself. "I've had a collagen injection in my lips, you see," he offered the vendor by way of explanation, pointing to the lips in question.

"You paid?" asked the man, moving in for an even closer look. "Seriously? You paid?" he continued, incredulous. "You paid. You *paid?* To look like that? To look like *that*," he went on. "Come on... you're having me on, yeah? It's peanuts, then, isn't it? It's peanuts, then."

The coffee vendor tilted his head, from one side and then to the other, like a dog attempting to work out the origin of a strange, unfamiliar sound.

"I'll have you know, my fine fellow, it's all the rage," replied Stan, who was immediately annoyed at the lack of quality in his response. Stan flicked his scarf over his shoulder with dramatic flair and reached for his drinks, picking them up again. "In fact, you should get some collagen into this coffee," suggested Stan. "Might get a bit of life in it." Stan smiled, happy that he'd recovered somewhat with this second comment of his, and then set about going on his way.

"Here, mate!" shouted the chap over the noise of the howling wind.

Stan reluctantly turned back around, and was greeted by the sight of the vendor holding two sausages about his mouth. Stan was near to taking offence, assuming that... well, he wasn't sure what he was assuming. It just seemed vaguely offensive to him for some reason though he wasn't certain why. But then he noticed that the fellow was, in fact, placing the sausages around the perimeter of his mouth — one on the bottom and the other over the top — in the form of lips.

"It's all the rage!" shouted the man with a coarse, delighted laugh. "And I didn't have to pay a fortune to look like a prize plumb!"

Stan's retaliatory banter was, well, rubbish — with Frank being the more clever of the two of them in that regard — and so he took the constructive feedback on the chin, next to his drool, and carried on his way taking a mental note to never, ever, buy a coffee from there again. He also wondered if, in future, he might simply say that, *yes*, he *did* in fact have a nut allergy. Though he disliked lying, it was, after all, a fairly good explanation — and one, not to mention, that would generate sympathy as opposed to derision. *Hrmm...*

Stan didn't have to look too far before spotting a familiar mop of grey hair dancing erratically in the firm breeze. He stopped for a tick, not only to clear his mouth of spit, but to take a moment. He lowered his head, taking several deep breaths; a burst of nausea ran through him, causing him to rest against a black handrail. He looked over at the figure slouched on the bench, staring out to sea, and he knew that within the next few minutes his life could very easily be dealt a hammer blow of bad news.

"You know," said Stan, handing a coffee cup over. "This is where I found you the day you learned about, em... you know."

Stan took a seat, and, now he had a free hand, placed it on his benchmate's knee and squeezed. Stan took a cursory glance up to make sure it was indeed Frank's knee he was holding onto, and not a stranger's.

"These waves are hypnotic," replied Frank, with an *unsurprised-to-see-you* inflexion. "Anyway, I was thinking the same thing. And, if I'm not mistaken, you gave me a cup of pisswater that day also," Frank added, prising off the lid and peering into the cup's brackish interior.

Stan sat in silence, staring up the River Mersey, watching the marine traffic glide languidly by. He and Frank sat under the shadow of the Royal Liver Building, near to the Pier Head, where the Isle of Man Seacat would be called home to port.

Frank struggled with a mouthful of the fetid liquid before having no recourse but to pour the cup's remaining contents onto the pavement. "I'm sorry, Stan."

"It's all right, Frank," Stan replied, unsure if Frank was referring to pouring out the coffee, or to something else. "It can't be helped," he added, in either case.

"Do you remember Mickey Freeman? From school?" asked Frank, without preamble.

"I don't think so—?" replied Stan, after a moment's reflection.

"You do!" urged Frank. "Mop of red hair? Pasty-looking skin? He looked like the head of a matchstick."

Stan half closed his left eye, giving the appearance of deep thought. But it could just as easily have been the collagen.

"Mickey...? ... No. No, sorry. You've got me there, I'm afraid."

"You do," insisted Frank once more. "He pissed himself in Geography class!"

"Ah! Yes!" Stan replied, raising a solitary finger in recognition. "Why didn't you say so at the start? Yes. I do remember him now, poor bastard."

"Mickey Freeman," Frank declared.

"But I think it was History class, actually? Now I think on it," Stan said, smiling in warm recollection. "That kid pissing himself was the talk of the school," he went on. "And, as I recall, that took a lot of attention away from me, a lot less scrutiny of my... preferences in certain areas, shall we say. At least for a bit."

"Yes," Frank agreed.

"I should really look him up and thank him for that," Stan mused aloud.

"You can't," said Frank. "He's dead. Heart attack last week."

Stan's right eye half-closed, joining its partner.

"Yet you look pleasantly pleased by that revelation?" he proposed. "Judging by the contented grin on your face?"

"Not at all," replied Frank, replacing his expression with sombre contemplation. "I saw him a few months back. He told me he was training for another marathon."

"I'm not really sure what's going on with this conversation, Frank? Where this is—?"

Frank patted his friend's thigh before continuing his lament.

"Mickey looked twenty years younger than me, easily, when I saw him," he said. "Full head of jet-black hair, lean, and... well... fit. Well-fit. And healthy. He told me — in between star-jumps — that he didn't drink at all, he ate healthily, and bed early every night."

"Uh-huh?" Stan replied, not really liking the sound of this conversation, actually.

"Basically, the opposite of me," Frank admitted with a shrug of his shoulders. "He was pleasant enough," Frank went on. "But he didn't really hide the fact that he was in some way judging me. I'm not happy the guy's dead, don't get me wrong. But it just shows that you can eat well, exercise, and do everything as you should, but if the Grim Reaper's got his claws on you then there's bugger-all you're gonna be able to do about it. And then there's the opposite of that, and equally true — that you can eat shit food, smoke, and drink too much, and in turn outlive a marathon runner."

"In that case, Stella's going to be immortal," interrupted Stan.

Frank gave an easy laugh.

"Frank, I know the point you're making, I think. But in view of your visit to the doctor today... I'll be honest, I'm not being filled with confidence here by way of this convo," Stan offered. "Frank... Frank, what did the doctor say?" he asked, lowering his voice and dropping his head down, afraid of the answer his friend might very well give.

Frank increased his grip on Stan's thigh. "He said I've got two to three good years left in me."

Stan brought his hand up to his mouth. "Oh, Frank. I'm so sorry."

"Don't be. I'm not," replied Frank. "It's great news!" he said.

"It... it is?" asked Stan, confused.

"Sure. Although drinking that coffee you just gave me could have reduced that figure by at least a year," Frank said with a wink. "Look, Stan," Frank went on. "I'm heading towards my mid-sixties. When I first got this shit inside of me, I thought I'd be gone by now. I went into that doctor's office today waiting to be told I'd be gone by Christmas. Only he didn't. I'm telling you, Stan — and I think I've said this before — I'm convinced that our adventures over the last eighteen months have extended my life. I've gone from death's door, to potentially having a couple more good years."

Stan nodded sympathetically.

"Right now, I'm going to concentrate on living rather than focus on dying, Stan, and, who knows, they're bringing out new medicine all the time, y'know? So... I've got too much stuff I want to do. The charity is going from strength to strength, we're going to get the keys to the farm soon, and we've got a TT winner to prepare for next year's TT. I haven't got the time to die. I simply haven't!"

"I'll be right next to you for the journey," replied Stan. "All the way," he added, for good measure. "And death..."

"Yeah?" said Frank.

"Death can fuck right off," replied Stan, with a somewhat uncharacteristic, but healthy, dose of profanity.

Frank looked into Stan's eyes with deep intensity — like old lovers, reunited. "I wouldn't have it any other way, me old mate!" he agreed. "Come on," said Frank, pushing himself up from the cold bench. "I need to phone Molly and let her know how everything went. And my lovely former wife even dropped me a text to wish me well, so I expect I'll let her know as well."

Now standing, Frank stretched his arms out, taking in a lungful of the bracing sea air.

"Stan," he asked, turning on the spot. "Can I ask you a question?"

Stan, busy fiddling with his scarf, replied, "Well of course you can," with a sincere bob of the head. "Anything at all."

"Have you seen the state of your lips?"

Stan lowered his scarf, pressing his fingers to his mouth. "Peanith, Frank. I muthst have an allergy," he said, adding back in his recent speech impediment for comedic effect.

"You're allergic to penis, Stan?? Blimey, that's going to put a right damper on your—"

"I said peanuts!" Stan insisted.

Oh," Frank answered him, with perfect deadpan expression, knowing full well what Stan had said but not letting on — enjoying, as he was, winding his friend up. "I could've sworn you said—"

"Peanuts!" reiterated Stan. This ready-made false explanation was not working out so easy as Stan thought it might.

"Ah. I didn't know you were allergic to peanuts?"

Stan gave a *that's-a-stupid-question* laugh, before replying, "Well obviously I didn't know, either," he said. "Right up until very recently. *Obviously.*"

Stan pulled his scarf across his face, covering his deformity like a sort of Phantom of the Opera. "Here," he offered suddenly, gripping Frank's arm with sufficient force to redirect Frank's forward progress. "Why, eh... that is... Why don't we, em... go *this* way, instead?" he suggested, pointing out a new route.

"Uh... okay?" Frank answered him, obligingly, if somewhat confusedly.

"I know it's the long way," Stan proffered. "But, you know, it'll give us an opportunity to talk about our plans—?"

As they spun on the spot, Stan's eyeline remained fixed on the path he'd previously walked. What he saw, and Frank did not, was that the purveyor of putrid coffee he'd encountered earlier had followed him with his mobile cart, apparently eager to taunt his prey a second time. There he stood, not far away, with the aforementioned offending prop sausages at the ready, held up to his face in furtherance of another volley of abuse.

But Stan was willing to take a dying man on a detour, two miles through the freezing cold, just to deny this supplier of substandard coffee with additional entertainment.

"I went to Craggy Sally's grave today," said Frank, by way of conversation, and completely oblivious as to the true nature of their returning via the 'scenic route.'

"Oh," replied Stan, looking over his shoulder. "How was she?" he asked, barely listening.

"Yeah, she was wonderful. She asked after you. Did you hear what I just said?"

"Sorry, mate," offered Stan, tuning back into the conversation. "I went yesterday, myself. I left flowers."

"I saw them," acknowledged Frank. "And lovely they were."

"Cheers, mate."

"I told her all about Stella becoming a shareholder in the business," Frank went on. "And that she's got a boyfriend."

Stan smiled. "She'd be proud of Stella. Stella's not everyone's cup of tea, mind you. Well, hardly anybody's, to be honest. But... still."

"She's our Stella," said Frank, smartly finishing off Stan's rambling. "I know precisely what you mean. And we certainly wouldn't be without her."

"Truer words were never spoken," Stan agreed.

"Back to the Isle of Man tomorrow, Stan," Frank added, a declaration that brought a smile to both their faces.

"Hopefully we'll get the keys to the farm soon, also," said Stan, rubbing his hands together, either in gleeful anticipation or to warm them up. Or, again, with the cold weather, perhaps both.

"Assuming that smarmy bastard Rodney Franks came good on his end of the deal."

Frank wiped the seaspray from the mouth of the Mersey from his forehead. "We'll need help," he declared.

"With what?"

"The farm."

"Ah," replied Stan. "I think I'm on the same page as you there. Do you mean...?"

Frank's eyebrows rose in a knowing fashion. "Do you think they'll do it? They've got jobs, after all."

"We can only ask," suggested Stan.

"It would be good fun, wouldn't it?" asked Frank.

"It would be, at that. Frank-n-Stan's Farm wouldn't be complete without Dave and Monty."

Frank chuckled away, first to himself, and then including Stan.

"Frank, Stan, Dave, and Monty on a farm. Fucking hell. What could possibly go wrong?"

"What, indeed?" Stan chimed in, with the raising of an imaginary glass for a toast.

# Chapter
# TWO

The soothing illumination of candlelight danced off the tasteful French wall art, casting a gentle glow on the faces of those in the vicinity. Background music, loud enough to be heard, but not overwhelm, kissed the ears of the diners engaged in generous conversation who broke their gaze only to top up their wine glasses. The captivating ambience was surpassed only by the astonishing aromas emanating from the kitchen.

L'expérience restaurant was a staple of Manx cuisine, regarded as one of the finest eating establishments on the Island, and it was clear to the casual observer that romance was very much the order of the day on that bitterly cold Thursday evening. That is, it was the order of the day for all but Frank Cryer, who sat, head bowed, fiddling with an expensive-looking salt cellar doing his best to not look uncomfortable.

"Can I get you another glass of wine?" asked the petite waitress with an unaffected smile.

Frank placed the palm of his hand across the surface of his glass. "No, thank you," he said, but she didn't immediately move away. "Are you trying to get me drunk?" he added, painfully, filling the awkward silence for no required reason.

The waitress — Chantelle, according to her name badge — tittered noncommittally in a manner that suggested she was accustomed to such inane chatter.

"I didn't mean—" stuttered Frank, lowering the salt cellar. He ran his finger under the collar of his shirt, before continuing, "I didn't mean to suggest you were trying to get me drunk for nefarious purposes," he said, pointing to his half-full glass. "And I'm not, by the way. Drunk, I mean. And I've got a daughter who's probably older than you, so..." he said, laughing in an *oh-bugger-please-don't-stand-in-front-of-me-anymore* tone.

It was a natural break in the conversation, the laugh, and any normal, rational, reasonable person would have simply stopped talking at this point. But Frank was none of these things.

"I'm meeting someone," he went on, undaunted, pointing at the vacant seat across from him. "After all, I'm not some sort of weirdo that would come to a fancy restaurant on a Thursday night on my own. You know..." said Frank, gesticulating animatedly... "Sat there with a book or something, a sad, pathetic creature that..."

Frank's diatribe veered off suddenly, taking a bit of a tumble, as he recalled the smartly dressed businesswoman at the table — the table for one — directly behind him, where she was presently sat nursing a glass of wine, and reading her book.

"Not *you*, of course," suggested Frank, turning and pointing down to the aforementioned woman's book. "I didn't mean *you* were a weirdo, or, for that matter, sad. Or, *erm*, pathetic." He coughed sharply, hoping to expectorate the stupidity out of himself, for the sake of his survival. "I think it's nice that you're comfortable to come out, on your own. That's not strange," Frank insisted. "That's not the slightest bit strange. At all. Not the, *em*, littlest bit. Not..." he said, trailing off, and holding out his hand with thumb and forefinger pressed nearly together. "The littlest..."

The stylish woman in a navy-blue suit raised her right eyebrow, just slightly. "I'm on the Island with *work*," she stated coldly, looking down her nose, over the top of her book, as she addressed Frank. It was obvious from her manner that she considered it a profound imposition to have to even *speak* to one such as Frank, much less acknowledge his existence, considering him far below her station. She stared at him, hard, for a few long moments, with a withering gaze icy enough to coat its victim in hoarfrost. Once satisfied, she readjusted her position, and she returned to the private isolation of her book.

Though she had not spoken another word after *book*, Frank nevertheless heard the word *cretin* in his brain, loud and clear, as if directed at him through some sort of psychic telepathy.

"Ah!" replied Frank, with his hands held aloft. "Well I'm sorry about the *weirdo* comment. And the *pathetic creature* comment as well," he added, not-terribly-sincerely, his hackles raised at the woman's overly cold response.

The woman's eyebrow returned to resting position, but once again, Frank's inability to shut the hell up at the opportune moment overtook him. "It's a good idea," he offered, motioning towards her book. "It *is* a good idea. At least, with the book, people will know you're not a... you know... dressed like that..." he told her, with a cringe-worthy type of pointing-by-way-of-fanning-his-hand, to indicate her business attire.

"Will know I'm not a *what*?" the woman demanded, affronted, and rearing up now like a proud Thoroughbred.

Frank's collar was once again the subject of his finger's keen attention. "*Shit*," he whispered, looking to a still-present Chantelle for assistance, but met only with a shrug of her indifferent shoulders.

"Are you saying I look like a prostitute?" the businesswoman insisted, slamming her book — titled *How to Get Along with Complete Twats*, as it should happen — down on the table.

"I didn't say that!" maintained Frank. "I *thought* it, mind, but didn't *say*... Look, I'm sorry, alright? I'm on all sorts of medication, and.. you know. Well maybe you don't know. Anyway, *em*... Anyway, I'll leave you to your book, yeah?"

Frank turned back to his own table, fully expecting to be struck on the back of the head with the hard, well-heeled spine of a book. "I will have that glass of wine, after all, thanks," asked Frank, lifting his goblet in his disconcerted-yet-unflappable server's direction.

Back in the kitchen, Chantelle reported back to Chef Murphy. "Table six might be some time yet, Chef," she informed him.

"Depending on how long he chooses to hang on. Or if he does at all. Looks like he's been stood up," she clarified.

"Stood up?" repeated Chef Murphy. "How long so far?"

"I dunno. Forty minutes, maybe?" said Chantelle in reply.

"Excellent! And does this look like there could be tears, by chance?" the chef asked, rubbing his hands together eagerly, a gleeful sparkle in his eyes.

Chantelle shook her head. "Possibly. Very possibly. He's certainly a bit… unhinged? … Unbalanced?" she mused, looking for just the right word.

"I've got crying!" insisted a scrawny youth, in a Scottish drawl.

Chef Murphy doubled in bulk, like quick-rise bread dough, from his already considerable mass, and turned his fiendish, dancing eyes towards the dishwashing station. "Have you, bollocks!" he cried, pointing in the direction of the whiteboard stuck on the back side of the kitchen door. "You've got *taken-away-in-an-ambulance*. I've got *tears-at-the-table*! Chantelle's got… Here, what've you got, Chantelle?" he enquired.

"Are you still on that stupid bloody game?" she asked.

"The sweepstake is up to three hundred quid," Murphy returned, running his hands through his hair — hair which looked like it'd been trimmed in the dark, and by a one-armed trainee, and with kitchen shears. Which, in fact, it had.

This information as to the current monetary reward piqued her interest. "Three hundred pounds, you say?" she said, suddenly very interested indeed. "Well, then. In that case, I've got *drink-thrown-in-face*. But…" she went on, stroking her ear as she thought for a moment… "This guy could realistically have any, if not all, done to him tonight. He mentioned medication, and the woman behind him looks like she's about to trepane his skull with her stiletto."

"Show me!" Murphy cackled, fit to burst, edging towards the kitchen door with two kitchen porters, and with Chantelle and the owner of the Scottish drawl in hot pursuit. Five heads, looking for all the world like they were missing their bodies to those that might be observing from outside the kitchen — and stacked like a totem pole — then peered around the edge of the door and into the dining area.

"Him with the blazer on?" asked Murphy, glancing down with his eyes only to the top of Chantelle's head.

"Yes," Chantelle's voice whispered, emanating from the top of her head, and making its way back up to that of Murphy's.

"He definitely said he was meeting someone?" queried Murphy, sounding not entirely convinced.

"Yes. I told you that!"

"Nah, I'm not having that," proclaimed Murphy. "He's got those leather patches on the elbow."

"What's wrong with patches on the elbow?"

"Just looks to me to be a boring geography teacher or the like, the type whose breath smells of stale coffee. And so someone who wouldn't be meeting a girl, I shouldn't think."

"Maybe he's meeting his carer?" issued the Scottish voice at the bottom of the stack of floating heads.

"You could be right, there," Murphy nodded, catching his chin on the head below him.

They were silenced for a moment as they watched Frank look up to the ceiling in either frustration or desperation.

"*Ohhh,*" said Murphy. "I'm sure I saw moisture on his cheek. And his eyes look like they're welling up."

They monitored Frank's progress, as he alternated between entreatments to the ceiling and staring-straight-down appeals to the table, interspersed by regular discreet glances at his watch. At a certain point, Frank performed a new move — grimacing for a moment and clutching at his chest.

"Oh!" exclaimed the Scottish voice. "That wee man's having a funny turn! Should I phone an ambulance?"

"You'll do no such thing," chided Murphy. "He's only removing his wallet from his blazer pocket. He's fit as a fiddle, he is. Well, physically, at least, if not emotionally. Emotionally, he's having a bit of a wobble. Maybe, I should...? Yeah. I should definitely go and talk to him..."

Murphy removed his head from the stack of spectral noggins and tuned his ears into the romantic music radiating throughout his fine establishment. It was Adele's "Someone Like You."

"Ohh, turn that up," he said to nobody in particular. "This is a good'un, and a sad'un, and if he's been stood up by someone then that should be guaranteed to get the tears flowing indeed. And if it doesn't..." Murphy considered philosophically... "Then this fellow must be truly dead inside. In which case he's got far larger problems than being stood up by a date."

Murphy wiped his hands on his immaculate apron, offering a smile to the patrons enjoying their meal as he sauntered through the restaurant with a spring in his step. Presumably, he was figuring out what he would spend the proceeds of the sweepstake on. Upon approaching Frank, he replaced his smile with what appeared to be an attempt at compassion, but, with his shifty eyes, as well as the mood lighting in the room, it was difficult to know for certain.

"You having an enjoyable evening, sir?" Murphy asked of Frank. "You, eh, waiting for someone?" he added incidentally, indicating, with a grin, the empty seat.

"Yes. Yes I am," replied Frank, looking at his watch, and smiling, with one side of his mouth, to emphasise the point. Frank was uncertain as to why he was being quizzed in such a manner by the kitchen help. "Do you, *em*... do you need the chair?" he asked tentatively.

"Ah," replied Murphy. "No, no. Nothing like that," he said, while casting a quick — and unnoticed to Frank — glance back in the direction of the column of ethereal floating heads watching on with intense interest.

"Ah," said Frank, echoing the apron-clad man. He was not sure what else to say.

"Was it a first date?" the chef went on, helpfully. "Maybe she looked through the window, and, you know... kept on walking?" Murphy proposed, gesturing illustratively with his fingers to mimic either said date buggering off or the stabbing motion of two knitting needles — it was difficult to tell which, since repeated kitchen mishaps had resulted in the severing of several tendons in Chef Murphy's hands.

"What? Why would she...?" Frank began, alarmed at the chef's line of thinking. "I don't think..." he went on, but trailed off. He paused, attempting to work out, for a moment, why the chef in a packed restaurant was stood in front of him, quizzing him about his love life, or perceived lack thereof.

"*Ehm...*" replied Frank, after a pause. "It's our first formal date," he answered the chap cautiously. "But, not the first time we've been out. If you know what I mean."

"Sure, sure," replied Murphy instantly, head tilted to one side. "It's never nice being stood up, though, is it? Perhaps... maybe she's met someone else? Say, at work?"

Frank wore a confused expression, like he'd smelt a fart and was trying to figure out who'd previously owned it. "What...? What are you...? Seriously, man, what are you on about?"

The chef moved his head from side to side, smiling as he did so, as if to shake away Frank's concerns.

"It's never nice. Being jilted. Especially, well, at your age, am I right? You may never find another," Murphy went on jovially. He then raised his index finger and pointed it at the wall-mounted speaker. "Sad, this song," he suggested, brightly. "You're going to be okay, then?" he asked, now resting his hands on the table, but in a sort of tone which suggested he sincerely hoped Frank *wasn't* going to be okay. "I know the pain you're going through," he commiserated gleefully. "They say it gets easier. But, I'm not so sure it does. It really doesn't, does it? No, it never does."

Chef Murphy stood there, his broad, cheerful smile perfectly preserved. After a brief pause, he asked, "Is there anything I can do?" He gave a thumbs-up signal behind his back, for the benefit of those watching from the kitchen, to indicate that everything was going splendidly.

Mouth agape, it took Frank a bit before sorting himself out to an extent that he could respond. Eventually, he came out with a reply...

"You could find out where the waitress went with my wine, actually. If you don't mind. In fact, can you make it two glasses of wine?"

"Certainly!" Chef Murphy happily agreed, taking this to mean that Frank was doing especially poorly.

"—Because here's my date now," Frank finished, looking to the window.

"Oh," replied Murphy, clearly disappointed. "Oh," he said again, watching his world before him crumble. "Are you with him?" he asked directly of Jessie once she'd arrived at the table, before she'd even had a chance to remove her scarf. He asked this in a mixture of disbelief and despair.

"Yes," confirmed Jessie, waving over to Frank. She unbuttoned her coat, turning to hand it to Murphy, who she took to be the cloakroom attendant.

But her coat only dangled there in the air, because Chef Murphy had already buggered off, quick smart, returning, from whence he came, to the kitchen.

"What an odd fellow," remarked Frank.

A half-snort, half-cough could be heard, from the table next, from the smartly dressed book-reading businesswoman. Frank gave no reply, as he decided he well deserved it.

Frank moved, momentarily, around the table to ease Jessie into her seat. "I like your hair, Jessie," he told her, smiling awkwardly. "You really do look lovely," he added, for lack of anything more clever to say.

For a lady of a certain age, Jessie carried herself with a youthful exuberance. Women fifteen years younger than her would scratch eyes out for her complexion, a complexion, it must be said, which was complemented by her radiant smile.

Jessie took a generous mouthful of the wine that'd arrived, being placed on the table by the now-attentive server. "I'm so sorry I'm late," she said to Frank. "Were you okay waiting for me?"

"Of course, of course," he lied, not troubling her with any details. "Is everything okay?" he asked. "On your end, I mean?" he added, clarifying something, notwithstanding, that clearly didn't require clarification.

Jessie took the menu, running her finger down the page. "I don't speak French," she whispered to Frank.

"There's a translation underneath each description," Frank offered encouragingly.

"Oh yes! So there is," she laughed, releasing an infectious twinkle from her eyes.

Frank hadn't received a response to his earlier question, but, rather than repeat the query, he sat, watching Jessie nibbling her lip, deciding what she wanted to order.

"Anything take your fancy?" he asked.

"Everything! But I think I'll try their onion soup. It's very good, apparently, from what I've heard."

"Oh? What have you heard?" Frank asked inanely. Inane was what he was best at.

"That it's very good," Jessie reiterated.

"Ah," Frank replied sagely.

She continued thumbing through the menu. "This is our first formal date, Frank! And what a lovely venue to spend it..." Jessie said, trailing off towards the end, catching the eye of the woman sat behind Frank. "I'm really sorry I'm so late," she added, quickly looking back to her own table. "I was on the phone to that insufferable buffoon."

"Who? Stan?"

"Of course not Stan. Stan is lovely," tittered Jessie. "I was on the phone to Dave."

"Dave Quirk? Your son? Why, what's he done?"

"Oh, he's got some daft notion in his head. He's only gone and quit his job is all."

"What?" Frank replied, a wide grin spreading across his face like an oil stain on a rag.

"You're smiling?"

Frank tried to avoid direct eye contact. "Am I?"

Jessie leaned closer, lowering her voice to barely a whisper. "Frank, don't look. But there is a woman sat behind you glaring at the back of your head."

"There is?" he replied nervously, pretending he didn't know what Jessie could possibly be referring to. Then, relenting, he leaned forward himself to join the huddle. "I might have implied... somehow or other... who knows how these things happen... purely a misunderstanding... it's funny, really, when you..."

"*What?*" Jessie pressed.

"Well it's like this," Frank said. "I sort of... completely by accident, mind you... you know..."

"No I *don't* know," Jessie corrected him.

"... Implied that she was a prostitute. Somehow," Frank offered by way of explanation.

"A substitute?" asked Jessie, raising her voice slightly to be heard over the music. "A substitute teacher?" she said, confused as to why such a thing might have caused offence.

Frank shook his head and repeated, a bit louder, "No. That she was a *prostitute.*" He said this, unfortunately, at the same time as the music ended.

"I'm not a bloody prostitute!" bellowed the well-to-do voice from behind Frank's head. "I'm visiting the *Island!* With *work!*"

Frank didn't turn around. There was no need. He lowered his head like a naughty dog. "So..." he continued cautiously, attempting to change the subject. "You were saying... about Dave?"

Jessie's face was etched with confusion and possibly an element of fear. "Frank, what in...?"

"Look, I'll tell you later," Frank assured her. "So." He coughed. "Dave?"

"Yeah," she reflected. "He's got some notion about working in the great outdoors! He's quit his job for one with no prospects. I despair with the boy at times."

"Did he mention where this new particular job was, *erm*, particularly?" Frank enquired expectantly.

Frank coughed again. There was apparently something stuck in his throat.

Jessie looked at Frank.

Frank looked back at Jessie.

Jessie looked at Frank some more. "It's you, isn't it?" she said, finally. "Well, you and Stan. You've offered Dave a job on the farm, haven't you? And this is what he means by the great outdoors."

She'd solved the puzzle, like a Rubik's Cube, turning the bit into place. But there was no prize to be had for it.

"Another drink?" offered Frank accommodatingly, pointing to her glass of wine, a glass that was already all but filled to the brim.

Jessie laughed. "You and bloody Stan! I should have known! At least we know Dave can keep a secret. Because he wouldn't tell me what the job was. Couldn't get it out of him at all, the rotter."

"I asked him not to mention it to anyone till we got the keys. Sorry, Jessie."

She placed her hands atop of his. "It's fine. I feel better knowing it's you two crazy idiots that are employing him, at least."

"He's not the only idiotic buffoon we've got on board, either."

"Ooh... let me see," teased Jessie. "I'm a good guesser. And I'm predicting one Shaun 'Monty' Montgomery in the mix as well?"

"You are indeed a good guesser," Frank gave her, only *guesser* inadvertently came out sounding like *kisser*.

Frank's phone — which lay on the tabletop — at that moment saved him, erupting into light, and drawing the eyes of the both of them. A summary of the text displayed, for their benefit:

> Frank. Mum knows I've quit. She's gone mental. More than usual. Oh, and touch my mum and you're dead.

Jessie, it would appear, was rather adept at reading upside down, as she gave out a little chuckle. "Oh, it'll be an adventure, I suppose," she said, referring to the endeavour in general. "Besides, he's a grown man and I should really stop treating him like a little boy."

"It's a long time since anybody thought of Dave as a little boy," agreed Frank. "Or little, at least. Anyhow, sorry I didn't tell you about the job. That was actually one of the reasons for inviting you out tonight."

Frank waved a bunch of keys to Jessie, playfully, like one would entertain a baby. Naturally, this backfired as he soon sat staring at the keys himself, mesmerised. They were, after all, quite shiny.

Jessie clapped her hands in delight, snapping Frank back into the present in the process. "You got the keys to the farm!" she exclaimed.

"That I did!" beamed Frank, proudly. "Henk finalised all the legalities this morning. And so the charity can use the farm for at least the next three years."

"Three? I thought it was two?"

"So did I. But that idiot, Rodney Franks, has already told Henk that he'll object to any and all plans for a hotel. He said he'd fund a campaign by the local residents to support him, also."

"That's good news for the charity, at least."

"It's brilliant!" gushed Frank. "We'll just need the money to do the place up a bit now."

Jessie leaned back as two bowls of French onion soup were placed on the table before them. "Thank you," she said graciously to the waitress. "It smells absolutely wonderful."

"Excuse me, may I get the bill," said the voice from the table behind Frank, not really as a question, taking the waitress's attention away momentarily.

Jessie gave a fleeting glance to the woman standing behind Frank. "It needs a lot of work?" Jessie asked.

Frank used a piece of bread to break through the cheese layer covering the soup as the music from the current song playing once again came to a natural conclusion. "Needs work?" he scoffed, loudly for emphasis. "It needs a load of work," he said, making certain to catch the attention of the woman behind, before continuing, "It's one of those where it looks good from a distance, but, the closer you get, all the cracks come into view and you can see just what a desperate state it's in."

Jessie motioned with her spoon to catch Frank's eye, in a hopeless attempt to shut him up. It didn't work. And the woman, with coat on, stood directly beside him with a face like a bear chewing a wasp.

"And the smell. Oh, the smell," Frank went on, fanning his nose with his hand for good measure. "Stinks, doesn't it? Just awful. Smells like it should be doused in bleach for a week. And I'll tell you what, once you've been in there, you can guarantee you'll be itching for a month."

The bibliophile woman crouched to the floor, near Frank's foot, where she discreetly removed something from her handbag. She stood brandishing a foil wrapper, which glistened in the dim lighting.

"Excuse me, sir. I couldn't help but overhear that tonight was your first formal date with this lovely lady. I didn't want the climax of the evening, as it were, to be ruined, so I thought I'd give you the courtesy of retrieving this for you," she said, placing a condom onto the table. "It must have fallen out of your pocket, I imagine," she said calmly. "Also," she continued, raising her voice and slapping her palms down on the table. "I'm not a bloody prostitute!" she exclaimed, interrupting those pretending to be engrossed in their meal, with one ear tuned into the unfolding drama. She threw notes on top of her bill and marched towards the door, throwing a scarf over her shoulder, before coming to an abrupt halt, reconsidering. She then turned back to Frank's table, and, once there, picked up the glass of wine in front of him, dispatching the contents smartly into his face.

Frank wiped the wine from his cheek, extending his tongue to catch a couple of dribbles in the process. All eyes were on him. "I would *never*, you know," he announced, pointing towards the door at the exiting figure of the woman. "I wouldn't. Not with a prostitute. She's wasn't a prostitute anyway, I don't think. She's just on the Island working. She's a *working girl*, I guess you could say. It's what she told me."

"Not helping," Jessie told him, talking through the closed fingers covering her face. "Perhaps a change of tack?" she suggested gently.

"I'm not some sort of sex pest!" Frank continued, undeterred, raising his finger to bring the point home. Unfortunately, when he did so, he did so with a flourish that very much resembled his digit thrusting itself up into an invisible orifice... and twisting around inside.

"And this!" he said. "It's not mine!" he protested. "It's not even my brand!" he proclaimed. "I only use lambskin!" he further declared.

He picked up the foil packet, daintily, with tip of thumb and forefinger, and with little finger extended, as if he were carefully lifting a used teabag up by the string, afraid it would drip its remnants on the table. He held it as far away from him as his arm would allow.

"Can you please take this away?" he asked of Chantelle, the waitress, but received only a blank, unobliging stare in return.

"I'll put it in my pocket, then," Frank said, more to himself than anyone else, since Chantelle was not interested.

"Jessie, that condom's not mine!" he said, turning to her. "I would never be so presumptuous or crude." Then he noticed her handbag, which she'd placed in front of her on the table. "I'm really sorry to cause you any embarrassment. Don't go, Jessie, please!" pleaded Frank, in a panic now, certain he'd made a right dog's dinner of things.

"Oh, I'm not going, don't worry," she chuckled, reaching into the bag. "Here, I only wanted to show you this," she said, teasing him with a cheeky wink, and lifting out a similar foil packet. "Now we've got one each!"

Frank made a noise akin to a giggle, wiping the remnants of wine from his face. "Today's turning out to be a rather good one, it would seem." He watched Jessie tuck her packet away again, perhaps for later. "Two more glasses of wine, please!" Frank ordered, without looking up, but Chantelle was back off to the kitchen, having already escaped when the opportunity arose.

"Three hundred pounds!" Chantelle hooted in delight, arriving back at the kitchen and materialising through the door triumphantly. "Give me that sweepstake, the pervert just had a drink thrown in his face! That three hundred quid is mine-all-mine, boys!"

Murphy appeared at hand, quick-smart, followed, as well, by the owner of the Scottish drawl.

## FRANK & STAN'S BUCKET LIST #3: ISLE 'LE MANS' TT

"Bastard!" screamed the Scotsman, as only a Scotsman can scream, and with a kitchen hand towel scrunched up to his face to both block his wailing — so as not to upset the customers — and to cling to for comfort and security as a baby would its special lil' blankie. "I knew I should have phoned for a bloody ambulance!"

## Chapter
# THREE

"I can't see anything!" bellowed a voice with a haunting echo. "It's bloody useless. And it stinks of faeces!"

"Turn your torch on, Monty!" shouted Dave in return.

"*Whaaaat?*" came the resonant reply.

Dave didn't attempt to hide his frustration. "*Thhheeee toooorch*, Monty. Turn. It. On."

"I'm not bloody stupid, Dave! Give me some credit, mate! The torch *is* on! I can't *see* anything, and it smells of *faeces*, I'm tellin' ya!"

"What do you mean, faeces?

"Faeces!"

"You mean shit?"

"Yes of course I mean shit!"

"Well why didn't you just say *shit*, then?"

"I was trying my best not to be vulgar, Dave!"

"*Since when?*"

"Fair point."

Dave's hands scuttled up the back of Monty's torso, applying pressure close to Monty's midriff now, rather than the previous position near his ankles.

The adjustment caused Monty to scream out.

"Don't you dare let me go, Dave!"

It was a tempting proposition, Dave had to admit. But, instead, he knelt on Monty's buttocks in a useless attempt to look around

Monty's shoulders, and down into the hole. "I can't see anything, either," he remarked, squinting his eyes against the blackness of the abyss.

"Well I wouldn't expect that you could!" Monty answered.

"And you're right about the smell, Monty... unless, that's you?"

"Don't be daft! If that was me then you'd need to be phoning an ambulance right about now!"

"Yeah, but you're *always*—"

"Help me up, Dave! I'm starting to feel faint!"

"Have you unblocked it?" asked Dave.

Monty used the last of his strength to push on the broom handle held in his hands.

"No, but I think something's about to give. The smell of faeces... er, shit... is certainly getting worse. Maybe that's a good sign?"

"You need to unblock it!" Dave roundly encouraged him. "Then I'll let you up, yeah? Come on, Monty, they're relying on us, mate!"

"Please let me up," whimpered Monty. "My eyes are burning, and I think something's alive down there..."

"All right, all right. Wait there," Dave told him.

"Where else would I be going, presently??"

Dave pushed himself upright, leaving his foot planted firmly on Monty's arse, preventing him disappearing down the...

"Help...!" screamed Monty, but his desperate plea was not sufficient to prevent him sliding deeper into the pit, as the pressure applied from Dave's foot alone was evidently lacking.

Monty's legs were the only thing above ground, poking skyward — at an acute angle — like the *RMS Titanic*, moments before she was lost to a watery grave.

Dave made a desperate lunge towards Monty's waist, clamping his chubby hands around the leather belt, only seconds before his friend was likely to have been claimed by the deep.

"I've got you, Monty! Hold on, old son!"

"No, *you* hold on! I'm scared, Dave!" screamed Monty. "I've dropped my torch and my face is planted in the dirt— at least I *hope* it's dirt. And I swear I can hear something down here! I'm not joking!"

Dave stooped over Monty, who was presently little more than a dead weight. The strain was etched on Dave's face. He used every ounce of strength to pull Monty skyward with a force that Excalibur itself would have found impossible to resist.

"I'm going!" screamed Monty.

Which came as a surprise to Dave, whose hands remained in exactly the same position.

Yet Monty was indeed going, slowly, like a cork being eased from a bottle. Dave fought valiantly, but he was no match for gravity or a greased-up Monty — who was now sodden with sweat, from stem to stern, to boot.

Dave planted his feet for one last-ditch effort, but it was in vain. Monty collapsed in a heap belowground, and the release in strain sent Dave flying backwards, where he came to halt face-down upon the earth.

Such was Dave's vice-like grip, however, that Monty's now-empty wellies remained fixed firmly under Dave's armpits. Unfortunately, at least for Dave, his efforts had also relieved Monty of his trousers — which had been catapulted, along with Dave, when Dave fell back.

Due to the preceding pitched battle, the wet grass was now caked in mud, mud which obscured Dave's vision.

"I can't see anything," pleaded Dave, using his forearm to wipe the mud from his face, but to no avail. He used the article of clothing he'd removed from Monty and gratefully wiped the excess mud from his eyes and mouth, taking advantage of the moment to blow his nose into the fabric held in his hand as well.

Dave chuckled as, once his vision was cleared, it became apparent what lay in his grasp. "You'll need to give these trousers a proper wash," he told Monty, giving his nose a final wipe for good measure.

And yet, after a few blinks, and his eyesight further restored, it became obvious to Dave that something was amiss. The 'trousers' he'd been using to wipe his face were suspiciously, and unnervingly, generally free from mud.

Dave looked down to his hand, at what in fact lay there — the gusset area of Monty's cream Y-fronts, Y-fronts that Dave sincerely hoped were soiled with only the remnants of mud from his own face, and not... other leavings.

"For the love of...! Monty, I've got your bloody underpants!" he said, using a wadded bunch of his own t-shirt, taken up in his spare hand now, to furiously remove any intimate essence of Monty which might have been taking up residence on his face.

"I was just looking for them," Monty declared. "Oi, help me out?" he pleaded.

Monty had somehow managed to work himself upright and stood on his feet, though his feet were perhaps lacking solid purchase, given, as they were, positioned in a shithole. Though his body was vertical and oriented with head northward, he remained, alas, for the most part subterranean. His head, in fact, appeared from the hole — visible only from the jawline up. He looked very much like an elephant seal peering out of an ice hole.

"Here. Dave. Are you sniffing my undies?"

"Yes Monty, that's exactly what I'm doing. I just saw them, lying there, looking all inviting, and thought, *I know, I'm going to sniff Monty's underpants.*"

"That's what I figured," remarked Monty, immune to Dave's sarcasm.

"Did you clear the blockage while you were down there?" asked Dave. "If we can't get those toilets flushing, we're never going to be able to get this place open," he said, looking back to the farmhouse.

Monty nodded, catching his chin on the corner of the drain, covering it further with unpleasantness in the process. "I think so," he replied. "Well, there's now water running about the height of my ankles, at least."

"Yeah, that's probably not water, I expect. But good job all the same, mate," came Dave's reply.

"Please. Help me out, Dave. I can feel things hitting my legs— terrible things. I'm sure they're logs, of a sort, but I'm guessing they're not the wooden variety. If you catch my drift." With a whimper, Monty raised his arms like a baby hoping to be picked up by its mummy.

"I'm not touching you, Monty. You're covered in shit."

"Faeces, Dave."

"Shit!"

"Alright, shit, then."

"Shit," Dave said again, but this time more thoughtfully, as he wondered what to do about it.

"Get a hose?" Monty suggested.

Dave stood up, removing underpants from the palm of his hand. "There isn't a hose, Monty."

"I can't just stay in here, Dave."

"*Hmm*," said Dave, as if ruminating on this.

"Dave, I can't just stay down here!" Monty reiterated desperately.

Dave crouched down, hands placed crossed over one knee. He looked towards the farmhouse, and then back down to Monty. "Frank and Stan are back!" he shouted to his comrade-in-arms.

"Can they help?" asked Monty hopefully.

"They've got some woman with them," Dave began.

"Surely now's not the time, Dave?" chided Monty.

"What?" asked Dave, distracted, not following along.

"No time for love, Dr Jones," Monty clarified.

"No, Monty, she must be from the council or environmental health or something. Frank told us we had to get the toilets working before they came back."

"I'd say they are?" suggested Monty.

"Yes, I can see that they're back!" countered Dave.

"I meant the toilets, Dave. In working order, that is. Judging by the smell down here, at least. Now please help me out. This is starting not to be fun anymore."

Dave shook his head. "Bloody hell, Monty, we've got new jobs… we're trying to *impress*, fergodsake, and presently I'm covered in sweat from your ballsack and you're stuck down a hole like a confused mole, half-naked, and with me waving your underpants around like the bloody Union Jack!"

"Sounds like top marks for effort to me," countered Monty. "Wave!" he added abruptly.

"What? Yeah, that's what I said, waving your underpants around like—"

"Wave," Monty repeated. "They're waving at you," he explained.

"Ah-*haa*-ha," offered Dave through gritted teeth, waving awkwardly in the direction of the house in surrender, Monty's white underpants still in hand. '*HI THERE*' he mouthed, with no volume audible.

Frank and Stan, along with the as-yet-unidentified woman, waved enthusiastically in return. "We'll be over in a minute, Dave!" shouted Frank, presumably unable to see Monty's excrement-covered head poking out of the earth. "We're just giving Eileen a tour of the house!" he added with a thumbs-up.

Dave folded his arms, rubbing his chin. "Eileen... Eileen," he mused. "Ah! She's the woman from the charity trust," the cog in his brain coming to rest and the memory settling into place. "Frank said they'd made an application for funding and that she was coming around to..."

"That's really interesting," interrupted Monty. "Please, do carry on. Let me put the kettle on while you tell me all about it. Oh no, I'll have to rain check, actually, due to currently being drowned in faeces and *god-knows-what-else*."

"Hmm?" said Dave, still distracted and only half-listening. "Yes, a cuppa would be lovely right about—"

"GET ME OUT OF HERE!"

Dave dropped Monty's undies, finally, uncertain why he'd been holding onto them this whole time. "Round this side..." said Dave, troubleshooting aloud, and shuffling around the narrow opening of the drain... "There's more grass than mud. Do you want to put your undies back on?" he suggested. "Please say yes."

"I can't! The water level is getting too high, now. Besides, you've seen what I'm packing down below loads of times before now, so there's no need for bashfulness on your part. Just, please, before I come out, *please*, you need to understand that the water is cold down here. *Very* cold. Yeah?"

Dave reached down, and the two of them held onto each other's hands with the intensity of two lovers in imminent danger of being forcibly separated. Dave bent his knees — good practice when lifting heavy objects — and gripped hold of Monty with every ounce of strength he could muster. He arched his back, taking the strain as his tentative grip on the grass threatened to break... only to send Monty plummeting back to the rancid depths.

"Work with me, mate," pleaded Dave. "How bloody heavy *are* you, anyway?"

"I'm carrying a little holiday weight, is all, Dave. If you must know. Plus I'm waterlogged. Now keep tugging at me."

"Here, can you not say that?" asked Dave, caught temporarily off-guard.

"What?"

"You. Asking me... that. Please don't."

Monty's head emerged slowly from the drain, almost as if Mother Nature were, herself, experiencing the joy of giving birth.

Dave recoiled as Monty eased ever closer. "*Eergh*, Monty. You stink of shit!"

"Grab hold again, big fella. Keep pulling— I'm coming this time. I'm coming!"

"Monty..."

"Don't stop. Don't stop this time! Keep tugging till I'm done!"

"Seriously, Monty, you have to stop this. *Think* about what you're saying..."

Dave dug his heels in, pulling for all his might — he did *not* want to go through this again — and his efforts were eventually rewarded when the top half of Monty's torso slapped, like the aforementioned elephant seal, onto the cold grass beneath.

"Give me a minute," suggested Monty. "I need to get my breath back."

"Get your breath back?" countered Dave. "I'm the one that's done all the bloody work! And-oh-dear-god-in-heaven-I-can-now-see-your-arse-cheeks."

"Magnificent, I can only imagine," reflected Monty jealously.

"Yeah, that's not the word I had in mind to describe it," Dave lamented.

Monty lifted his head, his good eye honing in on Dave and his other veering off to the left. "Dave," he whispered with a cautionary tone.

"Seriously, Monty, that's not the word I—"

"No. Dave. Listen. There's an angry-looking goat behind you."

"Yeah, I'm not falling for that one again, me lad. Every time we're in a paddock, yeah? Every time. You're all like, *Oh, Dave, watch out, there's an angry-looking goat behind you.* Only this time I'm not falling for it, okay? This time—"

"No, for real, this time," Monty said, trying again.

Dave wasn't for fooling and shook his head sternly. "Just how stupid do you think I am, mate? Do you seriously think, if I turn my head right now, I'm going to find...?"

Dave turned his head to illustrate his point.

"Oh," he said. "Oh, bugger," he said, turning his head to look directly at a considerably cross-looking goat.

"Do something, Dave?" Monty suggested.

Dave held his hands aloft, as if he were turning himself over to the police, in an *I-give-up* motion. Unfortunately, the goat did not appear to be familiar with this universally recognised display of submission.

"Like *what?*" Dave asked desperately to Monty through the corner of his mouth, eyes locked on the goat. "You think I've got all the answers? Because that bastard's got horns," he said. "Nice goat..." Dave cooed to the goat, taking a tentative step back and offering soothing, gibberish words as he did so, hoping they were noises the beast might find appealing and mollifying.

The goat advanced, snuffling and snorting, and for a moment gave the indication that it might well attack. The goat, however, turned its attention to the clothing cast aside on the earth. It ambled over, catching the scent, and rummaged casually for a moment or two in the clothing pile, appearing, suddenly, quite content.

"That horny bugger's got my underpants!" protested Monty from the mouth of his still-partially-inhabited hole. "Stop it!" he demanded of Dave. "Stop it doing... whatever it's doing! Hang on, what *is* it doing...?"

"I'll do no such thing!" replied Dave. "He's not attacking, and that's good enough for me! Besides, he looks like... yes, he looks like he's enjoying them, and who am I to interrupt?"

The goat stared impassively at Monty, chewing what was left of his underpants with no apparent concern for their previous employment. With Monty's undies swiftly dispatched, the goat turned its attention towards the pair of jeans remaining, quite invitingly, there on the grass.

"It's going for my jeans, Dave. Stop it, please!"

"Hang on," replied Dave, reaching into his pocket.

"Thank goodness!" Monty came back, certain that Dave had come up with some sort of cunning plan.

Dave removed a device from his pocket. "Hang on," he said again. "Why am I not filming any of this?" he asked, rhetorically, as he began capturing video with his phone.

With Dave offering no indication of assistance, immediate or otherwise, Monty pushed his feet against the other side of the drain, forcing the portion of his torso that yet remained below ground, above ground. It was a struggle, what with gravity working against him and all, but Monty's well-padded frame soon lay on the surface of the field, naked from the waist down, and with a goat watching on inquisitively, munching on his clothes.

He jumped up, like a salmon returning home — okay, like an elephant seal returning home — and clapped his hands furiously. If he could only balance a ball on his nose, Monty might have found a home in the circus.

"Shoo!" he barked, but the goat was not for disturbing— it was dinnertime.

"Jayzus. Just how cold *was* it down there?" asked Dave in horror, lowering his phone (though only lowering it for a moment).

Monty flailed his arms and bellowed a noise, best likened to something a moose would make after getting a hoof caught in a beartrap. The verbal assault offered, in fact, a modicum of success, with the goat dropping the jeans. Monty instinctively smiled to camera for a moment, whilst simultaneously yelling, "Stop bloody filming me, Dave!"

Monty's smug grin disappeared quicker than his appendage had in cold water as the goat lowered its head, scratching its front leg on the grass with menace.

"It's going to charge!" shouted Dave.

"Do goats charge?" Monty asked in a panic. "I thought it was just bulls that charged! And I'm not even waving anything around!"

"You're certainly not, mate!" Dave agreed, with a hearty laugh at poor Monty's expense.

The goat lifted its head — presumably, locking onto its target — but its impressive horns, in the process, caught on the waistband of Monty's abandoned jeans, draping them down over its face as a result, rendering it temporarily blind. Startled and confused, the goat charged.

Fortunately for Monty the assault was unsuccessful, with the goat missing him by a wide margin. Still, there was the matter of the trousers.

"They're *my* jeans! You can't *have* them!" screamed Monty at the goat, looking in vain towards Dave for assistance. And why he thought Dave might offer assistance is anyone's guess, since...

"Best get after them, then," was all Dave offered, with a shrug and a wry smile.

For a fairly small creature, the goat could certainly motor. The breeze caught Monty's jeans, lifting them from its face as it ran, but the horns weren't willing to let go of their prize just yet. The goat leapt like a spring lamb, shaking its head furiously, but the jeans just wouldn't budge.

Dave fully intended to continue videoing, but the sight and speed of Monty's pale buttocks disappearing to the hedgerow in the far corner of the field very much appeared like too much effort for him to follow after, and his contented smile was disturbed by a rather dapper-looking Stan approaching at pace.

"It's going brilliantly," suggested Stan, once there, peering down into the drain and then cautiously back over his shoulder. "I don't see Monty. Did you get rid of the shit blockage?" he asked.

"Faeces," replied Dave. "And that's no way to talk about Monty."

"What?"

"Faeces, Stan. Faeces."

"You mean shit?"

"Well, yes, of course."

"Well why didn't you just say shit, then?" asked Stan.

Dave sighed. "It's a long story, mate."

"*Ohhh*-kay," said Stan, trying to decide whether or not he should enquire further.

"Anyway," replied Dave, saving Stan the trouble of deciding. "I won't bore you with the details. But, yes, I believe we've sorted the blockage. And Monty is currently off exercising the animals."

Stan was of course unable to appreciate Dave's moment of comic genius. And, besides, he was more concerned, at present, in removing a fleck of mud from his designer Wellington boots. Stan was indeed embracing the outdoor life, in his own way, by boasting a fabulous tweed jacket and trouser ensemble, replete with the designer Wellingtons.

"Eileen loves what we've done with the house and the outbuildings, and, well, I think we're a shoo-in for the lottery funding," he whispered with an enthusiastic shake of the fist.

It was a shake of the fist resembling dice being shaken, or, more unfortunately for Dave, Stan having an impromptu wank.

"If we get this money," Stan went on. "It'll really take the charity farm to the next—"

Stan stopped dead, mid-sentence.

"Dave is that, Monty?" asked Stan, after a pause. "Why is he—?"

"It is indeed," said Dave, providing no additional information.

"He's got no shoes on and half his trouser leg is missing?"

Dave, though unsurprised, turned to confirm this before turning back and stating casually, "Ah. Yes. He had a bit of an... association, shall we say... with a particularly..."

"Not interested, Dave. Look, here comes Eileen and Frank. Go and give Monty the heads-up. I need you two to be, well, *normal*. At least for a bit. And I *had* hoped for fully dressed, as well, though that's not looking too likely just now."

Monty trudged towards Stan and Dave, stopping periodically — presumably — to ensure he wasn't being followed. He looked down, pointing. "I got them back!" he shouted in triumph, wiping copious amounts of sweat from his face, before continuing. "The little bugger took them, but he didn't know he was up against Shaun Monty Montgomery, nossir!"

Stan put an exasperated hand to his forehead. "Dave," he commanded. "I don't care to know what you two have been up to, but you make sure you two simpletons don't fuc... Eileen, how good to see you again," offered Stan, nervously taking his hand from his head then thrusting it towards her, which was unusual, possibly a bit weird, bearing-in-mind Stan had only been out of her company for five minutes, maximum. "You like what we've done with the barn?" he asked, one eye on her and one eye on Monty.

Eileen flicked her arm out, taking note of the time before opening her pristine leather binder. She was well-turned-out, possibly from the horsey-set and Dave smirked at the spectacle of Frank and Stan talking like they were landed gentry, and who were now busying themselves in idle chit-chat with Eileen.

Stan ended his closing anecdote with a high-pitched nasal laugh that sounded like the whinny of a Grand National winner. "So you like what we've done with the place, Eileen?"

Frank and Stan arched their necks to spy on the notes Eileen was furiously writing. She lifted her head and went to speak but the sound of Monty's voice carried on the breeze.

"It's eaten my bloody underpants," he announced, once again pointing in the vicinity of his crotch.

Frank took a pace to the left in an attempt to obscure her view, but it was, well, useless. She looked at Monty, towards Frank, then back to Monty. "That man has his trousers on back-to-front," she exclaimed, taking a pace back in the process. "He also has no shoes on."

"That's our Monty," laughed Dave by way of explanation. "Ahh, Monty..." he continued, before veering off.

Frank laughed for no apparent reason. "Yes, Eileen. He comes here for exercise. He loves the fresh air," suggested Frank, sniffing the country air for good measure.

Eileen took a further pace back. "Exercise? With no shoes on?" she asked.

Stan took a step forward. "He's, well, unusual," he offered by way of explanation. "He likes to gallop around the field— back to nature, ah-ha," continued Stan, waving his arms for emphasis. "Dave's his carer... helper if you will, aren't you, Dave!" confirmed Stan, staring at a bemused Dave.

"I am," confirmed Dave, playing along to he-wasn't-sure-what. "Monty just loves it here. So when we heard Frank and Stan were taking over, we were delighted when they said I could continue to exercise Monty hereabouts."

"I see," replied Eileen, unable to break her gaze from Monty. "Is that blood on his face? Is he okay?"

Dave turned to Monty then back to Eileen. "He's fine. It's probably from the berries."

"The berries?" asked Eileen.

Dave put his arm around Monty. "Sure... Monty loves nothing more than sticking his head in the bushes to eat the berries."

Monty had one eye on Dave and one on Eileen. He wasn't sure, exactly, what was going on, but appeared to go with it.

"Are they not poisonous?" asked Eileen.

"Probably," replied Dave with a friendly slap on Monty's back. "It'd probably explain quite a lot now you mention it."

An awkward silence ensued which Stan tried, unsuccessfully, several times to break, before Frank stepped in. "So, Eileen. Do you think the lottery trust will be impressed by what we've done with the place?"

She cleared her throat taking another fleeting glance at her watch. "Yes. Yes, I think so. Very much," she stammered before getting into her stride. She looked back up towards the farmhouse and back to the expectant Frank and Stan. "Splendid," she continued.

"What you've done here is remarkable. You've turned a run-down farmhouse into a place to give homeless and vulnerable people the opportunity to turn their lives around or, perhaps, a place of safety. What you've done with the outbuildings is, well, wonderful. To give these people the opportunity to learn new skills whilst they're here, is inspiring. And able to do this in a location as beautiful as this," she continued, waving her arm to introduce the countryside. She took a pace forward, placing a gentle hand on Monty's shoulder. "I'm sure you'll be very happy here," she told him, slowly but not unkindly. "You've got your trousers on back-to-front, dear boy."

With that, Monty turned on a sixpence revealing two perfectly round holes, positioned perfectly to provide a portal onto each of his buttocks.

Monty twisted his neck without removing his arse from Eileen's line of sight. He slapped each cheek in turn. "The goat ate my underpants and then the back of my jeans. I put them on back-to-front so you didn't have to see."

Frank shuddered. "And here you are, Monty. Quite happily, showing it off."

"I'm sure you'll be very happy here," repeated Eileen, quite possibly even slower than the last time before she returned her attention to Frank and Stan. "I need to present this to the board, but I think I'm quite confident that the funding will be approved, which, will go some way to helping your project?"

Frank offered a visible jig. "That's wonderful, Eileen, it certainly will. We've a long way to go with the fundraising, but that will be a wonderful help. Please," offered Frank ushering Eileen towards the farmhouse. She looked back once more. "Nice to meet you all. Oh, and Monty, do be careful with those berries."

With Frank and Eileen at a safe distance, Stan placed his palms on his thighs and took several deep breaths. "What the hell just happened?" he asked. "In fact, forget that. Monty, have you actually been eating berries?"

Monty wiped his mouth with the back of his hand. "No, the goat kicked me. It's blood."

"You've been here five bloody minutes and you've started a fight with a goat?" asked Stan. "I didn't think we had any goats. Are you sure it wasn't a sheep?"

"That's what I said!" confirmed Dave.

Monty scoured the field, presumably looking for his new friend. "It was a goat! There's no way a sheep could eat my underpants, half my jeans and give me a bleeding nose."

Stan took up position in between Dave and Monty and the three of them stood in line looking up to the farmhouse and the converted barns with contented grins on their faces. He put his arms around his friends and bobbed his head. "We've done well here, guys. This place is going to be something special. With the charity across the UK and this place, Frank 'n' Stan's Food Stamps is really going to be on the map. We can really help people here; just need to keep the momentum with the fundraising. We just need to get people over to stay in the place now!"

Stan provided a motivational pat on the shoulders of Dave and Monty. "You guys, you know you're very much a part of this? Sure, Lee is running the charity, but you are as much a part of this as..." Stan paused, lowering his arms and his head. He retched before gasping for air. "Monty," he gasped, with tears streaming down his face. "Monty, you stink of shit!"

"*Meehhh!*" screamed Dave, in his best effort to mimic the bleating of a goat. It was unconvincing, but sufficient to launch Monty several feet skyward.

"Bastard!" yelled Monty, he knew it was Dave, but still took a moment to scour the field, once more.

"Ah... you guys," laughed Stan. "We're going to have a lot of fun working here, together... a lot of fun," he repeated for no obvious reason. "Monty, for the love of god go for a shower. But not in the house, Dave... you know what to do."

Dave rubbed his shovel-like hands together. "Roger that, Stanley. Come on, Monty, we've got an appointment with the hosepipe! All we have to do now is find one!"

*Chapter*
# FOUR

The inadequately proportioned carpark was jam-packed with vehicles seemingly abandoned at will, with more hopelessly trying to nudge their way in. Rebecca gripped the black metal railing at the top of the stairs, staring intently to the building opposite, and her resolute gaze broken only by the eruption of laughter from the group of women on the opposing side of the concrete stairwell. She smiled when she looked over, but the gesture was not returned. She looked at her watch again.

"First day?" asked a gentle voice behind her.

"Sorry?" replied Rebecca, flicking her brunette fringe to one side.

"I'm Susie," continued the friendly voice. "Is it your first day?" she repeated.

"Oh. Yes. Is it that obvious? I'm Rebecca. Rebecca Hul..." she paused. "Rebecca Howard," confirmed Rebecca, offering a hand. "I nearly forgot my surname there," she joked, her cheeks flushing for a moment.

"Lovely to meet you, Rebecca. I can always tell the first-timers—They have that wide-eyed excitement. Or maybe it's a look of abject fear. I've got three here, myself, so it's like second nature to me by now. Or, then again, maybe it's the double gin I have before I do the pick-up."

Rebecca stared blankly.

Susie smiled. "I'm joking, Rebecca, but I could do with a stiff drink before driving into that carpark. It's a bloody nightmare.

That doesn't sound like a Liverpool accent, by the way. Are you new to the area?"

The sound of laughter in close proximity erupted, once more. "Stuck-up bitches, that lot," announced Susie with no concern for the volume of her voice. "Only interested in you if you drive a car worth over sixty thousand or you're married to a footballer. More plastic in that lot than the recycling centre.

"Ah, okay. Thanks. I'm from Manchester. We recently moved to Liverpool. That is, me and my son. We're not far from school, which is fortunate. Just on Whitby Street," she explained, pointing to a street that was a quarter of a mile away and impossible to see from where they stood.

"I'll see you around, Rebecca. I need to go in and speak to the teacher. First week and I'm being called in to see the teacher already! Not sure which one of the kids is responsible for this invitation. Hey, you should join me, yeah?"

Rebecca shuffled her feet uneasily. "To see the teacher?" she asked, uncertainly.

"No!" shouted Susie, now virtually at the bottom of the stairs. "For that large gin! Remember what I said!" she told Rebecca, throwing a glance at the group of women.

Rebecca smiled, offering a conciliatory grin to the group of women, but that wasn't returned, either. She looked to her feet, conscious that the toes were ever-so-slightly scuffed, and ruffled her hair in a manner that suggested she'd ran out the door without looking in a mirror. She folded her arms in an attempt to conceal her green jumper that'd faded in the wash, but her self-reflection was interrupted by the chiming of the bell. Doors were flung open with exuberant contempt and in milliseconds the gentle calm was demolished by the squeal of liberated children.

Fashion concerns were cast aside like the school doors when Rebecca caught a glimpse of Tyler skipping through the playgroup without a care in the world. He couldn't whistle, but his pursed lips gave the impression that he was an old hand at it. "Mummy!" he yelled upon seeing her, bursting into a more energetic trot.

Rebecca knelt on one knee and scooped Tyler into her arms. As she spoke, she couldn't help peppering his cheeks in between each word. "I've... *muah*... missed... *muah*... you. How... *muah*... was it? I... *muah*... want to... *muah*... hear... *muah*... all about it."

"It was okay, Mummy."

She tousled his mop of blond hair. "Just okay? Your first day at big school and it was okay. You'll need to do better than that, young man, or this lollypop is going back into my bag."

Tyler waved at another boy currently being subjected to a lip-based assault upon his person similar to that which his own mother had perpetrated.

"That's my friend Harry!" he cried. "I've got a lollypop, Harry!" he shouted over the sound of igniting engines.

Harry's mum appeared to have had a comparable idea, as he also now had a lollypop in hand, and the two boys waved them through the air at each other in solidarity like sparklers on Bonfire Night.

"Can we get a car, Mummy?"

Rebecca crouched down. "We don't need a car, Tyler. Look at all these angry faces in the carpark. Besides, we get to walk home from school, so you can tell me all about your day!"

"Skip?"

"I can skip, Tyler... you just try and stop me. Come on," she insisted, leaving an arm trailing as the skipping home commenced.

🏍

The absence of a car was fine when the weather was dry, but living in a flat, nowhere near the bus route, and pouring rain, wasn't the ideal start to a day. Still, Tyler was the first to embrace the positive, seeing this as an ideal opportunity to wear his red wellies.

"This coat is too tight, Mummy," he exclaimed, before locking another puddle into his sights. "Can I get a new coat, Mummy?" he asked. "This one doesn't fit so good."

"We'll see, Tyler," she replied, but it was clear she was distracted. A car had slowed when it neared them, so she instinctively reached for her son's hand. "Come here, Tyler."

She quickened her step whilst taking a discreet glance over her shoulder, but the rain in her eyes obscured her vision.

"Can I get a new—?"

"Tyler, not now!" she snapped, now pulling at his arm.

"Mummy, why are you yelling?" asked a confused Tyler.

"I'm sorry," Rebecca told him. "Look, honey, I'll see what I can do, okay? It's just, right now we need to..."

Rebecca gripped Tyler's hand and guided him quickly towards the hedgerow behind them as the car came to halt alongside them. She stood in front of her son and reached for the phone in her pocket. She wiped the raindrops from her eyes, preparing to dial, at the same time as the car's driver-side door window lowered.

"Get in," coaxed a gentle voice.

Rebecca didn't answer. She was trying to call 9-9-9, but her phone's surface was slippery in the heavy rain and she was having a difficult time of it.

"Get in!" the voice repeated, more forcefully this time. "Rebecca, it's Susie! From school! It's tipping down, let me give you two a lift!"

Rebecca looked up, seeing that it was, in fact, only Susie. "Oh. Right. Oh hello, yes," she said, still breathing hard and trying to calm herself down. "We're fine, I think? But thank you. You've got all your children in the car, I see. We'll walk. We're... we're fine," Rebecca told her, and thanked her again.

"Nonsense! It's a seven-seater, loads of room! Now jump in, it's pouring down!"

Rebecca hesitated. She appreciated the offer, but on the other hand she didn't want to impose.

"It's not a problem, Rebecca! Honestly!" Susie assured her. "Is it, guys?" Susie asked of her children.

*"Nooo!"* came the unified response of high-pitched children's voices. Susie then offered a series of gentle commands to the car's occupants, and, before Rebecca had time to protest further, Susie's children had smartly rearranged themselves and dressed up with military precision.

Rebecca had no choice but to accept the invitation of a ride at this point, lest she appear ungrateful — and she *was* grateful — and so acquiesced, herself taking a newly cleared seat up front and Tyler a spot in back with the other kids.

"You must be mad walking when it's like this?" asked Susie turning the heating on. "Do you not drive?"

"It wasn't so bad when we started out," Rebecca answered. "But then the sky just opened up on us."

"Mummy sold our car!" Tyler, possessing no filter, shouted from the back seat. "For money!"

"I'm, *ehm*, between cars... at the present time," explained a somewhat embarrassed Rebecca.

Susie was gracious enough not to press the point. "I come past this way most mornings," she advised Rebecca. "When we get to school, I'll give you my number and you can call me if ever you need a lift, yeah?"

"We're fine," Rebecca replied. "But thank you."

"Nonsense," Susie said again, though not in an unkind manner. "You can walk when it's nice, and you call me when it's raining sideways. There. It's settled."

"You're very kind. Thank you."

"Mummy, can I unzip my coat now we're in the car?" Tyler spoke up from the backseat. "It's too tight and I can't breathe!"

"Of course, honey," Rebecca told him, ashamed by what Susie might think, that she couldn't dress her son in a coat that fit. "How did you get on with the teacher the other day?" she asked Susie, trying to change the subject.

Susie looked concerned, but, after a pause, came back cheerfully. "Fine," she said. "But this one here..." she indicated, with a thumb pointing behind her in the direction of the back seat... "is Michael. And Michael, apparently, thought it would be a wonderful idea to type the word *boobs* into the school computer."

The word 'boobs' — quite understandably — brought a collective round of giggles from the rest of the car, including Tyler.

"Oh," replied Rebecca, looking towards Michael — who made every effort to disappear into his seat.

"I told the teacher that he wouldn't do it again, didn't I, Michael?"

"Yes, Mum," came the dutiful reply, from someone who likely had every intention of doing it again, actually.

"There we go, guys. Everybody out!" instructed Susie, once they'd reached the school. "And Michael, remember, computers are for *learning*, right?"

"For learning about *boobs*," Michael whispered as they got out, loud enough only so the other kids could hear, resulting in another round of giggles.

"It's not funny!" Susie scolded her son, calling after him. But, then, whispering so only Rebecca, still in the car, could hear her, "It *is* pretty funny, actually. Though of course I can't tell him that."

Rebecca wasn't sure how to react, so called out to Tyler, instead, "Tyler, what do you say for the lift?"

"*Thaaank yooou!*" Tyler shouted back, but he was already all but gone, running off alongside Susie's kids, as well as scouring the tarmac for additional puddles to waylay.

Susie turned to Rebecca in the front seat. "Rebecca, would you like a lift back?" she asked. "I don't have to be to work for a bit. Maybe we could go for a coffee?"

"Thank you, Susie, that's so very kind of you. But I've got some things that need doing, and it looks like the rain is dying out, so I'll just walk myself back. But I really do appreciate it. And thanks for the ride."

Susie pulled away, and Rebecca looked towards the school. For the first few days of school, Tyler had stuck to her arm like glue in the morning. It was good to have seen him playing with the other kids. Now, with the school bell ringing and all the students safely inside, Rebecca made her way along.

"Lovely day for it!" exclaimed the lollypop man, offering her, and several others, safe passage across the road.

"Good for the ducks," Rebecca replied automatically. She smiled, and was about to say something else, but the vibrating phone in her hand took her attention away.

"Yes, hello," she answered, whilst mouthing a *'thank you'* to the jovial lollypop man. "Yes, this is Rebecca," she continued, adopting the tone of consummate professional. "Yes, okay," she offered in response to the person on the other end.

She stepped into an empty bus shelter a little further on to escape what remained of the rain, with a finger pressed into her other ear to drown out the traffic noise. She lowered her head, listening intently.

"I understand, and thank you for letting me know so soon," she said into the phone after a pause. "I know I don't have that much experience," she agreed, trying her best, despite what she was being told, to sound cheery and optimistic. "Though I'd more than make up for that in enthusiasm, and… and… hello? Hello?"

But there was no longer anyone there at the other end.

She held the phone a moment longer, staring at the screen. "It's not going to be like this forever, Tyler," she whispered. "I promise."

She delayed the departure from her temporary refuge, looking to the furious grey sky, the rainstorm evidently deciding it wasn't quite finished after all. She was already soaked, so a little more rain wouldn't hurt her, she reasoned. And, so, the thought of Tyler jumping in puddles without a care in the world inspired her to do the same. She jumped out on the spot, into a generous patch of rainwater collected on the pavement, and, satisfied as to the results, she jumped onto another, and then another. For those passing in their cars, she may very well have appeared mad as a box of frogs.

But embracing this child-like whim was liberating.

"*I'm singing in the rain,*" she sang. "*Just singing in the rain.*" She ran her hand along a metal railing, using the ring on her finger to tap out a beat. This bursting into song offered her a momentary distraction from the current saturation she was receiving, a drenching which nevertheless caused her to quicken her pace.

She came to an abrupt halt at the end of the lane adjacent to her house and deliberately wiped her face once more, spreading a mixture of both raindrops and makeup across it focussing, all the while, on her drab, concrete front yard. A man wearing a dark hooded top was there, leaning forward, peering through the letterbox opening of her front door.

Her breathing became ragged, her heart rate increasing, as she saw the strange man shift position furtively to her front window, peering in. He then eased backwards, away from her front door, focussing his attention on the floor above, perhaps looking for handholds or footholds to clamber up there. Then he looked back, up and down the street, presumably checking to see if the coast was clear. Apparently satisfied that it was, be busied himself again with the front door.

And then inexplicably he gave up, just like that, walking off.

Rebecca kept him in view from her position of cover, ensuring he wasn't coming straight for her, when she was startled by a voice beside her. "Are you okay, luv?" asked the postman, mail satchel in hand.

Rebecca had forgotten to breathe, and had to exhale before she was able to reply. "You startled me!" she said. "There's a man!" she explained. "A man was at my door, at number twenty-three, and it looked like he was trying to break in!"

"I see him," said the postman. "Sketchy-looking fellow. Wearing a woolly hooded jumper. He's getting into his car… and now driving off. Is he causing you problems? You want I should phone the police?"

"No, but thank you," she said, though not sounding very certain of her answer.

"I don't mean to be rude," the postman offered. "Especially with the fright you've just had and all. But… you've got a bit of makeup smeared across your face. Just there. And, *erm*… there. And… there as well. Sorry. Just, you know, in case you didn't know?"

"Do I?" she replied, nerves a-jangle. She steadied herself. "I'm going for the Alice Cooper look," she told him, thinking on her feet.

"Ah! The Alice Cooper look!" said the postman reassuringly. "Well then you've done a smashing job!"

They both had a laugh.

"Would you like me to escort you to your house?" the postman asked, his chest expanding proudly. "It's no trouble at all."

"You're very kind, but I'll be fine," she answered him. She had a habit of saying things like this, it seemed.

"I expect so," came his reply, returning a warm smile. "Nobody's going to mess with you, after all, looking like, *em...*"

Rebecca looked at her knight in shining armour, head cocked, uncertain.

"Well. That," the postman finished, unable, unfortunately, to prevent the words from issuing forth.

With the spell well and truly broken, Rebecca merely patted his arm, taking a further cautionary glance about the street as she did so before continuing.

The postman looked uncomfortable with himself.

"Thank you. You've been kind. Rude, mind you, there at the end. But kind," Rebecca teased him.

With that sorted, she eased open the partially rusted gate to her front garden. It squeaked in protest. The moment she saw the notice glued to the glass pane on her front door, she knew who the mysterious caller had been and breathed a little easier — at least it wasn't him, she thought. She peeled the notice from the cold glass running her fingers through her hair with her spare hand, digging her nails into her scalp.

She prised the letter open, separating the flap with her fingers.

"This isn't happening!" she shouted, but there was no longer anyone there to hear her, and the words in bold type before her confirmed otherwise, regardless:

## NOTIFICATION OF EVICTION PROCEEDINGS

Rebecca sat there, on the front steps, in the rain, wrapping her arms around her knees, pulling them into her chest and sobbing. She crumpled the letter up into a ball, and tossed it down at her feet. "I don't know what to do!" she screamed.

She picked the letter, now dotted with rain, back up, and she unfolded it carefully.

She stared down at it.

"I don't know what to do."

"Tyler, you've got five more minutes to read your comicbooks before your tea is ready, okay?"

That was a statement, as any parent would be well familiar, greeted by a resounding round of silence.

Rebecca unfolded the receipt, removed a fairy-shaped magnet from the front of the fridge, and used it to affix the receipt there. It served as a reminder to herself, with the bolded letters, **Receipt for one (1) 18K Yellow Gold Ring**, staring directly back at her, though she adjusted the magnet to cover over the receipt's distinctive and immediately recognisable three-sphere pawnbroker's symbol.

"It won't be for long, Mum," she thought aloud, looking down on the faint tan line where once a ring sat, and, then, "Two minutes, Tyler!" she called, before interrupted by a knock on the door.

She stood in the narrow hall, struggling to make out a figure through the frosted glass.

"Hello, who's there?"

"Oh, hi!" returned a female voice. "Is that Rebecca's house? *The* Rebecca? My name is Susie! You may know me as... *Susie*," the voice relayed, in a light-hearted and jovial manner.

Puzzled, Rebecca unlocked and opened the door, just a crack, while placing a firm foot on her side.

"Ah, Rebecca! I've been to your neighbours, who I think might be smoking something illegal, if I'm being honest. Still, at least they told me where you were."

Rebecca opened the door fully, smiling politely, but with an expression that must have indicated otherwise, something to the effect of, *What the hell are you doing here?* because...

"I was going to bring that gin!" said Susie by way of explanation.

"Sorry?" asked Rebecca.

"That gin... Another time, maybe? Ah. Another time, maybe."

"No, no, sorry, it's fine. I just wasn't expecting... Here, do you want to come in?"

"Sure," replied Susie, politely choosing to ignore the apparent lack of furniture and smell of damp. "Look, I'm sorry to disturb you, but you left the umbrella in my car and the forecast wasn't good for tomorrow...?"

"You've been knocking on doors to find me because it's going to rain tomorrow?" asked Rebecca.

"Well, that and to drink the gin," said Susie apologetically. She placed the umbrella behind the door — a door in which the bottom portion was broken, covered by a piece of plastic, which was itself shattered.

"And that umbrella isn't mine," Rebecca told her. "I didn't have one with me earlier."

"Oh. Well someone left it in my car, so it's yours now, I suppose," Susie answered her, in not the most convincing of lies.

"I'm sorry about the state of things here, Susie. It's a temporary arrangement, this place," said Rebecca. This was spoken with an attempted sort of confidence, but Rebecca's lack of conviction betrayed her. "It's... not the greatest of places," she conceded.

"It's fine. Don't worry about it. Really," Susie assured her, but then remained quiet for a moment.

Rebecca looked at her, not sure what else to say.

"Ah," Susie went on, filling the gap. "Well. I was going to speak to you tomorrow, if I saw you again at school. But I didn't want to make you feel bad or anything..."

"Oh, no," Rebecca replied, fearing the worst. "What is it? Has Tyler gone and done something? Has he upset someone?"

Susie raised her hand to allay her fears. "What? No, no, nothing like that," she said. "Nothing like that at all. It's just... I couldn't help but hear about you selling your car and all, and about Tyler's coat not fitting him anymore."

"Sorry about that," Rebecca answered, casting her eyes down to the floor.

"No, listen, there's no need for apologies, okay? Look, it's just that the weather is supposed to continue to be rubbish and... Right, I'm conscious that I'm prattling on like a madwoman. But, listen, luv. I've got three kids, yeah? I've got three kids, Rebecca, okay? And I've got clothes coming out of every bloody cupboard in my house, believe me. And they outgrow them just as quickly as I buy them, don't they? And so I've brought you a few bits, and there's a lovely winter coat that's only been worn a handful of times. They're in the car. I'll just go and fetch them, then. Is that alright?"

Rebecca didn't speak. She couldn't. She only continued looking down at the floor.

"Oh, dear," said a very worried Susie. "I'm sorry. I'm so sorry. I've embarrassed you, haven't I? I really didn't mean to do, honestly I didn't. I'm an idiot, I am. Should I... should I go?"

Rebecca's shoulders began to heave. With her head still bowed, she put her hands to her face. "I'm a good person, Susie," came her muffled reply. "I'm a good mother, I promise," she sobbed, with tears now in full flow. "But I'm struggling to even buy my son a new coat!"

Susie moved closer, gently stroking Rebecca's upper arm. "We all have difficult times, Rebecca," she told her. "I can see you're a wonderful mother. I know that for a fact. It's obvious that... obvious that... Hang on. Is something burning?"

"Oh, no!" wailed Rebecca. "I've burned his bloody dinner now!" she cried, a statement that, along with it, brought only a further flood of tears.

"You sit down, I'll get the dinner out of the oven," suggested Susie. "You take a deep breath and compose yourself. I'll give Tyler his dinner, as you've got a bit of, *erm*, makeup... smeared on your face?"

"That seems to be a recurring theme lately," Rebecca answered her, in between sobs.

"You go get yourself sorted, okay? I'll take care of this here, don't you worry."

Once dinner was indeed taken care of, and Rebecca had eaten some of the overdone-but-still-palatable roast herself, and with Tyler off playing happily in the other room, Susie sat with Rebecca round the kitchen table and listened. She didn't judge, not once. Just listened, for over an hour. It was several cups of tea's worth of time, to be exact.

"You must think I'm an absolute fool, Susie," Rebecca said, after a bit of heart-to-heart. "If you'd told me what I've just told you, I'd have to think you were bloody stupid for staying with a horrible man like that."

"Not at all," Susie assured her. "It's never as simple as all that, is it?"

"My god, I'm a strong, intelligent woman. At least I like to think I am," Rebecca went on. "I don't know how I let it get to this stage, sat here, in this damp-infested hovel."

"This Robert. Did he hit you?" Susie asked.

Rebecca shook her head. "Occasionally. But not often. In a way, I wish he had," she told Susie. "It would've made it easier to leave him. And I would have had proof, you know? A visible badge for the way he's treated me. But he's too clever for that. But he treated me like a possession, something he owned. It started off so gradually that I didn't notice... Or maybe I chose to ignore it, to pretend it wasn't happening."

Susie nodded sympathetically. No judgement.

"I had a job. I had a career. I'd be going off to work and he'd tell me that I looked fat, and that I should wear something else. Always undermining my self-confidence, my self-esteem. If I told him he was hurting my feelings, he'd turn it back on me and say he was just trying to help me and be nice, and then I'd feel guilty. Every time he did it, he'd make it out to be my fault. I almost believed him. How stupid I was..."

"Don't punish yourself," Susie said to her, taking Rebecca's hand in hers. "Just don't. You hear?"

"I don't know how I didn't see it coming," Rebecca continued. "It got to the point where he'd scream at me all the time, always wanting to know what I was doing every minute of the day, who I'd spoken to. If I was five minutes late coming home from work, he'd..." Rebecca pressed her face into her closed fists. "He'd lock me in the utility room! And why the utility room? So I could get some washing done while I was in there, I guess. Why did I allow that? Why did I allow any of it??"

Susie gave her hand a squeeze.

"And here I am, two years later," Rebecca said, looking back up. "No job. No money. I'd saved a few hundred pounds in order to get away from him, but that's all used up. It didn't last long at all. And now I haven't got two coins to rub together. And he made sure I was alienated from my friends and family. So now I've got nothing, and nowhere to turn. The ring my mum left me when she died, I had to sell it. That's what I had to do earlier. That's why I didn't want a ride back from you," she sobbed.

"Does Tyler miss his dad?" Susie asked. "Does he know about all of—?"

"Yes, he misses Robert, believe it or not. I always tried to make sure Tyler was never caught up in it. All the domestic drama, I mean. It's hard, though. And Tyler doesn't understand why he's not able to see him. He has no idea how bad things were."

Susie released her grip, patting Rebecca's hand.

"Look at me. I've gone on too much," Rebecca said. "It's getting late now. Susie, thank you for the clothing you promised. I know Tyler will love his new coat. And thank you for listening to me ramble on. It's actually been a huge relief just to finally be able to talk to someone about it."

"It's fine, Rebecca. It really is. And I mean this, if ever you should need to talk, I'm happy to be there for you. Maybe you can come around to mine! Bring Tyler along, and we can drink some gin! Not Tyler, though, obviously."

"You really do like your gin," Rebecca remarked, allowing herself a laugh, which Susie shared.

"I don't want to make it sound like I'm obsessed with gin!" Susie told her." It's just... I work with a woman who, dear as she is to me, makes the gin necessary."

They shared another laugh, and then Susie went to fetch the bag of clothes she'd brought. When she returned, she gave it to Rebecca, along with a firm embrace. "Stay strong," Susie told her. "You're a wonderful mother, okay? and don't let anybody tell you otherwise!"

Rebecca felt a tremendous weight lifted. She'd tried to carry on all by herself before, stiff upper lip and all that. She'd been so embarrassed, and hadn't dared talk to anyone about her troubles. But now that this gin-loving, rather-pushy but perfectly-lovely person had made her way in, the loneliness and despair were gone.

"Oh, dear," she said, picking up Susie's purse from the kitchen table. She placed it in her own handbag so that she'd remember to give it back to her at school the next morning, before emptying the contents of the bag of clothing onto the tabletop. The clothes were immaculate. She smelt the winter coat and smiled, clutching it to her chest. "Oi! Tyler!" she shouted. "Look what I've got for you!"

She walked from the kitchen and laughed when she saw the outline of a figure in the frosted glass once more.

"Ah! I'm glad you noticed!" said Rebecca, unlocking the door. "I was going to bring it to school with me tomorrow, but you probably need your driving licence, don't you?" she went on, starting to pull the door open. "Oh and by the way, Tyler's going to absolutely love his new—"

The door flew open as if caught up by an angry gale, pushing Rebecca back and striking her squarely on the temple. She staggered backwards, reaching out for something to hold onto to steady herself, but clutched only empty air. Her legs buckled. She raised her hands in defence, but couldn't prevent a hand taking hold of her by the hair, throwing her like a ragdoll back into the kitchen.

*"Leave me, you fecking cow?"* screamed the towering figure looming over her. *"I told you you're nothing without me!"*

Robert held his face just inches from hers, spattering her with saliva as he screamed out semi-coherently, the smell of alcohol on his breath overpowering. *"Make me look like an idiot, you slag?"* he raged on, pausing only to take a breath, which was then followed by a volley of fists smashing into her face. There was no way for her to stop him. He sat on her chest, punching her at will.

Rebecca lifted her right arm, weakly, in a desperate attempt to protect herself, but it collapsed to the floor, along with the rest of her, when she lost consciousness.

---

"Hey sleepyhead!" Susie called gently, but there was no response. "Can she hear me?" Susie asked of the nurse by the bedside busy reading the monitors and checking on Rebecca's progress.

"She's a little drowsy just now, but she can most likely hear you," the nurse answered her with a compassionate smile.

"Hey Rebecca. Can you hear me? It's me. It's Susie."

Rebecca opened her eyes, emitting a strained groan as she did so, as if even lifting her eyelids were painful. Which it probably was, given her current state.

"Where am I?" Rebecca asked, and then, immediately followed by, "Where's Tyler?"

"You're in hospital," explained Susie. "Tyler is absolutely fine. He's with my husband and apparently having a lot of fun on their computer games. Don't worry."

"Take it easy, now," cautioned the nurse, as Rebecca eased herself up the generous stack of pillows into nearly an upright position, placing a cautious hand to her blackened cheeks, and then towards her split lip.

Rebecca stared at Susie for several seconds, as if unable to trust her eyes. "What are you doing here?"

"I thought I'd come to see you," Susie returned with a laugh.

"But you're in bed as well...?"

"I know. The things I'd do for a friend."

"I don't understand..."

Susie lowered her book, swinging her legs around to take a sitting position on the edge of her *own* hospital bed. "I forgot my purse last night. Couldn't drive without my driving licence, now could I? I wasn't even halfway home when I realised, so I came back to get it. Your door was wide opened, and some lunatic was smashing lumps out of you. So, I smashed lumps out of *him*."

"You... Wait, you *hit* Robert??"

"Oh I sure as hell did. And more than once!" Susie confirmed with a wide grin.

"I... I hit my head," Rebecca told her, reaching up groggily to feel her forehead. "I was... I couldn't fight back..."

"Don't you worry," said Susie. "I got in enough shots for the both of us! I took my shoe off and beat that bastard with it! I drew blood! It was going quite well, too, until the arsehole headbutted me."

"I'm sorry..."

"I thought you said he wasn't the woman-beating type?"

"I'm so sorry..."

"Don't be!" Susie assured her. "I got that bastard good! He got what he deserved!"

"Where is he now?" asked Rebecca.

"Robert? Oh, he ran off holding his head. I think he had a piece of my heel stuck in his skull, to be honest. Ruined a good pair of shoes in the process, that's the only downside! Anyway, the police are out looking for him if they haven't found him already."

Tears started to run down Rebecca's face. "Tyler... my god, he was there the whole time. What if he *saw*? I can't..." she sobbed. "... I can't get away from him, no matter what I do. He told me he'd find me if I left him. And he did. Somehow he did. I can't escape him."

Susie eased down the edge of her bed until her feet made contact with the floor. She padded the few steps between them, and then reached for Rebecca's hand and held it in hers. "The police will find him," she assured Rebecca. "They'll find him. They will."

"I know they will, but what then? I've got no money, no job, and a small boy to look after. What am I going to do?"

"They'll put him in jail," continued Susie.

"For how long? A few weeks and he could be back on the street! I can't put myself through this anymore. I can't put Tyler through this anymore."

Susie squeezed Rebecca's hand. She wanted to offer some words of comfort, something to take away the pain. "I think I have an idea," she told her. "I don't think I told you. I work for a taxi company. But thing is, the guys I work for, the owners of the—"

"There's help out there," said the nurse. She'd been gone for a moment or two but was back, and handed a folded flyer to Rebecca. "Sorry to interrupt. And I don't mean to pry. Well, to be honest, that's a lie. I do when it's needed. And this is one of those occasions. Now, these guys," she continued, tapping the flyer. "Started off by offering food stamps to the homeless. Frank and Stan's Food Stamps."

"That's—" Susie started to say, but the nurse wasn't finished.

"But they've now extended their reach to offering hostels, these guys," the nurse said.

"A hostel?" asked Rebecca, with trepidation. "In Liverpool?"

"Those are—" said Susie.

The nurse nodded. "Sure. We refer a lot of our homeless patients to the hostels around here, and these guys are wonderful. There are others, also, of course. But I recommend this. I hear very good things about them, and I think they'll be able to help you."

"Those are actually—" said Susie.

"I know you're trying to help," Rebecca replied to the nurse. "But if he found me where I *was*, then what hope do I have *here*? At one of *these* places?"

"You'll have company," suggested Susie. "Right? He won't do anything if other people are there. He can't. He wouldn't dare. See?"

"Apologies. I didn't really explain myself properly," the nurse went on. "The charity helps out people across the country. Not just Liverpool. They have several hostels that are designed for people in your situation. It's not just for the homeless who need a warm bed for a few days. They also provide shelter and offer people work experience and training to equip them to get work! You should phone them?"

"She knows what she's talking about," Susie added, now that the nurse had finally completed her delivery. "Frank and Stan, as I was trying to say, is who I work for."

"What?" Rebecca said, clutching her hospital blanket up to her chest. She looked at Susie and the nurse suspiciously now. "What is this?" she said. "Some kind of intervention??"

"No, no!" Susie told her. "I actually had no idea the nurse here would have information on this. It was—"

"I see cases of domestic abuse all the time, in my profession," the nurse explained. "I stay prepared."

Rebecca remained unconvinced. And she started putting pieces together, even though those pieces began showing an inaccurate picture... "This is why you befriended me?" she asked Susie accusingly. "I'm just a charity case to you?"

"No! No, please don't think that!" Susie pleaded with her. "I honestly had no idea! I just wanted a friend. A normal friend. As opposed to the woman I work with, Stella, who's the reason for my fondness for gin like I told you! And you seemed so nice. Really. That's all there was to it. The fact that you need help now, and that Frank and Stan, my bosses, can help you... that's just... what's the word? Serendipity. It's just serendipity..."

Rebecca wasn't sure what to think.

"Look, I don't believe in fate or any rubbish like that," Susie pressed on. "All I know is that you're my friend and I want to help. And I know people who can help. Yeah? Okay?"

Rebecca brought one of her hands down from her chest, allowing Susie to squeeze it once again. They stayed like this for a bit.

"I'm sorry. I'm not used to people helping me. It... takes a little getting used to. Thank you, Susie. Thank you both," she said, looking to the nurse as well. "I'm sorry to involve you both in this."

"Stop apologising!" Susie told her. "This is what friends are *for*, okay? This is what friends *do*."

"Sorry," Rebecca said again, to which Susie laughed, and Rebecca along with her.

"Oh. Would you mind awfully asking your husband to bring Tyler in?" Rebecca asked, now things were on a more even keel.

"Already sorted. He'll be here in about... ten minutes," Susie replied, looking at the time displayed on her phone. "Now take this," she continued, handing over her phone. "And phone my friends?" she asked, tapping the brochure the nurse had given her. "I'll leave you alone and see if I can secure us a cuppa."

"Oh, and one more thing," said Susie, popping her head back in for a moment. "If the police don't take care of Robert? My friend Stella will," she told Rebecca with a grin.

"Okay...?" Rebecca answered, unsure what to make of Susie's claim.

With Susie now off, Rebecca stared at the brochure. It was irrational, she knew, but she was ashamed. She was embarrassed that she was phoning a homeless charity for help. The thought that she couldn't look after her son burned through her, but she knew that wilful pride should hold no place in her decision-making at present.

She dialled the number, and she grimaced when she caught sight of her swollen face reflected back to her from the screen of the phone.

"Hello," she whispered. "Is this Frank and Stan's?"

She listened for a moment, taking a quick glance around the ward to make sure nobody could hear her. Despite herself, she was still embarrassed about calling. "Sorry?" she continued. "I didn't quite hear your name."

She cupped her spare hand over her mouth, so no one else could hear.

"Yes, hello, Lee," she said. "It's nice to speak with you as well. My name is Rebecca, and I hope you can help me. I've been directed to you, and I've nowhere else to turn."

*Chapter*
# FIVE

"Lee, yes... hello, I can hear you, crystal clear!" announced Stan, with an incredulous expression like he was the first human discovering fire. "This is wonderful, Lee, it sounds just like you're only in the next room! You wouldn't believe that I'm in the Isle of Man and you're in Liverpool." After he'd finished marvelling at the excellent reception, he asked, "How's your and Stella's new flat?"

"Great, thank you, Stan," replied Lee. "Look, can you see me?"

"See you? No, of course not," came Stan's reply, uncertain as to what Lee was on about. "How do you mean, *see* you?"

"Ah. Stan, you do realise that with this new technology you can not only talk to me, but also see me as well?"

Stan laughed. "Lee, I'm not *that* stupid," he said.

"No, Stan. I'm serious," Lee assured him. "This is a *video* call. I can both hear and see you. Well, I can see *something*, but I'm not entirely sure what I'm looking at."

Stan's eyes panned slowly across the living room, scrutinising the area, looking for a hidden spy camera.

"I can't see you, Lee?"

Lee took a breath, but not so deep as to give the impression of frustration. "Stan, is Frank there? He's an old hand at this."

"He's in the bath."

"Right-*ho*," replied Lee, with an enthusiastic emphasis at the end. "What can you see on the screen?" he asked.

Stan looked at his right toe, wondering what that had to do with anything. He was about to ask but then thought better of it. He didn't want to appear a complete muppet, of course. "On the screen?" he said instead, repeating back Lee's words.

"Yes, on the screen," answered Lee as gently as he could muster.

"Well, at the moment I think it's... yes, it looks like *Top Gear*," Stan told him. "Yes, definitely *Top Gear*. And it must be an older one because Jeremy Clarkson is still in it. He mustn't have punched that producer chap at this point. Awful business, that. And it's too bad, as well, because the new *Top Gear* just isn't—"

"*Top Gear*?" interrupted Lee. "What do you mean, *Top Gear*?"

Stan paused for a moment. "I mean *Top Gear*. You asked what was on the screen. That's what's on the screen, Lee," said Stan, not understanding what Lee was not understanding. "You asked me what's on the screen," Stan reiterated.

Lee went quiet. If Stan could see him, he would have found Lee to be presently chewing his own fist. Fortunately — for the sake of Lee's continued employment, perhaps — Stan could not see him.

"Stan," Lee asked, once he'd composed himself. "Stan, when I said the screen, are you by chance looking at the television?"

"Well yes," replied Stan. "What else would I be looking at except the telly? You're not making an awful lot of sense, Lee..."

"Jaysus," Lee whispered under his breath. "Stan, when I asked what was on the screen, I didn't mean the *television* screen. I meant the screen on the *iPad*, mate. Will you tell me what you can see on the viewscreen, please, just now?"

"Very funny!" replied Stan.

"I'm sorry?" Lee came back, somewhat nonplussed.

"How can I look at the screen? You're having me on, right?"

"What? No," said Lee, his natural Irish charm beginning to crack under the strain. "No, I'm not having you on, Stan, I promise. Just look at the screen, if you don't mind?"

"How am I supposed to talk to you if I'm looking at the screen?"

Lee went quiet again, and then asked, after a moment's respite, "Stan. I don't suppose Frank is out of the bath?"

"No. No? No. Why are you—?"

"*Staaan*," Lee interrupted, drawing out his words as one might, for instance, when addressing a cornered, frightened dog who you're attempting to convince not to attack and to instead be a very-good-boy. "*Staaan, wheeere* are you *hooolding* the *iiiPaaad*?"

"Oh dear. Lee. Have you been drinking, Lee?"

"No, Stan. Stan, are you holding the iPad to your ear, like a phone?"

Stan laughed again. "Is this a trick question? No. No, now I *know* you're taking the piss, right? Right. Because of *course* I am. Of *course* I'm holding it to my ear. Otherwise, how else I am meant to hear you??"

"*Jayzus, Mary, and Joseph...*"

"What's that? I can't quite make you out now, Lee. You're mumbling. Are you... are you praying? Are you... I mean I didn't know you were religious...?"

"Only a bit. And only at certain times. Nevermind. So. Stan. I can see you've never used one of these devices before. Okay. So, Stan, with the iPad — and voice calling — it's not like a traditional phone, yeah? You don't need to hold it to your ear. You hold it in front of you. Like you're reading a book. Now. Try that, then."

There was a lull. And then...

"OKAY!" shouted Stan. "RIGHT! I THINK I'VE GOT THIS NOW! CAN YOU STILL HEAR ME, LEE? LEE, CAN YOU STILL HEAR ME??"

"Stan. You don't need to shout. They're very good at picking sound up. Even from a... very slight distance. "

"OKAY, LEE!"

"Ah, now I can see a bit more. I think I'm looking at your carpet."

"Bloody clever these things, aren't they!" Stan announced, gobsmacked, yet fortunately at normal volume now he'd finally gotten used to the new-fangled device.

"Yes. Remarkable, Stan. Okay, Stan—"

"What will they think of next??"

"Quite a lot, I expect. Anyway. Stan. At the minute, you're focussed on your carpet. What can you see on the screen?"

"That's amazing?" answered Stan.

"What is?"

"I can see my carpet in a little box, and you. There you are. Such a handsome chap! Can you see me waving, Lee?"

"No, Stan. Unfortunately not," Lee replied, though a careful examination of his tone might have revealed that he, in fact, felt fortunate for this small favour, as he pictured in his mind's eye Stan waving giddily at him like a young schoolgirl.

"That little box you can see," Lee went on, with the patience of a saint. "The one that isn't me. That's what your camera is focusing on, and what *I* can see. And right now all I see is carpet. You need to turn it round."

"Right-*toe*, Lee!" complied Stan happily. "I'm on the case! I'm on the case, like... like..."

But Stan was too distracted by the task at hand to relate to Lee what fictional detective he may have had in mind. Stan turned the iPad over so that he was now looking at the shiny silver rear surface, as instructed. "How's that?" he asked.

Lee cleared his throat. "Yes, there you are, but yer wobbling a bit. Can you see me?"

"How can I see you?" laughed Stan. "You told me to turn the iPad around, silly."

"What?" growled Lee. It could have been the lilt of his Irish brogue. But then again it could well have been a growl. "Have you turned the entire iPad around?" asked Lee, already suspecting the answer.

"Yes! You bloody told me to!"

"*Jayzus wept...*"

"Lee, are you praying again? Is this not a good time to talk? Should I call back later...?"

"You don't need to turn the whole iPad around, Stan," Lee told him, as calmly as his tattered nerves would allow. "Just turn the camera around," Lee advised him. "Right, mate, just go back to where you were a moment ago, you know, when we started..."

"Okay," replied Stan simply.

Lee released a melodic whistle while he waited for Stan to sort things out on his end, like he was the hold music at a call centre. "You did it?" he asked, after a few moments.

"Yes," replied Stan.

"Wait. Have you put the iPad back to your ear?"

"Yes."

Lee released a muffled groan. It was muffled because his fist was in his mouth once again. "Stan. I didn't need you to go back to that stage, not all the way back to *that* stage, mate. Okay, so... right, remember I said about not needing to hold them to your ear, like a traditional phone...?"

"Ah, yes. How's that?" asked Stan, holding the iPad out, finally, like a book, once again.

"Perfect. Well, not perfect as I can see the carpet again. The problem is that there are two cameras, see? And you've currently got the wrong one... No, no, Stan, don't turn the iPad over again..."

"Ah, okay."

"Stan, all you need to do is keep the iPad in the exact same position. Don't turn it over or put it back to your ear. Okay? Are you with me?"

"I'm with you," Stan replied, like someone on the wrong end of a hostage negotiation. "Okay so now what?"

"There are two cameras," Lee instructed. "One looking forward, yeah? — to the carpet — and one pointing back towards you, Stan. Presently, you've engaged the camera that's looking at the carpet. All you need to do is change the camera. There should be a button on the screen you need to press, and you need to change the camera with that. Once you've done that, instead of looking forwards, it'll look back — one-hundred-eighty degrees — so I can see yer pure white chompers and sultry golden suntan."

"I'm pressing a button, Lee."

Lee watched on incredulously as the image on his screen slowly rotated... but with no image of Stan becoming visible.

"Stan, what exactly are you doing now?"

"I'm turning round a hundred-and-eighty degrees."

"Yes. Of course you are, so it is," remarked Lee, unsurprised, at this point, as the image he could see moved from the carpet, past what looked like the base of the couch, and then over to looking out onto the patio doors, where the image came to an abrupt, shaky halt.

"I've spun around on my seat," proclaimed Stan happily. "I was looking towards the television, but I'm now looking towards the back of the room, towards the wall."

"Stan, I meant the camera needed to change position. Not you," Lee explained. "Stan, I think it's probably best if I call you back in five minutes when Frank is out of the bath...?" suggested Lee. "And before I launch my electronics into the food blender?"

"What? I didn't catch that last bit, Lee. What am I supposed to watch...?"

But just then...

"Is that you, Lee?" boomed the familiar and oh-so-very-welcome voice of Frank from the background.

"Frank, thank god. Frank, can you help out Stan with the camera as I'm currently looking... Ah, there we go. Thank you, Frank. Stan... bless him... but Stan was driving me to distraction, and I was certain I'd lose my—"

"It *is* wonderful, this modern technology!" interjected Stan, waving like a blithering idiot.

"—mind," finished Lee.

"I'm just out of the bath," announced Frank, pulling up a seat next to Stan and adjusting the camera like an old pro.

"Yes. That would explain why yer naked torso is now filling up my screen, Frank. Please tell me you're wearing a towel down below," implored Lee.

"You're safe, Lee," Frank assured him with a chuckle. "Anyway, where's Stella? Where's your better half?" Frank went on. "Oh, hang on, there she is," he added. "And better *three-quarters*, I should say, given the relative dimensions of you pair."

Frank and Stan would have covered their eyes but, alas, it was far too late for that. Far, far too late.

"You're a laugh a minute, as usual, Frank," Stella piped up from behind Lee, rummaging for a fag from god-knows-where, since...

"I'm guessing she's just out of the bath as well? Only she didn't receive the memo about the towel, like me?" Frank enquired rhetorically.

"Hell's bells!" shouted Lee, spinning round, fairly lively, mortified, and dropping his tablet in the process. "Stella, I'm on FaceTime, and the lads have just seen you... *au naturel.*"

Stan looked at Frank with a very pained expression, and the two listened and waited patiently.

"It won't be the first time," replied Stella. "Nor will it be the last. I've said it before, couple of dirty old gets, them two. Anyways, I thought you were phoning them?"

"To be fair, so did Stan," Lee told her. "He's about as useful as a bloody chocolate teapot!"

"That's our Stan," agreed Stella, placing fag-to-mouth and lighting up.

Stan leaned closer to his tablet, looking at a blank screen. "I can *hear* you, Lee," he said. "The reception is crystal-clear, if you didn't know," he added, leaning in ever closer still, so that his nose was practically touching the device, despite this being not-at-all necessary as the reception was, after all, crystal-clear.

Then, as if by some sort of dark alchemy, like the answer in a magic 8-ball moving into view from the murky depths, Lee's face suddenly appeared once more, in full view, causing Stan to snap back with a jerk.

"So," continued Lee, scarlet-faced. He looked over his shoulder, and then moved closer to the screen. "Is she out of camera angle now?" he whispered.

"Sure is," replied Frank, gratefully. "Yes," Stan agreed.

"So," Lee said again. "There's a reason I wanted to video call you lot tonight, and it's not because I wanted to take a gander at yer darlin' mugs. Or, Frank, yer mostly unattired body. No offence."

"None taken," Frank answered him jovially.

Like a rabbit from a hat, Lee whipped out a folded letter and, with precision, snapped his arm smartly to open it up with a sudden jerk. Then, he seductively teased it in front of the camera, building the tension. "I have here," he said slowly, not wishing to give the mystery away so quickly. "I have here... something that's going to make your..."

There was a pause.

"Yes?" asked Frank, on tenterhooks. "Well get on with it, man," he told Lee.

Lee paused further, with a far-off expression in his face. Then, not to Frank, he said...

"Babe, I'm still on the phone! Yes, on the... Why would I know where your lighter is, I don't smoke, luv... Hang on, didn't you just light a cigarette...? If you didn't have your lighter then, how did you manage to...?"

Lee went to speak to Frank and Stan once more, but it was clear his attention, at least for the moment, was elsewhere.

Frank and Stan looked down on their iPad as Lee's head bobbed in and out of camera shot. "Sorry, guys," he offered, returning momentarily, and then, back to Stella, "Stella, you cannot light your fag on the cooker. Remember, we've got an electric hob, not gas. You'd be there all day, darlin'. I'm sure you've got a spare lighter in your bedside drawer. I put one there in case you woke up in the night and wanted a ciggie. That's how thoughtful I am... Yes. Thoughtful... Thoughtful, I said. Yes..."

Lee looked back to the camera, just in time to see Stella, there on the viewscreen, still naked as a jaybird and captured in all her glory ambling from the kitchen to the bathroom in the background, a vague, dark figure swinging its arms, looking very much like the Sasquatch caught on the infamous Patterson–Gimlin film of 1967.

"Babe!" shouted Lee. "Babe, they've just seen you starkers again!"

"What did I tell you about them two?" replied Stella, completely undisturbed. "They can't get enough once they've started, cheeky devils. Anyways, enough about them two bellend boys," she shouted, from the other room now. "I'm in the bedroom table, but I cannot find the lighter! Which drawer is it in??"

# FRANK & STAN'S BUCKET LIST #3: ISLE 'LE MANS' TT

Lee moved his head back from the camera, craning his neck away, in Stella's general direction. "Babe, it's in the second drawer down! It's next to Brad Pitt!" he shouted back.

Frank and Stan were, again, looking at a shaky screen, listening, but any dialogue at this point was barely audible...

"Right. I'm back. Sorry about that," returned Lee, coming into view after a tick, but...

"Lee!" growled Stella, now a floating head by the doorframe behind Lee.

"What now, Babe?"

Frank and Stan could just about make out Stella's permed head, fag hanging, as per usual, off her bottom lip. "Like what you see! I'm sure you do! Cheeky devils!" shouted Stella, pointing towards the screen, before turning her attention back towards Lee. "There's no lighter in my drawer next to Brad Pitt!" she said to Lee.

"Are you sure?" Lee called back. "I put it there earlier! Next to the purple one?"

"Purple one?" replied Stella. "I thought Brad Pritt was that cream-coloured one!"

Lee placed his hand over the microphone, but it had minimal effect, as Stan and Frank could still make out the sordid details of the conversation, to their chagrin. Or, to their delight. They couldn't decide which.

"No, darlin', Brad Pitt is the purple one with the extra thing that pokes out like a little finger! The cream-coloured job is Guy Martin! The nine-incher!"

Stan's eyes suddenly went wide.

Frank, uncharacteristically, had nothing to say. He just sat there, his own eyes darting back and forth, trying to work out how he could scrub this from his mind.

"Ah!" replied Stella, matter-of-factly, as if this sort of conversation were not the least bit uncommon. "That's where I went wrong, didn't I! Only I was looking at the six-incher!"

"The six-incher? That's Daniel Craig, silly!"

"Daniel Craig? Then which one's Idris Elba!"

"The larger black one! The one with the nubs all over the shaft for extra pleasure!"

"Ah! Of course it is! What was I thinking! What *else* would that one be! I *am* silly!" Stella called back. "Oh! Here it is! I found my lighter! I'd forgotten I'd moved it! All this time, I had it in my—"

"THIS LETTER," Lee said abruptly, with all that sordid business now sorted, and returning to the matter of the original call. He cleared his throat. "This letter," he continued, ignoring the dumbfounded faces staring back at him. "I'm going to hold it up to the screen so you can read it, alright? Here, can you see it?"

Stan screwed his eyes up. "I've not got my reading glasses, Lee. And Frank..." said Stan, looking over to his partner. "I think Frank is catatonic at present. Can you just read it to us, please?"

Lee read it out to them. The contents of the letter were as follows:

> To: Mr Lee Watson c/o Frank & Stan's Food Stamps
>
> Dear Mr Watson,
>
> On behalf of the Charities Committee, I'd like to congratulate you on the commendable work undertaken by your organisation.
>
> I'm delighted to confirm that your charity has been shortlisted for the accolade of Charity of the Year.
>
> The presentation will take place on October 15th at The Continental Hotel Glasgow.
>
> We'd be delighted if you were in a position to attend and ask if you can confirm how many members of your organisation will be in attendance.
>
> I look forward to seeing you on the evening.
>
> Evelyn McCrane
> Charity Coordinator

Frank and Stan looked at each other, to Lee on the iPad, and then back to each other.

"That's unbelievable, Lee!" raved Stan. "Well done!"

"Lee, seriously. Well done," Frank chirped, finding his voice again, and echoing Stan's words. "This is a testament to your hard work. Bloody well done!"

Lee grinned like a schoolboy. "It's grand, I agree," he answered them. "Just grand. I was sleeping on the street not long ago, and now this! I've got my own flat, a beautiful girlfriend, and..."

Lee lowered his head and went silent for what seemed like an eternity.

"This is all down to you lot," Lee went on, wiping his cheek with the back of his hand. "Sorry. Nothing to get scundered about, I know. It's just... you lads believed in me, and because of our collective work, we've now got hostels and food drop in centres all over the country. You changed my life," he said, lowering his head once more and dabbing at his face again. "Not to mention the lives of many others."

"Lee?" asked Stan, after a respectable silence. "I think maybe there's something wrong with the sound on this iPad. All I can hear... is a low hum... like a constant buzzing noise?"

"Hmm, I can't hear anything," Lee came back, after he'd gathered himself back together. "Oh, wait, hang on, yes I can."

"And?" replied Stan.

"Sorry, I'm so used to it that I couldn't hear it at first," Lee explained, by way of not really explaining.

"Yes?" prompted Stan.

"Oh. Sorry. It's, *em*, not the technology in your hands, I'm afraid. Rather, it's the technology currently in *Stella's* hands. In the, ah... in the vicinity of the bedroom," he clarified. "Stella, darling. Can you come in here and stop doing what you're doing? Please stop for just a moment, luv!" he shouted to her.

"I'm smoking!" she shouted back.

"How in hell are you smoking, and, at the very same time...? You know what, nevermind. Can you just come in here, please?" he asked.

Sure enough, Stella was indeed smoking. She always was one for multitasking. "What?" she demanded, dabbing a bead of sweat on the sleeve of a hastily-flung-on dressing gown.

"Do you fancy a trip to Glasgow, Stella?" asked Lee.

"No," she replied automatically. "I'm sure they've still got a warrant out for my arrest."

"What arrest?" asked Lee, confused.

"Or was that Dublin?" Stella mused aloud, flicking ash into the pocket of her dressing gown smartly. "Anyway, dun't matter. It's not my thing," she said.

"But we've been shortlisted for an award," Lee told her, waving the letter.

"Will there be free food?" she asked, interest now piqued.

Stella moved closer, into shot, and whilst it looked like the sash around the waist was holding fast on her night-time attire, Frank and Stan closed their eyes, fearing the worst, afraid it might yet give way under the considerable strain at only a moment's notice.

Stella took the letter in her hands and pored over it, with eyes glancing up at periodic intervals. Gently — and, for her, gently was not the way she ordinarily did things — she folded the letter carefully back up, once she was done, before handing it back off to Lee.

"I'm proud of you dickheads," she offered, with a sincerity that belied her form of address. "Seriously. I'm very proud." She placed a hand on Lee's shoulder, grabbed his head with her other hand, and then promptly thrust his head into the crevasse of her ample bosom.

Once released from the depths of her cleavage, and air returned again to his lungs, Lee grinned widely. "Stella, but that's not the only surprise," he said to her.

"Oh?"

"Have a guess who the compère for the evening is?"

"How the fuck should I know," she replied, somewhat cross. "You know I don't like bloody guessing games. Just out with it."

"It's a TV personality and sportsperson who you're particularly keen on."

"Just come out with it!" she shouted, but then, "Wait, hang on. Sue Barker? Is it Sue Barker??" she replied quite suddenly, and to Lee's bewilderment.

"What? Sue Barker? What on...?" Lee covered the microphone, again, but it was equally as useless this time around as it was the last. "I'll give you a clue," he whispered to her. "You've just been getting rather friendly with him, in your own fashion."

No reaction.

"In there," Lee further explained, pointing over towards the bedroom.

"Brad Pitt?"

"No, not Brad Pitt. Who'd you have for afters?"

Stella's jaw dropped, as did the fag stuck to her lip along with it.

"Not Sue Barker," Stella confirmed.

"Not Sue Barker," Lee verified.

"Then it's got to be... *Guy Martin*??"

Lee released the microphone and announced with great fanfare, to both Stella and to the iPad, for the benefit of Stan and Frank at the other end: "The host is none other than TV star and Isle of Man TT legend, Guy Martin. Stella's guilty pleasure."

Frank clapped his hands. "Again. Lee, this is a fantastic achievement, and it really humbles me that..."

"WHAAAT?" Stella screamed, cutting across Frank. "You're telling me *Guy Martin* is going to be at this gig? THE Guy Martin??"

By now, she'd firmly gripped Lee's shirt, throwing a glare at him so intense it would melt the Riiser-Larsen Antarctic Ice Shelf. "You're not lying???"

"No," replied Lee. "I promise. I promise you I wouldn't lie, particularly with your hands so close to my throat. But... if this isn't your type of thing?" he teased her, which, with Stella, was a game that could play havoc with your life expectancy. "I mean, if this isn't your sort of affair, like you said, then you needn't feel obligated to come along..."

Stella paced back and forth like a rabid, crazed animal. She peeled the fag from her lip, and, if this weren't unusual enough, a rare smirk emerged.

"Guy Martin?" Stella asked, in a trance-like state. "Guy Martin. Guy Martin," she kept repeating, like a mantra. "Guy Martin..."

"So you'll be coming with us, then?" asked Lee. "It's not too late to back out, you know. I'm sure there are other people — so-and-so, maybe? — who might go in your—"

"JUST YOU TRY AND STOP ME GOING!" said Stella, making her position absolutely clear. "I NEED TO GO!"

"Well if you're certain, then," Lee said with a laugh.

Stella, serious now, and much more sedate, said, "In fact I need to get back to my previous appointment with Guy Martin. Don't tell Brad, though. He gets very jealous."

Neither Frank, Stan, nor Lee said a word. Some things were best left unsaid. Best to leave her to her own devices, they surmised. Literally. To her own devices.

"Really great about that award, Lee," said Frank, after a bit.

Lee nodded appreciatively. "Oh, and something else I was going to mention," he told them. "I think we're going to have our first resident for the farm. It's a friend of Susie's. And we've got a few more lined up on top of that."

"Already?" asked Stan. "We're a few weeks away from being finished, still."

"I know, Stan. This lady is exactly what the farm was set up for. It's domestic violence, and she needs to get away to someplace safe. So this is perfect. She's also got a young son. For now, we've got her comfortable in one of the hostels over here."

"Brilliant," Frank joined in. "We should be finished up for early December, hopefully. We've had a farmer agree to come along to help out with preparing farming lessons to offer, and we've been inundated with people wanting to get involved with traditional crafts. I, for one, am looking forward to seeing Stan having a go at basket-weaving!"

"I'm sure I'll be marvellous at it," sniffed Stan.

"As well as the hostel, this is going to be a real community initiative," Frank carried on. "Also, Lee, with the new barn, we've been able to increase the residential rooms from eight to twelve, so we've more to fill."

"Nice problem to have!" Lee returned. "Also, we need to think about the name. At least in relation to the farm. I'm not sure it really goes, does it?"

"How do you mean?" asked Stan.

Lee stroked his chin. "Well, at the minute, with the charity being called Frank-and-Stan's Food Stamps, that implies we're just about providing food stamps, right? Which we're not. We've got thirteen hostels across the UK, and now this one in the Isle of Man."

Frank nodded along in agreement, stopping briefly to adjust the towel still around his waist. He wanted desperately to scratch his balls, but felt now was not the most opportune moment to do so. And thus he remained respectful, leaving his balls, for the time being, at least, unscratched.

"I do agree, Lee," he said. "We probably need to keep Frank and Stan in there somehow, of course. And not just from an ego perspective, but more of a brand type of thing, you understand."

"Frank and Stan's Hostel?" suggested Stan, but then, quickly, "No, that's rubbish. It sounds like a prison or something."

"That will work in the UK just fine, actually," said Lee. "Since that is indeed what they are— hostels. The place in the Isle of Man, though, is a bit more than that, isn't it? It's more than simply a bed for the night. It's also somewhere to learn new skills, and to build confidence levels."

"The TT Farm?" asked Stan.

Frank and Lee thought for a moment, before Frank opined, "It's not the cleverest. But it does get the job done, I suppose. And if it wasn't for the TT, we wouldn't be here in the first place. And if it wasn't for the TT, we wouldn't have been gifted the farm. Albeit temporarily."

"Plus it's smack-bang on the TT course!" added Lee, warming up to Stan's initially-somewhat-dodgy idea.

Frank looked over to Stan, and in the absence of any objection, declared, "Okay, guys. Frank and Stan's TT Farm, it is. We look forward to welcoming our first guests in a few weeks, and Lee, we look forward to seeing you and Stella in Glasgow next month. We also need to get our heads together for how we'll be funding our grand plans for the farm. We definitely need to ramp up the fundraising effort, if I'm not mistaken."

"The charity trust should help?" enquired Lee.

"Sure, but we've grand plans," explained Frank. "We're not going to have the farm forever, so it'd be good to have the funds to buy another place as soon as Henk needs this one back."

Stan widened his grin, moving closer to the screen. "I can't wait for Glasgow. I'm going to have to get some fresh underpants for the trip!" he said.

"I know. It's... exciting?" replied Lee, not entirely understanding Stan's meaning. "I'm going to treat Stella to a new frock, myself," he added, looking over his shoulder to the direction of his dear one presently retired to the other room. "Well, not a *new* one, exactly, since she hasn't got an *old* one to begin with. But, a lovely gown. And, perhaps some new jewellery for this big occasion. She's an unpolished diamond, that one. A real lady. And I'm going to make her look like the true royalty that she is!" he told them.

"Lee!" Stella shouted from the bedroom.

"Yes, luv?" Lee answered attentively.

"Lee, you're going to have to run down the shops. I'm not sure there's much life left in Guy Martin's batteries!"

"Right-*ho!*" came Lee's jolly reply.

## Chapter
# SIX

"Is that the last biscuit, Monty?" asked Dave, staring at it like a hungry, stray dog stares into a butcher shop window.

"This one?" replied Monty, extending his tongue to take a long, luxurious lick of the chocolate coating. "I think it might be, indeed, yes," he confirmed, dispatching it in one fluid motion.

"Bastard."

Dave leaned back against a large tractor tyre, placing his hands behind his head, releasing a contented groan as he stretched. "It's not a bad life, Monty. Would you look at that view," he said reflectively, using his chubby hand to introduce the panorama that was the rolling Manx countryside. "Just there," he said, pointing. "That's where the steam train to Peel used to run," he relayed to Monty, indicating a field at the south side of Frank & Stan's TT Farm.

"It's not too bad at all, me old chum," Monty agreed, joining him resting against the tyre, nursing his cup of tea, and admiring the view. By virtue of his lazy eye, he had, perhaps, an arguably even better appreciation of the expansive vista. "Nossir, not half bad," he reiterated for good measure. "And you're a TT winner," he added casually and for reasons apparent only to himself.

"Ay? Where'd that come from?" replied Dave. "But you're correct in that assessment. And I'm not complaining."

Monty slapped his friend's thigh. "I dunno, I guess I'm proud of you, is all. My mate, Dave Quirk. A TT winner."

"*Mmm*," said Dave, like a dog getting his belly rubbed, closing his eyes contentedly.

"Do you remember our first TT?" Monty set forth.

"Sure I remember," replied Dave, without missing a beat. "The copious amounts of alcohol that made me forget things were before and after it— not during." He smiled at the thought.

Monty let his gaze wander, perhaps in awe of the countryside, perhaps in recollection. "Do you remember our first machine, all those years ago, when we were doing the club racing? Before the TT?"

"Remember it!" Dave came back, opening his eyes again. "Ha! That bloody thing nearly *killed* me! I spent weeks working on that contraption. Still, I learned what I know now from that beastie. It nearly bankrupted the pair of us, though, in the process. It was lucky you came into some cash right about then or the dream could have ended there."

Monty slurped on his cuppa, wiping the remnants of biscuit from the side of his mouth with an expert curl of the tongue. "I didn't have any," he remarked, after a bit.

"Any what?"

"Cash," replied Monty. "I didn't have a pot to piss in."

"What? But you paid for the tyres and the bodywork from your inheritance."

"There was no inheritance. I didn't even have an Uncle Sam."

"I thought it was an Auntie?" queried Dave.

"Whatever. Either way, they didn't exist. I knew you wouldn't have just taken the cash, so I made that whole bit up. I sold the washing machine and the fridge. I think I may have sold the lawnmower, also, and a few other things as well. The wife went absolutely mental. I *almost* sold the garden gnomes, but then thought better of it at the last minute, thank goodness."

"I *would* have!" protested Dave, sitting up abruptly.

"Would have what?"

"Taken the cash! I wouldn't have thought twice about it, actually."

Monty bobbed his head. "Fair enough. Still, I'd do it again in a flash. The happiest time in my life. Again, thank goodness I kept the garden gnomes."

A goat wandered over. Judging by its markings, it was the same as that which had terrorised the pair previously. Presently, however, the goat was considerably more placid. Their former adversary now placed its bum on the ground, taking up position sitting by Monty's feet. It ruminated agreeably, chewing again the contents of its last meal, as it likewise took in the most pleasant of views along with its new associates.

"That mower, Monty," Dave commented. "You didn't sell it. I borrowed it."

"Eh?"

"I borrowed it," Dave repeated. "I forgot to give it back."

Monty drained the remaining contents of his cup. "It was all about sacrifices, back then," he said accommodatingly. "Hang on. Here, what are you laughing at?"

"I've just remembered that I sold your mower," admitted Dave.

"How's that funny, exactly? I think that's called theft," suggested Monty.

The goat stopped chewing, suddenly, and looked over to Dave. Monty would have looked over to Dave disapprovingly as well, but there was no need since one of his eyes was already on him anyway.

"Your wife was that annoyed about the washing machine and the fridge that I bought her, well, you both, new ones," Dave explained. "I sold your mower to put the proceeds towards it. But I forgot the mower was yours to begin with. Funny, when you—"

"Wait, so you bought the new ones?" Monty cut in. "But she said she inherited some..."

"Yeah," remarked Dave.

"We're a bunch of lying bastards," Monty laughed.

The goat, sensing all was once again well, turned to look back over the field, and resumed its rumination and mastication.

"Do you ever think about me and you, Dave?" Monty cast out.

Dave pressed his lower lip out, like a fish. "Well I always thought you were happily married, Monty. But I'd be lying if I said the thought hadn't crossed my mind. I'm only human, after all. You look like you'd be a very generous lover and I hope, one day, god willing, to find out for certain if my suspicions are correct."

Monty turned into Dave, as if preparing to lay a kiss firmly upon cheek.

"Here, mate, I was only—" Dave protested.

"I meant about us in the TT, you twit," Monty assured him, letting him off the hook. "Me and you. What we've experienced."

"Not really, no," replied Dave, stroking the goat with his foot.

"Oh," said Monty, his spirits sinking, torpedoed suddenly, like the RMS Lusitania.

"Of *course* I do, you soppy sod! You *made* the TT for me, Monty," Dave told him, with great sincerity. "Now, granted, I know I wouldn't have won that TT with you on board, this last time... uh, no disrespect intended..."

"No offence taken," Monty told him. "But, do continue," he instructed, shaking an invisible sceptre.

"Sure, that TT trophy will keep me warm on cold winter nights," continued Dave. "But it's the experience, ultimately, the friendship and comradery that I'll look back on fondly. Happy memories. And speaking of. You remember when I submitted that picture of you in your leathers to the calendar shoot in that gay porn magazine?"

"I do indeed," Monty returned, his feathers not the least bit ruffled. "Bought a copy for myself, I did. And I was quite the celebrity for some time after that. I'm sure I still get the odd approving glance every now and then. In fact, now I think on it, the first time your dad met me, he did that *I'm-sure-we've-met-before* routine, as a matter of fact."

"Cheeky!" answered Dave, approvingly. "Anyway, Monty. As lovely as this trip down memory lane is, my old son, you've still not explained to me why the tractor is covered over and why you look like a smurf?"

"A smurf?" asked Monty, cocking his head with interest.

"Yes, you're covered in blue paint, or whatever that is," said Dave with an up-and-down wave of his hand, highlighting said azure pigmentation.

"I always had a thing for her when I was younger, you know," confessed Monty, by way of nothing, and suddenly examining his arms as if noticing the colouration there for the very first time.

"Who?"

"Her. In the Smurfs."

"Smurfette? You worry me, Monty. Oh god, now I'm thinking about a young Monty and a very blue Smurfette, doing... doing unspeakable things. I think you may well have just ruined my childhood there, Monty...?"

Monty placed his cup on the grass and drew himself up, taking care not to upset the now sleeping goat. "Stand up and close your eyes, Dave," he asked of Dave.

"This is like that night we had in London, all over again, isn't it?" said Dave, but he did as instructed nonetheless.

Monty positioned Dave manually, as Dave was currently blinded on account of his eyes being tightly shut, turning him around and placing him several paces back from the tractor whose back tyre they'd just been leaning up against while seated.

"Okay," Monty instructed. "Open your eyes."

Dave put his hands on his hips, fully expecting to be underwhelmed by whatever Monty was about to show him, as Monty introduced the surprise as might a cheap game show host. Still, Dave was glad to be rid of the lingering images of a gaily frolicking Monty and Smurfette, playing out like a film reel on the back side of his eyelids.

"Holy shitsticks, Monty," declared Dave once he'd indeed reopened his peepers. "I prepared myself to only *pretend* to be impressed, you know, like a parent at the school concert. But seriously, that there is a thing of absolute beauty."

Dave approached the tractor — which they'd only uncovered that week — and stroked the paintwork like that of a prized stallion. The once-rusting and grubby red paintwork was now a polished, vibrant blue, and with an unmistakably familiar yellow-custard splodge emblazoned across the front and with the number "42" featured in the middle — a memorial to their beloved sidecar.

Monty took his thumb and wiped a couple of watery drops from about his eyes at the sight of it again. "It's a bit rough in parts, after a fashion, but it's the first time I've used a spray gun, yeah?" he acknowledged modestly, managing a grin. "Oi. And look at the windscreen," he said.

Dave welled up. He well and truly welled up. He couldn't have welled up more if he were wearing wellies, such was the extent of his welling.

"You've put our name across the top of the windscreen, haven't you?" said Dave, seeing, of course, that Monty had done just that.

Monty shrugged.

"Come here, you," Dave sighed, wrapping his arms around Monty and holding him tight. Dave gently caressed the top of Monty's head, and said, "You know, that tractor would probably have gone quicker than our first sidecar, Monty."

"I miss it," announced Monty, looking up with his capable eye.

Dave held the embrace for a few more seconds, before it became much too awkward to continue it. He let go of Monty and coughed, the cough resetting his 'Man' parameters neatly back into place. "Miss what?" he enquired. In a manly tone.

"Me and you in the TT, Dave," explained Monty. "I thought I was happy without it in my life. But I think the injury has sorted itself, and I might just see about getting a ride with another outfit for the next go-round."

Dave took a step back, crossing his arms across his chest in the process. "Another outfit, Monty? You'll do no such thing!"

"What's the alternative? You've already got a passenger, that idiot, McMullan. And you're a TT winner now."

"Harry McMullan can fuck right off!" Dave insisted. "I've not heard a bloody word from him since the TT, and I know he'll only be keeping me warm in case he can't get another rider. Plus, the guy's a complete tool to start with."

Monty didn't say anything.

Dave moved closer to his partner-in-crime, for a second time, placing a hand on his friend's shoulder. "Monty, if you'll be my partner, once again, I'd have you back in a heartbeat. IN A FUCKING HEARTBEAT. You hear me, me lad?"

"You've won a *TT*, Dave," Monty protested. "You can't go from that... that *grandeur*... to simple mediocrity with me. I mean, keep in mind, most of the time we didn't even know if we were quick enough to qualify," he admonished him.

"I'm *already* a TT winner, Monty. I'll not be any happier than I am about that now, even if I were to win another, or another still. It's not about that for me. It's sitting on our crappy sofa outside the awning, sharing a beer, chatting to any idiot passing by who'll listen to us. *That's* the TT for me. The thrill of finishing a race with *you* meant more to me than winning the bloody thing with that McMullan sod hanging about. I'd honestly enter this *tractor* if it meant I could race with you once more. I know it'd make Frank happy, he'd love to see us back together, and without being overly morbid... you know what I'm saying."

"Oh, right, that's gone and done it, then," sobbed Monty, fanning his face. "Come here, you lot!"

For two big units, as they were, they certainly knew their way around a tender embrace.

"Here's to Dave and Monty!" proclaimed Dave to the heavens. "TT teammates once more!"

"Teammates!" Monty joined in.

"Can you hear it, Monty??"

"Can I hear what?"

"'Ride of the Valkyrie!' Can you hear it in your head??"

"I can hear it!" cried Monty. "I can really hear it!"

"To glory!" Dave shouted.

"To glory!" Monty exclaimed, and they both danced on the spot, stuck together like Chang and Eng, the famous Siamese twins.

"*Ahem*," sputtered a hoarse, phlegm-less cough, interrupting, abruptly, the Bromance of the Ages.

Dave lifted his chin from Monty's neck. "Can we help?" he asked, breaking free with a sigh.

The cough belonged to a stout middle-aged man with a furious expression. "I've just been up to the farm and the builders there said I'd find the boss down here. Is that you, Papa Smurf? Or you, Sandor Clegane?"

"Did he just refer to you as *The Hound*?" Monty asked of Dave.

"If Frank and Stan aren't about, then, yes, we're in charge, I guess you could say," replied Dave, batting away the newcomer's presumed insult. "I'm sensing a little hostility here?" noted Dave amiably, though taking a protective stance in front of Monty.

"I'm Roger," explained Roger. "I've just been driving past on my way to Peel and I couldn't help notice that the buildingworks have begun!"

Dave looked at Monty, and then back to Roger. "Roger that, Roger," he said in his best American accent, unable to resist. "Yeah, *erm*, thanks for the update? I wondered what all the men in high-viz jackets were doing? Be sure to pop by again with any further updates," he told Roger with a playful sort of sarcasm.

Roger's eyes narrowed. "How are they building?"

"Shovels, diggers, and I think one of them has a saw?" presented Monty sagely.

Roger didn't reply immediately, rather, taking a moment, like so many good men before him, to ascertain where Monty's line of sight was focussed. "Is he taking the piss?" he asked of Dave, eventually, once he'd given up what he decided was a useless endeavour vis-à-vis Monty's eyes. "How the hell have you managed to get the builders in? I was only here a few weeks ago and there's not a chance in hell you could've had it removed by now!" he scolded them sternly.

Dave stared at this Roger fellow blankly. Then he turned to Monty. Monty, in turn, looked to the sleeping goat. The goat, as it was still sleeping, could offer up no opinion on the matter.

"I'm sorry. Removed what?" Dave enquired, finally.

"Asbestos!"

"Bless you," came Monty's automatic reply.

Dave held his palms aloft in submission. "Okay, soldier," he said. "Let's begin again. And you are?"

Roger's angry, stubble-chin-featured expression didn't soften, but he did explain...

"Right. I was here to do a full asbestos survey on this place and the barns only a few weeks prior. I haven't heard anything back since then. You could have hired a competitor of ours, but that seems unlikely, as there aren't many asbestos-removal companies over here at all that could handle a job of this scale. And so finding one willing and able to take the project on, having them perform their own survey, procuring them for the job, *and* having the work completed, or in the process of completion, could not *possibly* have been done in the span of a few weeks. And yet here we are, renovations well underway. Hence, my great concern."

"Frank and Stan had you do an asbestos survey. Which came up positive. And then let the workmen in?" asked Dave. "I'm not buying it," he said, shaking his head. "That doesn't sound like our Frank and Stan at all."

"Believe what you want, but it's true. Four days, me and the boys spent attending to it," countered Roger. "Here, I'll even show you the report," he suggested, with frustration in his voice becoming more apparent. He took his phone out of his pocket and used the flattened tip from one of his strangely nail-less fingers to scroll through until he found what he was looking for. "Here!" he announced, poking the screen of his phone with a dull meaty thud.

Dave and Monty moved in like two dogs eating spaghetti in a Disney cartoon, though it was unclear, at the moment, who was to be Lady and who The Tramp.

"I'm going to overlook, for a moment..." gasped Dave... "the amount of zeros on the estimate part of this report."

Dave took the liberty of prodding the screen on Roger's phone, scrolling through himself. "Hold on," he said, finding something. "This wasn't given to Frank and Stan at all. It was given... to one Rodney Franks."

"Our nemesis!" exclaimed Monty.

Roger looked up and to the left, searching to recall. Asbestos, he never forgot. But he wasn't the best with names. "Was that who I spoke with? Smarmy little git with a face you wouldn't get fed up of punching?"

"That would be Rodney Franks," confirmed Monty.

"There's lots of asbestos, is there?" asked Dave, but it was a question that required no explanation, since the number of zeroes on the estimate had already provided him with the answer.

"Loads of it," Roger replied, happy to hammer the point home. "Loads and loads of it, I'm afraid. The place is full of it. In the wall panels near the chimney stack, in the interior tiles, in the soffits, with the pipework. I could go on."

"We need to get them builders out of there... Monty?" Papa Smurf was dispatched, double-quick, to clear out the building.

"On it!" said Monty, before only the back of him was visible.

Watching Monty recede into the distance, Dave leaned against the tractor, taking care not to kick the goat that slept throughout what was to follow.

"So that tosspot, Rodney Franks — and I'm being exceptionally kind here when I use the term *tosspot* — knew the place was full of asbestos but did nothing about it?" he asked.

Roger shrugged his shoulders. "I wouldn't know what this Rodney Franks character did or didn't do. All I know is what I see before me now. To be fair, your builders up there would have realised the place was covered in asbestos? Though of course that's not an excuse for this unsavoury Franks... tosspot," he said, adopting Dave's polite euphemism.

"I didn't get a good look at the quote for the work," grimaced Dave. "May I see that again, please? Also, how long d'ya reckon it'll take to fix all of this properly?"

Roger looked up to the farm using his finger like a laser pointer. A dull, stubby laser pointer. But still. "It's a big job," he said. "No two ways about it. I couldn't be one-hundred percent, but with enough men on... maybe three or four weeks? The other problem is that we might need to now rip out any work the builders have already done in order to get into it. This is the quote," advised Roger, pinching the screen to zoom in, as if the figure required any additional emphasis.

Dave stared down on the phone for what seemed an age. He scratched his head, when it didn't need scratching, more of a distraction than anything else, because he presently felt like dropkicking the sleeping goat into the neighbouring field. He licked his lips as the moisture in his mouth evaporated.

"This," Dave ventured eventually, with a series of rapid raps on the viewscreen as if he were tapping out the distress-call letters S.O.S. in Morse code. "This... oh shit. This is a nightmare."

Dave slid down the tractor tyre, sitting on the grass, as before, but with his knees pulled into his chest this time.

"We were going to do great things here, Roger," he told Roger in a faraway sort of melancholy despair. "This was going to be a community farm and a hostel to help those that need helping," he went on. "And not just that. This was my dream job. I was going to be working with my closest friends, in the great outdoors, looking at that view," moaned Dave, too drained of energy, currently, to even point. "And now... That doesn't look like it's going to happen now. Not anymore. Fuuu..." he said, expelling the last of the air in his lungs, and not even bothering to finish the expletive.

Roger the surveyor's initial vexation subsided and, given the circumstances, he felt compelled to comfort Dave in some small way. "Eh, it'll be fine," he said, patting the top of Dave's head with one of his raw, un-taloned hands. It was all he could think to do.

"S'alright," Dave whimpered miserably.

"I should, you know, ah..." Roger told Dave, taking a few steps back in retreat. "Well, then, *em*... phone me if you need me?"

Monty sprinted back down the field, a streak of blue, like a young Sonic the Hedgehog. Or, rather, a getting-on-in-years and slightly-out-of-shape Sonic. Nevertheless, Monty could still introduce a bit of speed to the equation when the situation called for it.

"They're all out of the house and the barn, but they told me they still want to be paid!" Monty gasped, bent over to catch his breath before a sitting Dave.

Roger took his leave, with a now-sympathetic expression on his weathered face. "I can get the boys around to start straight away!" he shouted, from a safe distance away.

Monty knelt next to Dave. "It'll be fine, Dave. We've overcome worse than this," he said, immediately sensing the profoundness of his friend's despair. "We'll have a word with Frank and Stan, and I'm sure they'll sort it out and everything will work out just fine.

Besides, they've got the money from the charity trust people, haven't they?"

Monty felt a strange urge to pat Dave on the top of the head. He wasn't sure from whence the impulse came, but before he could act on it, Dave shook his head and replied...

"They get that at the end, when the building work is complete. That money is to pay for beds, computers, ovens, and all that sort of stuff. I'm not exactly sure who's funding things at the moment, but I'm guessing some of it is coming from the existing charity. But, knowing Frank and Stan, I'm pretty sure most of it, at present, will be coming from their own pockets."

"Come on, Dave, we're all about the glass being half-full, here, aren't we?" Monty came back, trying his best to raise Dave's spirits. "Keep your pecker up, mate!"

"The glass might be half-full, but the bloody bank account is going to be empty," Dave answered, not rising to the challenge. "Frank and Stan are going to be devastated by this. Absolutely gutted. Monty, I've seen with my own eyes how much it's going to cost to make this place habitable, and there's not a hope in hell they're going to want to stump that amount of cash up after what they've already spent."

"It's that bad?"

"It's not good. They've only got the lease on the farm for a couple of years and there's not a snowball in hell's chance they'll spend that sort of money when the place is likely going to be ultimately demolished anyway in order to make way for the hotel. Sorry, mate, but I think the TT Farm is going to remain a pipe dream."

"Bugger," Monty commiserated.

"And I also think," Dave added, "that we better have a word with our former bosses or get ourselves down the job centre, quick-smart!"

The goat, still sleeping blissfully up until this point, suddenly awoke, stood upright, and began making chewing motions. When it realised that there was in fact nothing left in its mouth to chew on, it wandered off, presumably in search of same.

## Chapter
# SEVEN

"It's nice out here," remarked Stan, running his tongue around the top of his ice cream as he would across the tip of a...

"You want some?" he asked Frank, pressing it into Frank's face like a reporter's microphone.

"I'm good, thanks," came Frank's reply.

"It's not like you to turn an ice cream down, Frank," remarked Stan, feelings hurt.

"I could get my own," Frank suggested. One that's less, I don't know... desecrated...?"

Stan pouted for a moment, but only for a moment, before attending to his ice cream once again, this time attacking it with gusto. "Suit yourself," he said happily, between lip smacks.

Frank didn't respond. He took a deliberate lungful of the bracing sea air. He smiled as a plastic ball, propelled by the gentle breeze, was chased down by a determined boy along the beach. "I love it in Peel. Well, to be fair, I love *everywhere* on this Island. But there's something about Peel, in particular. The heritage, and the sense of nostalgia are..." he paused, searching for the right word. "Humbling?" he ventured. "I mean, look at Peel Castle."

"Right. I'm looking at it," replied Stan, carefully following instructions. "Now what?"

"You could almost close your eyes," Frank went on, "and imagine you were on sentry duty when you clapped eyes on a flotilla of Viking invaders."

"Oh," said Stan, realising he was only meant to imagine here and that there were really no further instructions other than this.

"You wonder what would have gone through your head," mused Frank.

"Probably a Viking spear?" Stan suggested helpfully.

"You could be right, Stan," Frank agreed with a chuckle.

Frank turned his attention back to the pursuit on the beach, a pursuit which had now been joined by a black border collie and what looked like the boy's sister. The squeals of delight carried perfectly on the breeze, interrupted only by the occasional bark from the boisterous dog.

Frank and Stan sat on the multi-coloured wooden benches for over an hour, after their Viking and ice cream-related exchanges, with barely a word between them. It was late September, but mild; families packed the small seaside town, taking advantage of the favourable weather. It wasn't an awkward silence between the two of them but, rather, one of pleasant contentment. Stan made short work of his ice cream treat, Frank dreamt further of Viking invasions of times past, and the pair of them simply carried on enjoying the splendid view.

Eventually, Stan looked up and down the promenade, and then back over to the ice cream shop. "Did Dave and Monty go for a pint of lager or something?" he asked. "Only they went into the shop with you earlier, but I've not seen them since."

Frank's hands were tucked inside his jacket, so he pointed with his foot. "Over there. On the beach," he said.

Stan raised his hand to defend against the sun, shielding his eyes. He craned his neck forward, focussing on the two grown men kneeling in the sand surrounded by several children observing their efforts. "Are they making sandcastles?" he asked.

"I expect so. They were trying out a few different bucket-and-spade combinations when we were in the shop. Daft buggers," Frank answered him.

Stan turned his attention directly to Frank. He went to speak, but stopped mid-delivery, words evading him momentarily.

"Yes?" said Frank, distracted, not quite in the present and images of Norsemen coming ashore still playing through his mind.

"You remember when I said I wouldn't bring up your illness unless you wanted to talk about it?" said Stan, finding his words.

"I do," replied Frank, his eyes coming into focus.

"Do you want to talk about it?" prodded Stan gently.

"Not particularly?" came the reply, with Frank pulling up the zip on his coat and burying his chin in the fabric.

Stan proceeded carefully, taking a few moments to get his question ready, like a dog circling round before finally settling down to bed. "Is there anything you're not telling me, Frank?" he asked delicately.

"No, Stan. I promise. I'll be honest, I've been a little tired lately. Perhaps I've been doing a bit too much? I'll maybe have a few early nights to sort things out," he offered up.

"You're still on the treatment, Frank? You've not taken yourself off it?" Stan enquired sympathetically.

"What? No, of course not," insisted Frank, looking at Stan quite earnestly. "I won't give up, Stan, I promise you that. I'll fight this thing right to the end, believe me. Like you said before, Death can bloody well fuck right off! Am I right?"

"Right as rain," Stan agreed with a laugh.

"No, shan't be getting rid of me that easily, old boy," said Frank. "And, besides, it's Molly's birthday today!"

"I sent her a card and flowers," Stan told him, smiling gently.

Frank smiled as well. "I found a picture of her sat on my knee," he related. "It was maybe her first day at primary school, and she was probably no older than that little boy there running after his ball," he said, pointing out the young one still gambolling on the beach. "My goodness she was a pretty little girl, my Molly. She had this cheeky little glimmer in her eye, and a smile that'd melt your ice cream."

Stan looked around, confused, to see if there was more ice cream about that perhaps he might've missed. Confirming that there was, sadly, no more ice cream to be had, he replied, "I remember, Frank. She was a little cracker. Still is."

"I know Molly and I have not always had the perfect father-daughter relationship, Stan. But I've always loved my little... my little..."

Frank couldn't continue, his voice breaking under a wave of emotion. He pitched forward, placing his head in his hands, shoulders heaving.

"Here, here, what's all this?" asked Stan, sliding across the bench, placing a comforting arm around Frank's shoulders.

"I'm sorry, Stan, it's just..." Frank began, but the emotion caught his words up in his throat again.

Stan held onto his friend tightly. "You don't apologise to me, Frank Cryer. There's no need. In fact, this here is what you need. It's just what you need." It was unclear, with the last remark, if Stan was referring to the good cry Frank was having, or the flurry of pats he was giving Frank's heaving shoulders, or perhaps both.

The emotion had made its way over to Stan's face as well, and he found himself wiping at his cheeks. "I've just had a spray tan and now it's going to be laid to waste," he admonished his dear friend.

"I don't want to go," whispered Frank. "I love everything in my life. I'm scared, Stan. I think of Molly and how quickly she's grown up and I hoped one day that I'd be running along the beach myself, chasing after my grandchildren. That's not going to happen now, Stan. That's not going to happen, is it?"

Frank's watery eyes pleaded, and with every fibre of his being Stan wanted to give Frank endless assurances to the contrary, but he knew that he couldn't.

"Will you tell them, Stan?" Frank said.

"Tell who, what?" Stan answered.

"My grandchildren, Stan. If Molly has children. Will you sit them down when they're old enough and tell them about me?"

Stan's bottom lip began to quiver of its own accord. He secured it between his whitened teeth, nodding to Frank as he did so. "Of course," he began, but had to stop to clear his throat. "*Of course* I will, you daft bugger," he continued. "I'll tell them about the kindest man I ever met and how, out of all these billions of people on this little planet, I was fortunate enough to travel through life's journey with one of the most generous, compassionate, and loyal fellows that I could have ever imagined calling my friend."

Dave placed his red bucket at Stan's feet. "Right, what's all this?" he asked, but, try as they might, Stan and Frank were unable to string a coherent sentence together between them, blubbering as they both were at present.

Monty placed his red spade in Dave's bucket, throwing an enquiring glance at him. He was hoping for some sort of an explanation, but Dave appeared equally as perplexed as regards to the current sobbing state of their friends.

"Male menopause?" suggested Dave, whispering to Monty.

What the cause of Stan and Frank's lamentation, it didn't matter. Instinctively, Dave and Monty sat either side of Frank and Stan, as that's what friends were for, giving them a good cuddle.

It seemed to do the trick, since Frank regained his composure in short order.

Frank looked at them each in turn. Clearing the emotion from his voice, he said to them, "If I sat here all the day, I don't believe I could think of the words to convey the positive influence you three have had on my life. Thank you. I mean it."

"There's more of us?" Monty asked, confused, afraid his wonky eye had been betraying him all these years. But he quickly ascertained that Frank was merely referencing Stan along with he and Dave, and he got back to the business of hugging in which they were currently engaged.

A wee head appeared above the retaining seawall in front of them, just then. A pigtailed girl with a sand-covered face wore a stern expression. "We've not finished, you two!" she admonished them. "Please, mister?" she said, now directing her attention over to Frank and Stan. "Please can they come back to play? Only we've not finished the sandcastle!"

Like children, Dave and Monty stared expectantly at Frank and Stan, ready to hang on their every word, every utterance magical and unexpected.

"Oh go on, then," said Stan, finally, fearful the pair might burst if kept in suspense much longer. "You can go and play for ten minutes, or at least until Henk shows up," he instructed them.

Dave and Monty were up in a flash, bucket and spade in hand, and making haste towards the sandy shoreline before you could say *Jack Robinson*.

"Play nice!" Frank called after them with a chuckle. "And make sure you let the other boys and girls have a go with the bucket, too!"

---

The bustling throngs on the promenade parted like the Red Sea, with concerned parents scooping children in their arms for safety's sake. A towering figure strode through their midst like a force of nature. "You steaming droppings of disease-infested excrement!" bellowed its voice, only adding to the keen apprehension of those assembled.

The figure progressed forward, unstoppable, leaving those in its wake scurrying away like crabs. As it moved ever closer to Frank and Stan's bench, it began shaking its mammoth clenched fist, only adding to the terrible effect.

"Henk looks very cross," suggested Frank to Stan, confidentially, before offering a conciliatory wave to the approaching figure blotting out the sun.

Henk towered over the still-seated Frank and Stan, glowering at them. Or just glowering in general. It was not yet evident.

"Ice cream?" asked Stan, pointing towards the shop behind, helpfully.

Henk stamped his foot down, shaking the earth. "That cravat-necked, unhealthy, undernourished *zakkenwasser*!" Henk yelled, looking to the sky, appealing to the gods. Or shouting at them. One or the other. Regardless, Henk's insults may not have come across the smoothest in English, but they were absolutely brilliant in their original untranslated Dutch.

Frank raised his hand, like a schoolboy about to ask a question, and nevertheless, without gaining permission, remarked, "I'm guessing the meeting with the planners wasn't positive?" Frank knew their friend Dutch Henk well and, now it was clear his fury wasn't directed at them, could see that it was safe to speak freely.

"You should have an ice cream," repeated Stan. He was never proficient at reading a situation well. Either that or he simply felt that ice cream was a good solution to any problem.

Henk's usual double-denim clothing combination with a black leather waistcoat was accompanied by a loosely fastened black tie. The veins in his forehead bulged and throbbed. His hair danced about his head, kept aloft by a wind that seemed to be more forceful at that raised elevation, giving the appearance of Medusa's writhing serpents.

Henk sat on the seawall, in front of Stan and Frank, looking particularly grim. "I am going to *kill* Rodney Franks," he said, spitting out the name of Rodney Franks like an ominous curse, dire and malevolent.

Frank and Stan looked at each other. They were no fans of Rodney Franks, either of them, but they wondered where this was leading.

Henk removed a raft of papers from inside his denim jacket, the breeze taking them up like a cheeky Manx gull scooping up someone's chips, resulting in them flapping wildly.

Frank stood up, ensuring he retained a respectful distance. "What happened, exactly, at the planning meeting, Henk?" he said, speculating as to the source of Henk's agitation.

"They have turned down permission for the TT Hotel," Henk told him, without preamble. "The planning department had been given many objections to the building because of what they referred to as its greenbelt location."

Stan joined Frank in the standing position. "That can't have been orchestrated by Rodney Franks, surely?" he asked.

"He had something to do with it," explained Henk. "As I came out of the planning meeting, he was waiting in the carpark. He had a giant cake on a table with candles. As I walked past him, three men with trumpets appeared!"

Frank turned to Stan, mouthing the words *'real trumpets?'* in puzzlement, trying to work out if Henk was speaking literally here or metaphorically. Simultaneously, Stan turned to Frank and enquired, similarly mouthing the words, *'real cake?'* In the end, neither considered it wise to pursue such a line of questioning directly with Henk.

"So I am fairly certain he had something to do with the planning objections," Henk went on. "Several of the objection letters indicated that there had been Viking treasure found on the site previously. So, the planners said that even if there had not been objections to the hotel, I would still have needed to complete a full archaeological dig. Which would have taken many months."

Stan cast Frank an admonishing look. *'Vikings'* he mouthed accusingly. Then, when Henk looked away for a moment to the heavens once again, Stan, all blame immediately cast aside, mouthed the additional silent words, *'Should we tell him about the asbestos?'* enquiringly.

Frank shook his head frantically, and then took a seat next to Henk on the seawall. "You can try again?" he said to Henk. "You must be able to appeal the decision?"

The knuckles of Henk's fists were white as sun-bleached whale bones. "It has taken me months to get to this stage, Frank. I could continue, but there would be no guarantee. Rodney Franks put a clause in the contract that I can return the property and the land back to him at a reduced rate within one hundred and eighty days. You see this? This genital herpes of a person knew all along that I would never get the planning permission within that time frame."

Stan took a step closer. "You can't give him it back?"

"I have spent nearly two hundred thousand pounds on lawyers and architects. If I continue on, I could spend *another* two hundred thousand pounds with no guarantee of planning permission. And to make matters worse still, I would need to employ *Illinois Jones* to check for Viking treasure," replied Henk gravely.

No one was brave enough to correct his film reference, nor felt it was the time for such things. Henk continued...

"I will get my revenge against Franks, good fellows, you may be certain of it. But he has won this battle, I am afraid, and I cannot let personal feelings get in the way of business decisions. I would be foolish to persist at this time. I am sorry, the two of you, but I am going to sell the farm back to the pus-filled abscess of infected tissue that is Rodney Franks. It would seem I have no choice in the matter."

"No. No you can't, Henk," pleaded Frank, sliding closer to him, but, even then, marvelling admiringly at the peculiar manner of Henk's strange insults. "You see, we've got everything in place. For the charity. We've got the first residents to arrive in a few weeks. We've got funding in place, and volunteers to help us with training courses. Frank and I have spent about fifty grand on the place already ourselves!"

Henk's aggression eased as the passion on Frank's face was apparent. "I am sorry, fellows, I know the importance of this place to you, but I cannot waste funds by spending more money on something I have already spent money on that is not good. You are businessmen. You can understand?"

Stan shrugged his shoulders, he couldn't argue with the logic. "At the risk of giving you more bad news, Henk…"

A look of panic crossed over Frank's face, but only temporarily, because he knew it needed saying, what Stan was about to say.

"Full disclosure, Henk. But you may get less from Rodney, in the end, than you imagine."

"What?"

"We've had the chap around from the asbestos company, a surveyor. It would appear that our collective arch-enemy had an asbestos survey completed. A rather extensive one, actually. And then didn't bother to tell anyone about it."

Henk produced a silver hip flask from his pocket, removed the lid, and dispatched several generous slugs, before offering it over to the other two.

"No, I've just had an ice cream," replied Stan, for no discernible reason, as that had never prevented him from combining the two in the past.

Henk didn't say anything, and Frank took Henk's silence as an invitation to provide additional details. "Henk, the place is lousy with asbestos. I saw the inspector's estimate, and it'll cost between seventy and a hundred thousand pounds to remedy this asbestos situation. I can only imagine that Rodney would subtract that amount off of any offer he'd make you for the farm. As I see it, you could either let us fix the place up and continue with the farm for a couple of years and hope you get planning permission, or you sell it back to the man you despise at a loss. Neither option ideal, granted."

Henk drained the rest of his compact container, making short work of it. Only then did he speak. Choosing his words carefully, he said: "I am going to rip a leg off from Rodney Franks' body, and then I am going to beat him with it. If that does not kill him, I will then take an arm off and use that to beat him also."

Henk said this calmly, but there was an intensity to his voice that was immediately evident. Henk pondered these thoughts of dismemberment and grievous bodily harm for an unnerving length of time. Then, he announced: "There is a third option."

"Another limb?" Stan threw out.

"No," Henk said. "Although that is always a good option."

"Go on," Frank returned, assuming Henk wasn't referring here to further mayhem.

"The two of you buy the property from me for the charity," Henk told them. "I will give you a very good deal," he went on. "You pay me what I have paid out to lawyers, architects, and everyone else that has had their hands fishing into my pockets for the last several weeks. If you return to me what I have paid out, I will be satisfied. In this way, you may take the farm outright. Even if you need to spend money for removal of the asbestos, you will still be getting a very large bargain on what the property is worth. Most importantly, it will make Rodney Franks a very, very angry fellow. And this will be very good."

"You're serious??" asked Frank.

"I am very serious," Henk answered him. "But I have only one very important condition," he added.

"Name it?" replied Frank, both agreeably and immediately.

"You must take the storage area for all the horse and cow excrements, yes? And you must commemorate it, I believe is the English word, by naming it after Rodney Franks. You see?"

"I do indeed," Frank told Henk. Frank glanced over to Stan, hoping to see in Stan's eyes the gleam of approval, but Stan held a vacant expression. Stan did this, it must be said, when working out numbers as he and numbers had a somewhat strained relationship.

Stan looked off to the distance, raising a finger as if to speak, then lowering said finger, and then raising it again, the hamster on its wheel housed in his cranium running furious overtime. "Frank..." commenced Stan with his summary findings once sufficient brainworks were produced.

"Yes?" said Frank, anxious for Stan to bloody get on with it.

"Frank. By my reckoning, we need to pay Henk two hundred thousand. The asbestos business is going to be another hundred thousand. Plus, we'll need to probably rebuild what we've already built so that the removal men can actually get that asbestos out. So, we're looking at about four — maybe five — hundred thousand pounds total. Frank, you know I'm ever the optimist. But, on this particular occasion, I think we may just have to say..."

"That, yes, we'll do it," Frank quickly agreed, extending to Henk a firm handshake to seal the deal.

This was, of course, not the response Stan was expecting of Frank. "We will...?" he said, thoroughly nonplussed.

Frank patted his longtime friend on the back. "Definitely! This is too important to give up on, me old pal. And we'll get the money from somewhere, Stan, no worries."

Stan's raised eyebrows found themselves both in agreement, however, and unconvinced. "Remember, we don't know how much the gynaecologists will cost, though, Frank," Stan advised him.

"Yes, but—" Frank began. "Hang on. The *what*? What are you on about here, exactly?"

Stan expelled an exasperated sigh. "To find the *Viking treasure*, Frank," Stan reminded him.

"There will not be any to find," Henk assured them. "Rodney Franks most certainly would have gotten one of his paid henchmen to place that in the mind of the planning department merely so that the property would cost me more money."

"Can we just step back for a moment, please?" requested Frank. "I'd like to address..." he said, turning to Stan... "a *gynaecologist*? A *gynaecologist* doesn't go digging around a field for *treasure*, Stan. A *gynaecologist* sifts through entirely different crevices *altogether*. Archaeologist, Stanley. *Archaeologist*."

"Of course, of course," replied Stan dismissively, with a wave of his hand, anxious to deflect attention away from his faux pas. "No need to get hung up here on unnecessary details," he chided Frank.

"*Unnecessary*—?" Frank began animatedly, but Stan quickly cut over him.

"Anyway, we could actually use that to our advantage, if need be, an archaeological dig," said Stan. "That's *archaeological* dig, Frank, by the way, not *gynaecological* dig," Stan instructed him. "*Obviously.*"

"What?? *I'm* not the one who—!" Frank began, but to no avail.

"Imagine how cool it would be," Stan steamrollered over him, "to have farm residents or local kids learning history on a live *archaeological* site!"

Frank's consternation gave way to appreciation, as this was a wonderful idea. "You're right, Stanley," he conceded. "That's some fine thinking on your part," he had to admit.

"So. Henk," said Stan, now taking the lead, with an exasperated yet amused Frank watching on. "We'll get you the money as soon as we can, and the charity gets to keep the farm. It might take us a little while to pull that sort of cash together, however."

"Fellows, I dislike doing this," Henk said, pulling on his tie to straighten it. He pulled on it so hard that the knot tightened itself up and reduced to the size of a small walnut.

"Then don't do that...?" suggested Frank.

"No. Fellows," Henk went on. "I dislike having to do this, especially where a charity is to be concerned. But I must tell you that time is of the importance here. I will not bore you with such details, but I will have a mountain of tax liabilities and other expenses if that farm remains to be in my name past a particular date. And we Dutch are not fond of mountains."

Stan and Frank listened on.

"If I don't give it back to that plague-ridden Rodney Franks," Henk continued, "or sell promptly, then I will end up having to pay a considerable, watery-secretions-inducing amount of money extra. I hate to be pushy, fellows, but if you want the farm, then we need to complete the transaction in five weeks by the latest date. If you are not confident of that deadline, then I will unfortunately need to hand it back."

"You could give us the farm and we'll pay you later? If we don't manage to raise the money by then?" asked Stan, in hope rather than determination.

Frank shook his head. "We can't, Stan. We're a registered charity," he explained. "We have to do everything by the book, and by the letter of the law. If we don't think we can get the money and do it properly, it'll have to go back to Rodney." Frank's posture dropped like a wet sack of Irish spuds. "Stan, it's too much of a financial liability for the charity in that amount of time," he confessed. "I think, at this time, regrettably, we should perhaps..."

"Definitely do it!" agreed Stan in a familiar fashion, adopting Frank's earlier method. "You'll help us?" he asked, turning to Dave and Monty, who'd just ambled up from the beach and were now joining them.

"What's that?" asked Dave, pulling up his trousers to conceal his builder's bum from Monty — who was still a pace or two behind — though Monty was not complaining of this.

"Raise some money to buy the farm," Frank explained.

"Of course we will!" Monty came back enthusiastically, not hesitating even the least little bit. "Dave and I can do a sponsored wet t-shirt competition!" Monty brainstormed on the spot, joining his elbows together in an effort to illustrate his voluptuous bosom for the benefit of the others.

Dave joined him in the pose. "I don't think sponsored wet t-shirt competitions are a thing, Monty. I will, however, in the interests of science, spend an inordinate amount of time researching the topic. This very evening, in fact. How much do we need to raise?"

Frank took a deep, audible intake of breath. "Five hundred thousand — give-or-take — in about five weeks," he rattled off.

"Oh," replied Dave, rubbing his palm over his mouth. "That's a lot of tits needed, then. Our breasts have always kept us in good stead, mate, but I'm not sure they'll be quite enough to get us through this particular campaign, Monty."

Monty, for his part, seemed entirely unconvinced regarding Dave's unfavourable appraisal to his plan.

"But, if we should buy the farm..." Dave mused. "Hang on, let me rephrase. If we should *purchase* the farm... collectively, I'm saying... does that mean we get to keep our current groundsmen jobs, full-time, forever?"

"Forever and ever," confirmed Stan with an assured nod.

"*Yerrrrsss!*" shouted Dave, offering an ill-timed high-five at Monty — ill-timed because Monty's good eye was not prepared for it and so not properly directed. Nevertheless, Monty shared Dave's keen enthusiasm.

Frank clenched his fist and thrust it up into the air, accompanying it with a spirited roar. "It's on, chaps! We can do this! What are we waiting for, then? I'd say we've got a bloody farm to buy!"

## Chapter
# EIGHT

"Is it, eh, the BBC you work for, Jenny?" enquired Stan. "I'm not sure if I mentioned the last time we met, but I did a bit of acting work when I was younger." He raised one finger as he said this, as if to see which way the wind might be blowing. "I was in a Western," he declared, whipping his hand back towards his belt to reach for an imaginary pistol, to show off his skills, but the only thing discharged was his mobile phone from his pocket which bounced on the ground. "Oh, bother," he said, scooping it up and inspecting it for damage. "It worked better when I was on set, that bit. I promise, Jenny," he told her. Moving closer, he asked her, conspiratorially, "You must have an eye for acting talent, Jenny, yes? I'm sure you get asked all the time for recommendations?" Not waiting for an answer, he added, "All mine," tapping on his front teeth to show her that they were, in fact, the genuine article. "I know they look like falsies but, honestly, I can assure you they're not. The camera falls in love with my teeth, let me tell you!"

Jenny stared, and continued to stare, even after Stan had finally shut the hell up. She was either in awe of Stan's gunmanship, or she was unsure of what she'd just witnessed. Most likely the latter, judging by the narrowed eyes and the slightly curled-back top lip. "I work with ITV Sport," she told him. "So, *em*, yeah, don't really have the ear of the top movie producers, I'm afraid. Sorry?"

"Well if you ever did..." Stan encouraged her, now tugging at his hair to demonstrate that it was not a wig or toupée, in a further effort to show off his remarkable pedigree.

Frank arrived on scene, struggling with a petrol can in either hand, and had a spanner held in his mouth for lack of a third hand. "Thanks for the help, Stan," he mumbled, then spat the spanner onto the grass for later. "I saw you doing your dodgy John Wayne impression yet again, by the way. Were you boring Jenny with the time you were in that commercial?"

"I thought it was film?" asked Jenny, feeling unfairly misled.

Stan looked uncomfortable, but only for tick, and rose to the challenge valiantly. "It was *on* film," he advised her, smiling with an exaggerated smile to offer up his teeth once again for consideration. "So it wasn't a *feature* film, *per se*. But it was still filmed!"

"It was a local advert. For eggs. When he was a boy," Frank clarified for Jenny's sake.

"Four thousand people, Frank!" Stan protested, pouting, his ego somewhat deflated.

"How's that? *What* was four thousand people, Stan?" enquired Jenny, even though immediately regretting stoking that fire by encouraging him.

"The number of people that would have seen that advert," replied Stan, proudly reinflating his chest. "In fact, I was *just that good* in that advert that I was asked to turn on the Christmas lights, back home!" he said, pointing to home, which was about seventy miles away, in Liverpool. "At Christmastime, I mean," he added, for purposes of elucidation as well as illumination. "It was quite the honour."

Frank placed the petrol cans he was carrying on the ground, flapping his hands about in an effort to restore bloodflow into his fingers. "That was at Sunday school," he said, determined, for some manner of intent which eluded him but yet he was nevertheless a slave to, to piss in Stan's cornflakes. "That was at Sunday school, Stan, and the only reason the teacher asked you to do it was because of the cracked casing on the electrical cord for the string of lights. She was worried about getting electrocuted and so dragged up the closest available kid to do it for her instead. And that, Stanley, just happened to be you."

"Anyway, enough about my storied acting career," Stan said, glossing over Frank's unkind words. "Dave did well to get this place all to ourselves," he observed, glancing around Jurby Road & Race Track admiringly.

"It wasn't cheap," remarked Jenny, in between helping to position her crew's equipment. "The station manager is going to go mental when he sees the invoice for procuring this place. I thought we were paying for a couple of laps to get some action shots on film. I didn't realise we were hiring the entire track, plus paying for an ambulance to be on standby," she said. "Plus, apparently, paying for extras to be on hand," she added, nodding in the direction of a racing club regular stood firmly in place some distance away, smoking a cigarette and observing the goings-on. "Neil?" she said now, turning to her cameraman. "How's it looking?"

Neil's thumb, held in the vertical position, rose up from behind the camera. "All good, Jenny. Light is perfect, and I should be ready to go in ten minutes or so," said Neil.

With a well-practised precision, Jenny ran a brush through her hair whilst fluidly applying a smattering of makeup. "Can you guys tell Dave and Monty to get ready?" she asked, directing the question to Stan and Frank.

But the sound of an engine bursting into life in the distance answered her question. Frank peered over the fence separating the safe area of the track from the racing part, holding his hand up for Dave, fingers spread, to indicate five minutes. Dave sat deathly still at first, apparently thinking he was being commanded to stop. But he quickly realised what Frank was signalling, and saluted in acknowledgement and then gave an 'A-OK' sign.

"Dave's all aboard," confirmed Frank. "And I can see Monty heading over. I do hope his injuries have sorted themselves out by now. He does seem to be walking somewhat... gingerly?"

Stan joined Frank peering over the fence, like two inquisitive horses looking for a bucket of oats. "Gingerly?" echoed Stan. "He's walking like the Tin Woodsman from that Judy Garland film before Dorothy pulled the WD-40 out. There's no way he's going to get his carcass into that sidecar."

The pair were then joined by Neil the cameraman as well, and they all watched as Monty traversed the tarmac straight-legged, without bending his knees, and swinging his arms like pendulums to develop the required motion to propel himself forward. Dave looked back, waving his co-pilot on encouragingly.

"What are we looking at? Should I be recording this?" remarked Neil, but didn't want to look away, keen to see what was holding the pair's rapt attention. The sidecar was somewhat in the distance as compared to the readying camera crew, likely sufficient for Monty to believe he was safe from prying eyes, but close enough for the three gawkers to nevertheless continue observing.

Neil closed one eye, wincing, as he saw Monty finally collapse in a heap, across Dave's back. "These two won the TT?" he asked of the others, incredulously. "The *actual* TT Races?"

Frank nodded, filled with profound satisfaction all over again just thinking about it. "They did indeed," he told the cameraman. "Well, not both, technically. Just Dave. And that was the very sidecar he was racing when he won it."

"*Hrm*," said Neil. "I can't make out who's who from this distance. But I'm going to hazard a guess here that Dave is the one already in the sidecar, rather than the one that's just rolled off of it and now lying prostrate on the ground like a tranquilised hippo...?"

Try as he might, Monty couldn't appear to right himself. An animated Dave turned off the engine, dismounted his machine, and could be seen frantically attending to his fallen comrade.

"This is Monty's comeback," Stan told the cameraman. "He didn't finish the TT, so the leathers he's wearing didn't really get much in the way of a proper run-in," he offered as explanation. "I think he may also be carrying a few extra pounds than the last time he wore them, if I'm not very much mistaken. Which might be a slight complicating factor as well," he proposed.

A few extra pounds may have been a mild underestimation, judging by the general futility of Dave's efforts. Still, Dave did eventually manage to pull Monty back to an upright position, and the pair could now be observed attempting a series of lunges, presumably to loosen and work in the leathers upon Monty's person. Which, to be fair, appeared to be working, as evidenced by the gradually increasing mobility in Monty's knee joints.

"Are we quite ready?" asked Jenny. "Only there's a penalty payment if we overstay our allotted time. And can someone tell me again why the heck we're paying one-hundred-pound-an-hour for an ambulance?"

"It's part of the race regulations to have them always present," Stan chimed in. "No ambulance, no racing, I'm afraid. Section Six, *Safety*, subsection—"

"I, *er*... I think the ambulance might be warranted, actually," Neil offered, interrupting Stan's impressive recitation of code, as he continued watching Monty, who'd lost his balance presently and was back down on the ground — this time like a turtle on its back, his arms and legs working furiously in the air without gaining any sort of purchase whatsoever. "Best to keep the ambulance round just to be on the safe side anyway," Neil suggested.

"Jenny, I meant to ask," said Frank. "You think people will be interested in Dave's story? I mean, I assume you must. Otherwise you wouldn't have gone to the trouble and expense of agreeing to meet us here for a follow-up interview?"

"Oh, yes, absolutely," Jenny replied. "When we last interviewed them, before the previous year's TT, the pair were hoping for a top-ten finish. Since then," she recapped for an imagined audience, "Monty, because of injuries sustained, stepped down, however, to graciously allow his friend a shot at victory, allowing Dave to carry on and in actual fact win the big time. And yet this year, despite Dave's last-year TT win with brilliant, if somewhat irascible, fill-in teammate Harry McMullan, Dave decides to forego another fair shot at an assured win, and, instead, insists upon racing this year with Monty Montgomery, reuniting with his dear, longtime friend once again, and racing *only* with Monty, having it no other way." She paused, taking a breath and admiring her own summary, before continuing: "Yes. Oh, yes. This is TV *gold*. Honestly, people love the whole rags-to-riches theme. Trust me, if this was a plot in a book it would be snapped up and made into a film. What we'll do, Neil," she instructed, "is let them ride around for a few laps and we'll meet them near the start line. Let them build up a bit of a sweat. It'll look more authentic. Okay?"

"Sure. You got it," agreed the cameraman.

Frank and Stan grinned like children in a toy shop as Dave and Monty's sidecar roared back to life.

"I can't tell you how much I love that noise, Stan," Frank told his partner reflectively. "You know how you smell something, and it reminds you of a time in your life? Like freshly cut grass— That always brings me back to playing in the school field when I was a boy. Well, similarly, hearing that engine spring to life does the same— I'm instantly transported to warm summer evenings watching the racing, a few drinks at the Bushy's beer tent, and surrounded by wonderful friends."

Stan leaned his head forward, over the wall partition, nostrils flaring, several pulses in a row. "You'll get that smell-recognition you were talking about as well, Frank, in just a moment," Stan told him, wafting the acrid odour — or, to a racing fan, tantalising *aroma* — of burnt fuel in Frank's general direction with a fluttering motion of his hand.

Frank took in a lungful of cold, fresh Manx air. He closed his eyes to appreciate the sound of the engine accelerating up through the gearbox.

"Monty doesn't look overly comfortable, Frank," Stan observed.

Monty tucked his head in but his left leg, which should have been doing the same thing as his head, dangled out of the sidecar precariously, appearing to forget its destination entirely.

"He doesn't, Stan," Frank agreed, opening his eyes back up to take a confirmatory glance. "Hopefully it's an issue with his leathers, rather than an instance of his previous injuries in protest? Oh, wait, there we go. It's back where it should be. The leg, that is. Maybe he was just stretching it?"

"Probably best not to speculate in the case of Monty," Stan observed. "As it could be any number of things to which we're not privy, and to which we likely wouldn't *wish* to be privy."

"Well-spotted," Frank agreed with a laugh.

Jenny attached a discreet microphone to her jacket, giving her teeth a run-over with her tongue to remove any excess lipstick that might be taking up residence there. "Have you got enough for the intro, Neil?" she asked of her inveterate cameraman.

"I will in a moment," he replied, one eye still trained into the camera lens. "*Juuuuust* let me get them going round that last corner, *aaaand*... Ah. There. There we go. Brilliant."

"Great. If you can get them pulling in? And then I'll jump in when they stop."

"Gotcha," said Neil accommodatingly.

Jenny assumed a position of relative safety behind a protective tyre wall, taking a final look over her notes. "Right. Here we go, Neil," she advised him, as the sidecar eased back into the pits. "Oh, and for the camera," she said, "don't forget from last time that Monty is the bloke with the..." she trailed off, placing her palm over one eye, for illustrative purposes, and circling it round in a Daniel-*san* wax-on, wax-off motion.

"Hang on. What...?" asked Neil, before the memory of their previous encounter with the lads made its way back to his recollection, clicking into place. "Ah. That's right," he said looking to Frank and Stan for help. "Now, which one of your friend's eyes is his good eye, again?"

Frank went to speak first. "It's... *ehm*... That's a good question, actually... Stan? It's the left... I think? Wait, or is it the right?" He closed each of his own eyes, in turn, as he said this, trying to work out which was Monty's wonky one, and which the good one. "Stan?" he said again, looking for assistance.

"It's the left, Frank," Stan replied with an assured confidence, before. "Or... wait..." he went on, a wave of doubt kicking in. He turned to face the other way, and then forward again, and then back. "Now I think on it... is it the left eye when I'm *looking* at him, so it's actually the *right*, or... You know, Frank, I'm really not so sure now..."

Jenny shook her head, as one might do when evaluating career choices, which by curious coincidence was precisely what she was in fact currently doing. "Guys," she said. "Forget about the eye for now, okay? I don't want to become fixated on them when I'm on-camera. The eyes, I mean. Not Dave and Monty. Fixated, I mean. Not— Ah! Okay, right, Neil, this is us," she said, changing tack, and like the flick of a switch, going from a pained impatience to adopting the persona of the consummate professional as Dave and Monty pulled in.

"Jenny Seagrave here, folks," she said to the camera. "And I'm back in the beautiful Isle of Man. Now, some of you may recall, when I was covering the Isle of Man TT races over the summer, our feature we did on back-of-the-van racers who really encompass what the great event is all about. Way back in June, we caught up with Dave Quirk and Shaun 'Monty' Montgomery. You may recollect that Dave and Monty were optimistically eying a top-ten finish. Well, things didn't quite work out to the original plan. I'm delighted to be here at Jurby Road & Race Track in the north of the Island, where I'm thrilled to be joined once again by our intrepid pair. I'll just give them a moment to get out of their sidecar."

Dave jumped out, sprightly-as-you-like for a larger fellow, and stood obediently next to Jenny as indicated. He looked to his left, and then to his right, fully expecting to be joined by co-pilot Monty, who was at present suddenly conspicuous in his absence.

"Is your friend... okay?" asked Jenny, spotting the source of the delay. Monty, as it happened, had managed to change position, somehow, from frontwards-facing to backwards-facing in his seat in the sidecar, with his legs dangling out the back, like a very large crab whose legs wouldn't fit in the boiling pot.

Monty looked over to Jenny and the camera with a friendly wave, but with little give in either his leathers or his joints, it didn't appear as if he had the leverage to stand up. And, indeed, he gave them a twirling motion with his finger like he was mixing a drink, directing them to carry on without him.

"Look at this, folks!" resumed a high-energy Jenny. "As a reminder of how physically taxing this type of racing is, a few laps in the sidecar really takes it out of these guys, and our Monty here can barely stand up!" She said this cheerfully, rolling with the development as only a seasoned pro could do.

"It's probably more to do with the Guinness," Dave shot back over his shoulder, running to help his friend. And with no small degree of effort — and a mental note to visit his GP for possible hernia — Dave extricated Monty from their machine, and in record time had Monty standing beside him, pretty-as-you-please, before Jenny.

"Dave, if I can come to you first?" said Jenny, now that was all sorted, conjuring a microphone for him from thin air, like a bouquet of flowers, and handing it over. "I had the pleasure of interviewing you in TT week the year previous, and—"

"It was all my pleasure then, and is most certainly again," returned Dave, for which, just as he did in the referenced TT week, he received a death-stare in response for both interrupting and for his being overly familiar.

With Dave sufficiently cowed into submission in short order, Jenny carried on...

"You may remember, Dave, that we discussed your aspirations for a top-ten finish. Well, things didn't quite go to plan, did they? And would you mind explaining why that was, for the benefit of our viewers?"

"The bike was going well, and I was entirely confident in our prospects," Dave began elaborating, as instructed. "But sadly, my mate Monty here..." he said, using both hands to present Monty to the audience. "Sadly, Monty's injuries couldn't stand up to the TT. It's pretty savage out on that track even when you're at a hundred-percent top physical condition, see? But with any sort of injury, well, you've simply got no chance. So Monty very magnanimously, of his own accord, retired." At this, Monty took a low bow for the camera. "I thought that was curtains for my TT effort," Dave continued. "But, with the help of my sponsors, Frank and Stan, as well as our good friend Dutch Henk, I managed to get not only a new, faster machine but a new passenger for the outfit as well. And just in time, too."

Jenny smiled in appreciation of Dave's summary. It wasn't as good as hers, of course. But it would do. "Your new passenger was, of course, Harry McMullan," she said. "Now, if I recall, in our last interview there was no love lost between yourself and the brothers McMullan. You must have made up with Harry McMullan, then, in order to achieve this beneficial arrangement?"

Dave adopted the usual crossed-arm, hand-rubbing-the-chin thing he did when thinking. "I think I called him a tosser, last time? If I'm not mistaken?"

"I think you did just that," replied Jenny through gritted teeth, and with a forced laugh. "And I think you *also* promised that you *wouldn't* say such a thing again on-camera."

"Sorry, Jenny. But to be fair, didn't you say the exact same thing about him, off-camera, when we—?"

Again, the death stare, along with pointed throat-cutting gestures, indicating to him that he should immediately cease-and-desist.

"Anyway, my opinion remained the same even with him as a passenger. Don't get me wrong, that guy has got loads of talent, and he's a true professional. Just, like I said, a complete toss–"

Death stare.

"Pot. Tosspot, is what I meant to say," Dave said with a cough.

"So Dave, for those who may not be aware, with the combination of the new passenger and the new sidecar, can you tell the viewers if you managed to get your top-ten finish?"

A satisfied smile erupted across Dave's face as he held out his hand to Monty, in an obviously rehearsed motion. Monty stared blankly at the extended hand in front of him, before producing a Cadbury Crunchie from his breast pocket that he'd been hoping very much to save for later, and handing it, hopefully, to Dave with a cheeky wink.

"Not the *Cadbury Crunchie*, Monty. Why would I be asking for a *Cadbury Crunchie*? Although I will take that, actually."

Monty looked both pleased that he'd made Dave happy with his gift, and yet unhappy that he no longer had his Cadbury Crunchie he'd until-just-recently been saving for later.

"Remember the *thingy*, Monty?" Dave coaxed gently. "The *thing*?"

"The thing?" asked Monty.

"Yes, the *thing*," said Dave.

"The thing I had to go see the doctor for? To get the antibiotics for?" Monty ventured.

"Not *that* thing!" Dave told him. "The *other* thing. The thing we *talked* about. For *this*," he said, moving his upraised palm around in circles like he was making popcorn on the stovetop, but meant to signify the whole *this* that was the current circumstance at which they were presently engaged.

"Ah! A-*ha*! A-*ha*-ha-ha," replied Monty, suddenly catching on, and disappearing from shot.

This was much to the frustration of Jenny, who was by this time ready for packing up and heading home, looking forward as she was to running a bath and treating herself to some much-needed relaxation, attending to her needs under cover of the warm water.

Monty returned momentarily, bringing with him a trophy he'd retrieved from Frank, at-the-ready for the occasion. "Here you go, Dave," he said, making a show of presenting it to him.

Dave clutched the trophy and pressed it into the soft-cushion waiting embrace of that which was his man-boobs. "This is my replica trophy for winning the TT race," he said to Jenny, as well as to the folks at home.

At this, Jenny returned a genuine smile. Though, at this stage, it was likely more in appreciation that the interview was back on-point than it was in appreciation of the trophy itself.

"Just to unpack that for a moment. I interviewed you for our back-of-the-van racer feature, and then you managed to only go and win the blooming race, Dave. That is an absolutely spectacular achievement, and one for which you must be extremely proud. It really is a tale of rags-to-riches— No offence meant, of course."

Before Dave could respond to this, Jenny turned her attention to Monty. "Monty," she said. "If I can come to you now," she pressed on, hoping to soon bring the interview to a conclusion. "How did you feel when you had to pull out, and when your friend won?"

Right on cue, though certainly not planned, Monty became moderately misty-eyed. He lowered his head, wiping his eyes with the heel of his palm. "It was one of the proudest days in my life to see that man there stood on the top step," said Monty, looking back up, his eyes shining.

"You mean that, don't you, Monty?" asked Jenny, seeing the sincerity in his still-glistening eyes, the fact that those eyes were facing in two entirely different directions notwithstanding.

"I live for racing, Jenny. I was gutted when the injury ruled me out of the TT, but I've always said that Dave had the ability to get on the podium. Would I like to have won a TT with him? Absolutely I would have. But I took just as much enjoyment from being there to watch him win, regardless, and it's something I'll never forget." Monty then leaned in to Dave, giving him an impromptu embrace.

Jenny dabbed at her own eyes. "Gosh, now you've got *me* welling up," she said. "Monty, you've decided to come out of retirement," she continued, soldiering on. "Can you tell us why that is?"

Monty's eyes were briefly in agreement, and properly aligned. They did that, paradoxically, when he was deep in productive thought. This wasn't often, mind you. It was a rare occurrence, coming round only occasionally, like Halley's Comet.

"Racing is an unrelenting and insatiable itch that, once scratched, needs scratching again and again. I love every aspect of it, not just the racing, but cold nights rattling around a damp garage making adjustments to the suspension, or even wondering where I'm getting the money from to buy the next tyre. I get to travel all over the country to race at different tracks, and get to meet some real characters along the way. Then, to top it all, I get to spend two weeks camping at the TT, spending time with my friends at the greatest show on Earth. It really doesn't get much better than that, truth be told, and to give it up is hard. I thought I could, but I just couldn't. And I didn't want to get in Dave's way, so I was going to team up with another rider. But Dave, sorry milksop that he is, well, he just wouldn't hear of it, bless his heart."

Jenny stepped in a little closer. This was a great story point for the audience, and she wanted to delve into it a bit more. "So, Monty and Dave are going to be reunited at the next TT? Just to be clear?" she asked.

But Monty was afflicted by a case of the sniffles, getting himself a little worked up emotionally over his last statement, so Jenny turned to Dave with a follow-up question:

"Dave, that must have been a big decision, all things considered, to part company with Harry McMullan and another potential place up on the coveted TT podium. Did Harry understand your rationale?"

At this, a look came over Dave's face like he was constipated and had just sat down on the toilet desperate for relief, yet only managed to produce a small fart. He looked at Monty, and then over to Frank and Stan. "Guys. Have we actually *told* Harry?"

"I don't think..." Stan began tentatively.

"... we've told him?" Frank finished for Stan. He giggled, and the giggle spread, contagious, throughout the four of them.

"I suppose he'll know when he sees this interview, won't he?" Monty said with a laugh, at which point another round of giggles ensued.

"Harry McMullan will have long forgotten about me by now anyway, I expect," Dave offered. "He'll drop me and team up with someone else as soon as it suits him, and probably already has. His idiot brother, most likely."

"Yep. Idiot brother," repeated Monty, for no particular reason.

The camera panned away from Dave and Monty, now giving Jenny its full attention. She spoke directly to camera and, not wanting things to degenerate into further name-calling, began to wrap up the interview. She couldn't help but notice Frank and Stan, however, waving furiously in her peripheral vision.

Try as they might, Frank and Stan's efforts to attract Dave and Monty's direct attention were failing miserably.

"Try this," suggested Stan, handing a half-eaten Scotch egg to Frank, and without further invitation Frank dispatched the meaty missile with precision, catching Monty on the bridge of the nose and breaking apart into sections. Monty, with cat-like reflexes where food was concerned, snatched every bit of the treat, in a juggling motion, straight out of the air, popping each bit into his mouth as he went along. This was not the expected result of the egg-based assault. Still, it produced the desired result in that it served the purpose of gaining Monty's attention.

'*Tell them about the fundraiser!*' mouthed Frank and Stan in unison.

Monty cleared his throat. "Jenny," he whispered, though much too loudly to really be considered a whisper. "Can I just...? Only I wanted to... If I might...?"

Jenny ignored him at first, before finally relenting and giving him a *this-had-better-be-bloody-important* glare.

Monty had breadcrumbs all over his face at this point, looking like he'd been infected with some form of strange leprosy. "This interview..." he told her, continuing on in his loud stage whisper. "Is it going out this week? Only, I wanted to tell your viewers about something, if that's not too terribly much trouble...?"

"Let's have it, then," said Jenny, pretending to listen, but really thinking about her fast-approaching therapeutic bubble bath.

"Me and Dave are working on the farm, called the TT Farm, which our sponsors Frank and Stan have set up. They do a lot of charity work in the UK. Anyway, this farm is a hostel for vulnerable people who need a change of location, and, being a working farm, we're using it to provide traditional skills and crafts," Monty related smartly, remembering the verbal script Frank had gone over several times with him. "We've been given the opportunity to buy it, but we need to move pretty quickly."

Jenny's upper lip was beginning to curl up again, as it had done earlier, in a manner which suggested to Monty that he had perhaps eight seconds or so before she became irrevocably bored and turned the camera off. This expression caused Dave to jump in...

"You see, Jenny. We need to raise about five hundred thousand pounds in only five or six weeks' time. So, we're going to put on something a bit special on the Isle of Man next month. Something the Isle of Man has previously never seen the likes of."

This managed to reclaim Jenny's attention. "Oh?" she said, genuinely curious now.

# FRANK & STAN'S BUCKET LIST #3: ISLE 'LE MANS' TT

"We're quite excited, to be honest," Dave began, wanting to build up the tension, but Jenny was looking at her watch already, and so he cut to the chase. "We're going to put on a Family Fun Day, here, at this very track," he announced, with a fanfare of jazz hands.

Neil, ever the professional, panned the camera around on that statement over the Jurby track, before returning it back towards Dave for him to resume speaking.

"As well as the Fun Day, we're going to have the Isle of Man's first ever twenty-four-hour race. Non-stop racing for a full day and night. What we're looking for is for teams to enter and people to show up and support it. There's going to be celebrities entering and everything. And here's the thing— because it's only a small racing track, we don't want racing cars as they'll be too quick. And because we're *back-of-the-van* racers, we thought the best sort of vehicles for the race would be vans! An actual *van* race! And as we're sidecar racers, we're also thinking of allowing sidecars, of course, but not for the full race. They're a bit temperamental, tend to be the sidecars, so maybe for a maximum of an hour, maybe two."

Jenny nodded her approval. "That's actually a great idea, guys. A twenty-four-hour race on the Isle of Man. It'll be like Le Mans."

Monty went to speak but the words wouldn't come out quickly enough, with Dave beating him to it. "Ah!" exclaimed Dave, in a moment of clarity and brilliance. "What about, for the race name, then, *The Isle Le Mans TT?*"

"That's absolutely genius," replied Jenny, a sparkle in her eye.

"Thieving bastard!" Monty shouted at Dave. "That's what I was about to say! That very thing!"

Jenny turned her back on them both, as Monty continued attempting to reclaim the moment for his own from Dave. But it was far too late for that.

"So there you have it, folks!" said Jenny, well and truly wrapping things up. "*Two* exclusives today! The *first* being that Dave Quirk and Monty Montgomery will reunite for next year's TT races! And, *second*, the Isle of Man is going to be having its very own Le Mans race!"

*"Called The Isle Le Mans TT!"* shouted Monty from the background. *"The name that I thought of myself before Dave stole it from me!"*

Once the camera crew were packed up and on their way, Frank rushed over to Dave and Monty, finger poised in the air. "Ah, two points I'd like to make, gents, if you'd be so kind as to hear me out? Right, firstly, I thought we were just going to have a Family Fun Day? That is, with maybe a few laps in the sidecars? And secondly, *what celebrities?* We've not got any bloody celebrities lined up for this!"

Dave placed his oversized hands on Frank's shoulders — which, considering Dave's height relative to Frank's, was more or less their natural resting position.

"We can do this, Frank," Dave told him earnestly. "I had a moment of inspiration or epiphany, or whatever you call it."

"An epiphany! That's right!" Monty agreed happily.

"Look, you and Stan have done a great deal for us two idiots," Dave continued. "I know how important this farm is to you, and, no disrespect, a crappy little family fun day isn't going to get you five hundred grand. We can get race teams to enter this— All the big boys will want to be in on this at the ground floor, believe me. We can do the fun day, yes, but *this* is what's going to bring you the money in, right? You wait and see."

Dave leaned his head down, planting a firm kiss on Frank's forehead. "We're going to *do* this, guys," he said, in case the kiss wasn't convincing enough in and of itself, extending his arms to scoop Stan and Monty up, all inclusive-like, into the circle of love. "I've got a stirring in my loins over this one," added Dave, which was perhaps not the best turn of phrase to use at present, in view of their proximate proximity, as it were. "And my loins never steer me wrong. *The Isle 'Le Mans' TT*. Ha! Pure genius!"

"Which I thought of first, by the way," moaned Monty.

"There, there, Monty. It doesn't matter who came up with the idea. All that matters is that we all pull together to make it happen," Dave assured him, giving him a comforting pat on the back for good measure.

"That, and establishing proper credit where credit is due for the naming," Monty agreed.

## Chapter
# NINE

Sleep eluded Frank. He'd been stood in the bay window of his bedroom for what felt like hours, contemplating. His view of the TT Grandstand only a couple of hundred metres up the road never failed to bring a smile to his face, as did the view down to the distant lights of Douglas Harbour. A recurring, unwelcome theme was ever-present in his thoughts, though. He'd found his utopia, he knew, but this understanding was tinged with the realisation that he should have done this years ago when the commodity of time was still on his side. He knew it was futile to think such things, for if he hadn't lived his life as he had then he wouldn't be stood precisely where he was today. And, if he hadn't married a blood-sucking leech, then that unholy union wouldn't have produced a wonderful daughter. *Things happen for a reason*, he mused.

This evening's slumberless night was not completely consumed by pangs of regret, however. Rather, considering the day which lay ahead, it was accompanied by a giddy feeling similar to that of a small child desperate to discover if Father Christmas had paid a visit whilst he slept.

Only Frank wasn't sleeping at the moment. And so, although he knew he'd packed his tuxedo, he checked, yet again. He also made certain his two bowties were in there. He didn't need both, but he always packed two — placing the first inside one of his polished shoes and the other inside his jacket pocket. This way, he reasoned, though he might lose one of them, he'd be unlikely to lose the both of them. One could, of course, never be too careful.

"Cufflinks," he said aloud, snapping his finger in the process. He took them out of the smart leather box on his dressing table, holding one aloft in each hand. "I hope I've made you proud, Dad," he whispered, placing a tender kiss on each of them in turn. He put them back in the box and then rubbed his thumb over the embossed lettering on the lid — his father's initials. "It's a big day today, Dad," he announced with a smile, to both himself and the ghost of his dear father.

"That you up, Frank?" came the reply, but it was no spectre or phantasm. It was only Stan. "Knock-knock," Stan announced, as he pressed his way in. It wasn't difficult, as the door was already ajar.

"Alright, then?" Frank asked amiably.

"I couldn't sleep, Frank," Stan told him. "Honestly, I've been up for hours just looking out over that view."

"You too?" Frank asked sympathetically. "If anybody walked past, we would have looked like a couple of weirdos stood at our two bedroom windows in the middle of the night."

"But we *are* a couple of weirdos," Stan reminded him.

"Fair enough," Frank replied with a laugh. "Say, have you packed your bags?" he asked.

"I did that by midnight, and I've checked them three or four times since." Stan joined Frank, peering now out Frank's window as opposed to his own. The view was much the same, at this early hour, as it was in fact at any hour. Delightful.

"Do you think we'll win?" asked Stan reflectively.

Frank didn't respond immediately, offering a humming noise as a placeholder. "I can't say that I haven't thought about it, Stan," he said eventually. "That's why I've been up most of the night. Well, that and my bladder, of course, which has now got the capacity of a thimble it would seem. Anyway, I'm just happy the charity has been nominated, Stan. That's good enough for me. Anything more is just an added bonus."

"Yeah... only you don't mean a single word of that, do you," Stan answered him, given as a statement rather than a question.

"Don't I?" said Frank.

"Frank. Of course you don't, Frank," Stan chided him. "You think I don't know you?" he said with a laugh. "You believe all those losers at the Oscars, for instance, would likely sacrifice their left arm for the chance to ram that trophy up the winners' arse."

"True enough," agreed Frank. "You've got a point there."

"I want to win this award tonight, Frank, and I'm not ashamed to admit it," Stan remarked. "And there is an irony that I'm not being overly charitable here, considering the award is for Charity of the Year. Still. I can live with myself."

"I'm sure you'll persevere, powering through the shame," Frank said with a chuckle.

"We can *do* this, Frank," Stan advised him. "Give me a *roar*, Frank."

"I'm in my underpants, Stan."

"So? Give me a roar."

Frank acquiesced, with his first, reluctant attempt resembling no more than the sound of a cat chewing on the telly remote control.

"Roar, goddammit!" shouted Stan, now shadowboxing a volley of punches against Frank's midsection to prompt an appropriately lively response.

"GRRRROOOOAAAAR!" roared Frank. "How about that, Stanley? You've just let the lion out of the cage, I'm afraid!"

"Yes, I can see as much, Frank. You need to put it away."

Frank was having none of it. "Too late for that!" he told Stan, roaring a bit more, and raising his makeshift claws for emphasis.

"No, Frank. I mean the lion has flopped out of the cage. Little Frank has escaped from the zoo. Is what I'm saying."

"Oh," said Frank, tucking himself back into his shorts. "I did think it was getting a touch breezy. That explains things."

🏍

"She *wasn't*, Dave," explained Monty, patiently at first, before becoming less so. "She's *paid* to be nice to people. She's a bloody air hostess. It's what they do."

Dave spread his hands over the front of his kilt, flattening it out, and then checking to make sure the sporran was properly adjusted.

Once satisfied, he returned his attention to Monty. "You didn't see the glint in her eye when she asked if I wanted peanuts," Dave told him. "She must like a man in a skirt, I expect. A man who's clearly comfortable in his own skin."

Stan checked his phone for directions, looking up from the pavement to the buildings around them rising above. "Are you two still on about that air hostess?" he asked, turning to the pair. "Dave, I hate to break it to you, but I think *I'd* have had more of a chance with that hostess. And I don't think I've kissed a girl for fifty-one years!"

"That is a very hurtful thing to say, Stan, and I'm deeply offended," Dave said, not-at-all offended.

"So what *is* with that kilt?" Stan enquired.

"I wanted to look my best for the occasion, didn't I!" Dave answered. "Unlike *some* people," he added, casting an eye in Monty's direction. Monty also cast an eye in Dave's direction, though he was currently looking straight ahead. "Anyway. It's Manx tartan," Dave went on. "I bought it for a wedding years ago and, what with coming up to Scotland and all, I thought I'd give it a go. Oh, and before you ask, Stan... no, I haven't," he announced, lifting up the front of his kilt for inspection.

Stan rolled his eyes. But only after them lingering for just a moment.

"Are you blushing, Stan?" asked Monty.

"And why would I be blushing? You think I've never seen a cock before?" replied Stan with a wink. "Anyway," he continued, "it looks like Frank and Jessie know where they're going."

Frank and Jessie walked several paces in front of the others. It could have been to distance themselves from the three people behind, or it could have been simply that they were in a beautiful city, lost in each other's company. Frank held their bag in his left hand and without looking, or even having to look, scooped Jessie's hand up with his right. Frank pulled her gently closer and, once that more intimate proximity was properly sorted, placed a protective arm around Jessie's shoulder.

"Would you get a load of the two lovebirds," remarked Monty, but not unkindly.

Stan shared the sentiment. "I'm really happy for the both of them. Arm-in-arm, like love's young dream. I think it's sweet."

Monty slowed, taking Dave by the arm with him, but before Monty could speak, he was met from Dave with, "Monty, whatever it is you're about to say, whatever it is you're about to tell me, I have a sneaking suspicion it's going to involve my mum, somehow, as the subject. So *don't*. For the love of god, just *don't*."

Monty gasped for air. "*Moi*? I was only going to make the suggestion that you should tell the receptionist that Jessie is your mum, and that she's on her first weekend away with her new boyfriend. And that, if you ask nicely, she may just ensure your room isn't next to your mum's, because, well... *cough*... you know... you probably wouldn't want to hear her headboard knocking off the wall like a woodpecker's beak all night long. See? That's all I was going to say."

"Bastard," replied Dave. "Right bastard," he repeated, this time with an involuntary shudder at the very thought.

The rapid pitter-patter of approaching footsteps caused Dave to glance over his shoulder, and then turn around. A young boy, six or seven years of age, was running towards them at maximum velocity — and a welcome reprieve, for Dave, from Monty's crass remarks. The child stopped at Dave's feet, struggling to catch his breath after all the exertion. "Excuse me," said the wee one, panting. "My dad. Over there," he continued, pointing back down the street from the way he came. "Is on crutches. So he sent me over. Are you by chance Dave Quark?" the boy asked.

"Dave *Quirk*, yes," Dave corrected him gently.

"*The* Dave Quark?" the boy said, undaunted, seeming to like his own pronunciation better.

"Yes, indeed," came Dave's reply, with him now giving up on correcting the boy's pronunciation. It could, after all, have simply been the boy's Glasgow accent, and Dave didn't want to appear rude to an obvious admirer.

Dave glanced over to the others, who had now turned round themselves, as well, to see what the commotion was about. Dave wore a proud-as-punch expression, nodding his head continuously in a *'You see? You see?'* fashion, as he looked to them all in turn, lingering on each of them, savouring this moment. "It would seem I can't go anywhere these days, even as far away as Glasgow, without attracting attention since the TT win," he said, lest there be no doubt.

Dave pulled a pen from his pocket, crouching down so he could look the young lad in the eye. "So, you and your dad want an autograph, I expect?" he asked, rhetorically, as he was fairly certain of the answer. "Happy to oblige," he said amiably, smiling, pen poised at-the-ready, waiting patiently for the boy to produce either a slip of paper or a photograph for him to sign.

The boy smiled back uncertainly, unsure if this was just another instance of adults not making an awful lot of sense, as was often the case, or if there was something more to it than that. The boy looked back down the street again, this time pointing helpfully to a man stood resting on crutches. The man had his neck craned forward, and his head cocked first this way, and then that.

Dave gave the fellow a cheerful wave, and the man waved back, somewhat hesitantly. "Your dad?" Dave asked the boy.

"Me da," the boy confirmed.

Dave had pulled a piece of paper from his pocket, and was about to ask who to make the autograph out to, when the boy continued...

"Right," the boy said, pausing a tick to remember what it was he'd been instructed to say. "Right, then," the boy began, rather smartly. "Me da can't run on them crutches," he continued. "So he done sent me instead. He sez you look like Dave Quark, and wants to know if you is indeed Dave Quark."

"That would be me," Dave told the lad, wondering now where exactly this might be heading. His hand, pen still in hand, lowered to half-mast.

"Right. So. Good. Me da sez he wasn't sure, but that you looked an awful lot like that Dave Quark that ran out on him in a poker game after you lost and owed him money."

Dave's pen hand drooped down by his side, limply, at this point. "*Erm...*" was all he said.

"Me da sez, if it's really that Dave Quark fella, then it's a good thing he's up again this way. Because me da never thought he was gonna get his money after all these years from that thievin' bastard Dave Quark. And he's on crutches and can't run. So he sent me to ask. Cuz I haven't got crutches and I can run fast enough to catch up with a fat bastard like Dave Quark even though me da can't right now. Cuz he's still on the crutches."

The wee lad smiled proudly, pleased that he was able to remember all the things he was meant to say.

Dave sighed, pulled his wallet from his trousers pocket, and counted out a handful of notes. "Tell your da there's two hundred quid thee," he told the young one. "And that includes extra for interest."

Dave stood, and he watched the little boy race back to his father. Once there, a whoop of joy could be heard, even from that pronounced distance, and the boy's father punched the sky in victory like Rocky Balboa atop the steps of the Philadelphia Museum of Art. "Thank ya, Dave Quark, ya fat bastard!" the boy's father shouted, and Dave gave a feeble wave in return. The boy's father even, at this point, attempted a jump for joy. This did not go well, being, as he was, still on the crutches. Still, he seemed happy enough, shouting once more, "Ya fat bastard!" as he turned to hobble merrily away, money in hand.

"Fans everywhere," Monty agreed. But he left it at that, choosing not to further poke the bear, so to speak, since Dave was now skint and this meant that Monty would now have to spend his own money.

With Dave's admirer taken care of, the group continued on, making good progress, and soon found themselves in front of an imposing glass-fronted hotel. Luxurious red carpet invited guests from the street, directing them up a flight of steps with a shimmering gold revolving door at the summit, where stood an elegant moustached gentleman on sentry duty.

"They've got a *doorman*," gawped Monty, with eyes widened. "And *red rope* heading up the stairs."

"That doorman's got a top hat on," added Dave. "A bloody *top hat*. Stan, are you sure this is the right place?"

"As Frank and your mum are already halfway up the steps, I think it very well could be," Stan assured him.

"As long as Frank doesn't punch the air once he gets to the top," said Dave miserably.

Monty walked up the pristine carpet with his mouth agape. "I've never stayed in a place like this, Stan," he confided. "When me and Dave go away, the hotels we stay in usually have an hourly rate and rubber sheets. That sort of thing."

Frank took a step back down the stairs, seeing the others were still a few paces behind. What with the sheer opulence of their accommodation now on full display, he felt the need to impress upon them the relevant matter of financial clarification as they approached. "Don't forget, guys, this is all on me and Stan," he told Dave and Monty. "So don't worry about letting your hair down and enjoying yourselves. It's our little treat."

"Let our hair down, he says," whispered Monty to Dave. "*Now* he tells us. After I've already gone and got a haircut for the occasion."

"Isn't it always the way?" Dave agreed with a laugh, taking the steps two at a time.

It was still early afternoon, but the reception area was a hive of activity, with people presumably preparing for the gala dinner that evening. The line for the check-in desk was doubled back on itself, but rather than a feeling of frustration, the Isle of Man contingent soaked up the atmosphere, marvelling at their plush surroundings. It was apparent that this place was the real deal, suited to a traveller with a certain degree of sophistication and panache. Of course, not all present necessarily possessed this level of sophistication and panache, and in fact some murmurings closer to the front of the queue could be heard in this regard.

"You need to extinguish that, madam. If you'd be as kind," said a velvety female voice.

A plume of smoke rose like that emanating from an Indian campfire. What it was signalling was not yet apparent. The request had been eloquently delivered by a polite woman in a dark pinstripe jacket and skirt. "This is a no-smoking hotel, madam," she continued, with a timely finger to the no smoking sign.

A further puff of smoke appeared, before a rather gruff voice announced, "Fine. But tell those idiots to hurry up. I've been in this queue for twenty minutes and I need to drop a few friends off at the pool." This was Stella's way of speaking politely.

"I'm sorry? Are there more in your party?" the hostess enquired.

"I need to see a man about a dog," Stella rephrased. And, then, seeing no recognition in the woman's eyes, she spoke more plainly. "I need to have a shit. A massive one," Stella explained, in a manner of speech more to which she was accustomed.

"Ah. There's a restroom at the rear of the reception area," the apparently unflappable staff member replied, without upset.

"Trust me on this, sweetheart. I've been eating cold chicken tikka in the car for the last three hours, and while I do love my curry, it does tend to do a number on my insides. If you know what I mean. Some things need doing in the comfort of your own loo, if you know what I'm saying, so you better make it snappy because I'm nearly touching cloth." And then, turning to her gentleman companion, "Lee, I'm going outside to finish this cigarette. No sense letting a good fag go to waste."

As Stella stepped straight through the queue on her way out, rather than taking the only-slightly-longer way around it, Stan, further back in the line and near to Stella's incursion in the ranks, lowered his head, hoping not to be noticed. Frank, however, did not share Stan's modesty. "You arrived okay, Stella?" he asked, making himself clearly known.

Stella placed the temporarily extinguished ciggie behind her ear, offering a cursory nod to both Frank and the rest of their party. "You need to give Lee your credit card," she instructed Frank, with no further explanation or acknowledgement. She walked the walk of a person clearly clenching their buttocks. A hushed silence followed Stella, as the present calibre of guest on hand were fearful of attracting this unusual woman's attention, or, worse, her wrath.

Stella stopped just before the revolving door. "Lee!" she shouted across the lobby. "Lee, tell the girl on reception to send a few extra bog rolls up to the room, just to be on the safe side! This is going to be a multiple-wiper, I can feel it, and I don't want to run out! Cheers, luv!" Once outside, she removed the fag from behind her ear, setting to work on it again, in earnest, and giving a casual wink to the moustachioed attendant. "All right?" she asked the doorman. To which he tipped his top hat accommodating and replied, "All right," most agreeably.

"I need a drink," announced Stan. "And a large one at that."

"Since you lot are paying, I'll be happy to join you," volunteered Monty.

"That sounds like a fine idea!" agreed Dave happily.

Stan paced back and forth across the polished marble hotel foyer floor, stopping by a mirror on the wall at each pass, to check and see if his bowtie hadn't moved since the last time he'd checked to make certain it was positioned properly just moments before. He offered a courteous smile to those he encountered arriving in their finest eveningwear, in between the pacing, and the checking of his tie in the mirror, and of checking his watch for any number of inestimable times. He recognised several of the faces walking by him, though unsure from where. Stan had a number of famous former acquaintances from his and Frank's days, years ago, as talent agents. Or, it could be they were simply celebrities he recognised. In either case, he offered a hearty welcome to all, to a point where people began to think he was a member of staff, looking him up-and-down for a glass of something with bubbles — unfortunately to no avail on that front. He was waiting for Frank to make his way down from their rooms. Stan was already dressed in his finest, but Frank was taking ages.

Frank stood in the centre of the wide, gently spiralling staircase leading down from the second floor, finally making his grand entrance. He extended a hand, inviting Jessie to a place beside him. Her sequined red ankle-length dress shimmered from the light of the chandeliers overhead. Before they continued on, Frank reached out to take his daughter Molly's hand from where she stood on his opposite side. Stan now stood poised, with his camera at the ready, and those coming down from the top of the stairs held back for a moment to allow for the group's picture to be taken below.

Stan captured the moment of Frank, stood proudly there, flanked by the two ladies most dear to him. As Stan lowered his camera, he couldn't help letting his eyes linger fondly, and he took a moment to blow an affectionate kiss in their direction. "Oh my," he said to himself, taking a handkerchief to dab at the corner of his eye. Stan hated himself for thinking it, but he knew one day he'd be looking at the photograph he'd just taken of that beautiful scene he'd witnessed a moment ago, but that he'd likely be viewing it through the lens of sadness and loss.

"You look wonderful. All of you," proclaimed Stan, leaning in for a generous cuddle as he met them at the foot of the stairs.

"You don't look too bad yourself, Stan," Frank answered him. "Very dapper, I must say."

"And did you expect any less?" replied Stan with a grin.

"Not at all," Frank agreed. "I wonder if…?" Frank began, but then, turning his head, he got his answer. "Oh, my," he declared. "Look at the Dynamic Duo making their way down the stairs."

Dave and Monty sauntered down that posh staircase like they owned the place, dressed to the nines, resplendent in their tuxedos. "My son's even combed his hair," said Jessie, chuffed pink.

"They certainly clean up well," Stan marvelled.

For two gentlemen more used to having their heads buried in the mechanical workings of a sidecar, they blended into their surrounding perfectly, except, perhaps, for one minor detail, as evinced by an intermittent flash of white about Monty's ankles as he'd made his way down the steps.

"Monty, are you wearing white socks?" asked Frank, peering down in the general direction of Monty's feet.

"I am indeed," Monty replied, pleased as punch. "They match my handkerchief," he said, pulling up his trouser legs an inch or so in confirmation to show off his colour-coordinating skills.

Frank closed one eye, like he'd just been stabbed in it. "Normally, Monty, for formalwear, you'd wear bla–" he began, but thought better of it. "You know what, Monty? You look splendid. You *both* look splendid," he said. "*Thank you*," he added, both to Monty and Dave at their efforts to look presentable, and also to the waitron who was carrying a trayful of glasses of champagne, as Frank had just lifted off two of them — one for himself, and one for Jessie.

The waitron, a middle-aged man of impeccable breeding, perfect posture, and a back as straight as Monty's was crooked, tarried, steadfast in his goal of emptying the tray perched upon his upturned palm. "*Ehem*, would you care for a refreshment, sir?" he enquired of Monty, to that very end.

The champagne server stepped to his left, likely in conflict for which of Monty's eyes he should be looking at. But, as the waitron moved, so did Monty, with the two of them moving this way, and then that way, in order to reconcile their difference. It was slow at first, but then picked up speed, this sort of no-touch Viennese waltz. "A refreshment, sir?" the waitron asked again, now giving up entirely on the prospect of effective eye contact and their impromptu dance.

After performing several more dance routines with the help, Monty and the rest of the group made their way to their assigned table. The brass section of the assembled band drew to a climactic crescendo, and then silence, as the final guests had taken their seats in the opulent ballroom. That is, apart from a pair of still-empty seats on Team Frank & Stan's table. Frank's eyes darted around but, with the mood lighting such as it was, it was difficult for him to see. "Where's our Lee and Stella?" he asked, looking to the others, hopefully, for any insight.

"There's dozens of tables in here... maybe they're at the wrong one?" Stan whispered, conscious of the hushed silence.

"I saw them running back to their room," Jessie informed them. "Stella said they were going for a quick one, and I don't think she meant a cigarette."

"Jeezuz, Mum," Dave said with a shudder. "Anyway, here's Lee now," he offered, pointing his thumb over his shoulder like a hitchhiker. "And if anybody deserves a charitable award at this affair it's got to be *him*, after what he's just had to suffer through."

"Sorry, guys, there was a big job that needed doing upstairs," Lee told them as he joined the table a few moments later.

Dave produced a sturgeon-faced frown of admiration and approval. "You're not wrong there, Lee. That's enough of a job for *two* men," he said, but his comments washed over Lee's head, as Lee was currently looking back to the room's entrance in anticipation of Stella's follow-up arrival.

All eyes in the room except Lee's were on the raised stage, rigged with lighting and an imposing videoscreen backdrop, eagerly awaiting the host for the evening. A spotlight raked over the stage, further building the tension. At the sound of footsteps, heads began to turn in anticipation, like wedding attendees waiting for the bride to appear. The spotlight operator, clearly caught off-guard at suddenly having an actual target to highlight, struggled to adjust his aim accordingly, sloppily, like a rum-drunk, one-eyed harpoonsman.

Finally, the light locked on Stella, who walked casually, with no regard for the hundreds of people now looking intently at her. In fact, such was her air of confidence that people started to applaud, fully believing that she was part of the show, perhaps even the master of ceremonies.

There was no doubt that Stella was at the high end of some sort of spectrum, and that a psychologist could spend a career on her. Still, it was impressive how she couldn't possibly care less about unwanted or unexpected attention, where others in a similar situation might wish to find a nearest corner in which to cower.

"Frank!" Stella shouted over the din of silence, peering through the darkened room past her eye-of-the-storm spotlight. "Oi!" she shouted, which was the first indication that she was perhaps not part of the official proceedings after all.

"Over here!" Lee called out, with an enthusiastic wave.

The spotlight followed her as she made her way over, perhaps to guide her safe passage, or perhaps because the operator believed she was a noteworthy spectacle worth illuminating for the curious. Stella's black hobnail boots announced every step she took, obligingly, and her black mini-bandeau strapless dress left little to the imagination, regardless of whether the observer should desperately wish it. The front of the dress, which had the unenviable task of securing Stella's cleavage, was bearing up... if only just. It wasn't this attracting muttered voices, however. Rather, it was the rear perspective. Stella, as it turned out, in her haste after the 'big job' upstairs, had failed to adjust herself, and the rear of her dress was now tucked into the back of her pink undergarments — undergarments which became lost in the crevasse of her buttocks, affording onlookers a generous view of her extremely overly-generous posterior.

When a brave attendee pointed out Stella's fashion faux pas, whether out of helpfulness or abject horror, Stella simply nodded appreciation, entirely unbothered, and sorted herself out. Lee, ever the gentleman, stood, removing the chair for the arrival of his Queen, and welcoming her to the fold. Once seated, Stella looked over to Stan. "Right, then. Well pass that wine this way, you greedy bastard," she admonished him, wiggling her empty wine glass to stress the point that it was, in fact, empty and in proper need of filling.

Food was soon dispatched, as were several additional bottles of very expensive red wine. Stella stood to loosen a notch on her belt after wolfing down her meal, as well as both her cheesecake dessert and Lee's. Lee, for his part, sat back in his chair, himself defeated by the impressive fillet of beef all on its own.

As Stella stood, Stan stared across the table. "Is that a *toolbelt* you're wearing, Stella?" he asked in disbelief. Little did he know that, after this evening, toolbelts with dresses would be all the rage in Glasgow and beyond, thanks to Stella's spotlight celebrity catwalk moment.

"You shouldn't have your eyes down there," she scolded him, pointing back up to her face, indicating where Stan ought to be looking. "You may have noticed this dress is somewhat form-fitting, and so lacking in places to stow things," she explained. "And so my toolbelt is perfect for holding my money, fags, hip flask, and various and sundries." She opened and closed the various compartments to illustrate their efficacy, refastening each Velcro-secured pocket in turn, before sitting back down.

Stan didn't dare ask what her various bits 'n bobs might consist of. Instead, he busied himself replenishing glasses. "That host..." he observed, glancing up to the stage... "And I'm not an authority on the subject... not as much of an authority as *some* here might be... but that doesn't look much like Guy Martin, I don't think?" After receiving no response to his roundabout form of querying, Stan posed his question directly to Lee. "Lee, where's Guy Martin?"

"Ay? Oh. Good ol' Guy Martin is up in the room. On charge, at present, if I'm not mistaken," Lee answered him. "Why do you ask?"

A brief grimace flickered across Stan's face. "No, I mean the *actual* Guy Martin," he clarified. "I thought you said he was hosting this thing?"

Lee gave a micro-shake of his head in response, and then leaned in close to address Stan further so as not to upset Stella with what he was about to say. "I got it wrong," he admitted. "Guy's only handing out one of the prizes, as opposed to being the host for the whole thing. Stella was not a happy bunny when she found out."

While Stan was having this conversation with Lee, the *actual* host for the evening had brought the formal proceedings to proper order with a well-timed tap on his microphone, at which point he had introduced a small girl. Lee was just beginning to detail precisely how cross Stella had in fact been, sharing with Stan some of the amusingly un-ladylike curses which had issued forth from his dear one's mouth, when a round of rapturous applause brought their attention back to the affair at hand.

"What did she win a prize for?" Stan whispered, but Lee was just as clueless as he was since the both of them had missed and hadn't heard the emotional back-story. Jessie, on the other hand, was consumed in tears — just as most of those in the room were. For fear of appearing heartless, and unsure if television cameras were in attendance, Stan wiped an imaginary tear from his cheek in solidarity. In unison, the crowd offered sympathetic murmurings as the little girl blathered on about something or other in her acceptance speech, followed by the sound of muffled sobbing, and then another round of applause as the host said something to the effect of, *"And there you have it."* At this, the little girl stood on tiptoes in order to say a final *thank you* into the microphone before accepting her prize and making her exit.

"You'd think she was bloody Mother Teresa or something," Stan said to Lee, confidentially. Only it didn't turn out to be confidential, as Stan spoke too loudly just as the applause abruptly ended — leaving much of the audience to hear his unfortunate pithy observation clear as day.

Angry eyes focussed their fury on Stan, with the little girl on stage opting not to deliver her final words, but to instead bugger straight off instead, sobbing. The prize-giver stood there rooted to the spot, with the girl's undelivered trophy still in his hands.

"What an inspiration to us all," Lionel, the white-suited host said flatly, the moment ruined. The audience offered up a timid round of applause, keeping a disapproving eye on Stan in the process.

"This is shit," announced Stella some great while later, with no attempt to disguise her frustration. "What time are we going? It's either that or they need to bring more food out. Because this, as it stands, is shit."

In fairness to Stella, hers was a sentiment which by this point appeared to be shared by many. Indeed, on the adjacent table, one elderly gentleman was asleep on the shoulder of his female companion. Frank glanced at his watch, and had to admit as well that she certainly had a point. It really had turned out to be an extraordinarily arduous, never-ending slog of one rubbish award after another. Salvation finally, blessedly, came in the form of Lionel announcing the penultimate award for the evening.

"And so," Lionel continued on from his previous droning monologue. "To present the Fundraiser of the Year award, I'm delighted to invite on stage TV celebrity and racer Guy Martin."

With that, an uncommon occurrence was manifesting itself at Team Frank & Stan's table, as rare as hen's teeth, one could say, or rocking horse shit: Stella's teeth were slowly appearing, a strange configuration taking hold, creeping across, and finally overtaking her face. She was, in fact, smiling.

Like a chink in a dragon's armour, it was unusual to see this soft white underbelly exposed. Granted, in Stella's case, it was a very *large* underbelly, as well as being *particularly* soft.

"I'd ride him like a new bicycle on Christmas Day," proclaimed Stella aloud, her eyes locked on target and boring into the beefcake on display at the stage like drill bits.

At this, a well-presented lady well past middle age, sat with her back to Stella at the next table over, turned round and leaned over, confiding, "I've named my vibrator after him."

Stella nodded her head sympathetically. "You and me both, sister," she said, with an approving wink. "You and me both."

Frank pressed his elbows into the table, leaning forward. He was showing a keen interest in Guy Martin as well, though of a slightly different type. "That's who we need for our Isle 'Le Mans' TT," he declared. "We could do with a third racer on our team. If we get Guy Martin on board, think of the publicity. Dave, we *need* him."

"You're telling me this as if you're expecting me to make it happen," Dave remarked. "Do you think I've some sort of magic wand up my sleeve?"

"Dave is rubbish at magic tricks," Monty added.

"Didn't you used to race on the same track as him?" suggested Stan, chiming in.

"I once sat next to Sean Bean on a train," Dave answered. "But that doesn't mean I know him, or that he managed to get me a part on *Game of Thrones*. Though I did ask."

"You would've been good as one of them Wildlings north of the wall," Monty opined wistfully.

"Thank you, Monty, that's lovely of you to say," Dave answered Monty appreciatively. "Anyway," he went on, "Just because I happened to be in the same races as Guy Martin doesn't mean I've got Guy Martin's ear."

"He'd be brilliant," Frank carried on, undeterred. "How do we get hold of... Hang on, where's Stella going? Stella, what are you doing?" he asked, in reference to a now-standing Stella, wine glass in hand.

"I'm going to ask Guy Martin to join us at the event and be on our team," she replied with a faraway, monotone effect, as if she were in some kind of hypnotic state, completely mesmerised. Which of course she was. And, upon issuing her pronouncement, she began advancing towards the stage.

"Someone grab her! Lee!" shouted Frank desperately. And then, calling after her, "Stella, he's on stage presenting a prize! You can't just—"

"What about that, ladies and gentlemen," announced Lionel, returning to the stage once more after Guy Martin had done his bit. "A very worthy winner, I'm sure you'll agree. And that brings us onto our final award of the evening, the Charity of the Year. Now, unlike the other awards, we don't read out the shortlist, but rather head straight into the winning charity, who, by the way, will be receiving a fifty-thousand-pound donation to their cause!"

"Holy shit," said Frank, going pale, and completely forgetting about the errant Stella. "I didn't know about this prize money. We can really *do* this, Stan," he said encouragingly.

Time slowed to a crawl, with Frank and Stan virtually on each other's laps. Frank looked around his table with a contented grin, confident as to what was to come, as Lionel teased the silver envelope open, ever so slowly, to draw out the anticipation.

"And, the winner is..." he said, and then, after a dramatic pause... "Mrs Tillypickle's Hedgehog Sanctuary!"

"Oh, fuck off!" shouted Stan, in a somewhat uncharacteristically expletive-laden outburst.

"It's okay, Stan. There's always next year," said an equally gutted Frank, trying his best to console Stan. But a "next year" seemed unlikely, as...

"Beaten by a bloody *hedgehog* hotel?" Stan was screaming. "Seriously? Fucking seriously??" he continued, in full-on Tourette syndrome fashion now. "That's right, I said it! You can fucking fuck right off!" he shouted. "FUCK. RIGHT. OFF."

"Stan... Stan..." Frank attempted, massaging the air in front of him, as if that might calm Stan down. But Stan wasn't listening.

"Oh, brilliant, here comes security!" said Stan, still shouting. "Well that's just great, isn't it! It's okay, I'm going! *Believe* me, I'm going!" Stan carried on, much to the amusement of a returning Stella, who cackled away in delight.

"*That's* the spirit, Stan!" she said, complimenting him. "*Now* you're learning!"

"What, *all* of us?" asked Frank of the stern-looking security guard. "Great, well, all right, then. Come on, guys, let's go," he said to the others.

"Apologies for the disturbance, ladies and gentlemen," offered Lionel from the stage. "Security is dealing with the troublemakers presently."

Stella stood ramrod straight, extending two fingers to the stage. "Oi! Didn't Stan tell you to fuck off?" she called out. "He *did*! And *up yours*, Lionel!" she said, with an upward motion of her two raised fingers, making it eminently clear, lest any doubt should remain, that she was *not* making a 'V-for-Victory' sign. At all. "And sort that suit out!" she added for good measure. "You look like you've nicked it from a corpse!"

"That... certainly escalated quickly?" put forth Jessie, somewhat shell-shocked, once they were all in the hotel lobby.

"You have to understand," Molly told her, a comforting hand on her shoulder. "This is all *perfectly normal* for a night out with Stan and my father."

"Yes, I'm starting to realise that," said Jessie, along with the sort of giggle a madwoman might give. "I hope it's just the function room they're throwing us out of, though, bearing in mind we're staying at the hotel?"

"Bloody *hedgehogs*," lamented Stan. "Still... I suppose I may have overacted just a little."

"At least the night's not a complete washout," Dave offered. "We still got a good meal out of it, yeah?" he said, trying to look on the bright side of things.

"More productive than you might think," interjected Stella.

"How so?" asked Dave, and the others turned as well to Stella to see what news she had to reveal.

"Well. While you lot were faffing about, as usual," she began, reaching into one of her toolbelt pockets for a celebratory fag, but then, remembering she was not allowed to smoke there in the lobby, placing it behind her ear instead. "I've actually procured Guy Martin for our event. He's on the team."

"Jeez boy, she's something pure special, that girl," declared Lee in reference to Stella, flushed with admiration. "There's no man alive that can resist the charms of this heavenly beauty, am I wrong?"

"Stella, how on earth did you—?" asked Frank.

"Where exactly did you go?" Stan cut in. "I saw you walking up to the stage, but then you disappeared. Did you go backstage after Guy did his bit?"

"I got things *done*. Like I *always* do," Stella answered, enjoying her moment of glory.

"Like a weary sailor at the mercy of the siren's song, so it is," Lee carried on. "Poor bastard didn't stand a chance," he said, properly chuffed.

At that moment, Frank spotted Martin making his way over from the event and heading towards the men's loo. Frank gave him a friendly wave. "Happy to have you in the fold, Guy!" he called out, cheerfully.

Martin froze just as he was pushing through the bathroom door. Like a deer caught in headlamps, he was glassy-eyed and stared at them vacantly. There was what appeared to be an odd mixture of excitement and terror over his face. Mouth open, but unable to speak, he gave a curt nod to Frank after a moment or two, and then made a hasty exit into the loo, disappearing from sight.

"Stella, what did you *do* to that poor fellow?" asked an incredulous Frank, turning to her for answers.

"Things needed sorting. She *sorted* them. It's what she *does*," Lee reiterated, echoing Stella's words.

Stella didn't answer. She merely licked her lips and took the cigarette from behind her ear, placing it into her mouth carefully and affectionately, receiving it like an old friend. Remembering herself, she then tucked it back up, for the time being, where it had been. "No rush," she said to herself aloud in a calm, placid voice. "Plenty of time for more of that later." Her eyes lingered on the now-empty doorway of the men's loo. "Loads of time," she said.

*Chapter*
# TEN

Frank sat back in his leather chair, resting his feet on top of his desk, staring at a spot on the wall.

Stan followed his eyes to the object of Frank's attention. "You may have been rather presumptuous with the shelf, Frank."

"What's that?" Frank said, shaking loose of his contemplation.

"The shelf. I was saying it was a bit presumptuous."

"You're not half wrong, Stan. A shiny trophy should be nestled on that shelf. When we decided to build the office in the house, I wanted something to go on that wall. That trophy would have been perfect, but now every time I look at it I'll think of those bloody hedgehogs."

"Bloody hedgehogs," Stan repeated, commiserating from his side of the office. "Frank, when you think of hedgehogs, though, what image does that conjure up in your mind?"

"What?" asked Frank, laughing. "I'm not really sure I fully understand the question. Dinsdale, I suppose? Spiny Norman?"

Stan tapped the fingers of his right hand rhythmically, gently playing them across the surface of his desk as if it were a piano, while he pondered a burgeoning thought taking shape in his brain. "Besides that," he told Frank. "See, the thing is..." he went on... "The thing is, the only time I ever see hedgehogs for real is at the side of the road. You know?"

"Selling lemonade?" Frank ventured, unsure where Stan was heading with this.

"No. With a tyre mark embedded in their back," Stan explained patiently. "And because of that — *see?* — because of that, the image I have in my mind isn't one of cuddly little spiky things, but rather of something that looks like it's been flattened by a steamroller, and with a grid pattern over it like it's been cooked on a grill. Do you know what I mean?"

"Stan, I've long since given up trying to work out what goes on in that mind of yours, if I'm being honest," Frank responded. "I've got enough trouble trying to figure out my own."

Dave eased open the door with his foot. "Knock-knock, ay-up, gents," he said, juggling several cups of coffee in his hands along with an assortment of sugar-coated snacks. "That's yours, Stan," he told Stan, now indicating to Stan with a nod which coffee he should take. "And, Frank, this one is yours," he went on, performing the same routine. "Black as pitch, same as your dark heart, just as you like it."

"I do so have a heart!" Frank protested. "It's in here somewhere, I'm sure of it," he said, looking down to examine his chest and thumping on it with two fingers to search for the aortic organ.

"It's on holiday at the moment?" Stan offered with a chuckle, playing along.

"It was there only a moment ago," said Frank, feigning alarm.

"You're looking on the wrong side," Dave offered. "You won't have one there on the right side, not unless you're a Time Lord," he said, setting out the treats and then placing his own coffee down.

"Pity I can't regenerate," came Frank's reply, gone from jocular to suddenly melancholy. "Eh. No Monty with you?" asked Frank, spirits raised again, and examining the contents of his cup to make sure Dave had in fact gotten it right.

Hands now free, Dave held a thumb and forefinger to his ear for illustrative purposes. "He's on a call just now," he said. "Let's just say the phone hasn't stopped since we got back from Glasgow..."

Dave dragged out 'ow' in Glasgow for dramatic effect, but his audience were not impressed, preoccupied at the moment as they were tucking into the selection of doughnuts on offer. Dave went on...

# FRANK & STAN'S BUCKET LIST #3: ISLE 'LE MANS' TT

"Since you put me and my learned colleague, Mr Montgomery, in charge of Isle 'Le Mans' TT, things have been moving at quite a pace."

Still bugger-all interest from Frank and Stan. Frank had gotten hold of a glazed chocolate cake job, and was currently dunking it into his coffee with enthusiasm. Stan, for his part, had got his hands round a custard-filled and was presently squeezing it and licking off the excess thick, viscous custard that issued forth and came running lazily down the side.

"It's a wonder we get anything done here at all," a dismayed Dave said to himself, since no one else was listening.

"Did you tell them?" enquired an animated Monty, entering the room at an exuberant canter, scanning the faces in the room for any form of reaction.

Dave sat on the corner of Stan's desk, smiling sadly, and swept his hand through the air in a gesture meant to express something along the lines of, *Witness the state of things, me lad.*

"We've offered a first prize of fifty-thousand pounds to the winner of the inaugural Isle 'Le Mans' TT," announced Monty, not to be undone, and holding both hands out to emphasise his point, like Spider-Man shooting webs.

Stan guffawed between gobs of custard. "Very good," he said, nearly choking on his treat. "Nice one. You almost had me there."

"He's being deadly serious," Dave attested. "The prize for first place is fifty-thousand pounds. Look, it's even on the flyers and posters we had printed."

Frank was ready to join the frivolity and come to Stan's defence when he caught sight of the poster in Monty's hand. In one fluid motion, he spun about on his chair, swinging his legs into action and leaping forth like a panther. "What the hell, Monty?" moaned a keening Frank. "What the hell??" he said again, frantically pawing at the relevant bit on the poster confirming what Monty and Dave were telling him.

Dave nodded. "That's right, boys. Fifty-thousand clams to the winner, baby!"

"Are you completely and utterly *mental*, Dave?" said Frank, turning the poster around to examine the rear, blank side in a hopeless attempt to search for something — like an explanation, perhaps — that couldn't possibly be there.

"Mad as a box of frogs," Dave admitted happily. "What's that got to do with anything?"

"How many of these have you handed out?" cried Frank. "We need to get them back out of circulation!"

"All of them, Frank!" replied Monty, receiving a high-five from Dave for his enthusiasm in response. "That's why we're late. We had to drop off the last of them."

"Okay. Right," said Stan, trying to be the calm voice of reason. "Dave, you do realise we're trying to raise money to buy the farm, yeah? We do not have that amount of money to be giving away for prize money, as that would be counterproductive. You understand this, yes?"

"But you do," replied Dave.

Stan glanced over to Frank, at a loss. "Dave," he said. "Dave, we really *don't*."

Dave rubbed his hands together in delight. "I am very pleased, chaps, to tell you that we indeed do. You see, since one Guy Martin added his name to our little event, a lot of people have become very interested in signing up. We've spoken to the management at Jurby Race Track, and we've been given permission to have twenty-five vehicles on track at any given time. That can include sidecars, as well as vehicles of the four-wheeled variety. I've told them we're going for vans. Entrants can, if they wish, race sidecars for a maximum of two hours and then for the remaining twenty-two it has to be in a van. To keep things on a fairly level playing field, the van has to be of the stock variety you could buy from your local dealer, and the only permitted alterations are suspension, tyres, and brakes. Oh, and racing seats and roll cages, of course — the usual racing safety equipment. Other than that, they're completely standard so that it comes down to the ability of the driver. And three drivers per team, taking turns at the wheel in two-hour shifts. As for the sidecars, on the other hand, anything goes. The quicker the—"

"That's all well and good, Dave," Frank cut across. "But, you know, as to the certain matter of—"

"Ah. Well," replied Dave. "Let me finish."

"You never let him finish!" Monty interjected, chastising Frank, despite the fact that Frank was not routinely in the habit of preventing Dave from finishing anything.

"Fine," Frank sighed. "Let's hear it, then?"

Dave looked at Monty with a satisfied grin, and then back to Frank and Stan. He took a large breath before speaking, because this was big news he was about to deliver...

"I've told the people what have been in touch that there's a ten-grand entry fee."

"TEN GRAND!" screamed Stan, the voice of reason no longer, ejecting large chunks of doughnut from his mouth and sending them sailing through the air in the process. "Who in god's name is going to pay TEN GRAND?? Dave, are you *mental*?"

"He's mental," Frank confirmed.

"They've already *paid* it, Stanley," announced Monty, intent on getting some more words in.

"*Who* has?" scoffed Frank.

"*They* has," replied Dave, pulling a bank statement from his pocket and holding it out for inspection. "We're fully subscribed. The race sold out in less than a day. So you see? Fifty grand in prize money is not at all unreasonable when compared to the entrance fee everyone's paid."

"You're taking the piss?" asked Frank.

"You're having us on, surely?" echoed Stan.

Dave shook his head. "I'm not. And I wouldn't. Not about this. Excluding our own entry, we've had twenty-four people paying ten grand a pop. We've currently got one hundred and ninety thousand pounds, all told, *after* you take out for the prize money."

"I'm feeling faint," declared Stan, back of the hand pressed to his forehead. "Frank, is the room spinning or is it just me?" But Frank was too busy to answer, himself holding on tightly to his desk in an effort to combat the sudden vertigo.

"Have some sugar," suggested Monty helpfully, handing over another doughnut to Stan.

"I don't like this kind," said Stan, handing it back. He was overcome with emotion, yes, but not so overcome that he couldn't recognise a doughnut preference. "I was hoping for another custard-filled?" he asked hopefully. "And if there aren't any more of those, a jelly-filled would be lovely."

With Stan tucking into a fresh doughnut, preoccupied and content for the moment, Dave went on. "If you think about it," he said. "That amount of money isn't that much. These guys are going to have their vans on the track for a full day. But, the vans'll be plastered with advertising, don't forget. So they'll be getting loads of exposure."

"Loads," Monty added.

"Plus," Dave continued, "if this thing really takes off, they can say that they were in at ground floor on it and have bragging rights. Hence, the enthusiastic response."

Frank looked punch-drunk. "I'm staggered. Honestly, boys, I'm staggered. In my head I'd all but written the farm off, thinking there wasn't a snowball in hell's chance of getting the money. But that's nearly half raised, and in less than four days!"

"Don't forget the money from ITV Channel 3 for covering the event," added Dave, finger aloft.

Frank sidled over to Dave and Monty, scooping them up into his arms — which was no easy task, as both fellows were rather large. "ITV are covering this?" he exclaimed. "I say again, you are taking the piss?"

"Okay, look," said Dave. "How about the two of you just agree to take whatever we say as gospel truth for the next ten minutes, all right? Then we can get through a bit quicker?"

There were no objections.

"Right. That reporter, Jenny, who interviewed us before, she got in touch. Once Guy Martin and Peter Hickman were on board, she had no problem convincing her bosses, it would seem, of covering the event. It's a high-profile event with them lads involved, so likely to get a good viewing audience, which is why they're willing to pay for the honour of covering the event. So that's fifty grand we'll be getting from them."

"Go to the foot of the st–! Sorry, nevermind," Frank replied, immediately correcting himself.

"Hang on. Who's Peter Hickman?" asked Stan.

"Who's Peter...? Is that a deplorable question, Stan?" Monty asked, confused.

"You mean rhetorical?" said Stan.

"No, *deplorable*," Monty answered him.

"He's not wrong," offered up Dave, agreeing with Monty.

"He's in the *TT*, Stan," explained Monty, unsure if this was some kind of test.

"Ah," said Stan, giving a knowing sort of nod, though he remained entirely clueless. "Is he, *em*... any good, then? This Peter Hickman?"

Dave's eyes narrowed. "You *do* watch the solo machines in the TT, Stan, don't you? Peter Hickman, as you *should* be well aware, is pretty damned quick. You could say he knows his way around a racetrack, to put it mildly."

"Ah! Yes! *That* Peter Hickman!" replied Stan, with unconvincing assurance. "Why didn't you say so at the start?" he said, quickly performing a somewhat-less-than-discrete internet search on his phone. "Just, ah... checking for messages here," he told them. "Don't mind me. Carry on."

"How many people are going to enter sidecars?" enquired Frank, leaving Stan to his devices.

"Four," replied Dave succinctly, with an impressive, professional finger on the pulse, not often witnessed previously. "The teams entering sidecars are the ones with a special eye on first prize. Including our own Team Frank & Stan. Sidecars are only permitted for a maximum of two hours, remember. So tactics will come into play for when they're used."

Monty jumped in at this point. He was feeling like he hadn't spoken for a bit. "Henk's also on board," he told the others. "He thinks it's an amazing idea, this whole thing, so he's got the McMullan brothers together again on his team, since Harry knows by now that Dave and me are reunited." Monty sniffed. "Dave and Monty reunited," he repeated, savouring the sound of it.

Dave laughed. Not at Monty's sentimentality, but at the final point he'd made. "He really took it well, being dumped in favour of a fat bastard as replacement His ego must've loved that," he remarked. "No offence, mate," he said to Monty.

"None taken," replied Monty, patting his belly contentedly.

"You told him, Dave?" asked Frank. "Harry?"

"No, not at all. He must have seen that interview we did. Or Henk told him. Either way. You want to hear something interesting, though? That gobshite, Rodney Franks, had the nerve to try and enter a team into the race! The cheek of that... that..." he said, searching for the right expression. "What was it that Henk called him?" he asked.

"Among other things? *Very low-hanging scrotum,*" Stan offered up with a chuckle.

"Cheek, *indeed,*" Monty said, underscoring Dave's words.

"You told him to piss off?" asked Frank.

"Sure. He tried to get someone to enter on his behalf," Dave told him. "Because of course he knew we'd do precisely that. Tell him to fuck right off, that is. But I knew the guy was a stooge for Franks the moment I saw him, so told them in no uncertain terms just where to go."

"Just there," Monty added, pointing down, to the bowels of the earth, lest any doubt remain.

"Henk was particularly pleased when we relayed this to him," Dave went on. "Speaking of Henk, the only downside, to be sure, of Harry and me parting ways is that glorious sidecar the two of us won the TT with. It will of course be following him back into Henk's team. And that means Monty and I will be back on our own trusty little machine. We'll crack on, though, eh, Monty?"

"Sure will, Dave. We'll be cracking on like... like a thing that cracks quite a lot," Monty replied.

"Well said," Dave answered him.

"Don't forget, Dave," Monty advised him. "You need to ask them about the... the thing."

Dave stared back blankly.

"You know," Monty prodded. "The *thing*."

Dave was still staring blankly.

"The *thingy*," Monty told him. "The THINGY."

"Oh the thingy!" Dave came back, realisation finally striking. "Ah. Yes. Good point. The thingy. You see..." Dave said, now turning to Stan and Frank... "The thing is, chaps, we find ourselves at somewhat of a loss here," he went on.

"A loss," Monty added.

"As we've got a sidecar to race with but haven't got a van," Dave explained.

"It was only your idea for the race to be in vans!" Frank scolded him, though not angrily. "What do you think, Stan?"

"It's the least we can do, boys," Stan said, entering in. "I've had my eye on a VW Transporter, actually, for the farm. And so if you don't end up trashing it, we can use the van for the farm when you're done with it," he pronounced sagely.

Dave grinned. "Us, trash a van in a mere twenty-four-hour race? Perish the thought."

"Whatever happens, boys, Stan and I are very impressed with what you've done with all this. Seriously impressed. Proper impressed. And you're involved in something great here. I don't mean the racing, so much, but rather the farm. You and Monty are part of a legacy, and one I'm sure you'll both continue to be a part of long after me and this one are long gone. At the risk of sounding maudlin, well done, lads. And I mean that sincerely. Unbelievable work. And to think, when I first suggested that you lot come and work with us on the farm, Stan told me it was a bad idea, and that you pair were a couple of bumbling idiots."

"Hold on!" Stan protested. "I'm pretty sure it was *you* who said as much!"

"Minor details," Frank replied, shrugging off Stan's desperate remonstrations. "That's always been your problem, Stan," Frank chided him playfully. "You're forever focussed on the minor details but ignoring of the larger, grander picture."

"Yes, that's always my problem, all right," replied Stan, rolling his eyes.

"It's okay," Dave told them, finally. "We *are* idiots," he said thoughtfully. "But we're *your* idiots. And you, ours."

---

The phone had continued to ring for the next few days, and having to declare that the entry list was full ripped Dave's insides out, for he knew how much more money could be gotten for the farm had the race been on a larger scale.

The problem here was that there was but one purpose-built racetrack on the Isle of Man, and that was Jurby, where the event was due to take place. The other blue-ribband racing events on the Isle, such as the TT and the Southern 100, took place on public roads that were closed for the purposes of those particular events. The Isle of Man government were particularly eager to promote motorsport on the Island, and the Billown Circuit — home of the Southern 100 — would have been ideal at a little over 4.25 miles in length, accommodating an increased entry list perfectly. Unfortunately, when Dave pitched the idea to close the roads for twenty-four hours, a twenty-four hours *not* in July and for purposes strictly related to the Southern 100, the only response he got was for those on the other side of the desk to laugh and to continue to do so even as Dave left the building in defeat. Still, the Jurby circuit was perfect for their present needs, and as Monty said at the time, if the event grew in stature, then the Billown Circuit might still be a possibility for a future running.

It was evening, and Dave turned the pink Nissan Micra he was driving into the farmhouse drive. Dave slowed sufficiently as he made his way up the drive, allowing he and Monty a moment to admire their handiwork, the fence they'd erected the previous day. They really were embracing this working outdoor life of theirs. "Frank and Stan must be here," Dave declared. "The lights are on."

Monty hopped out as Dave parked. It was dark, aside from the farmhouse's interior illumination spilling out, casting a gentle orange glow over the courtyard. "But their car isn't here, and the builders look like they've long since gone," Monty said, stepping back and letting Dave take the lead while he maintained safe cover behind. "What if it's a burglar?"

"I don't think burglars put the lights on, Monty," Dave offered.

"They do if they want to get a proper look at what to steal," Monty countered, remaining unconvinced.

"Come on," Dave told him. "We've work to do on the sidecar. She needs to be purring like a kitten come race day. It's quite handy being able to store it up here, don't you think?"

"I've just seen someone," declared Monty, pointing up to the second floor of the farmhouse. "Seriously, Dave. Walking past the window," he said, breathing a little heavier now.

"Monty, you're hurting my arm," Dave told him. "Can you let go of it, please?" Dave looked up, briefly, but his attention was drawn to the barn, instead, where a thin strip of light shone out from around the frame of the closed door. "Someone's in our sidecar shed," he said gravely.

Dave picked up a garden gnome, holding it like a cudgel.

"Come on, Monty. Here's the plan, ay? You open the door, head in, and I'll have your back. Right? Right."

Monty gave a stifled cry. "Not the gnome!"

"Sorry, I forgot," Dave had to assure him. "Look, I'll just brandish it about, right? I won't hurt it, I promise."

"Well if you promise," Monty reluctantly acquiesced. "But I'm not going in first. You should. You're bigger, plus you're armed."

"It's a gnome, Monty, it's not exactly an M16. But, whatever. You open the door, yeah? And then I'll pounce in, okay? Right. Are you ready? After *four*."

"After *four*?" replied Monty, suddenly sceptical. "I thought it was *three*? It should always be on the count of *three*! That's how these things are done!" Monty held onto the door handle, not moving, his confidence — such as it was — now thrown off, and uncertain if he wished to continue. Especially what with Dave throwing a spanner into the works with his oddly improper counting and all. "Should we phone someone?" he proposed tentatively. "Might that be the best course of action?"

"Like who?" asked Dave. "Phone the police? And tell them what, exactly? That someone's left the lights on?"

"If wasting electricity isn't a crime, well then it should be!" Monty answered. "Hang on. What was that noise?"

"What noise, Monty?"

The sounds of passing cars could be heard off in the distance, further up the lane. But, now, with both their ears pressed up against the wooden door, something entirely more nefarious was revealed — a hideous rasping noise, like the dead risen from their graves, bones scraping together as they moved impossibly about.

"It sounds like it could maybe be a horse farting?" suggested Monty, searching desperately for some sort of rational explanation.

"If that's a horse passing gas then the only person you should be phoning is a vet, Monty," Dave countered.

They listened on, and there it was again, a high-pitched rasping — only this time it was followed by what sounded very much like laughter. It was an eerie, haunting kind of laughter, clearly not of this ordinary corporeal world.

Dave stared at Monty, and Monty stared at Dave, as they tried to interpret what they were hearing in any type of way that could conceivably make sense.

"There's someone, or *something*, in there," whispered a terrified Monty. But then, mustering a small degree of sense, and seeking a more worldly explanation for their perception, he asked, "What if it's the McMullan brothers broken in, and they're trying to sabotage our sidecar ahead of the race?"

"I like your enthusiasm, Monty," Dave answered him. "But I don't think the McMullans see us as that much of a threat, mate, to be honest." But the clang of something that was obviously metal dropping onto the floor interrupted him. "Right. That's no ghost, then. Open the door, Monty. I'm going in."

Dave readied himself with a series of deep breaths. His hands took hold of the gnome's crotch, pressing firmly, and stroking it like a worry stone, in a manner that was both comforting and perhaps a bit inappropriate. Monty nodded his approval. "I'm going in, Monty," Dave said again, his mind made up. "After four," he told Monty. And, then, with no preamble... "*Four!*"

Monty did his part, as instructed, present counting debacle notwithstanding.

"*Rraaaaahgggg!*" screamed Dave, opting for the shock-and-awe tactics he hoped might subdue any intruder. But he progressed no further than six or seven feet before his right leg caught a toolbox, sending him arse-over-tit in a sprawling heap. "Man down!" he yelled. "Man down! Send in the reinforcements!"

Monty looked around to spot the reinforcements, grateful that they had arrived, but then realised the reinforcements Dave was referring to were none other than his very person.

Monty didn't see what had felled his great friend and could only assume he'd been the victim of some form of terrible assault. He hopped, adrenalin pumping, on the spot, and his wayward eyes were typical of the conflict in his head — one pointing the way to safety, and the other to the barn ahead. Monty steeled his nerves, for the sake of his fallen comrade, deciding to follow the eye that led towards Dave. It was *damn-the-torpedoes, full-speed-ahead*.

"*Rraaaaahgggg!*" screamed Monty, replicating the war cry of his fallen comrade, but he progressed no further than six or seven feet into the fray as well before he too went arse-over-tit, tripping over Dave, and landing mere inches away from him. *At least we'll die together*, thought Monty. *It will be a glorious death.*

Dave rolled onto his front, unsure from which direction this new assailant had attacked, so swung the gnome still in his hands wildly about, making obscene grunting noises all the while.

Unbeknown to either of them, the only people involved in this mêlée were in fact, Dave and Monty themselves. "Where is he??" Monty shouted, popping up. "Get him, Dave! Get him!"

One of the gnome's boots caught Monty squarely in the jaw, sending him sprawling back to the barn floor. Along with this revised vantage point, however, came the benefit of their present circumstances being made apparent.

"Stop," Monty moaned, covering his face to guard against further gnome-based assault. "It's just me and you fighting, Dave. There's no burglar at all. Or ghosts, for that matter."

"There isn't?" asked Dave, thoroughly confused. "Monty, what are you doing on the floor there? And what was that noise, then?" Dave held out the gnome, still at the ready, though by now it looked more like a French loaf of bread rather than a weapon.

"It's a kid. Look. Over there," directed Monty, pointing.

Sure enough, the potentially-lethal intruder likely there to sabotage their sidecar — or equally-lethal spirit or ghoul — was in fact revealed to be only a small boy, sat astride Dave's sidecar, where he'd been making the pretend noises of a championship driver. The boy stared back at Monty, Dave, and the baguette-like gnome in Dave's hand, wondering what all the fuss was about.

Dave lowered his makeshift weapon, taking the gnome out of play, much to Monty's tremendous relief. "Hey, buddy, don't worry about the screaming," Dave told the boy, who now looked as if he was wondering if he ought to be frightened or not. "We were just playing," said Dave reassuringly. "We like to do that. We call it..." he trailed off, unsure what precisely to call it, actually.

"Gnome wrestling," said Monty with confidence, quickly coming to Dave's rescue, apparently well familiar with the subject.

"So what's your name?" asked Dave, turning back to the young one. "Would you like me to show you how I drive the sidecar? I'm Dave, and this is my official sidecar passenger Monty. We're here to fix her up, in fact, because we've got a big race coming up soon! You could help if you wanted?" Dave offered tentatively, hoping to allay the possible fears of their 'intruder.'

The boy nodded enthusiastically, and Dave walked over, offering a hand to help the wee one off the bike. "So. Where did you appear from?" Dave asked by way of conversation, but before any response could be given, the barn door flew open.

"Tyler, I told you to stay out of here!" the panic-stricken woman called out. "Oh! I'm so sorry!" she added, noticing Dave and Monty stood there. "I hope he's not damaged anything?" She closed the distance between them, and then scooped the boy up in her arms, pulling him into her chest, and stroking his hair.

"*Muu*-uum," the boy protested, wriggling in her grasp. "We were just gonna work on the motorbike!"

"It's fine," replied Dave, as the woman, obviously Tyler's mum, set her son back down so his flailing legs could once again find purchase on the barn floor. "He was just trying the sidecar out for size," Dave continued on, cheerfully. "I'm thinking of swopping out your boy for mine, actually. Got a race coming up, and he'd be a bit less weight than Monty. That way, we should get more speed going up the hills. What do you reckon, Tyler?" Dave asked amiably. "Sound good?" he said to the now-giggling boy.

The woman extended her hand. "I'm assuming you must be Dave? I've heard quite a bit about you. Grand Prix winner, is it?"

"TT, yes, close enough," Dave replied, taking her hand. "And this would be Monty."

"Ay-up," Monty offered up agreeably.

"I'm Rebecca. Well, Becks, you can call me. And this is my son, Tyler."

"Ay-up!" Tyler chirped, mimicking Monty's salutation.

"What must you think of me," Rebecca said, chastising herself, pulling back and pointing to her current state of dress. "The first time you meet me, and I'm wearing pyjamas and a tatty pair of Ugg boots."

Dave and Monty smiled back, humouring her, because truth be told they wouldn't have been able to identify one women's brand of boots from another. And, beyond that, they both felt that pyjamas were a perfectly acceptable form of attire and not at all cause for embarrassment.

"Frank and Stan showed Tyler the sidecar earlier," Rebecca went on. "But when I was running him a bath, he must have decided he wanted to win a Grand— sorry, TT race— himself."

"Ah!" declared Dave. "I've just worked out who you both are! Specifically, I mean. In reference to the farm, I mean. Sorry. It often takes me a while to get up to speed."

"Takes him a while to get up to speed," repeated Monty, nodding his head along for good measure.

"A while to get up to speed," Tyler agreed, nodding his own head along as well.

"So," continued Dave. "You're the guys from England who've come to spend some time with us, if I remember correctly?" he asked, looking to Tyler.

"A while to get up to speed," Tyler agreed, still nodding his head.

"Sorry for thinking you were burglars and all that," Dave went on, turning his attention back to Rebecca.

"We thought you were burglars," Monty clarified. "Well, Dave did, that is. I didn't, of course," he added, shaking his head at Dave's ostensible foolishness.

"Burglars," Tyler agreed, shaking his head.

"It's just that Frank said you were coming in a couple of weeks," Dave explained. "So we — me and Monty, that is — weren't expecting you to be here just yet." Dave stared for a moment longer than necessary after he said this, feeling his face get hot. Rebecca was dressed for bed, with her auburn hair tied back, and while she looked less than glamorous according to her, she looked entirely presentable to Dave, her eyes shimmering whenever she spoke.

"Oh. Well one room was finished in the other barn," Rebecca told him. She took a step forward, cupping the side of her mouth and lowering her voice. "I told Tyler we were staying at a friend's house in Liverpool, rather than try to explain to him what a hostel was. But then Lee said a room had become available over here, and I thought it was a wonderful opportunity to, you know, make a fresh start. Lee suggested we come over straight away, so that we could be settled in well before Christmas. And being here for Christmas means we can help out with the decoration," she told him. "I'm a wizard with decorations!"

"I'm a wizard also!" pronounced Tyler, popping his head up from the sidecar he'd scampered into, and his mother's efforts at speaking confidentially obviously for nought. "I painted a picture of my teacher's car, didn't I, Mummy? Will I still have the same teacher in my new school?" he asked.

"Probably not, honey. Anyway, we should get you to bed, little man, and leave these two to fix their... their bike thingy. It's really nice to meet you both," she told Monty and Dave. "And hopefully we'll get to come and see you when you're racing!"

"Ah!" Dave replied. "Well we'll likely see you around the farm as we're here every day doing whatever needs doing and fixing whatever needs fixing. If you'd like to see a bit more of our Island, I'd be happy to take you for a drive around? It's my mum's car, but she wouldn't mind."

"Sure, sounds great," Rebecca answered. "Wave goodbye, Tyler," she said, and Tyler dutifully waved goodbye to them, as instructed.

With the barn door closed, Monty gave a broad smile.

"What?" asked Dave, busying himself with a spanner.

"Nothing."

"Good, let's get on with the sidecar."

"You like her, Dave," Monty told him, his grin not abating.

"I bloody don't, Monty!" Dave answered, his face flushed yet again, betraying him. "She *was* nice, though, wasn't she?"

"She was lovely indeed, Dave. Very pretty, and a charming personality. But, honestly, I really don't fancy your chances."

Dave reared up playfully. "What? I say, my good fellow. I may be carrying some excess timber about the main deck, but what's not to love?"

"I was referring to the fact you said you'd borrowed your dear mummy's car and if you asked your mum really, really nicely that maybe she might possibly let you take it out for a date night," Monty said with a laugh.

"Is that how it sounded?" Dave asked, shoulders drooping. "Bollocks, now she's going to think I'm a complete plumb! I'm not very good at meeting women for the first time if I like them. And she is very pretty, isn't she? I have to admit, I... Hang on. Wait a tick, why are you doing that thing with your eyes, Monty? What's wrong with them? They're even more erratic than usual."

Monty continued to rotate his eyes, nodding towards the door. And then there came the sound of a throat being cleared, from that very direction.

"Sorry to, eh, interrupt again, guys... I just wanted to be clear. Which one of you was Dave, again, and which one Monty...?" Rebecca raised her finger like a wand as she said this, directing it one way, and then the other, like she were casting a spell.

Dave grinned like he'd got caught breaking wind, desperate to say something, anything, but his mind ran blank. "She'll be fine...?" he managed eventually.

"How's that?" asked Rebecca. "I don't under–"

"My mum," Dave explained. She always lets me borrow the car. Whenever I want. So it's... it's not a problem?" he told her pathetically.

The moment the barn door shut, Dave fell to his knees. "Bloody hell I'm going to be single forever," he groaned. *"Forever."*

"I can't argue with that," Monty replied, pulling a Toblerone from his pocket and tearing away at the wrapper. As he bit off a generous mouthful of the chocolate, he observed happily, "At least the gnome is intact. Thank goodness for that."

## Chapter
# ELEVEN

Susie peered over the rim of her coffee cup, making sure to maintain eye contact as she performed a magician's sleight of hand, hiding her packet of chocolate biscuits away. "Can I help, Stella?" she offered. "Do you need a hand?"

Stella shuffled through the door of the taxi office, with sweat running freely down her beetroot-coloured face and sporting impressive wet patches beneath under each arm. "Fucking hell. My legs are shaking like a shittin' dog," she announced, before making it over to her chair and collapsing. "That sadistic get at the gym had me on a bloody StairMaster machine for forty minutes. *Forty minutes*. That's not good when you're wearing a leather skirt. The *chafing*, is what I'm saying."

Susie laughed until she realised Stella wasn't. "Oh, you're being serious about the leather skirt at the gym?"

Stella's ability to make people feel they'd asked a very stupid question, with only the most minuscule of facial muscle movements, was truly remarkable. And neither did it let her down on this occasion. "Wearing a skirt at the gym..." Stella explained, as if to a small child... "Allows air to circulate in your nether regions, the important areas, and is like air conditioning for your—"

"Flowers!" exclaimed Susie, cutting Stella off in mid-sentence. "They arrived when you were out!"

"I saw them," Stella replied, inspecting the lovely bouquet of flowers on her desk without the slightest bit of interest. "You keep 'em," she told Susie. "Or you can chuck them in the bin for all I care," she said. She removed a packet of wet wipes from her desk, took out several, and massaged her thighs as she leaned back in her chair. Feeling this procedure required greater attention, she stood. "I'm going to sort out what the air conditioning missed," she said, taking tentative steps in the direction of the toilet.

"Lee also popped in, Stella. While you were out," Susie told her as Stella hobbled to the loo. "He wanted me to be sure I told you," she added.

"He did, did he? Very convenient, that, when he knows I'm at the gym and you're in here all on your own," Stella returned.

Once again, Susie was uncertain if this might be a comment she was meant to laugh at, and so she grinned noncommittally instead, with her mouth only, considering this action to be the safer option. But Stella never turned back, slamming the door to the bathroom behind her.

Susie grinned for a second or two longer, sufficient time to ensure Stella wouldn't be returning to deliver a punchline. She felt her face warm as she blushed, unsure if she'd upset her friend-come-boss, replaying the conversation they'd just had in her head, trying to work out where she might've made a wrong turn. But there was no malice implied in anything she had said, so she was none the wiser.

There was no smell of alcohol in the air, and it'd been weeks since Stella had sparked up a joint in work, so with no other clue, Susie propelled her chair, Flintstones-style, over to Stella's desk and the flowers. She listened towards the bathroom — something she instantly regretted — before reaching for the card. She held her hand over the message at first, feeling guilty for intruding on Stella's privacy. She didn't know what she was expecting to read, but once she pulled her hand away to reveal what was written there, it simply said:

*To the lady in my life.*
*Love, Lee.*

She put the card back, placing it as precisely as she could, before returning to her desk and busying herself with tasks that didn't need busying with. It wasn't long, however, before she decided another cup of coffee might be the tonic she needed right at that moment. She moved around the front of the shop counter, just as Stella appeared, clutching a handful of scrunched-up wet wipes. "If you're going in there..." said Stella, pointing to the toilet... "I suggest you should leave it five minutes. Ten to be safe."

"I was going to make us both something to drink," replied Susie. "Coffee, I mean," she added, seeing Stella perk up.

"You got it right the first time," Stella answered. "Put a finger of booze in mine."

This was yet another instance of Susie not knowing whether her officemate was serious or joking. Fortunately, Stella saved her the trouble of deciding.

"Nevermind, I've got a stash in my drawers," Stella told her. She must have noticed the look on Susie's face, because she quickly added, "My desk drawers, you silly thing."

At which point Stella returned to her desk, opening and closing several drawers before finally settling on the contents on one of them. She produced a bottle of Glenfiddich Ancient Reserve from its depths — procured during the trip to Glasgow at Stan and Frank's expense — held it up to inspect its label, examining it carefully, remarked, "Yes, this'll do nicely," and then proceeded to pour several jiggers into her awaiting mug. Once accomplished, she received her cup to the lips of her own awaiting mug, taking a deep, protracted draught, and then exhaled contentedly. "Better," she said. "Much better now."

Now that Stella was in a more relaxed state of mind, Susie sallied forth courageously, saying, "It's none of my business, Stella... and tell me to shut up if you want to... which I know you will, and have... but what's going on with you and Lee? He sent you the nice flowers, after all."

"Did he? How'd you know that?" asked Stella.

"I just, *ehm*, guessed it was him. I mean who else would it be? Right? Unless you've someone *else* in your life that's sending you flowers. But I don't think—"

Stella eyed her with suspicion, lighting a fag without breaking her stare. But then her expression softened again. "I'm sorry about that, Susie," she said. "About before, that is."

Susie smiled. "Oh, you don't need to be sorry, Stella. It's kind of you to say. Sure, it's not ideal. But, to be fair, there's no extractor fan in the toilet. But the smell doesn't last that long, honestly. Most of the customers don't even notice it anymore. I know *I* certainly don't," she went on, babbling nervously. "So it's not... I mean..."

"I meant about snapping at you earlier."

"Ah. Okay." Susie coughed. "Apology accepted, then."

Stella ran her fag-free hand through her tightly permed hair, interrupting the cigarette smoke halo circling around it like the clouds of Mt Fuji. Catching a glimpse of the sweat-infused t-shirt she was wearing in the process, she declared, "Would you look at the state of me. Honestly. Going to the gym. And what's the point of it? I'm perfect as I am, aren't I?"

"It's good for you, Stella," Susie offered deftly, rather than step onto a minefield.

Stella sucked on her fag like it was an asthma inhaler. "I know. Opens up the lungs," she said. She lowered her head, releasing a frustrated sigh. "He's a wanker, Susie," she offered up, in reference to Susie's question a few moments earlier.

"Come on, that's a bit harsh, isn't it?" Susie replied, with a curious flapping of her hand. She was either trying to wave away the notion of Lee being a wanker, or the smell emanating from the loo was still evident. Perhaps both at once.

Stella shrugged her exceedingly broad shoulders. "No. It's true. Listen. Every time I walk into a room he's on his laptop, slamming the lid down when he sees me. He must be... you know..." she said, shaking her fist like a craps player to illustrate. "As if I'm not enough for him! And that's not the worst of it. He's been going out without explanation, and when he is around he's constantly texting when he thinks I'm not looking."

"Oh," Susie replied.

"Something's going on," Stella said.

"Oh," Susie said again.

"Surely I'm all he needs?" Stella asked, waving her fag up and down her seated torso, as if the answer should be obvious. "Plus, I'm shit hot in bed, yeah?" she told Susie. "Let me tell you, I do things to him he didn't think were even possible. I could make a bloody Bangkok hooker blush. Strewth. But, I dunno, maybe he's just decided he doesn't want to be with a fuller-figured woman anymore...?"

"Is this why you joined the gym?" Susie asked.

But Stella only nodded in response, and with her face going through a series of strange contortions in apparent frustration, unaccustomed as it was to exhibiting proper displays of emotion and attempting in vain to work out the proper configuration.

Susie was in rather unchartered territory, and, like removing a thorn from a lion's paw, she approached Stella with caution, finally put a hand on her back, settling it down there as lightly as a butterfly. "But you can't improve upon perfection, can you," she told Stella gently.

"I don't know why I got involved with a man," Stella went on. "They cause you nothing but trouble. I think I was better off being single," she said. "Are you okay on your own?" she added.

"On my...?" Susie began, somewhat taken aback by the overly personal nature of Stella's enquiry, as well as Stella just assuming that she was single when in fact she was very happily married.

"Yeah. Those wet wipes don't seem to have hit the spot," Stella continued. "I'm feeling a bit clammy. Down below. If you know what I mean."

"Yes, I know what you—" Susie started to say, both relieved and alarmed.

"I should probably shower," Stella announced.

"Of course. You go. I've got things under control here," Susie assured her.

Stella packed up her kit bag, offering what looked like the faintest of smiles in Susie's direction as she made her way to the front door. "I'll leave this propped open, Susie, I think I was wrong," she said, looking over her shoulder.

"What's that?"

"That smell. It's got twenty minutes written all over it."

After Stella left, Susie was enjoying the influx of fresh air, and the noxious haze in the office seemed to clear just in time for the phone to ring. "Frank-and-Stan's Taxis!" Susie cheerily announced into the phone, but then her face abruptly adopted a more worried expression...

"No, Lee. She's just left." Susie paused for a moment, looking over to the flowers. "Yes," she replied to him. "They arrived about an hour ago. They're beautiful."

Susie listened for a few seconds more, before lowering her voice, taking a cautionary look around the waiting room. "Lee," she whispered into the handset. "Listen to me for a moment."

She took one final visual sweep before moving her head even closer to the receiver.

"Lee, Stella isn't stupid. She knows something's not right." Susie shot glances to the entrance door continuously as she spoke. "Lee, Stella knows there's something going on. She knows something's afoot," she said, her hands shaking. "Oh, god, Lee. And what the hell is she going to do when she knows that I'm involved...?"

## Chapter
# TWELVE

Panoramic countryside vistas were never too far from view in the Isle of Man. For a devoted city boy, the quieter life had taken some adjustment, but Stan was now a firm advocate. The location of the TT Farm provided a backdrop to rolling Manx hillside from virtually every window. Autumn was packing its bags for another year, allowing crisp winter mornings to make an appearance, and the canvas on display outside was evolving accordingly once again.

Stan pressed his thighs against the outdated radiator in their temporary office, nursing a cup of tea, as two plump robins fought over the fat ball of beef suet Stan had hung outside the window to attract their feathered friends. He ran his tongue across his teeth, removing the spoon from his cup, licking it clean, and fashioning it like a temporary mirror to examine his veneers. Satisfied they were in pristine condition, he angled it slightly, horrified at the sight of several errant, untidy hairs projecting down from his left nostril. He lowered his cup, searching through his desk drawer for a pair of tweezers in order to perform an unexpected mission of extirpation.

"Morning, Stanley!" boomed Dave, who was followed closely behind by Monty. "Are you admiring that view? There's a brass monkey in tears out there. Bloody cold, it is!"

Stan's nasal hairs were spared from their impromptu extraction, at least for the present time. "It's stunning, boys!" he answered

Dave. "Frigid. But stunning. I've actually been watching the birds for the last hour."

"I never fancied you as a birdwatcher, Stanley," said Dave merrily, now hammering in an elliptical-shaped wooden plaque up on the wall with little regard for Stan's shattered tranquillity.

"Oh, yes!" replied Stan, the joke going right over his head. Stan peered over Dave's shoulder, reading the sign which Dave was now busy straightening. *Race HQ – The TT Farm*, it read. "I like it, Dave," said Stan. "Nicely done!"

"It's good, isn't it?" Dave remarked, entirely pleased with himself. "Me and Monty spent most of yesterday carving the wording, but the chickens we added in for extra effect were a real nightmare, what with all that fine detail work, as if the lettering wasn't enough of a battle," he said. And, then, turning to his partner in crime, "Oi! Monty! Does this look like I've hung it straight to you?"

"You're asking me?" Monty had to remind him, pointing to his eyes and twirling his fingers around.

"Oh. Right," Dave said. "Stan? Whaddaya reckon?" he asked.

"Look's perfect," Stan told him. "Very professional."

"I should say so," Dave replied, with an absolute confidence rivalling that of Stella's. "I thought it was apt to call the TT Farm the race headquarters, yeah?" he said, admiring his handiwork. "Who'd have thought we'd be part of this," he went on, waving his hand extravagantly.

"This?" enquired Monty, turning around. He had busied himself with tea-making duty.

"All this," Dave said, with another grand sweep of his hand.

"Ah," Monty replied, returning to his task.

"Stan, it's like I'm a new man, I tell you," Dave told Stan. "I've struggled to sleep, but not in a bad way. It's because my mind is full of ideas for the farm! I can see it so clearly..." he went on passionately, looking off into the distance... "There will be people milling around, learning new skills, working in the great outdoors... It's going to be a real community. Oh, and two weeks to go to the big event, mind you. Monty's been keeping his eye on the long-range weather forecast every day."

"My good eye," confirmed Monty. "And it looks favourable. The racing will be fine in whatever weather, of course. I mean it'll go on as planned whatever the weather, I should say. But of course we're hoping for good weather all around, since it'd be a real shame if we have to move or cancel the Family Fun Day portion of the event."

"We've got loads of stalls lined up for the day," Dave agreed. "We just need the good weather for it."

"It should be fine," laughed Stan, although not unkindly. "The Isle of Man is known for its generous smattering of winter sun. We'll just need to remain optimistic and pray to the weather gods. Oh, that reminds me. Speaking of the race, I took a call, but it was relating to the Isle Le Mans."

"I came up with that name, remember. I thought of it first," Monty insisted.

"Fucksake, Monty, let it go, mate!" Dave told him.

"I'm just saying," Monty mumbled to himself.

"So do I need to phone someone back?" asked Dave of Stan.

Stan referred to his handwritten scrawl, but stared at it like it was penned in a foreign language. "I'm not sure I've taken it down correctly, actually. I couldn't really understand the fellow. As near as I could tell, I think his name was Gary Larkin? Does that make sense?"

Dave rubbed his chin, looking over to Monty's blank face. "I got nothin," Monty admitted.

"I'm afraid that's not one either of us know, Stan," said Dave.

Stan stroked his earlobe. "It's fine. I just couldn't understand him. He sounded a bit crazy, to be honest. He kept saying things like *'by 'eck'* and *'now, then,'* and he must have called me *'chief'* half a dozen times or so," he told them. "Oh, wait. There was something else," Stan went on. "He did reference his van, said something about it being very quick. In fact, he said it'd been around the..." Stan paused, looking at his notes again, tracing his finger along the lines... "See, this is where I'm confused. Because I couldn't make sense of what he was saying. Here," he said, tapping a spot on his notes. "Here it is. He told me his van had been around an ice-skating ring, yeah? But that doesn't make any sense, right? Because that's just nonsense."

"Wait, back up the bus, say that again?" said Dave.

"No, I hung up on him at that point, right?" said Stan. "Because I thought surely he was taking the piss. I imagine it must have been Frank, now I think on it. Disguising his voice? Taking the piss? It must've been Frank."

Dave stood over Stan, looking over his shoulder, trying to decipher his hieroglyphics. "The bit about the ice-skating ring," Dave advanced. "Stan, could that have been Nürburgring? And, could Gary Larkin, perhaps, have been our Guy Martin?"

Stan paused in thought. He brought his fingers up to his nose, and he began pinching absently at the long nose hairs he'd been addressing earlier, trying to spark something in his memory. "I suppose it could have been?" he said, finally. "If it was, could you tell him not to speak so quickly? It's difficult to—"

"Bloody hell, Stan, you've hung up on Guy Martin!" Dave shouted at him. "And that van he was talking about was the one he had on TV trying to break a record at the Nürburgring, and you thought it was some sort bloody ice-skating park!"

"It wasn't my fault?" was the only thing Stan could think to say.

"I'll have to manage Guy's expectations about the maximum amount of modifications permitted as sadly that van is a little over prepared for this." Dave muttered to himself, reaching for his phone. "Bloody Gary Larkin," he said, laughing lest he should cry. "Ay? What's this?" he said, his phone vibrating in his hand. "Oh. It's a number I don't know. Maybe this is *Gary Larkin* getting hold of me," Dave speculated, casting an evil eye over to Stan. "Hallo?" he said, engaging the call. "This is Dave speaking..."

Dave paced around the office like a caged animal, eventually coming to a stop before the vista window, and stood there, looking out. His body was not at all relaxed.

"Yes, hello. I *thought* I didn't recognise this number." Dave listened intently for a minute or so, as Stan and Monty watched on expectantly. "I'm sorry but we cannot accept your entry, I think this was made quite clear previously," Dave said once resumed speaking. His teeth were clenched together, and he was trying his damnedest to keep his cool. "Yes, I *know* you've got the van ready and all, but, as I said, it's just not possible."

The volume on the other end of the phone increased several decibels, causing Dave to pull his hand away by half an arm's length. His cheeks fluttered and flapped in agitation, with his body mass appearing to inflate and increase as a result, until the phone in his hand looked like a child's toy. "Listen, dipshit!" he said, phone now back to his ear and all semblance of civility cast aside. "I know you've probably surrounded yourself by a bunch of gormless, gutless wonders, but your intimidation tactics won't work with me! *No* means *no! Get* it? Now sod off!"

Dave ended the call, and took several deep breaths to steady himself. For a moment, it looked as if his fist might become part of the plasterboard.

Monty bit his bottom lip. "I'm a bit confused, Dave. I thought we *needed* Guy Martin? I know you said his van was a bit ambitious, But still. We could have talked him around, surely?"

"That wasn't Guy Martin. Believe me, I'm not that bloody stupid, mate," Dave answered him, still angling around, looking for something to punch. "It was that fucking idiot, Rodney Franks, asking for a late entry. But he's already *been told.*"

Stan nodded in approval. "He's a bit keen, is he not? What's that all about? It's going to be a great day, sure, but he seems unusually needy. Is it because he doesn't like to be told no?"

"Probably. He's got a new race team for next year's TT, and wanted to use this as a launch pad in view of the audience and participants, I expect," Dave speculated. "At least we know if Rodney wants in, then that indicates our race must be considered a prestigious event to be involved in. He probably knows that Henk is as well, which only means he's champing at the bit that much more. He must be going mad." Dave laughed. "He said to me, this tosser, that he'd give me one more chance to change my mind. Otherwise *what happened next would be down to me.* Fucking seriously? Who even speaks like that?? He's like a really bad villain from a *Scooby Doo* episode."

"Scoob and the gang," said Monty, for no apparent reason.

"Ah. Anyway," Dave went on. "I'm not letting that idiot upset me. I'm in too much of a good mood at the moment. I'll just ring Guy back and sort that business out," he said, brightening up, since after Rodney Franks it was impossible to be cross at Stan any longer.

"It's good to see you so enthusiastic, Dave," said Stan, happy to no longer be the subject of Dave's ire. "You too, Monty. And Dave, don't take this the wrong way, and I'm certainly not saying you were particularly scruffy before... but you look like you've made a bit of an effort...? Is that a new shirt you're wearing? And... you smell pretty good, as well?"

"He's in heat for the TT Farm's newest resident," explained Monty. "He *likes* her."

"I bloody *don't*," Dave protested, stomping his foot like a child. Well, like an especially large child.

"So the new alpaca that arrived yesterday?" Monty teased him. "That's what this about, Dave? I really don't—"

"*Not* the alpaca!" said Dave, along with another foot stomp.

"Not that there's anything wrong with alpacas," Monty assured his friend. "If that's what you really—"

"That'll explain the cologne, then, will it?" asked Stan, playing along.

"Nar, that's just horse manure," Monty offered, getting a laugh from Stan in return.

Dave, however, was not laughing. "ANYWAY," he said, shooting Monty a *you're-getting-it-later* stare. "Look at this, Stanley," he said, changing the subject, and holding his phone in front of Stan's face.

"What am I looking at here?" enquired a clueless Stan.

"I'll explain," Dave said, explaining. "I didn't think Henk could be any more of a legend, right? But when the entry fees for Isle Le Mans went on sale, Henk paid twenty-thousand for two places— one for his team, and one for us to auction off. Not only is Henk letting the TT Farm keep the money from that auction, he's also throwing the van in for the auctioned slot's team to race."

Dave moved over to the computer, conscious that Stan didn't have his glasses, and loaded up the page he was referring to for Stan to examine.

Dave had initially considered giving the auctioned entry to the highest bidder, but he knew that some idiot with too much cash — like Rodney Franks — would enter a team. Dave was a privateer racer at heart, self-funded, with motor oil flowing through his veins. Sure, he'd experienced the factory racing life, taking a TT victory in the process, but, for him, that wasn't a sustainable career path. The success of blue-ribband racing events, like the TT, was a healthy mix of privateers and those in the factory camp, Dave felt. In fact the majority of those with factory support were often those that'd once been privateers, and who'd never forgotten their roots, and were the first to lend out a spanner or to provide advice on suspension set-up to a beginner.

There is always the exception to the rule, however — the factory outfits who contribute nothing to the racing community, purely in it for what they can take out. Fortunately, this was exceptionally rare. Rodney Franks, on the other hand, epitomised all that was wrong with those with too much money. He, along with those misguided enough to closely associate with him, developed a pompous sense of entitlement. And this was the reason Dave didn't want to just take the cash from whatever highest bidder offered it for the auctioned slot, even when the future of the farm and their careers could have made that decision sufficiently more palatable.

"And I've purchased a trophy, by the way," announced Dave. "A nice one. As well as the entry, we're going to award this beauty to Privateer of the Year. I reckon it doesn't necessarily need to be a racer, either, necessarily. It could also be, instead, someone linked to the racing, like a marshal or charity fundraiser. Anyway, Stan," said Dave, pointing to the computer screen. "This is the charity fundraising page we set up for our event, and what we did here was let the public decide who their winner was going to be. For the auctioned place, I mean. Not the race itself, obviously."

Stan smiled. "I like it."

"So," continued Dave. "The public donate ten pounds, and for every donation they get a vote to nominate the winner of their choice. Of course we'll need to keep an eye on things in case that bellend Rodney tried to pull a Donald Trump and buy his way in."

Stan moved his face closer to the computer screen, squinting. "I see the names of Dave and Monty nominated. If I'm not mistaken?"

"What can I say about that? Except that the public has exceptional taste," suggested Dave, before pointing down to the total. "That's the amount we've raised, Stan. And the winner, with the most votes, as it turned out — and despite me and Monty's nominations! — is a chap by the name of George Spence."

"Dave, am I reading that correctly?" asked Stan. "Thirty-four thousand pounds? That can't be right? That would mean there's, let's see... divide by... carry the..."

"A lot of votes," confirmed Dave.

"A lot of votes," confirmed Monty, not wishing to be left out.

"A lot of votes," Stan confirmed.

"It sure is, Stanley," Dave told him. "And all going to the charity, me old son."

Monty pulled out a printout, unfolding it and snapping it open. "George Spence is a class act and one of the nicest guys in the paddock. You only have to read some of the comments that people have left about him to see as much. Here. Take a gander," he said, happy to contribute, and printout prepared in advance per Dave's instructions for Stan's consideration.

Stan took the piece of paper handed to him, running his finger down the page. "The Scotsman with the most TT finishes and one of the highest overall," he mumbled.

Stan's smile broadened as he continued to read the comments that'd been left:

> Dod, as he's known to most, epitomises the spirit of the TT.
>
> First came to the TT in 1978 and after twenty years got his licence so he could say he'd done the TT once. He didn't stop at one!
>
> Former steel erecter that used his skills to put up a shelter at his local track.
>
> The first guy in the paddock to offer to loan you something from his toolbox.

FRANK & STAN'S BUCKET LIST #3: ISLE 'LE MANS' TT

Has ridden everything around the TT course – would ride a donkey around the mountain circuit if it was race-ready!

"Wow, this guy sounds like a complete legend. I've got to say, he does appear to be a worthy winner indeed," observed Stan, his eyes continuing down the page. "Here, I like this paragraph, especially, from *TT Supporters Club Magazine*." He read it aloud to the others:

George 'Dod' Spence epitomises the spirit of the TT, an event which cannot do without the true privateer who battles often on a shoestring budget relying on dedicated friends to achieve his goal whether it be an improved lap speed, a replica, or just the satisfaction of completing the race distance. Dod is not a front-runner, but has stood on a TT rostrum and is the leading rider from Scotland in terms of finishes... We must not forget the role played by Dod and his like in the annuls of TT history.

Stan placed the paper back on the desk. "I think I *like* this fellow," he announced.

"It's the tattoos, isn't it?" Dave joked.

"No I'm serious. I don't know why, but that's made me a little emotional, reading that," Stan told him, dabbing at his eyes theatrically. "I know from being around the two of you what the TT and racing means in general, but this just brings it all home that much more, you know what I mean? To see so many people talking about the positive influence someone has on a sport, and their lives, is, well... it kind of gets you right *here*," he said, making a show of wiping his eyes again, but only to hide that fact that he seriously *did* need to wipe his eyes. "I've got to say, guys, this is a wonderful idea, and an exceptionally worthy winner. Great, initiative boys. Truly, great initiative. Blimey, this whole thing..." he began, fanning his face... "Has got me right in the..."

"Cockles? Of your heart?" suggested Dave gamely.

"Right in the cockles," Stan happily agreed.

"We should name the trophy after him," considered Monty, an idea forming in his brain. "I know we're going to give him an award for being privateer of the year. But I'm thinking that if this turns into an annual event, we could name the race-winning award after him as well?"

"Oh, Monty. I like that, me old son," Dave answered him, pursing his lips in approval. "That's a wonderful idea."

"Is it as good as the Le Mans name? My other great idea?" asked Monty, still sore about the misappropriation of his brilliantly original idea that was pulled right out from under his feet, and he cast one eye on Dave as he said this. Though, to be fair, one eye is all he could only ever manage.

"LET IT GO, MONTY," Stan and Dave said in unison. Monty just shrugged in response.

"You know, I can see our little event turning into an annual spectacle on the Isle of Man," Dave mused grandly. "It'll be a globally recognised event, with everyone battling it out for the prestigious trophy!"

Monty pursed his lips in contemplation as well. "I'm right there with you on this. I can just see the garlanding ceremony, where the winner reaches out, dripping in sweat and champagne, reaching for the... *George 'Dod' Spence Isle 'Le Mans' TT Trophy.*"

Before the others could say anything else, Monty added, hammering the point home, "FUCK ME THAT'S GOT A NICE RING TO IT, DOESN'T IT, LADS."

## Chapter
# THIRTEEN

"It's not a date, so just be yourself," repeated Dave, over and over to himself aloud. The traffic lights in Marown turned red, permitting further time for his self-directed pep talk. It hadn't been that long ago that he'd been hurtling through these very same traffic lights at one-hundred-forty miles per hour, on his way to his maiden TT victory. The pace today, however, was mildly sluggish in comparison.

"Just be normal Dave Quirk, and if it's a joke you'd think funny, or Monty, just remember that not everyone shares your sense of humour," he reminded himself, pointing at his reflection in the rear-view mirror. He shook his head several times in quick succession, executing a sort of *get-yourself-together-mate* routine, sending his jowls jiggling around like a slobbering bloodhound, until the car behind offered a polite toot on the horn as the lights turned green once more. Dave offered a friendly wave, all the while gibbering away to himself, and with his hulk-like frame against the backdrop of a pink Nissan Micra, his silhouette must have been quite a vision to the waiting driver behind.

The TT farm developed a little further each time Dave appeared for work; it never failed to bring a smile to his face as he turned left from the main road, up the drive, and into the cobbled courtyard. Frank and Stan had taken a calculated gamble by continuing with the buildingworks, but with the money from the race, Family Fun Day, sponsorship, and other endeavours, confidence was high that they'd meet their financial deadline. Indeed, press interest had soared through the roof, expanding as far as France and Germany. Tickets to spectate the planned race had been sluggish initially, but Guy Martin's efforts, legend that he was, had produced tremendous results, with a simple tweet or message on his social media platforms resulting in massive surges in ticket sales. The Isle of Man's ferry company had been inundated with bookings for the relevant days, and there was talk of needing to operate additional crossings to meet the demand. It was fairly evident that their idea had the makings of something special and, crucially, in addition to that, commercially viable.

Today, however, was not a workday for Dave.

Rebecca stood with her back to the barn door, dressed like she was ready for a polar expedition. She had more layers than an onion, and at first glance Dave didn't see Tyler huddled into her, wearing a red bobble hat and scarf that matched his mum's. Rebecca took Tyler's hand as Dave pulled up. "Nice car," she said.

"Thanks, Becks. Yeah, it's me mum's," Dave told her.

"That'll explain the pink," she replied, with a wink and a glorious smirk that lit up a rather overcast morning.

Dave, ever the gentleman — at least on this occasion — darted from the car to render assistance in opening the passenger door. "Oh and I've got something for you, little man," he said to Tyler, in tow.

Tyler peered inside the plastic bag and pulled out a black t-shirt, with the sort of less-than-unenthusiastic expression children were not yet adept at hiding. His eyes, however, widened once was revealed, emblazoned on the front of the shirt, the image of a sidecar bursting through the trees along with a trail of confused lights enhancing the impression of warp speed.

Dave knelt down on one knee. "Who do you think that sidecar belongs to?" he asked of the boy.

Tyler shrugged his shoulders. "I dunno. Lewis Hamilton?"

"Not quite, but I'm sure he'd be pretty quick if he raced at the TT. But, that," Dave explained, pointing at the image. "Is me when I won the TT last year."

"Wow. You have your very own t-shirt with your picture on it?" Tyler asked, duly impressed now. "Are you famous, Big Dave?"

Dave glanced at Rebecca. "Well... I don't really like to talk about it, Tyler," he said, trying to appear modest.

"But you're talking about it now," Tyler answered, with a child's inherently unfiltered bluntness.

"I suppose I am," Dave answered, giving a jolly laugh.

"Can I wear it now, Mum? Please?"

"Later," Rebecca replied. "It's taken me ten minutes or more to get you wrapped up in your current state and I'm not undoing it all now. So what do you say, Tyler?"

"What do I say to what?" Tyler asked, only half paying attention, engrossed in the t-shirt as he was. "Oh. Thank you," he offered, after a gentle nudge from Mum.

Dave clapped his broad hands. "Right, you two," he announced. "As you're new adventurers to this lovely Island, I thought we'd start our journey by heading to Peel, where hopefully the ice cream shop hasn't closed up for the winter. Then, I thought I'd take you up the west of the Island, and then on to Jurby where I'll show you the track where the racing is going to be. The sidecar is up there now. You can have a go, Tyler, if you'd like? In the passenger seat?"

It was as if Dave had offered Tyler a free pass to a fireworks factory which had been dipped in chocolate equipped with a vending machine dispatching free toys. But Rebecca was somewhat more reticent at the prospect, her protective maternal instincts automatically kicking in. "I don't know about that, Dave," she told him. "Are you sure it's safe...?"

"It's fine. I won't go fast, I promise," he assured her. "How about you jump on, too? I'll take you *both* on a very gentle spin round the pit area?"

"Can we?!–Can we?!–Can we?!" yelled Tyler, jumping on the spot like he was on a pogo stick.

"We'll see," Rebecca replied, throwing a glance at Dave of the sort only a mother was qualified or capable of delivering.

Once they were on their way, at Tyler's request, Dave delivered a corner-by-corner recital of the final lap of his victorious TT as he hit each spot along their drive. Tyler hung on Dave's every word, and fully believed competitors fired mushrooms and other objects at each other like those in Mario Kart — an embellishment Dave had thrown in to ensure his young friend's attention didn't wane, though he needn't have worried in that regard. For her part, Rebecca, as someone with zero previous interest in motorsport, also found herself getting carried away in the commentary, and was in fact rather disappointed when they broke away from the dedicated TT course at Ballacraine, instead heading straight on towards the idyllic seaside town of Peel.

"It really is quite a dramatic rags-to-riches story, Dave. Who would have thought that someone like... I mean, *em*..."

"You mean a big lump like me?" laughed Dave. "How could a big lump like me end up as a race winner?"

Rebecca blushed. "No, not at all. I was going to say... for someone driving a pink car like this."

A brief silence ensued as Rebecca, who clearly didn't yet realise that it was impossible to offend Dave, thought for certain she'd stepped her foot right in it. She was about to attempt another apology, but it was Tyler who broke the silence.

"Look what I found, Mummy," he chirped, leaning forward from the back seat and dangling what very much appeared to be a woman's undergarment. "It's just like yours, Mummy!" Tyler added, giggling, because undergarments were indeed a source of endless amusement, especially for a small child.

"What's he found?" Dave asked, keeping his focus on the road.

Rebecca's blushes returned once more, back in full force this time. "It's a bra, Dave. A black one."

Dave went quiet for a moment, terrified by the discovery and what Becks must think of him as a result. and searching desperately for an explanation. Any kind of explanation at all.

"Ah," Dave said, finally. "It's not... please don't think... Only it's my mum's car, yeah? So it must be hers." And this was a point he was at great pains to stress, and something at which point they all had a jolly good laugh at... That is, until he considered how his mum's bra could possibly have ended up in the backseat of her car. Maybe it had spilt over from a load of laundry? But that didn't explain why she'd be carting around a load of laundry in the backseat of her car. And then, of course, the solution hit him…

"Bloody Frank," he muttered to himself.

All thoughts of women's underwear and what Frank might or might not have done with them were soon forgotten, however, as they reached their destination. "This is Fenella Beach," proclaimed Dave, pulling the little pink bullet into a space with a perfect view of Peel Castle opposite. "That there is where the Vikings lived," announced Dave, summarising a thousand years of history for Tyler, who was clawing to get out of the car. For folks who'd spent most of their time in a cramped city, the vast, open spaces in the Isle of Man must have seemed a treat, thought Dave. Throw in an ancient castle, a picture-postcard beach, and a shop that sold ice cream, and Peel really was a child's dream come true, not to mention an adult's as well.

"How the heck?" asked Rebecca in reference to Tyler's present attire. "How did you manage to get your new t-shirt on without me even noticing? Let me bundle you up again once we get out of the car again, okay?" she cautioned.

Dave briefly shuddered at the recurring thought entering his brain once again. "The backseat of my mother's car is quite the changing room, it would appear," he said. "Don't ask," he added in response to Rebecca's enquiring glance. "Come on, you two," he said, steering the subject hurriedly in another direction. "Let's get this party started!"

"Ice cream time?" asked Tyler, tongue hanging out like that of a panting dog.

Dave pointed to the steep hill leading out of the carpark. "That, my young friend, is affectionately known as Ice Cream Hill. Not only does it provide the most spectacular views of the castle and Peel, but it is written in Manx law that you have to climb it, enjoy the bracing sea air, and enjoy every step of the way. Then, and only then, are you allowed the reward of an ice cream. In fact, I have to take a photo of you stood at the top, otherwise the person in the shop isn't allowed to serve you an ice cream at all."

Tyler looked at his mum for verification of this dubious claim, but she was perfectly straight-faced, indicating that Dave wasn't having him on after all. "And what if you don't show them a picture?" Tyler asked, looking up to the summit in worry.

"Ah. Well. You mean aside from just not getting an ice cream?" replied Dave, stalling his response for thinking time. "Right. See that?" he continued, explanation devised. He stifled a grin as he pointed across the water. "That is Peel Castle."

"Where the Vikings live?" Tyler answered, remembering what Dave had said earlier.

"Yes. Only they don't live there anymore. That was a long time ago. Now, the castle is where they throw people in the dungeon. People who've attempted buying an ice cream without having their picture first taken," Dave explained solemnly.

Tyler's suspicion rose, this all becoming a bit much, even for a small child, to swallow. Still, it didn't stop him looking over to the magnificent castle perched atop St. Patrick's Isle. But then he began to laugh. "Well what if you'd didn't have a camera? What then?" he asked, too clever for Dave's machinations.

"Simples. You have to draw a picture in that case," Dave replied instantly. "You see, camera phones have only been around for ten years or something, only a few years before you were born, and that castle has been stood for a thousand years. So, before cameras and the like, you had to draw a picture. And if it wasn't a good one, mind, then not only didn't you get anything in the shop but at the discretion of the shop manager you might still end up in the castle's dungeon as a lesson to others," Dave warned him, and, story-spinning business finally complete, said, "Now, come on, let's get going!"

"Don't forget your camera!" shouted Tyler, who was suddenly halfway up the steps at the foot of the steep hill, waving the others along, urging them to follow in his wake.

Never in the long and distinguished history of the Isle of Man had a child climbed that hill as quickly as Young Master Tyler managed to achieve. It was unlikely that retreating forces with

Viking steel threatening an internal inspection would have been able to match the impressive pace.

"Take a photo, take a photo!" he commanded from the top of the hill, triumphantly.

Dave straggled behind, trying valiantly not to expose the fact he was blowing smoke out his arse. And also because he was having a difficult time of it travelling up the hill himself. The first initial steps were easy, but then...

"I need oxygen..." Dave declared weakly, audible only to those in close proximity. Of which there was only one...

Rebecca put her hand under his arm, giving him a push up the final hurdle. She'd deliberately kept her attention on the path ahead so as to achieve the maximum impact when she turned to face the view that Dave had promised. She wasn't disappointed. She put a hand to her mouth, pulling Tyler in front of her. A brisk, salty wind whipped in from the Irish Sea, accosting their cheeks. Rebecca's eyes fell on the castle, with the backdrop of the west coast of the Island stretching into the horizon. Her attention drifted over to the beach, where a hardy dog walker battled against the stiff breeze, before scanning over to the sight of the vibrant town centre, with expansive, rolling countryside providing the frame to this captivating scene.

"Oh my," she said, wiping a wind-induced tear from her eye. "Dave, you weren't joking," she offered, taking a lungful of the crisp air. "That is one of the most wonderful things I've ever seen. I could stay here forever."

"So could I," replied Dave softly, though for a different reason, but his response was carried away on the breeze. He smiled as Tyler pointed out the cathedral, until his brief reverie came to an abrupt end as thoughts of ice cream returned to the forefront of the boy's mind, marked by a series of hopping motions. "Will you take our picture now, Big Dave? *Pleeease?*" Tyler pleaded. "So we don't end up in the castle *jaaail?*"

"I think he's deserved it," Dave put forth. "Mum? What do you reckon?"

Rebecca laughed. She handed a tissue to Dave to wipe the perspiration from his forehead from his trek up the hill, though the wind from the sea had done much of the job already. "I think you've both deserved it," she said. "And if the ice cream is half as good as the view, I'm sure it'll be the best we've ever had."

In short order, the frozen treat, procured without incident and no jail time, was soon a dairy-based crust on Tyler's wee chin, and the pink bullet that was Dave's mum's little Nissan headed at a gentle pace towards Jurby, in the north of the Island. "He must be dreaming about motorbikes," remarked Dave, in reference to the young one occupying the back.

Rebecca looked into the rear seat. "Oh, you mean the snoring?" she said. "I suppose it does sound like an engine. It's funny. At that age, snoring is cute, isn't it? Is that what you sound like, Dave? When you're asleep?"

"Dunno," Dave answered. "I'm usually asleep when I'm asleep, so I couldn't say. Fair play to the young chap, though. He dispatched that ice cream quicker than a seagull eating chips, as we like to say here on the Isle."

"Yes, it's quite remarkable, isn't it, that children cannot manage to eat even a meagre portion when it's tea time, especially if vegetables are involved," Rebecca observed. "But they can polish off a double chocolate ice cream scoop with an extra Cadbury's Flake thrown in without even blinking an eye."

Dave didn't answer, as he was currently trying to work out if this were all real or simply a dream, and his eyes alternated intermittently between the road and the contented, sleeping child in his rear-view mirror.

"I'm not boring you already, am I, Dave?" came Rebecca's voice, assuring him that this was, in fact, real.

"Oh, bollocks," Dave said. But it wasn't in response to Becka's question. Rather, it was in reference to the wail of a siren behind them, along with accompanying flashing blue lights.

"I wasn't speeding, was I?" asked Dave, pulling over.

"No more than you were speeding up Ice Cream Hill," laughed Rebecca.

Dave's eye went wide. But it wasn't in response to the police officer he saw advancing in his side-view mirror. Rather, it was in admiration of Becka's deft comedic jab. "The cheek of you!" he said, laughing along with her.

Dave wound down the door window, the sound of their laughter spilling out. The officer was not amused.

"You think this is some sort of joke, do you?" the stone-faced officer asked. "I can assure you that it is not," she said severely.

Before Dave even had chance to respond, the police officer began walking in a very deliberate manner around the perimeter of the vehicle, paying particular attention to the tyres and lights. She had her hat tucked under her arm as she performed this inspection, and she stopped now and again only to shoot icy glares in Dave's direction. With her lean face, long neck, and slim but sturdy figure, she reminded Dave of a whippet or a greyhound. This was clearly a woman who enjoyed the responsibility bestowed on her, and Dave imagined her tenacious and fleet of foot on the occasion someone might be foolish to attempt to run from her.

When she eventually appeared back at Dave's window, she rested her hat on the roof of the car, staring towards the distant treeline as she spoke. "You're not so quick today, are you, sir?" she said, directed to the horizon.

Dave looked over to Becka, palms up, and with a shrug of the shoulders. "I'm sorry, officer? I don't understand," he said to the police officer's torso.

"You thought you were quite the TT racer at or about ten p.m. yesterday evening, didn't you, sir," she replied, still watching something in the distance, as a statement rather than a question. And despite her addressing him as "sir," there was no respect implied in her voice. In fact, when she said *sir*, she spat it out almost like a curse.

Dave took the comment as an odd sort of compliment, given his history. Perhaps she recognised him? He wanted to respect the officer's authority, so he gave only a tentative response. "Thank you..." he said... "One does try?"

The officer shifted her attention from whatever elusive prey she'd been staring at off in the distance, bending down now and leaning in close to Dave's face. Her long, narrow face and far-set eyes made Dave uncomfortable. "Levity will get you nowhere with me, I can assure you, sir," she told him in no uncertain terms.

Dave wondered how someone who did so much assuring could be so utterly unreassuring. He also wondered, with not an ounce of fat on her, how she could possibly stand the cold. Because she was not shivering at all. Not at all. She gave the impression of being in entirely too much control to allow her body to shiver.

"I've got a good one for you. Since you're a comedian," she told him. She was not smiling as she said this. "Yes, it's very funny, and you may well enjoy it." She still was not smiling. "How does three penalty points on your licence for speeding away from me last night sound to you? Does that make you laugh, funnyman?" Now she was smiling. But the smile quickly turned to a scowl. "Your sort makes me sick to my stomach," she said, looking around the interior of the car. "And with a *child* on board as well. Shame on you," she said severely. "*Shame* on you. You're out scouring for your next depravity-ruining location, I expect? Well, this evening won't be going to plan quite as you expected, sir. I can assure you of that."

Dave motioned to speak but the words wouldn't come, as he was at something of a loss. The officer spoke again instead.

"Nothing to say, funnyman? Bit slow off the mark, are we? Though you weren't slow of the mark when you sped away from me, tyres squealing, last night at or about ten p.m., were you? No you were not. But no one evades me for long," she said. "Not anymore. Not again. Not ever again."

There was obviously some kind of backstory to this policewoman that Dave was not privy to, not to mention the fact she must certainly be confusing him for someone else and in regard to some other incident which he was most definitely not involved in. "Ma'am?" he said. "I mean... officer?" he corrected himself, unsure how to best address the woman, and uncertain also as to what on earth she was on about. "I was in the pub last night. At that time. At or about that time, that is. I think you've got the wrong fellow," he told her. He wanted to add, *I can assure you*, but thought better of it.

"Drinking? So there's that as well, is there? The list of charges is growing by the minute, I can *assure* you," she told him, not-at-all-reassuringly.

Dave tapped his fingers successively on the steering wheel, drumming out with them his displeasure. This was becoming absurd. So absurd, in fact, that...

"Has Monty put you up to this?" he asked with half a laugh.

"And who, or what, precisely, would this Monty person or thing be?" came the curt response, with the officer looking up from her notepad. It wasn't so much that she was interested in learning about whatever excuse she thought he could be coming up with. It was more that she was gauging whether or not she might possibly be able to add on another citation with any new information he was about to present, and she had her writing implement poised at the ready.

"Monty is... Look, that doesn't matter," Dave said, realising now that Monty was not involved in any shenanigans, though Dave wished desperately that this had been the case. "I wasn't drink driving, officer," Dave protested. "I wasn't even driving last night at all," he said. "I can *assure* you," he added, unable to help himself. "Can you please explain to me what I'm supposed to have done?"

The officer closed her notepad temporarily, in preparation for the dressing-down she was about to administer. "I *think*," she said, once ready. "I *think* I shall refer to it as *outraging public decency*. Though *you* people..." she said, looking down the length of her long nose... "*You* people may refer to it as *dogging*, if I'm not mistaken." She looked especially disgusted as she said this. "On Marine Drive, at approximately ten p.m. yesterday evening. And I can *assure* you, I do not get paid *nearly* enough to compensate me for having to see your naked arse cheeks pressed up against the window. And *you*, madam," she added. "Do you have no shame?"

"THAT'S ENOUGH," said Dave. "You leave her *out* of this. She was not involved *at all*, I CAN ASSURE YOU." He glared daggers at the officer. If the mix-up had been amusing at the start, it was humorous no longer. The officer could accuse him of anything she liked. Hell, at some point in his life, Dave knew, he'd probably done it. But impugning the honour of Rebecca was another matter entirely and this he could not tolerate.

The officer unsheathed her radio, ready to call in for back-up.

"Dave, it's okay," Rebecca told him, trying to calm him down. And then, turning to the officer, she offered, "Look, officer, I think this might be a simple case of mistaken identity?"

"Pink Nissan Micra. No. No, miss. I am not mistaken."

"Oh god," Dave muttered, the colour draining from his face. "Oh my god. I think I know what's—"

"This will explain your mum's underwear," Rebecca confirmed, seeing where Dave was headed and reading his thoughts.

"Officer," pleaded Dave in a much more conciliatory tone now. "I think you've got us mixed up with someone else, as my friend has said."

"Do you think, *sir*, that I am foolish enough to get a *bright pink Nissan Micra* confused? *No*, I am *not*. I can *assure*—"

"No, listen, officer. Please," Dave entreated. "What I meant to say is that the current versus former occupants of this car is where, I think, the confusion has arisen."

"I'm listening," said the officer, placing her radio back in its holster.

"Thank you," said Dave. "Listen, we weren't in the car last night. It's my mum's car. And... sorry, it makes me throw up a little in my mouth just to have to even *think* about it... but I'm certain it must have been her engaged in, *em*, outrageous public indecency, I think you said?"

"Close enough," said the officer.

"It was my mum," Dave continued. "It was my mum who was out last night carrying on in an, *em*, immodest fashion, to put it politely. God help me, that's a sentence I never thought I'd have to say out loud in front of a police officer, much less a woman I only just met a few days before."

"The only way to sort this out is to show me your arse," replied the officer. She was not smiling, nor did she appear to be joking.

Dave narrowed his eyes. "No offence, officer. But I don't believe that's proper police protocol...?"

The officer took a step back, framing her fingers like a film producer's viewfinder. "I'd recognise that arse again. It's the only way to clear you of wrongdoing. The image. It's burned onto my retinas. So you'll need to prop your cheeks up against the driver's window so I can see the— No, no, don't take your trousers down, man! There are children about! Merely place your buttocks against the window so I can scrutinise the dimensions."

Dave did as he was instructed. Or at least he tried to. Alas, it was like playing a game of Twister after one too many moves had already been made. He gave it a go, valiantly, raising himself up off the seat and attempting to swivel about in order to place his bum up against where the window would have been were it rolled up. But there was his oversized frame to contend with, particularly as compared to the relatively undersized dimensions of the vehicle, not to mention the very limited range of his joints. In short, there was simply no way for him to move his body into the position he was being ordered to move it into. Try as he might, it was impossible.

"Stand down, soldier!" said the officer, having seen quite enough to satisfy her. "For the love of all that's holy, stand down, son. It's clear you've got the flexibility of bog-wood."

"So we can go?" Dave asked, relieved, and blessedly reconfiguring his body into a much less pain-inducing form.

"On your way," the officer instructed. "You just tell your mum I'll be keeping an eye out for her. And If I see this car, and its occupants, engaged in any further *shenanigans*, I will have it towed away with your mum and her... *gentleman* friend, still inside." Of course, the way she said "gentleman" did not in fact imply that she in any way meant *gentleman*.

After the officer had gotten back in her vehicle and pulled away, Dave remained where he was, both hands clenching the steering wheel tightly.

"Dave?" Rebecca asked, concerned. "Are you okay?"

"FRANK," was all he said, through gritted teeth.

"The cheek of him," Becks remarked.

"What did you say?" asked Dave, turning to her, his grip on the steering wheel softening.

"I said the *cheek* of him," Rebecca repeated.

Dave stared at her for a moment, and then they both burst out laughing.

When they were once again on the road, a small head popped up from the backseat. "Mummy?" asked Tyler, rubbing his eyes. "Was Big Dave waving his bum at the police person?"

"Yes, honey," his mother told the sleepy boy. "Yes he was."

Which only generated more laughter inside the car.

Jurby raceway had been transformed. It was a stalwart of the Isle of Man racing scene, but it'd now been elevated to another level. It was still a little over a week to the main event, but the marketing departments of the entrants, it would appear, had been out in force. Every spare inch of available trackside space had been taken up with advertising hoardings. As Dave pulled up into the carpark, one ambitious advertiser, in fact, was in the process of erecting an inflatable bridge across the track itself. "Bloody hell," remarked Dave, climbing out of the car. "I mean bleedin' heck," he said, remembering the company he was in. "Would you look at this," he said. But Rebecca, and Tyler in particular, needed no encouragement in this regard as they soaked up the spectacle with their eyes.

Pit lane, ordinarily a strip of unassuming tarmac, was now a series of pristine, temporary garages adorned with the logos of the sponsoring companies. The transformation was remarkable. The track used for club racing now resembled a miniature Silverstone racetrack.

"I need to take a picture of this to show Monty, he won't believe this," Dave said in wonder, more to himself than the others.

"He's over there," said Rebecca, pointing to the first garage.

Monty waved furiously, pointing to their garage. "Oi! We got number one!" he shouted. "Come and have a look! This is choice!" he called out, not the least bit interested in hiding his excitement. "Heya, Tyler. What do you think of our van?" he asked, once Dave &

crew had joined him. In response, Tyler unzipped his coat for a moment to show off the brand-new t-shirt he was sporting for the occasion. "Noice!" Monty told him, giving the wee lad an enthusiastic thumbs-up.

Tyler marvelled at the metallic grey Volkswagen Transporter van, sat patiently in the garage, as did Dave. The standard wheels had been swopped out with racing slicks, and it sat with an angry stance on uprated suspension. It was like a caged bull, anxious for the gate to be opened so it could rip the matador limb from limb. Dave ran his hand over the bodywork admiringly. He'd seen her when she arrived, of course. But, now, covered in sponsorship decals and emblems, she wouldn't have looked at all out of place on any racing circuit.

Rebecca moved to the side of the van, motioning to Tyler to join her. "Wow, nice pictures, boys."

A three-foot-high picture of the TT farm dominated the side of the van with the caption, underneath:

## *Your TT Farm*
## *Growing in the Community*

A trio of headshots of Frank & Stan's TT Farm racing team — Dave Quirk, Shaun 'Monty' Montgomery, and Guy Martin — also graced each side of the van, floating angelically above the farm scene. Dave put his arm around Monty. "We look almost regal in them pictures, Monty," he said, admiring their images. The three heads on the van stared proudly back, waiting to bless their adoring fans in a few short days.

"She looks the part, Dave, doesn't she?" asked Monty.

"She does," Dave replied, casting a fond glance over to Becks, spanner in hand.

"I meant the van, Dave," Monty answered with a soft chuckle.

"I know, mate," Dave said, winking. "And I'm overwhelmed, mate. She's a real beauty. It's just a shame we're not allowed to rip out that two-litre engine and get something with a bit more grunt in there."

"What??" said Monty in alarm, before realising they were talking about the van again.

Rebecca handed Monty the spanner that Tyler had picked up and been playing with. "So I know you're *sidecar* racers," she said, emphasising the fact she'd remembered the name of that motorbike contraption they usually rode. "But, vans also?"

"Ah. Not so much," confided Dave. "Here's the thing," Dave said. "The idea was, we're back-of-the-van racers, yeah?"

Rebecca looked back at Dave like she didn't understand. This was because she didn't understand.

"Ah. Let me explain. A back-of-the-van racer is someone with little or no external funding but for whom racing is their passion, their life. They'll travel round the country to fulfil their ambition, often sleeping in the rear of their van in the process," Dave told her. "Hence the genesis of my brilliant idea for this race."

"I wondered how someone could race from the back of their van and not from the steering wheel up front," Rebecca replied with a giggle, nodding along, though still not entirely certain of the significance of the whole back-of-the-van thing.

"And I thought of the name for the race!" Monty entered in. "The *Isle Le Mans*! That was all my doing!" Monty looked over to Dave, daring him to challenge his assertion. But Dave stood down, allowing Monty his moment in the sun.

"Monty, that's brilliant!" Rebecca responded enthusiastically, causing a now-unhappy Dave to question his silence on the matter. Nevertheless, he carried on with his explanation instead...

"Now, along with me and Monty, that's Guy Martin's image up there on the van. You may not be familiar, so I'll explain that Guy Martin is—"

"I know who Guy Martin is," Rebecca cut in, a cock-eyed smile on her face.

"I'm sorry?" Dave answered, a bit taken aback that a non-racing fan like Becks would know who Martin was.

"I already know who Guy Martin is," she told him again, a contented grin now spread over her entire face.

"*Erm*, anyway..." continued Dave, momentarily at a loss before soldiering on... "We can take the sidecar out for two hours if we want, but it's all about this little beauty. The van, I mean. Guy's done a bit of van racing already. You may have watched that programme on the TV the other week, *World's Fastest Van*, I think it was called?" Dave suggested.

"Hmm? No. No, I don't think so," replied Rebecca, registering no recognition at all.

"No...?" said Dave, pausing to allow her to explain how, then, she might know who Guy Martin was. But she did not. The contented grin, however, remained on her face and showed no signs of abating.

"Oh...kay?" Dave went on, confused, but at this point seeing no clarification would be forthcoming. "Anyway. Em. Right. Where was I? Oh, yes. Okay, so, apart from Guy, we'll just be picking it up as we go along. We're not terribly bothered about where we place at the finish. At the end of the day, of course, it's all about raising some money for a very worthy cause."

"So you won't mind if you don't even win?" asked a genuinely impressed Rebecca.

Monty felt compelled to offer in his opinion just then, as his bullshit meter was pinging away, needle pinned. "Dave is playing it cool," he advised Rebecca. "I've known him too long for this. And what he's conveniently left out is that we've actually been getting a few lessons ahead of the race. Trust me, if me and Dave are going racing, we want to win."

"It's a fair cop," Dave admitted, pulling his lips to one side of his face and shrugging.

"It's for charity," Monty went on. "But I can promise that we'll be giving it everything we've got. As we always do. And all of the other fellows in this race will be doing the same."

"Fellows?" Rebecca interrupted. "There aren't any women racers?" she asked.

"Hmm, now that's actually a good point..." Dave mused, hand raising up to stroke his chin... "And has got me thinking..."

"You're not bloody replacing me again!" Monty admonished his partner. "We're a team!"

"I know, I know!" Dave protested. "I was just—"

"You were just *nothing*," Monty scolded him, not amused. "We're a team. *End of*," he said, glaring at an at-this-time still-chin-stroking and obviously-pondering Dave.

"Fine, fine!" replied Dave.

The conversation was interrupted, suddenly, by an irritating, nasally voice. "*You* lot," it said, directed at Dave and Monty. "Are you the valet parking? Because my car needs attention."

Dave turned, knowing what he was about to find. Sure enough, a smug face was revealed, of the sort one might never tire of striking with a cricket bat. There was only one man with that insipid, adenoidal tone that grated on one's nerves like fingernails down a blackboard when he spoke.

"Rodney *Franks*," laughed Dave, with an overly friendly inflexion. "Rodney, fantastic to see you again so soon," he said sarcastically. "Happy to help! Now I'll just show you over here, if you'd be so kind as to follow me to the exit, and we can have you back in your car in no time, on the road again, and headed on your jolly way!"

Rebecca offered a pained smile, casting her eyes to this cravat-wearing gentleman presented before her, attempting to work out whether he were friend or foe.

Franks raised his hands in mock submission. "Now, now, that's not a very nice thing to say at all, Dave Quirk. Especially to a dear old friend," he replied, making a point of looking Rebecca up and down as he said it. "I only wanted to come and see the track ahead of your little affair. Extend my best wishes and all. I'll be honest, I'm actually impressed with what's been done with the place in preparation for the race. It *very nearly* looks professional."

Monty stepped forward, buoyed by Dave's opening salvo. "The best part of it?" he said. "The best part of it is that this *little* race, as you've called it, is going to allow us to buy the TT farm from Henk, for the charity. So it's all for a *very good cause*, don't you think?"

Franks stared back at Monty but did not immediately respond. After several long moments, he pointed back at himself and said, "Oh! I'm sorry, Mister... Montgomery, is it? I'm sorry, Mr Montgomery, but I didn't realise you were speaking to me. What with the, *em*, you know..." he said, holding a finger up and stirring the air with it, in obvious reference to Monty's wonky eye. "I could see one of them looking at me, but the other..." he trailed off, looking over to the field beside them... "Was somewhere over there?"

Monty didn't react. It'd take a bigger man than Rodney Franks to ruffle his feathers in such a manner.

"Anyway. The *best* part of this whole sordid affair?" Franks went on, mimicking Monty's previous phrasing, and giving Rebecca an unsolicited once-over again. "The *best* part about this whole affair is that I'll very shortly be *owning* this little racetrack. Isn't that wonderful? In fact, the very reason I'm here today is to finalise the paperwork. I'm still *very* eager to build my hotel, you see. And who knows, perhaps I'll build it *right here*," he said, indicating the track with a sweep of his hand.

"I don't understand," said Monty, not understanding.

"You know that doesn't really surprise me in the slightest. And how about you?" Franks said to Dave. "Would you like to translate it for your intellectually challenged friend here?"

Dave stared at Franks. "What that means, I presume, is that this event will soon be mysteriously booked up, or unavailable next Sunday, if you're not racing in it?" Dave was exceedingly unhappy at this turn of events, but he refused to give Franks the satisfaction of showing it.

Franks pulled out an invisible diary. "Correct!" he said, folding the imaginary book back over. "And if you don't have your racetrack, then you don't have the money to buy your precious, quaint little farm. Simple enough. Even for a simpleton to understand. Isn't that right, Mr Montgomery?"

"If we don't have the money to buy the farm, it goes back to you?" Dave asked coldly.

Franks shook his head. "It's a possibility, though, sadly, unlikely. The Dutchman has the option to hand it back to me after a certain period, but as he said to me today, that's not going to happen so long as he has a hole in his... well, I shan't repeat his crass vulgarisms. But, he has a massive tax bill and associated costs if he keeps hold of the farm. Without your little event, you won't have the money to buy it from him, so that essentially leaves the large fool two choices. The first being to sell it back to me, which he has already indicated in his own inimitably profane way that he has no intention of doing. His second option would be to sell it on the open market. As it's riddled with asbestos, however, and he has no planning permission besides, it would sit on the market for years. He is rather between the devil and the deep blue sea, I should say."

Dave started stroking his chin again. "Right," he said. "So I'm just trying to work out what all this means, as well as why you're telling me all this. You've bought yourself a racetrack. Which won't have been cheap. Just to secure entry in this race? That doesn't make an awful lot of sense, Rodney, even for someone as daft as you. Entering a team isn't going to change your world, after all, even if you win the bloody thing. So, again, it makes absolutely no sense why you'd do this. Which only leads me to wonder... are you a bit dim?"

Franks nodded along as Dave had been speaking. To the casual observer, it may very well have looked like they were, the two of them, old friends. But they most certainly were not. Surprisingly, Franks did not appear offended by Dave's insults. In fact he was smiling now, and for all appearances enjoying himself.

"Not stupid at all, Mr Quirk, I can assure you." Dave winced as Franks said this. "But I can understand why you'd think it," Franks continued. "I won't lie to you, I want that farm. I'm in it for the long run and I'm fairly certain I can get planning permission for my hotel, at some point. For your elucidation, this is how I see this playing out, so do listen closely. And, for the sake of your associate Mr Montgomery especially, I'll try to keep it as simple as possible."

Neither Dave nor Monty were laughing, but this didn't concern Franks. He went on...

"I'll allow you to have your event next Sunday on my newly owned racing circuit. You allow my team an entry. I shall pay the entry fee, without incident. It is for charity, after all. We have a friendly wager amongst ourselves about whether my team or your team finishes higher up the leaderboard—"

"What bloody wager are you on about?" Dave cut across. To which Rodney massaged the air in front, shushing Dave as one might a small child.

"I will allow your little race for charity to go forward," Franks said magnanimously, like he was doing Dave a tremendous favour. "And, if you win, you get to raise the money you need for the farm. If my team finishes higher, however, then your Dutch friend needs to sell the farm to me. I'll even pay him full market value, despite that horrible, troublesome asbestos. Why he wouldn't wish to sell to me remains a mystery to myself, I'm sure," Franks sniffed. "But you must convince him to do so."

Dave rubbed his chin that much it was in danger of catching fire. "You'd do all this just to get the farm? What is *with* you and this farm?" After receiving no reply, he asked another question: "If we lose, then what are we meant to do with all the money we've raised?"

Franks gave an exaggerated frown. "Why is that a concern of mine?" he said. "I couldn't possibly care less. I don't know— Give it back? As it stands, presently you have no event as I will soon own the track. With my proposal, on the other hand, you at any rate at least have an *opportunity* to keep your farm, unlikely as that outcome may be. If you walk away from this, however, then you do not. It really is that simple."

"Sod that," Monty entered in. "We've got most of the money already. Let's just buy the farm from Henk, and tell this one to bugger off," he said, without looking directly at Franks. Which wasn't difficult, in Monty's case. But still. Though he did look to the lady present, apologising for his language. "Pardon my French, Becks," he told her. She waved him on, indicating that his language was just fine, actually, given the circumstances.

"Oh, *do* think about it, my dim-witted friend," suggested Franks. "If you don't have a track, then you don't have a race. And if you don't have a race, then you don't have the money you'll need. While you may have *some* money just now, you still don't possess *nearly* enough to purchase the farm at present."

Monty knew Franks wasn't wrong, but said nothing. Taking this as acquiescence, Franks blathered on...

"We'll draw up a little agreement so there is no confusion or backing out at a later date. I suggest you tell your Dutch friend of my proposal, and remind him that I will pay market value if you lose the bet. If you don't end up having the money to buy that farm of his from him, the place will sit empty for years, and it will cost him a fortune. Don't forget to remind him of that as well. He is a businessman, after all, and so he would be mad to refuse my offer." Franks looked at his watch. "I will need to know by eight p.m. this evening," he told them. "As I'm sure I've had an enquiry to use the track next Sunday. It would be poor manners if I didn't get back to them to confirm their booking, and it is not nice to be rude, now is it? You can see where it leads, can't you? Of course you can. Well. Toodle pip."

Rodney Franks pranced off to his car, not a care in the world, like he was cock of the walk. Which in fact he was. A cock, that is.

Monty punched the palm of his left hand with the fist of his right, wishing for all the world it was Franks he was punching. "There's no way Henk is going to deal with the idiot, is there?" he asked Dave.

Dave mashed the keypad on his phone. "I don't expect he will," he said, dialling Henk to fill him in on what had just transpired. "But if we can't convince him, then the Isle Le Mans TT is doomed to failure before it begins. And we lose the farm, Monty, we also become unemployed. If Henk isn't on board, then we're all well and truly... Well, we're all well and truly," he said, biting his tongue for the sake of present company.

"Who even wears a cravat?" asked Rebecca, filling the silence, still trying to get a handle on the polluting cloud of unpleasantness that was Rodney Franks. "And says *toodle pip*? Seriously? That's not even a real human being. That's... that's..." she said, trying to put into words how she was feeling.

Young Tyler had remained silent during the whole of the prior exchange. To him, it had been just another instance of grown-ups speaking gibberish, which is what they mostly spoke, in his six and a half years of experience. Coming to his mother's aid, he did finally make one observation, however...

"Mummy, he's like a cartoon," he said. "But not a good cartoon. A *bad* cartoon."

To which no one could disagree.

## *Chapter* FOURTEEN

Susie slapped her hands on her desk, gasping for air. She lowered her head, resting it between her knees. The elderly chap with an obvious combover, wearing a pair of slippers even though it was midday, paid no attention, sat patiently waiting for his taxi to arrive.

"Oh god, oh god, oh god," she chanted. She gripped the corner of the desk, turning her knuckles white, with her breathing getting more and more desperate like she were giving birth to a bowling ball. A very large bowling ball.

The old chap snapped his paper shut, taking a glance to the street directly to the side of the building, where the taxis collected those that'd ordered a cab. "Excuse me, luv?"

"I'm fine," replied Susie. "I'll be fine."

"I wasn't asking about that," replied the old fellow. "Any sign of my taxi is all I want to know?"

"Five minutes," Susie replied, which was the standard reply of any taxi operator, in any taxi office, in any part of the world. She ignored the inbound phone, which rang incessantly, taking several further lungful's of breath to steady herself.

"Pick up," she whispered to herself, repeating it several times in quick succession as she pressed her mobile phone to her ear. "Pick up," she said one last time, impatiently, before finally giving up and throwing her phone back into her bag. "Bloody hell. Where are you *going?*" she asked aloud, rising up and looking out the window with increasing desperation.

"Fifteen Willets Way, luv!" shouted the slipper-wearing chap, clearly put out at the brief delay he'd been experiencing. "I've told you twice already!"

"I wasn't speaking to you!" shouted an exasperated Susie somewhat less than professionally, which was unlike her. "I was wondering where someone's *gone*," she said. "I know where *you're* going, sir. It's on the computer."

"What is?" he asked, getting even more animated. "What's on the computer?"

Susie pulled her fingers into a claw, cracking her knuckles in the process, and breathing through her teeth. "Your address is on the computer," she told him.

"It's not a dress," he replied immediately.

"What?"

The man stood to reveal his ensemble, including his pyjamas, which were secured at the waist with what looked like the tieback sash from a pair of curtains. "It's a dressing gown, luv. Not a dress. There's a difference!"

"I said a... nevermind. Harry, why do you look like you've just got out of bed?" Susie asked their regular customer, softening now. "You only need a white nightcap and you could be Ebenezer Scrooge, you know."

"I'm making a pan of stew!" Harry explained. "I didn't have any carrots, did I? So I had to go down the shop. There wasn't any point in getting all dressed up just to head out for ten minutes, now was there? No, I should think not," he told her. "Logic!" he shouted, so loudly and abruptly that Susie nearly fell out of her chair.

"But you only live about three minutes away, Harry. Why didn't you simply walk?"

"What? Don't be bloody stupid. I'm only wearing my slippers!"

"So you should have got dressed, then!" Susie sighed. "Anyhow, Harry, you didn't happen to see Stella along your travels, did you?"

"Who's this Stella person?" Harry asked.

"You know Stella, Harry. She sits right here," offered Susie, pointing to the empty seat near to her.

Harry's eyes narrowed. "Are you trying to trick me?" he asked. "You can't trick me because I'm too clever for that. And there's quite obviously no one sitting there beside you."

"She *usually* sits here, Harry. When she's *in*. When she's *in*, that's where she sits," explained Susie, with the patience of a saint.

Harry stared blankly until a moment of knowing hit him. "Hold on. Is she the fat bird with hair like wire?"

Susie nodded reluctantly. "That would be her, Harry, yes. You've not seen her? When you were out at shops?"

Harry paused for a few moments, pondering, then replied, "You've asked the right fellow, as I have a photogenic memory. And I can tell you, with certainty, that she was in the toilet when I was here on the Tuesday of this week. When she came out of the toilet, the smell made my eyes bleed. The smell was that bad that I ended up walking home instead of waiting for a taxi. And it had just begun raining, and showed no signs of abating, and there was me without my mac. And yet I walked home anyway, because *that's* how bad the smell was. And when I'd gotten home, I discovered that my fruit had turned, and I blame that entirely on the noxious bathroom odour."

"Your fruit?" Susie asked, wondering if this were perhaps some kind of euphemism, or...

"The fruit I'd just purchased at the shop! Do pay attention!"

"Ah. But you haven't seen Stella today?" Susie tried to coax out of him.

"Today? No, of course not. I've already told you."

"I'm sorry about your fruit, Harry," said Susie.

"Hmm? What fruit? What are you on about, dear lady?"

"Your spoiled fruit?" she reminded him. "That you got at the shop?"

"Oh, that. I thought you were speaking in code. I'm very good at interpreting code. I'd done it during the war. I'm very clever, you see. I know my onions. And so I thought you were speaking in code, and perhaps flirting with me. I'm much too old for that sort of nonsense! But, with my dashing good looks, I can understand perfectly why you'd be so overcome with—"

"Oh, look, your taxi is here," Susie announced, relieved. "And just in time."

"Hmm? Just in time for what?" Harry asked, confused.

"Just in time for being on time," Susie told him. "Look, I'll tell the driver that this fare is on me, for your fruit, and for the odouriferous assault on your nasal passages. Okay? And there's your car outside, so you have a nice day, all right?" Susie motioned to the driver, and he came in to help Harry out to the taxi.

She could hear Harry carrying on as he was led away. "She keeps talking about my fruit!" ... "I think she was chatting me up!" ... "Imagine! At my age!" Susie offered a half-hearted wave, now distracted by her ringing phone.

"Lee!" she shouted into the phone, with no longer any attempt to retain her calm professional demeanour. "Where the hell have you been? I've been trying to reach you!"

Susie paced around the reception area, keeping one eye on the front door. "Lee, we're in deep trouble. Stella left me a message this morning saying she knows you've been cheating on her. She said Eric Fryer at the café told her he'd seen you with a woman."

She listened for a few impatient moments, then continued, "I *know* you know more than one woman on this earth. But she knows something's been going on, or at least thinks there is. Lee, Eric Fryer saw the two of us together, and if he walks into my office, for any reason, and recognises me, he's sure to tell Stella that *I'm* that woman, and... Oh, god, I don't want to *think* about what Stella would do. Lee, you need to sort this out! Lee? ... Lee, are you still there? Hello? Lee??"

Susie checked the phone, but the call was still connected. She placed the phone back to her ear...

"You're back. Oh, you've found a note from Stella? Why didn't you tell me that five minutes ago?? ... Okay, sorry, you've only just found it. But you'll need to excuse me for being somewhat cranky. Knowing Stella could turn up at any second here, only to separate my limbs from my body, is not exactly a prospect I relish. She scares me at the best of times, but knowing what she does... Good god, it doesn't bear thinking about." She paused, lest her anger and frustration get the better of her. "Well?" she said expectantly.

Susie smiled as a young couple entered. *'Just one moment,'* she mouthed, with her finger raised politely. *'Sorry about the wait.'*

She turned her attention back to her phone, cupping her mouth now for privacy. "*Well what?* What do you mean, *well what?* Lee what do you think I mean? What does the bloody note say?? Yes I'm listening, Lee..."

The male half of the couple, the couple now stood waiting by the counter, shifted impatiently from one foot to the other. "Thank you for your patience. Bit of a family emergency here," Susie told him, smiling apologetically.

"No, not you," she said, back on the phone. "I've got a customer here... What? Great, so Molly's going to the Isle of Man to support her dad, so Stella's gone with her. I guess I'm running the business all by myself, yet again. How marvellous! Now. How are we going to sort out this kerfuffle when she's on another piece of rock entirely? ... Yes, I know she can't physically harm me from over there, at least, but it's still not ideal, now is it? When are you due to go over to help at this racing event? Tomorrow? Okay, it'll have to wait until tomorrow, as Stella seems to have turned her phone off. What do you mean, what are you going to say to her? Lee, you're a grown man. You'll just need to grab the bull by the horns and tell her what you've decided, won't you? It may come as a shock to her, but at least she will then know, and we won't need to continue carrying on behind her back. She deserves that, don't you think?"

The fellow at the counter looked at his wrist, making a show of checking the time even though he wasn't wearing a watch, communicating that his patience was clearly wearing thin. His lady companion was now stood at the window watching the flow of traffic, perhaps looking to see if she could spot another company's taxi car they might procure.

"Lee, I've got to get back to work," Susie said into the phone. "I'll speak to you later."

There remain two modes of travel to the Isle of Man — by air, being one method, and by sea being the other. In November, the latter option could, on occasion, be a calculated gamble. If you also wanted to bring along your own transport, four hours on the ferry from the port of Heysham awaited. On a calm day the ferry was a sublime way to travel, but if the Irish Sea was angry then you were in for rather a tumultuous adventure. Molly, tasked with bringing more of her father's belongings over to the Isle, was beginning to regret her offer of taking them over by car. Not just because of the inclement weather, as it turned out, but also because of now having an unexpected, uninvited, and unhappy travelling companion in tow. Travelling with Stella did, however, have its advantages, on this occasion particularly on an overcrowded boat, as Molly was about to learn...

"There are no seats, Stella," said Molly, smiling politely at those already seated. Unfortunately, ferry passengers had a habit of taking a seat, then placing their belongings either side to avoid unwelcome neighbours — with any neighbour being considered, in fact, unwelcome — and the end result of which was that one person essentially occupied three seats. These types of people were exceptionally good at avoiding eye contact, often waving at people who didn't exist in order to back up their subterfuge. The vision of Stella in a leopardskin dress certainly exaggerated this reaction, with that many people motioning over their imaginary travelling companions that it looked like they were involved in a stadium-style Mexican wave.

Stella pointed towards the rear of the bar area, where a series of bench chairs joined together to create a large seating area. People there sat squashed together, some reading, some listening to music, along with one particularly inconsiderate woman lying down across the bench taking the space of four people. The woman lay positioning herself to face the wall, it seemed, so that she didn't have to look at the people who were left standing because of her, or had given up completely and were sitting uncomfortably on the deck floor. Those sat closest to Sleeping Beauty offered a frustrated tut-tut, and an occasional murmuring, but, being too British for their own good, they remained entirely too polite and their angst manifested itself no further than this.

Stella, on the other hand, was not any of these people. "Over there," she said, placing a half-smoked fag behind her ear. "Luckily, I see a seat opening up just now. Bully for me."

Molly was about to protest, but Stella was already making her move...

"Alright, princess. Shift yourself!"

There was no response.

"Oi! Yes, I'm talking to you!"

There was still no reply, but the woman was likely only feigning deep sleep, and so Stella carried on, undeterred. Not that the woman genuinely being asleep would have made the least bit of difference anyway. "Look," Stella suggested, not at all discreetly. "You're taking up about four bloody seats here. So shift your carcass. *Pronto.*" She said this with a snap of her fingers for good measure, to get the point across.

With no response yet forthcoming, Stella leaned closer so there would be no doubt as to her intentions. "Listen, luv. I've had a really bad day. All I want to do right now is sit down and have four or five pints of Guinness to sort myself out. So, you either shift your sorry ass, RIGHT NOW, or I'm going to *pick you up and throw you overboard.* DO I MAKE MYSELF PERFECTLY CLEAR?"

The woman may have been an idiot but she was not, apparently, a blithering idiot because she did indeed, at this point in time, perform the action that was instructed of her.

"And that's how it's fucking done!" Stella announced aloud to the present onlookers, now staring in wonder.

Stella took one of the now-vacant seats. "Good girl. It looks like you may retain your health today," she said, directed to the very nervous-looking woman now sat in a perfectly upright position next to her. "Molly," Stella said, pointing a thumb over to the bar. "Grab me a Guinness while you're up, yeah?"

"But I'm not—" Molly began, but of course it was useless.

"I'll watch your seat for you," Stella told her.

Molly rose to the occasion, although it was more a case of her realising she didn't really have any real choice in the matter.

"Oh!" Stella shouted across the length of the bar. "Scampi fries, if they've got them! Two packets! No, wait, better make it four!"

Stella pulled her mobile phone from her bra as she waited for her refreshments, casting a frustrated glance down at the screen. "Fucking bastard," she muttered, due to the absence of any unread messages. Or it could have been in reference to the screensaver picture of Lee on a trampoline, dressed as an elf. Or, it could have been both things at once.

Molly returned, offering a sympathetic smile to their now rigidly vertical neighbour, and took a still-available spot next to Stella, despite the shortage of seating, handing over her pint as she did so. "The boat's really busy, Stella," Molly said to her by way of conversation. "I was speaking to that group at the bar and they all said they're going to the Isle of Man just for the race on Sunday. You know, I think the boys could really be onto something with this event," she said. "Oh," she added. "And you know who else is on the boat, don't you?" But she didn't finish what she was going to say, now staring, as she was, at Stella's empty pint. Molly had only looked away for a tick, but the only evidence there'd been anything there at all was the white outline of foam presently on Stella's hairy upper lip.

"What? I was thirsty," replied Stella matter-of-factly. "Who?"

"Who, what?" asked Molly.

"Who else is on the boat?"

"Oh, yes. Your friend Guy Martin." Molly turned her head back towards the bar area. "Those blokes over there said they'd been chatting with him while he was queuing to get on. He was sat with his mate in that tricked-up Ford Transit van he raced on that show of his, according to them, so they were especially interested in that…" But by the time Molly looked back to Stella, her seat was empty, aside from two empty packets of scampi fries and her well-drained plastic beaker of Guinness.

It wasn't too much of a challenge, actually, to find out where Guy was seated, on account of the large group of people milling about, forming a circle to perhaps have a picture taken or to have something signed by him. A large proportion of those waiting were lovestruck women, as it would happen. Guy was obliging and happy to sign anything placed in his way, including a large pair of breasts, which were suddenly inches from his face. This was not an uncommon occurrence, women asking to have their breasts signed, so he didn't bat an eye. "Would you like me to personalise it, luv?" he asked routinely. And it wasn't until he pulled back a little to capture his admirer's response that the expression on his face changed to one of terror again — that strange mix of excitement and terror — as before, at the Glasgow hotel.

"Yes, please," Stella said.

Guy stared intently at Stella for several awkward seconds, and then relaxed. He knew from experience that a battle with Stella was one he'd never win, so he simply accepted the inevitable. "Bloody hell," he said, clapping his hands together. "Joey," he said, addressing his mate who'd accompanied him on the trip. "This is Stella. The one I was telling you about."

"I thought you were having me on, Guy," Joey replied, cautiously absorbing the wonder that was Stella in a skintight leopardskin dress. "I didn't think she was real. I thought you'd made her up!"

"Oh, she's real alright," Guy assured him. "And she's bloody brilliant at managing enthusiastic crowds, this one, among other things. You should see her in action. She's the best," he said, turning back to Stella and giving her a wink.

"When you're right, you're right," said Stella, taking the compliment with no modesty on her part. She looked over to Joey, whose eyes were transfixed. She waved her hand around her face. "Oi! You keep your eyes north of the border, you dirty get," she told him. "See? Or we'll have a problem."

Guy stifled a burst of laughter, with Joey looking like he was about to unscrew the porthole window and take his chances in the force-7 gale outside. "Right. You just see that you do," Stella further admonished him. "Anyway," she continued, addressing Guy now. "Your offer that we discussed before. Were you serious?"

Guy flicked his eyes over to Joey, for he knew how her question might be interpreted. "You mean about the personal assistant job, Stella?" he clarified.

"Yes, that."

Guy nodded, running his hands through his mass of unkempt hair. This had the effect of sending a mass quivering amongst the assembled women present in the queue, along with a collection of audible gasps. Strangely, for her part, however, Stella now appeared to be largely immune to Guy's special charms, or perhaps merely preferring of the battery-operated version of him.

"Absolutely," Guy told Stella. "You can handle people like nobody's business, you can drive, presumably, and you can provide the security services of three grown men!" he joked. "But... are you not happy in the taxi office? You're co-owner now, I think you were telling me?"

Stella still had two packets of scampi fries on her person, somehow, and she produced them from locations unknown given her skin-tight attire, ripping open the packets of fish-flavoured treats and swallowing their entire contents down in one go, one after the other, like a cormorant eating a pollock. With her snack sorted, she turned her attention back to Guy. "I was happy in the taxi office," she said to him thoughtfully. "I *was* happy, until just recently. But things have changed. That's what you get for trusting people, I suppose, and I won't be doing that again in a hurry, I expect. Anyway, I'm over all weekend helping Frank and Stan with their race, so I'll catch up with you there," she said. "And you can sign my tits there, if you like," she added. "I'll leave you to it for now, as there's others waiting," she told him, mindful of the remaining throng, or, just confident she could get her personal bits signed whenever she pleased.

Stella manoeuvred round in the tight space she'd wedged herself into next to Guy, and Guy lifted his legs like his mum was running the Hoover around his feet, to accommodate her, allowing her an easier route. Joey stared on in terrible astonishment as she took her leave. "Mate, I thought you were joking about her," Joey whispered, reiterating his earlier comment, once certain Stella was out of earshot. "Did she ever do wrestling? She must've done, now I think on it. I'm sure I've seen her on the telly?" But Guy only laughed.

"Everything okay?" Molly asked Stella. "Only you were gone for a good while."

Stella didn't respond at first. She looked out to sea. And, if they'd been out on the open deck, she could have blamed the salty wind for the hint of moisture at the corner of her eye. "Molly," she said, finally. "Have you ever questioned your career choices?"

"Of course. Don't forget I used to be a lap-dancer, after all. What's going on, Stella?" Molly slid up the already intimate bench seating, placing a comforting hand, somewhat bravely, on Stella's thigh. "Has Guy Martin upset you?" she asked. "Because, if he has..."

Stella smiled at the sentiment. "I'm alright, Molly. But thanks for that," she said, patting Molly's hand in a way that both acknowledged her kindness and indicated that she might perhaps consider taking it the hell off of her thigh forthwith.

"Mm-hmm?" Molly said, pulling her hand away, and encouraging Stella to continue.

"I'm just annoyed with myself, to be honest," she went on. "I'm annoyed that I've opened myself up to the point others can take advantage of my good nature. I was happier on my bleedin' own, without a man to complicate things. What do we even need them for? I've got two replacements in my bedside drawer which are better than most I've met, especially that ruddy punter, Lee. I suppose deep down I knew this day would come. After all," she went on, running her hand up and down in front of her body illustratively. "I'm an acquired taste for most, glorious as I am. I know that. And the last time I was with a man, before Lee, it turned out I was a bloody bet. But I thought Lee was different," she said, exhaling sharply. "I truly did. I can't believe I've been this stupid. Still, it's not all bad. I've just sorted a new job. I'll be providing personal services for Guy Martin. So there's that," she told Molly. "Oi, I'm going on deck for a quick fag."

"I'm sorry, Stella," Molly told her as Stella rose. "For what it's worth, I'm your friend. And I won't let you down, yeah? I promise. Can I do anything to help, Stella? Is there anything you need?"

"Well you could get yourself up to the bar while I'm out and get me another Guinness, now you ask, as well as two more packets of scampi fries. That's for starters. After that, we'll have to see." Stella smiled broadly. This was her way of saying thank you.

"Coming right up, then," said Molly with a laugh, long since accustomed by now to Stella's idiosyncrasies.

## Chapter
# FIFTEEN

Stan capered about the kitchen of the TT farm which, fortunately for two hungry stomachs, and unlike the rest of the farm, was further ahead on the refurbishment schedule. The builders had been stood down, for now, until the future plans were secured, but with Rebecca's assistance the place could, in parts, be considered homey. "It's days like this that make you glad to be alive, Frank. The sun's in the sky and not a cloud in sight and the forecast for the weekend is more of the same. We really did luck out on the weather," Stan said, dropping a pair of perfectly poached eggs onto Frank's plate.

"How's that toast coming along?" Frank asked, unwilling to tuck into his eggs without toast at hand.

"Coming up!" answered Stan, thrusting his spatula up in the air for emphasis.

"It was snowing this time last year," observed Frank, applying a liberal application of salt to his eggs, and then reaching for the HP Sauce. "Hang on," Frank said, freezing suddenly, and clutching his hand to his chest.

"What is it, Frank?" Stan said, alarmed, rushing to his friend's side. "Are you okay, Frank? Are you having a turn?" asked Stan desperately, looking Frank over like an A&E doctor. "Do we need to get you to hospital? Speak to me, Frank!" Poor Stan was nearly in tears at this point.

"No, it's just..." Frank began hesitantly.

"Just what?? Tell me, Frank!" Stan cried.

"It's just, I thought there was going to be beans as well...?"

Stan didn't know whether to be relieved or to hit Frank over the head with his spatula. "Monty ate the last tin," he told Frank. "I have to get more."

"That boy likes his beans," Frank remarked, oblivious to Stan's distress. That, or enjoying it. "Anyway, about that toast? Only I thought it'd be ready by now. Not sure why it's taking so long...?"

Stan uncocked his spatula-wielding arm with a sigh, letting it drop down and relax. "On it," he said. "Butter?"

"What a silly question. Of course, butter. But I'll do it myself. You never put enough butter on when I leave it to you."

"I'm just looking out for your health, Frank. God knows someone's got to. And speaking of which, you should go easier on the salt, by the way," Stan instructed, handing Frank his toast.

"Bollocks to that," remarked Frank. "Here, what's this?"

"What's what?" Stan asked. "What is it now?"

"Why's my toast so dark? Why'd you leave it in so long?"

"Well I was a bit distracted, wasn't I??" Stan shouted.

"Oi, easy there, Stan," Frank told him. "What's gotten into you this morning? Look at that sun shining. It's a lovely day! Pecker up, old chum!" Stan was standing back over at the kitchen counter, clutching his own hand to his chest now. "What are you doing over there?" Frank asked him. "Aren't you going to join me for breakfast?"

"Yeessss," Stan replied, sounding like he was trying to charm a snake. "Just give me a moment. I'm collecting the Branston Pickle for myself."

"Anyway. Like I was saying," Frank carried on cheerfully once Stan had joined him at the table. "It was snowing this time last year. Remember having that snowball fight with the neighbour's kids?"

"Yes. I do, at that," Stan told him. "You're implying it was a mutual battle, though. However, I seem to recall those little blighters launching an unprovoked attack when we parked up outside the house."

"You gave as good as you got, Stan. You were simply annoyed because you'd only just had a spray tan and looked like an orange snowman in the end. So. The weather's looking good for Sunday, then?"

"Perfect by all accounts, Frank," Stan said, taking a sip of his freshly squeezed juice. Frank was staring at his, hard, with a look of intense pain on his face. But Stan wasn't going to fall into the same trap twice. "What is it, Frank?" he asked calmly.

"Why have you got—?" Frank started to say.

"This is freshly squeezed, Frank. You don't like freshly squeezed juice."

"But—"

"And this is grapefruit juice, Frank. You prefer orange."

"But then—?"

"Monty drank the last of it, Frank. And that reminds me, I need to pick up more bread as well. He's toasted nearly all of it."

"For his beans," said Frank, the equation becoming clear in his head: beans + toast = Monty.

"But, yes. Perfect weather," Stan continued now that bit of business had been sorted. "And I know it cost a few quid having an indoor Plan B for our Family Fun Day, but having it outdoors is going to make such a difference. It also means all the stalls can get set up the day before and leave their stuff overnight without it getting soaked. Oh, and that reminds me," he said again, taking a small notepad from his pocket and jotting something down.

"Bread, beans, and orange juice," Frank reminded him helpfully. "Oh, and pick up some McVitie's Digestives, will you? I've had a craving for those lately. The chocolate-covered ones."

"That not what I was going to..." Stan began, but then dropped his shoulders in defeat. "Fine," he said, scribbling down Frank's order. And with *that* business sorted, Stan went on: "No, I need to arrange a couple of security guards to watch the site overnight. You know, make sure everything is where it should be on Sunday. So," he said. "Henk is keen with everything? What if it doesn't work out?"

"I wouldn't say keen, exactly, Stan. And we just need to hope that the boys come good in the race. I feel pretty bad, because the only time we really see Henk of late is when we're asking for something. I can see it in his face that he's sick to death of this place by now. Well, the swearword was in Dutch, but I didn't need to be a native to get the general gist of what he was saying. He told me in no uncertain terms that he wants this place to be a roaring success but that, after tomorrow, that's him done with it. He doesn't want to have to deal with Rodney Franks again, that's for certain. But, come Monday, either this farm will be in the hands of the charity or Henk will have no choice but to be selling it back to Franks. How's Team Frank-and-Stan's preparations going, by the way?" he asked, casting a glance over to the front kitchen window overlooking the field. "They've certainly been industrious, the lads, between eating all our food," he said, poking his egg with a toast soldier, just the way he liked. "That sidecar is going to run like a dream with the time they've spent on it."

Stan, mouth full, waved his fork around as he spoke. "They've not been working on the sidecar or the van of late, actually, as both vehicles are currently nestled in the garage at Jurby waiting for the big day. Ever since their new-best-friend Guy Martin appeared, they've been wasting time mucking about with that clapped-out old banger of a tractor that Monty painted. Take a look at them," Stan said, pointing his utensil in the direction of the window. "They're at it right now. I saw them as I was making breakfast."

"I'll never get tired of that view," Frank sighed.

"Monty's builder's bum?" Stan suggested.

"I can't see it from this distance," Frank said with a laugh. "But no. I meant the Isle of Man countryside, Stan. But Monty's arse does have a certain hypnotic appeal of its own, I suppose."

"That tractor they'd so lovingly festooned in the same colours as their sidecar has never seen so much attention, I expect," remarked Stan. "And judging by the rust patches it had, I'd say it'd been sitting in that field for ages, and through who-knows-how-many Manx winters. It's a waste of time if you ask me," Stan observed. "That thing is ready for the knacker's yard."

Frank couldn't disagree. "A bit like us in that regard, my old friend. Besides, you're only jealous because that old girl is getting more attention from the boys than you are!"

"Pish posh!" Stan countered, words he'd never uttered before, but he didn't know what else to say.

"Hang on," said Frank, craning his neck to get a look out the window from the kitchen table. "Guy's looking a bit happy with himself at present," he related to Stan. "Either that or he's caught fire? He's running around the tractor like a madman, and the others are jumping up and down and pointing and waving about. Do you think something's gone wrong? Should we go out and check on them?" he asked. "Stan...?" But Stan had already snatched up his coat and was heading out towards the field.

"What's going on? You haven't got it working, have you?" asked Frank, now out in the field once he'd caught up with Stan. Frank stood with his upper half keeled over, panting and trying to get his breath back. At least he could see Guy had not caught on fire.

So confident of their success were they that they'd in fact also fastened the original trailer to the rear of the tractor, an attachment presumably used in years past to transport the previous owners' workforce around the farm as it had a bench seat running down the interior of either side of it. "Jump in!" said Guy, offering a hand to Stan, who was first in the queue. Stan, for his part, appeared somewhat reluctant to comply, as if he were unsure he could manage to jump up that high to get in. More likely, however, he only wanted Guy's assistance because that meant Guy laying hands on him.

"You've got the honours," declared Dave, handing the key to Guy. "It was you that mostly coaxed her back to life. The bloody Tractor Whisperer, you are!"

Guy protested at first, but then graciously accepted the keys, pausing to look at each of the watching faces in turn, dramatically, as if he were about to board some sort of space shuttle on a one-way expedition to the stars. "You're certain, then?" he asked, receiving a sturdy nod from both Dave and Monty in return. "I love this," he announced, climbing aboard Tractor Number Forty-Two, with the polished blue & yellow bodywork gleaming in the mid-morning sun like a great boiled sweet.

After everyone else had climbed up into the trailer — requiring, remarkably, no assistance — Guy offered an oil-covered thumbs-up, ensuring his charges were all seated comfortably. "Ready?" he bellowed. "Here we go!"

And with that, the crisp, tranquil air was violated by the din of a decrepit diesel engine busting back into life. It rattled at first like the lungs of a lifelong smoker taking their first morning breath, and with each rotation of the engine all heads on board motioned in a rhythmic fashion, urging her along, until finally, in a wondrous burst of thick acrid smoke, the engine that'd been silenced for years announced its triumphant revival to the world in glorious fashion, and with the engine thereafter running quite smoothly and contentedly.

"Yes! You bloody beauty!" screamed Guy, applying the throttle confidently, and easing the big boiled sweet out of her premature retirement and into awaiting glory.

After its initial maiden voyage, they took it in turns, each of them, to captain the aged beauty for a lap or two around the field, with their teeth drying out from smiling so much. That is, apart from Stan, whose cosmetically enhanced gnashers retained an oily sheen throughout.

As the tractor commenced another circuitous journey, Monty at the helm, Frank leaned towards Guy, both settled in at the back now, planting a firm hand on his shoulder. "I understand Dave and Monty explained about the race being a little more than just an exhibition affair?"

Guy nodded, one ear listening to Frank, and with the other ear attending to the notes of the engine, like a choirmaster. "She'll be 'rite, Frank," Guy replied. "I've never entered a race thinking of it as an exhibition anyway. The only difference now is that I don't feel the slightest bit guilty, as an experienced competitor, about ragging the nuts off of that van and doing what I need to cross that finish line first."

## FRANK & STAN'S BUCKET LIST #3: ISLE 'LE MANS' TT

Frank smiled, looking back to the farmhouse for a brief second. "So you're up for finishing ahead of Rodney Franks' team, then? This place means the world to us, Guy. We've got impressive plans for it, and to see that bloody idiot turn it into a hotel would be truly heartbreaking."

"Oh, you needn't worry about my competitive streak, Frank. And you've got a couple of beauties in Dave and Monty, as well. We've had a few practice laps in the van, and those two boys can definitely drive. I'd say the lessons must have paid off. And of course we already know they can handle a sidecar."

Optimism overtook the anxiety in Frank's eyes. "The van's quick then, Guy?" But Guy's attention was taken by a loose bolt on the side of the trailer, which appeared to be his next project. This chap certainly was easily distracted by anything mechanical and shiny, Frank mused.

"The van," Frank repeated. "It's quick, then?"

Guy laughed, assuming the question to be a joke. "Bloody hell, Frank, stop worrying. But the van? Quick? Not a chance. It's a right bag of spanners. But it's reliable enough, to be sure. And the good thing about it, at least, is that every other bugger in the race is in something that's just as slow." Guy stared directly at Frank, his current focus no longer in doubt. "I'll drag every last horsepower out of that van, Frank, and trust me, I'll drive that bugger like I've stolen it. We just need to shift some excess weight, and that'll get a couple more miles an hour out of her."

"We can't put them on a diet now, can we?" Stan asked. "Ah... you mean from the van? Like seats, and that?"

Guy eyed Dave and Monty for a moment. "It probably wouldn't hurt to send them for a run around the farm, Frank. Every ounce saved can only help."

"Hmm. They'd probably gain any weight lost back within a day," Frank pondered aloud.

Guy slapped his grubby paw on Frank's immaculately clean beige chinos, with no concern for the perfect greasy handprint he left in the process. "If we don't beat them, Frank, it won't be for lack of trying!" he told Frank.

Guy cocked his head, directing his ear and listening to the engine note that purred like a kitten. It might best be described as a kitten with laryngitis, one could argue. But, for Guy Martin, that sound was a sweet as anything the Royal Philharmonic Orchestra could ever muster.

Guy focussed back in on Frank, grinning. "I'm pleased I've met you crazy bastards, Frank. I've got a feeling this is going to be a weekend to remember."

*Chapter*
# SIXTEEN

*... Good morning, folks. Chris Kinley here in what I'm delighted to report is a mild Isle of Man. We've got an absolutely fantastic day in store for you today on Manx Radio, which is the reason I'm out and about at seven a.m. on a Sunday morning instead of being tucked up in bed, but I wouldn't miss this for anything. The road-racing calendar is already over for the year, which is why I'm salivating at the prospect of what's in store for you today. I'm here in Jurby, and even though the sun has not yet risen it's a hive of activity in the north of the Island for the inaugural Isle Le Mans TT, a twenty-four-hour race around this circuit involving vans with only modest modification permitted, but, as a little twist, teams can, if they choose, bring out the sidecars for a maximum of two hours.*

*In addition to the racing, folks, there's also a Family Fun Day down here today. If I look around through the darkness I can see bouncy castles, fairground rides, food stalls, and all sorts of other activities at the ready. The doors have only been open a few minutes, and there must be a couple hundred people here already. It really does promise to be a delightful carnival atmosphere. Though we know some of the competitors involved, for the most part the teams are keeping the identity of their racers a closely guarded secret, and you can smell the competitive streak. I should probably remind them all that this is a charity event for Frank-and-Stan's TT Farm! Ha-ha!*

*What we do know is that we've got at least several celebrities in attendance racing today, including two TT legends for certain, and if those guys are involved you can be certain they'll be going for it! In fact, I've just seen one of them now, none other than the world's fastest road racer, Peter Hickman! Peter, if I can grab you a moment? ...*

*Yes, here he is! Thank you, Peter. Now, Peter, I bet you didn't think you'd be racing in the Isle of Man in November, now did you?*

PH: Well I heard *you* were going to be here, Chris, and I couldn't bear the thought of not seeing you until next year! Ha-ha! Seriously, though, when the sponsors got in touch to see if I wanted to do this, I signed up straight away. I was supposed to be at a wedding today, Chris, to be honest, but this event is something special, and could very well be history in the making.

CK: *Well as long as you're not the groom, Peter, I think you'll be fine! So. Four wheels instead of two, this time? What do you think?*

PH: Yeah, I'm looking forward to it. It's going to be a long day, but it'll be mega. It's great coverage for all the sponsors, and should be a great day out for all involved, racers and spectators alike.

CK: *Will your team be entering a sidecar?*

PH: Ha! Not a chance. I tried it once and ended up with three months' worth of chiropractor visits. So no sidecar here. But the teams with the sidecars will have a massive advantage, so will be the ones with an eye on the top step, I should think. We're just here to have a bit of fun, though, and maybe put a bit of a show on for the crowd.

CK: *Who's in your team?*

PH: I've got TT legend Lee Johnston with me, plus a chap from our sponsors who I've not yet met. As far as Lee, though, I think I may need to get him a cushion so he can see over the steering wheel when it's his turn to drive!

CK: *And blocks for his feet so he can reach the pedals?*

PH: That's a bit harsh, Chris. Blimey, I was just talking about being sat in the van for so long.

CK: *Oh... erm...*

PH: Ha! I'm just kidding with you, Chris! I was actually tempted to dress him up like a jockey, the fella's so short. Still might! Anyhow, I'm looking forward to having a tussle with Guy Martin's team, but they've got the sidecar being readied, I see, so they must mean business.

CK: *I imagine they do! And, thanks, Peter!*

*And there you have it, folks. A whole host of celebrities on show for you today, including the absolute TT lap record-holder and world's fastest road racer Peter Hickman. I'll be back with you throughout the course of the day if you can't get over here yourselves. But it does promise to be a treat, so do pop up to Jurby if you're able!*

Chris Kinley lowered his microphone and received the nod that they were off-air. He strolled over to Team Frank & Stan, peering round the garage door. "Morning, boys!" he shouted. "How's the preparation?"

Dave had his hands full, so lowered his sausage & bacon bap, wiping brown sauce from his chin as he did so, and then licking his fingers. "Heya, Chris. All right?"

"Sure, sure," Chris replied amiably.

"So you're a man in the know," said Dave, wasting no time. "So tell me. Who exactly is racing in the other teams?"

This question prompted Frank, Stan, and Monty to circle around Kinley like disgruntled footballers about a referee. "I'm not sure, boys," he told them with a shrug.

"Bugger off, Kinley, nothing gets past you," said Dave, shaking his butty in the air as he spoke. "So spill it!"

Chris took a careful look over his shoulder to add to the intrigue, before leaning in conspiratorially, causing those around him to tighten their circle ever closer. "Well..." Chris began, casting about several furtive glances before continuing... "I've not got much of a clue, as everyone is staying rather tight-lipped. I do know a couple of them, however."

"Yes...?" prompted Dave.

"As it turns out..." Chris said, looking over his shoulder once more... "There's one team with an absolute ringer. But you shouldn't let yourselves worry, because the other two are overweight, stupid, unhygienic and, well, gullible."

"Chris, it's a good job you've got in stature what you haven't got in humour. Oh, wait—" said Dave.

"Hang on, I'm confused," interrupted Monty. "Who's he talking about, Dave?"

"I rest my case," said Chris, laughing.

"He's talking about us," Dave informed his partner, ignoring Kinley for the moment.

"But that doesn't make sense," said Monty, still trying to work it all out. "Because then who's the ringer, Dave, if not you?"

"He means Guy Martin," Dave told him.

"Well he's got it wrong, then," Monty concluded.

"You see, Kinley?" Dave said, turning back to him, well and truly chuffed. "Not as stupid as you think!"

"Alright, but seriously," Chris went on. "Because I like you lads. And because you promise not to swear again when I interview you afterwards...?"

The lads shook their heads in agreement.

"Then I can tell you a couple of things. Out of all the teams, only seven are using the option to enter a sidecar. Including your friend, Rodney Franks. The other teams are—"

"Franks is NOT our friend," replied Dave, cutting across. "But about Franks. I know he's got his two cockwombles Napier and Thomas with him, and they're ace on a bike, much as I dislike them. But who's Franks' ringer for the van part? I know he must've brought in someone very good, since he won't be taking any chances here."

"Right, well I don't know his name," Chris told them. "Honestly I don't. But he's some form of racer from the BTCC, apparently.

Retired, I believe, but he must be fairly decent? Anyway, need to make my rounds, so good luck, chaps!"

"BTTC?" asked Stan to the others once Chris Kinley had moved on.

"That's bad news, then," said Monty, clenching and unclenching his fists. "BTCC, Stan. It's the British Touring Car Championship," he explained. "They're seriously good at driving. Proper good."

"And so what?" protested Dave. "We've got Dave Quirk, Shaun Montgomery, and bloody Guy Martin. That's a team to be reckoned with, Monty. Seriously reckoned with. And that's the team that's going to not only get us the farm, but also to keep the jobs we love, me lad. Believe it!"

Dave gripped Monty and planted a big sloppy kiss on his sweaty forehead.

"We can do this, Monty," Dave went on. "Napier and Thomas are fine enough on their machine, yes. But that's mainly because they've always had a better sidecar than us. We've put our heart into getting ours running like a dream, and sure theirs is quicker than ours, but what we don't have in horsepower, we have in passion, me old mate. In other words, it's on, chaps! It is SO fucking on."

"BUT YOU DO!" boomed a thundering voice through a perspex window in the corner of the garage. Henk removed his head from the window and walked around the front of the garage. "You have horsepower, my crazy bastard friends!" he yelled, even though he was standing right before them now.

"I don't understand," said Monty.

"I don't understand, either," said Dave. "How do you mean, Henk?" asked Dave.

"It is simple," Henk explained. "You take my sidecar, and I take yours. You see? Simple," he said again. "I have got the McMullan brothers driving in my team, but I am not interested in winning. In fact, the slower my team drives, the more the public sees my advertising! Ha!"

"Can we...?" Frank began to say. But Henk wasn't quite finished.

"You take their sidecar, yes? And we will take yours! I want you to finish higher than Rodney Franks so I may sell the farm to you! Not him!"

"Can we do that?" Frank was able to say.

"Buy the farm?" Henk asked. "You must! I do not wish for it to ever be in Rodney Franks' disease-carrying hands!"

"No, I meant, can we *do* that?" asked Frank, looking to anyone for any form of insight. "Change the sidecars this late?"

"Of course," replied Dave, rubbing his chin with the sort of contained excitement one might find inside an engine cylinder, spark igniting. "This is essentially an exhibition race, and it's not compulsory to race a sidecar, so on that basis, there are no rules covering it. The only rule is about the van not being overly modified, and it having a limit on its maximum engine capacity. Hell, in theory, we could strap a jet engine to the back of the sidecar if we wanted!"

"Hmm," said Frank.

"Hmm," said Stan.

"Hmm," said Monty, seeing as how everyone else was saying it.

"With Henk's sidecar..." Dave went on... "We're on machinery equal to, if not better than, Napier and Thomas'. And although they may have a BTCC driver on board with them, we've got bloody Guy Martin, and he's fast as fu–"

"I say, fellows!" exclaimed an all-too-familiar nasal-twanged voice. "Lovely day for it, yes?" asked Rodney Franks, with a smug grin perfectly ripe for the slapping.

"Do you ever *not* wear a cravat, Rodney?" asked a disgusted Stan.

Rodney stroked the fabric. "I *have* to wear it, unfortunately," he said. "I have to wear it to conceal the love bites from Mr Quirk's mother, don't you see."

Dave and Frank looked at each other, quite unsure who was supposed to be defending Jessie's honour. "Ah, piss off, Rodney, before I tell Henk what you were calling him last week," said Stan, to which Frank gave him an approving look.

Henk reared up. He was just waiting for an excuse, any excuse at all, to mash Franks' face to a pulp.

"Goodness gracious, this is supposed to be a nice day all about the charity," Franks chided them. "Oh, on that point, if you need any sponsorship, I'd be delighted to throw a couple of pounds in the pot." Franks looked down on the big blue boiled sweet that was their motorbike. "Oh dear. Are you sure that thing's going to last two hours around here?" he asked, with a disturbingly girlish giggle.

"Ah!" began Monty, index finger raised. "That's where you're—"

But before Monty had chance to finish, Dave poked him in the ribs with his elbow, giving him a certain look, and then turned back to Franks. "Mind how you go, Rodney," he told him. "Be sure not to bang your head on the spanner in my hand on your way out. I'd hate to see anything happen to you."

"I hate that suppurating prick," exclaimed Monty, which was surprising given Rodney hadn't actually walked away yet. "Oh, *I'm* sorry. It's my *eye*, isn't it?" explained Monty sarcastically. "Only I thought you'd already gone, didn't I? Because of my eye and all," he said flatly. He blew Rodney a kiss for good luck. "Mind how you go, now, Rodney," he added. "Watch out for Dave's spanner."

Dave looked at Monty, open-mouthed in astonishment. "Where'd you learn a word like that?" he asked after Franks had buggered off.

"What? Prick?" Monty said, confused.

"No, the other one. Suppurating."

"Well I like to read in my spare time, Dave. Didn't you know that?" Monty answered him.

Dave had to take his hands and manually close his mouth, because it wasn't closing by itself. "We won't tell him about the change of machinery," offered Dave, first staring at Monty with newfound admiration, and then to the others as well. "It'll be a pleasant surprise for them all later."

"Number three, boys!" shouted a marshal in a high-viz jacket. "They've just pulled out the numbers and you're third on the grid in the start position. And keep an ear out for an announcement in..." he said, looking at his watch... "Ten to fifteen minutes, which will be the first call to get machinery out onto the track for warm-up. We're looking good for a nine-a.m. start, guys, so a little over one hour for the actual start of the race," he added, before continuing on his way to notify the other teams of their positions and such as well.

"I'm starting to feel a little sick," said Monty, rubbing his belly.

"That'll be the three sausage baps," suggested Stan. "Anyway..." he continued, looking around the garage and the area outside... "Where's Guy disappeared to? Why isn't he here?"

"Well," Dave began, whirling his hand around, indicating the other garages around them. "Here's the thing, and this about sums Guy up rather neatly. See, some chap stuck his head round the corner hoping to find a particular type of wrench about two hours ago. And not only did Guy have that very sort of wrench the fellow needed, but he went off to see if he could help him fix whatever it was needed fixing."

"Ah," said Stan. "But then....?"

"Yes, well not only did he help sort that out..." Dave went on... "But the guys in the adjacent garage also had a problem needed sorting, and now he's helping them fix that, as well!"

"Strewth," said Monty with a hearty chuckle. "That's our Guy Martin."

"I never really knew Guy that well around the paddock," Dave continued. "Mainly because he rode two wheels, and us three, you know? But I'll tell you, he really is a proper genuine chap. There's absolutely no celebrity about that man, and the fact he's currently doing what he's doing marks him out as an absolute gentleman in my book."

"Not only that but he's got a cracking arse," offered Stan. "So there's that as well."

"*Yeeesss*, and on that note," said Frank, "I'm going to give the van a quick wash to get her looking pristine." He looked over to Dave and Monty. "Are we all set with everything mechanically now?" he asked. "She's ready for action?"

Dave rubbed his hands together gleefully. "All ready, Frank. Right now, I'm going to take my fine-looking passenger here..."

Monty tipped an imaginary hat in acknowledgement.

"... and swop sidecars with the McMullan brothers." With his hands all warmed up from the rubbing, he stopped, pressing his palms together like he was praying. Which in fact he was. "Oh god," he said. "I hope Henk hasn't told the McMullan brothers that he's given their sidecar away to us. I really, really, would like the pleasure and satisfaction of doing that myself."

At this point, Dave was interrupted by the ringtone on his phone indicating he'd gotten a text message. He pulled his phone out, read the message, and then, smiling broadly, shared it with Monty. To which Monty replied: "Noice." And then two more cricketers joined the crease...

"Morning, Molly! And a fine good morning to you as well, Stella! It's a lovely morning for it!" Dave greeted them cheerfully.

"You're certainly in fine spirits!" Molly answered him. "Looking forward to the race?"

"Ta! Talk later!" replied Dave, buggering off for a moment to make a call.

"That, and he's just had a text," volunteered Monty, in Dave's absence. "From Becks. She's bringing Tyler down soon, and Dave's also got the chance to ruin the McMullan brother's day. I don't expect—" But, with that, Monty went suddenly quiet. He was afraid to reveal too much, lest Dave should overhear, because he didn't want another elbow in the ribs. Dave hadn't meant for it, not knowing his own strength, Monty thought, but that last jab had really fucking hurt.

Monty's eyes shifted furtively, darting from side to side. Or, in his case, side to side to side. Either he was deep in thought, or possibly he was having some form of seizure. It was difficult to tell which.

It was disconcerting enough for Molly to enquire as to his well-being. "Monty?" she asked. "Are you okay?"

"I'm fine. I've just realised that we've got Becks and Stella in our camp," he said, smiling. "And that can't be bad."

Dave, back from making his call, grinned in admiration a second time. '*Nice save*,' he mouthed to his friend.

Molly smiled to be polite, though not understanding what she was smiling about.

Stella, on the other hand, released a course guffaw. "I like it, Monty," she said, scratching her arse in appreciation.

"I still don't get it?" said Molly, looking for an explanation.

"Don't feel bad, there's not much to get, Molly," Frank explained to his daughter. "Monty's merely excited because we'll soon have two kinds of beer on hand."

"Ah. Becks and Stella. I see," said Molly, seeing. "Now all we need, then, is a..." she began, before trailing off, no further feminine-sounding beer brands coming to mind.

As if on cue, Dave returned, though feminine of course he was not. His jovial mood now appeared to be considerably soured, judging by the look on his face. He waited until all eyes were on him before he spoke. "*Em*, not so good news, I'm afraid," he began.

"How so?" asked a concerned Frank.

"Well, you know how the TV production company are coming over and giving us a boatload of money to cover the event? Well, I just phoned to see where they are, and they're not coming, as it happens."

"Why?" asked Frank, simply.

Dave looked to the garage ceiling with a shake of the head. "The lady I spoke to was under the impression that the event had been cancelled. And so didn't send the crew over," he told them, looking back down at them again, his expression dour.

"What about the money they're paying us?" suggested Stan. "After all, it's their cock-up...?" He could just as easily have said *their mistake*, of course. But Stan liked the sound of 'cock up' much better.

It was clear from Dave's face that it wasn't a positive outcome in that regard. "She offered her apologies and said they might see us next year, but did offer their best wishes for the event. Which is nice, of course. Though doesn't help us much. Is there any way we can have a word with Henk about the final price for the farm?" Dave asked, looking specifically to Frank and Stan.

Frank pondered that thought for a moment before responding. "We can't, Dave," Frank told him, finally. "And I'm sure he would, if we were to ask. But it's not fair to ask him. He's moved heaven and earth for us on this whole adventure, and we've caused the poor fellow nothing but grief. And even after all that, he's offered us the use of his sidecar, which is beyond generous. Look, the weather's good, and we're putting on a wonderful show today, so we can only hope to make more than we've anticipated from the ticket prices and Fun Day goings-on."

"It's quite a financial hole to plug," Dave commented, sighing, and picturing in his head Dutch Henk sticking his finger into it and plugging it up quite nicely.

Frank bowed his head. "I know, but you two need to concentrate on the driving and let us worry about the money. If you don't finish above Rodney's crew, the TV money will be the least of our issues."

"We should have spoken to the BBC," Monty offered up, for no discernible reason. But, after a pause, he continued... "I was in the loo earlier, standing next to some bloke in white overalls who was wearing a white helmet. He didn't say much, of course, being stood at a urinal as he was. Although I did try to strike up a conversation. Anyway, he had a BBC logo on his back. Looked like he knew what he was doing."

"Peeing's not hard?" remarked a befuddled Stan. "Under normal conditions, surely...?"

"I meant like he knew his way around racing," Monty explained. "Although he looked a bit out of place, to be honest. Like he was selling drugs or summat."

"*Top Gear*?" asked Dave.

"I don't know, I didn't buy any," Monty answered, holding his stare for several arduous seconds, where he marvelled at the genius of his own joke, but received no reply.

"C'mon," was all Dave said. "Let's go swop them bikes."

As they set off to make their way to the McMullans' garage, Monty could still be heard seeking due recognition.

"Dave. Dave, I said, I didn't *buy* any..."

🏍

It was a remarkable sight to behold, as it wasn't often the sun shone in the Isle of Man in November, but the assembled spectators were appreciative, with the majority of the thousand-plus crowd casting aside the normal winter attire, bobble hats now poking out their jacket pockets. As far as race strategy was concerned, it seemed from the absence of sidecars on the starting grid that each of the teams who were employing them in the event were saving their ace-in-the-holes for later in the race. And so twenty-five vans sat idling at their respective starting positions, and with those starting positions chosen in order of their randomly drawn starting numbers.

Pit crew, friends, sponsors, and general gawkers wandered at will, taking in the visual spectacle that lay before them. No expense, it would appear, had been spared on the preparation of the vehicles, and the vibrant colours of the bodyworks on display were festive and exhilarating. Those in attendance knew the present event was going to be something both memorable and significant. And this was all the more remarkable given that the theme for the race had originally been proffered, admittedly, as a bit of a gimmick. And yet the array of vans lined up on the starting grid today would not have looked out of place at any racing event, anywhere.

Guy was fresh from assisting anyone who needed mechanical aid, ensuring all entrants were on the starting grid at the ready. His desire to get into the race himself was insatiable, but he'd have to hold out a bit longer as Dave had the honours of piloting the first two-hour leg. And so Guy was there at the van window, getting Dave pumped up.

Yes, Dave Quick, Sidecar TT Winner and minor celebrity around these parts, sat focussed behind the wheel, helmet on, rattling his gloved fingers on the sports steering wheel. This was a seasoned racer, arguably on the top of his game, ready to show all those assembled that he was ready to add another accolade to his trophy shelf. This was a true professional, the envy of the other drivers, admired by women, adored by small children and farm animals, truly, a shining example of coolness personified...

"I think I've soiled myself, actually," Dave announced to those in range of hearing. "Honestly, my stomach is in knots. Here, can you smell anything? Seriously, I believe I've shat myself. These overalls are so rigid I can't tell for sure, but I'm fairly certain my legs feel warmer?" He felt around, checking to see if anything was making its way out the bottom of his trouser legs. "Bloody hell, this track looks massive when I'm in the sidecar. But, sitting in a van, and along with all the other vans queued up as well, it looks tiny as hell. Fuck, fuck, fuck, I hope I don't let you guys down," he moaned, with Guy and Monty each taking his hand for support, with Monty from inside the van and Guy stood just outside.

Guy leaned in closer, allowing his mesmeric eyes to augment his encouraging words. "You can do this, Dave. You've gone down Bray Hill at one-hundred-and-fifty miles an hour, don't forget. You've done what most of these guys here can only fucking dream about, myself included. Dave, you've won a race at the bloody TT, yeah? It doesn't get any bigger than that. And if you can do that, mate, then you can do this, sure as I'm standing here. Now don't you worry. This van is running bloody mint, and remember you've got a team around you to make this happen as well. We're all working towards the same goal. So go out there and have fun, and beyond that, drive it like you've stolen it!"

"Yes, but what if I've—?" Dave started to say.

"If you've shit yourself, Dave, well, it just shows you care," Guy told him.

"That's... reassuring...?"

"Engines off for final instructions over the megaphone," said Monty, pointing to the race official stood on the start line, but Dave was currently wrestling with the Velcro on his new gloves. "Here," said Monty, reaching over and turning the engine off. "Dave, you can do this. *We* can do this," he said, looking at his teammates, but then quickly to Dave only, because Guy's eyes were starting to have a strange effect on him and he didn't want to fall into a trance again at such an important point in time. "Dave, it was my life's ambition to get on a TT podium with you. That may never happen. But winning an Isle Le Mans TT would be a brilliant second best, and something I'd be pleased as punch to accomplish. Now blow the bloody doors off this thing!" he said, slapping the dashboard.

The orange army who were so pivotal to the very existence of motorsport on the Island had done the organisers proud. Unpaid marshals had volunteered en masse to support the event and, once again, they showed what a spectacular, committed, and selfless group of folks they were. Their vibrant orange tabards could be seen peppered around the track, and this lot were as eager as those racing to see the action start. And speaking of the Orange Army, or at least one member thereof...

"Clear the grid, please!" yelled the race official, producing a firm burst on his air horn to reinforce the request.

Monty now stood outside Dave's window. Dave was holding his hand tightly. He broke his steely focus away from the track ahead, just for a moment, looking through the open window to his ever-present friend. "Monty," he whispered, before repeating it louder. "Monty... I'm feeling a bit emotional," he said. "You're my best friend, Monty. I love you, you know that?"

"I do," replied Monty, patting Dave's hand. "Now get this beauty..." he said, slapping the side of the van... "out there and show them how it's bloody done. Give them a good thrashing, mate!"

Monty wiped a rogue tear from his cheek and quickly made his way off the track, before realising something perhaps of some small degree of importance...

"Oh, bollocks!" he screamed to the nearest steward, just about the same time as Dave started gesticulating wildly from inside the vehicle. "Excuse me!" shouted Monty. "I've taken the bloody keys to the van! Can you give them back to Number Three, please? Otherwise, that bugger's going nowhere fast!"

With mere seconds to spare, Dave was reunited with his ignition key and the van's engine burst into glorious, combustive life. Team Frank & Stan watched on with childlike exuberance, wide-eyed and excitable, jumping and waving support, along with the ever-expanding crowd which swelled by the minute. Guy Martin put his arms around his crew, smiling at them each in turn like a proud papa. As rubber screeched on the start line, it never was clear if Dave Quirk, TT Winner, had in fact shat himself on the start line.

Isle Le Mans TT was a *Go, Go, Go*...

## Chapter
# SEVENTEEN

The cheery melody of a traditional fun fair mixed well with the alluring aroma from hotdogs and candyfloss. Throw in a backdrop of screaming engines, and with a smattering of warm sunshine on offer, you had all the ingredients you required for smiling faces, Manx and non-Manx alike.

One lone face was not smiling, however — that belonging to Stella, who sat perched on a stack of four car tyres about ten metres away from the track, watching the vans hurtling by with a casual sort of indifference. Frank had been keeping a watchful, fatherly eye on her, thinking she perhaps simply needed a little bit of time by herself for whatever reason. But when he noticed she'd not been smoking for a good half hour or so, he knew something must be terribly wrong, and felt the need to intervene. He approached from the front, in clear line of sight, to avoid startling her. Startling her was never a wise course of action, as that tended to provoke an attack of some kind be it physical or verbal. He waved as he approached, signalling he meant no harm and came in peace.

"Heya, Stella. Why are you sat on a stack of tyres by yourself? Are you all right?"

She gave out a protracted sigh. "It's good for my piles, sitting on tyres, as it spreads out your cheeks," she said, pointing in the general vicinity of her arse's enlarged blood vessels. "I've got a cushion ring I sit on at home, but I left in a bit of a rush."

This was entirely more information than Frank either needed or wanted, but he said nothing, allowing her, without complaint, to continue.

Stella indicated towards the distant figure of Monty, perched as he was over the crash barrier, his attention unwavering, glued to the racing action, and clicking what appeared to be a hand counter every time the team's van went by. "Right now, I'm trying to figure out why Monty is counting the laps," she remarked.

"I think Dave was yanking his chain earlier," Frank told her. "I overheard him saying to Monty that it was his job to count them manually, explaining that ordinarily it was all done automatically with some sort of computer system and a tracker on the van. A *transgender*, Dave told him."

"A transponder?" asked Stella.

"Of course," Frank replied. "I think he just wanted to say, *Now you'll be the transgender today*, to poor Monty. Which he did."

"Simple minds," observed Stella.

"Indeed," agreed Frank. "Funny thing is, I suspect Monty knows the difference, and not only that but can see right through Dave's counting ruse as well. He's not as stupid as he sometimes appears. I think he just does it for a laugh."

"Hmm," Stella replied noncommittally, having no dog in the fight one way or the other.

"Anyway," Frank continued, moving in a bit closer. "You look really sad over here on your own, Stella. You know how much we care for you. And I should probably tell you that Lee's arrived. I think he wants to see you, Stella."

Stella kicked her heel sharply into the tyre wall at the sound of Lee's name. "He can kiss my magnificent, splendiferous ass!" she shouted. "Well, he could if it wasn't so sore," she corrected herself. "All joking aside... though my arse really is sore... I have no desire to see that cheating bastard. He can sod off back to sleeping in bins for all I care."

"I know you're upset, Stella," Frank conceded. "He's told me as much. And I'm not privy to everything that's gone on between you two lately... But Lee has asked me to come over because he needs to show you something. It's very, very important, according to him."

Stella didn't reply, preferring instead to watch the vans as they came around again, even though she wasn't all that interested in them at present.

"Stella, I think you should go talk to him," Frank went on, his tone gentle as he could make it. "You know I'd never do anything to hurt you. You know that, right? You're like a daughter to me, Stella, so please trust me, okay?" he said, reaching out for her hand.

"Fucksake, I'll do it alright? If only to stop you getting all bloody maudlin on me and embarrassing yourself further," she said. And, with that, she jumped down from her stack of tyres, throwing him an irritated glance. "As long as you shut the hell up, I'll do it."

Frank escorted her away from the racetrack entirely, through the carpark, and over to an adjacent field. The field was empty aside from the trailer of an articulated lorry parked there, about twenty metres in, along with a lone velvet-upholstered chair with gold trim. Frank introduced the chair to Stella with a wave of his hand. "Take a seat," he instructed.

"I thought I told you to shut the hell up!" came her response. "Did I or did I not tell you to shut the hell up?" she demanded.

"Stella, please. If you would?" he said, hand still held out to the chair, and maintaining as mild a demeanour as he could muster given that he was being shouted at.

"What is this rubbish?" Stella barked. "I don't like surprises! What is this rubbish? It's rubbish!"

"Just take a fuckin seat!" yelled Frank, but not in an unkind manner despite his language.

Stella finally took a seat, though not liking it one bit. "I need my cushion!" she said, even though the padded chair was actually quite comfortable. She looked on with suspicion, and with those suspicions roused only further by the arrival of Molly, Jessie, Stan, and several other nosey buggers come along intrigued to see what the hell might possibly be going on here, especially as a pair of costumed performers appeared from either side of the trailer, dressed up as lions like in a pantomime show.

Before Stella had opportunity to leave, or to question why she was sat on a regal-looking chair in the middle of a goddamn field, the seductive dulcet tones of Hugh Jackman warbled from speakers set up on the steps of a temporary staircase leading up to the base of the trailer at its middle. The warble of Hugh's voice increased in intensity at the same time as a gaily dressed acrobat, appearing from parts unknown, performed three back-flips up the steps, landing in position to pull down on a green cord, with the resulting action releasing a tarpaulin acting as a false wall and with the contents of the trailer finally revealed.

Painted onto a large decorative sign in prominent lettering, and suspended from the roof of the trailer against the back wall by two gold chains, were the words:

## THE GREATEST SHOWMAN

Right on cue, a spotlight shone onto a solitary figure in the centre of the makeshift stage. The figure turned and looked to the light, and with a flick of the arm held out a black cane with polished chrome head that flashed against the illumination. The cane was then thrust down to tap-tap-tap the floor, replicating the beat of the music. This also served to signal additional performers, apparently, as more of them appeared from behind the trailer.

Stella looked up to Frank, who now stood with his hand resting on her shoulder. "Fucking hell, is that Lee?" she asked. "That looks an awful lot like Lee. Is that Lee?" To which she received only a wide grin from Frank in return.

Lee was utterly immaculate, dressed in an opulent waistcoated ensemble of red velvet that matched the chair on which Stella's sore bum was currently sat, replete with ornate gold detail. With a tap of the cane once more, one of the acrobats tossed a top hat to Lee, which he snatched up mid-air quite handily and placed on his head, completing his outfit.

## FRANK & STAN'S BUCKET LIST #3: ISLE 'LE MANS' TT

The volume of the music attracted additional spectators, who marvelled as more acrobats, a strongman, two men on stilts, and a wee little person recreated the opening credits scene from the film of the aforementioned name — *The Greatest Showman*, with Hugh Jackman starring, hence his recorded voice warbling over the speakers — with aplomb. Lee theatrically marched down the wooden stairs, attracting his co-stars like bees to a nectar-heavy flower in the process. Those stood behind Stella, though no wiser than Stella as to what the hell was precisely going on, nevertheless embraced the unfolding presentation, clapping and waving their hands as if they were also part of the performance. Stella, her earlier displeasure notwithstanding, found her foot to be also indulging itself, tapping itself along to the beat despite her now admittedly mild protests.

As the song built up a crescendo, on towards its finish, the entire cast formed a semi-circle in front of Stella as they all together belted out the lyrics the film's theme tune — not lip-syncing, actually singing — and with the actors in their lion costumes no longer stationary but now frolicking in front.

Stella was breathless as both the music and motion came to an abrupt halt, with the performers seemingly hit with a pause button as not one of them moved a single inch.

After several long, agonising seconds of no movement at all, Lee twirled his cane like a baton, in a fashion that would have made a seven-year-old majorette green with envy, and took two steps forward, adopting a final position resting on one knee, in front of Stella. He raised his eyes up to her, slowly, using every opportunity to draw out the tension. His left hand rested on the head of his cane, and his right hand was employed removing his top hat which was then held against his chest.

Lee didn't speak. At least not yet. Instead, like an auctioneer smashing down his gavel, he gave one final burst on his cane, thumping it on the ground, summonsing an acrobat to arrive in a mass of synchronised flailing limbs and coming to a controlled halt, mere inches from Lee.

Lee didn't look at the acrobat. Rather, he kept his eyes locked on Stella, though he lifted the end of the cane in a well-rehearsed motion to the acrobat. Then acrobat, in return, placed something onto the protruding, polished metal tip — a small shiny object — after which Lee retracted the cane, end carefully held up, to his side once again.

Not breaking eye contact with Stella, Lee now presented the pointed end of the cane to Stella. Stella looked up to Frank with her jaw agape, as she attended to the cane, taking in her hand and removing from it a platinum ring. Before she had chance to say a word, however, Lee swopped knees, turning his attention to a beaming Frank and Stan.

"With your permission, Frank and Stan?" asked Lee.

"Absolutely one hundred..." replied Stan. But his voice was breaking, and so overcome with emotion was he that he was unable to continue.

"One hundred percent," Frank finished for him. "Do carry on, Lee," he said, and just in time as well because he was getting a fair bit choked up himself.

Lee placed the top hat back on his head, cleared his throat, and took Stella's hand in his. "Stella, would you care to..." he began, but Stan and Frank were not the only ones having trouble speaking. He cleared his throat once again before continuing... "Stella," he offered most humbly... "That is, if you could see your way clear, would you do me the enormous pleasure of becoming my wife?"

Stella pulled her hand away, raising both her hands, now, across her breast and placing them, each one, on top of Frank and Stan's own hands which were sat, one apiece, on her shoulders. "I think I'd like that very much," she told Lee, tears openly rolling down her face, flooding her cheeks like the River Mersey. "That would make me very happy. And I don't generally *do* happy, mind, but... yeah. Yeah, I think that'd make me very happy," she confirmed.

The cast, now free of their statuesque poses, all cheered, raising their arms into the air in delight, and they were joined, additionally, by the congregated observers who offered hearty applause as well.

Only the lion-costumed performers did not join in, since they had wandered off and were presently capering and cavorting about somewhat farther afield. In fact it appeared as if one of them was, in fact, currently engaged in the process of mounting the other.

"Can I stand up now?" asked Stella. "Only my arse is—"

"Are your piles playing you up, luv?" asked Lee. "I've brought your ring over with me, and I even gave it a bit of a proper wipe-down for you."

"Now that's real love," replied Stella. "A ring for my finger and a ring for my arse. I say again, that is true love right there."

"It is indeed, at that," Lee agreed happily in his lilting Irish drawl. "So it is."

"Now come here and give your future wife a kiss, YOU GREAT TOSSPOT!" Stella instructed, in a strange, tumultuous mixture of happiness, aggravation, and relief.

After a passionate embrace, which included a little too much tongue action for the comfort of those stood near, Stella pulled back, appearing as if she might perhaps have something to say but wasn't quite sure how to say it.

"What is it, Stella?" Lee encouraged her.

"You and Susie..." she began... "I thought... fucksake, I owe you both an apology. I thought you were cheating on me, maybe even the two of you together, and now I say those words out loud, I can't believe I was so stupid as to—"

"You don't have to worry a bit about that," Lee assured her. "Not one least little bit. Alright? Me and Susie, we've been sneaking around your back for so long planning this thing and setting it up, it's a wonder you didn't murder the both of us by now."

"I thought about it," Stella offered, only half joking.

"Ha-ha! I'm sure you did!" Lee told her.

"There's one thing I'm left wondering about," said Stella.

"Yes?" said Lee.

"The whole Hugh Jackman movie theme. What made you...?"

"It's your favourite film, yes?"

In response to Stella's expression of surprise, Lee went on, "What? You think I didn't know that? You think I don't know what makes my woman happy? You think I don't know how to please her, then?"

"No. You know how to do that just fine," Stella admitted.

At which point more excessively sloppy, tongue-heavy kissing ensued, much to onlookers' discomfort.

Off in the field, some distance away, the two lion-costumed performers were indeed going at, with the one atop the other thrusting enthusiastically, and the one on the bottom springing its haunches up and down most accommodatingly. How they were accomplishing this remains a mystery, since the costumes did not possess the proper placement of holes allowing such a thing to occur. And yet, somehow, against all odds, they had found a way. Love always finds a way.

It was, in fact, a very good day.

*Chapter*
# EIGHTEEN

*... Chris Kinley here and I'm preparing myself for a very long day at the inaugural Isle Le Mans TT. We're just coming up to the two-hour mark and the racing has been gripping. You really should get yourself along here as it's been a terrific day so far. There are teams that are pushing hard, and others that are here for more a gentle, leisurely drive, just enjoying themselves without worry of winning the race...*

*I've been keeping an eye on the leaderboard, but at this early stage there's not much worth relating. However, I can see that the guys from the BBC, their Top Gear team, are setting the early pace. The teams we expect to be at or near the top of the leaderboard as we get further along are those who've opted to enter a sidecar, and that's reflective of the current standings. I won't read them all out at this time, not every one, because they'll all have changed position by the time I've got to the bottom of the board. But what I will tell you is that Peter Hickman's team are flying at the moment and sitting, after the BBC team's lead, in second place, with the Napier and Thomas outfit in third, the McMullan brothers in fourth, and Guy Martin's team taking up fifth...*

*Remember, as I said, this can all change in an instant. This really is an endurance test, not only for the drivers, but for the machinery, also. Adding to the excitement, presently, the vans are coming in for the changeover in drivers, and we've seen a few slick substitutions, while others, not so much...*

*Ha! I see one driver managed to get himself into the wrong van before correcting himself! Oh, I'll spare his blushes by having a quick word with Guy Martin instead, who's poised and ready for action. Maybe I can just get to him before he's off...*

*Bear with me folks...*

*And, yes, I'm here with Guy! Guy, you look focussed. I can see that you're really looking forward to this?*

GM: Now then, boss. I'm buzzing and can't wait to get out there. My mate Dave has been putting the hammer down, as you've no doubt seen. He's flying, and that's going to make my job a little bit easier, no doubt.

CK: *Any strategy or tactics from your side?*

GM: Do you like cats or dogs, Chris?

CK: *What?*

GM: I'm not sure myself, and I was just wondering what your thoughts were?

CK: *Ha-ha! This is like interviewing you on the TT grid, Guy. You always love throwing me a curveball. Well, then. I'll go for cats, Guy.*

GM: Champion. Right, I think this is Dave coming in, so we'll pick up on this later. Can I just say, Chris, there's collection buckets about today and all money raised is going to a fantastic initiative, the TT Farm, so please dig deep!

CK: *You heard him, folks! I'll just take a few steps back and see how this changeover goes. They'll be adding fuel and giving the van a once-over. Dave Quirk is just bringing the van to a stop, and his pit crew are straight in and, yes, giving the tyres a check and getting fuel into the tank. His teammate, Monty Montgomery, is doing a superb job getting the windscreen squeaky clean, I see. It does look like Dave's perhaps had a bit of a tussle out there judging by the dints on the rear quarter!*

Dave staggered out of the van, with this legs giving way beneath him. He'd unfastened the front of his racing overalls, and let the outfit hang down at the waist, with sweat glistening off his chest in the cool November sunshine. He reached for a bottle of water, whipping his helmet off to take several deep quaffs. Monty appeared in Dave's corner, so to speak, like a boxer's trainer, wiping down his charge. Chris Kinley went in to have a word, but judging by the furious expression, as well as the salvo of expletives issuing between gulps of water, Chis thought better of it, moving to the neighbouring garage instead to continue his coverage.

Dave drained the contents of the bottle. "That bellend!" he shouted, between gulps of air instead of water, now, to catch his breath.

"Who? Chris Kinley?" asked a surprised Monty. "What did he do? I think he just wanted to—?"

"No, Napier and Thomas!" Dave clarified, taking deep breaths, now, out of anger. "Or whichever shitstick of the two was driving Rodney Franks' van this last go-round. They tried to take me out half a dozen times out there. It was like the bloody stock cars at times! Unfuckingbelievable! If this race wasn't as important as it is, I'd have rammed into their own van, pulled the driver out bodily, and used his windpipe as a bloody boot scraper!"

"Other than that, how's the van...?" asked Monty.

"Perfect, she's running like a dream, but seriously, it's proper hard work out there for two hours Monty. Where are we on the leaderboard?"

"Fifth. But you've got the second-quickest lap behind the BBC's team."

Being a competitive sportsman, Dave's anger fell away at this consideration. "Hmm, second quickest. Say, that's not too bad, Monty, is it?" he said, looking over to the nearest scoreboard, just quick enough to see Guy Martin's first lap time beat his own. "Jaysus, Guy's absolutely flying!" he said. "Oh, god, can we not get security to rid us of this useless idiot?" Dave remarked, in reference to the approaching Rodney Franks, who he tried his best to ignore.

Rodney slow-clapped his arrival. It was unclear whether he was giving Dave applause, or if the applause was directed at himself, self-important twat that he was. "Looking good out there, Quirk," he said, not-at-all sincerely. "But, here, maybe not so much?" he added, pointing to Dave's partially exposed body. "Despite that, it really is turning out to be a fantastic event, isn't it? And you don't even have to thank me for letting you host the event here! It's my distinct pleasure."

"Your boys are either going to get suspended, or they're going to be subjected to a quick-onset fist-related tooth disorder, Franks," Dave answered him, disregarding Franks' not-so-pleasant pleasantries. "They smashed into me a number of times, you bastard, and If I was being cynical, I'd have to think it was because they didn't want us to finish."

"Perish the thought, Dave!" replied Franks, using Dave's Christian name as if they were fast friends. "I'll be sure to have a word with the lads and remind them that this is a charity event, after all."

"I'm sure you will," said Dave, and if looks could kill then Rodney Franks would currently have found himself drawn & quartered.

"And speaking of this being a charity event," Franks went on in his inimitable, insufferably annoying tone. "Have you managed to raise all the money you require? It would be such an awful, terrible shame if your team were to finish above mine and you *still* didn't have the requisite funds to buy the farm."

"*You'll* have bought the farm in just a minute, if you don't shut the hell up," Dave muttered under his breath.

Monty held his arm across Dave's chest, as having a driver arrested for murder at this stage of the race wouldn't have been the most productive idea, strategically speaking.

"The charity will have more than enough money to cover the cost of the farm, Rodney," Monty told Franks, in a remarkably calm voice considering present circumstances.

"Oh that is indeed great news, Mr Montgomery. I was rather concerned, you see, as I did hear talk you'd had a rash of bad luck regarding one of your sponsors."

"And what knowledge would you have about that, *Rodney?*" Dave said, spitting out Franks' name as a curse, and pressing against Monty's fortunately still-outstretched restraining arm.

Franks, in response to Dave's obvious insinuation, did his very best impression of Edvard Munch's *The Scream*, with his hands held to either side of his head in horror. "Why, I'm not entirely certain what you're suggesting, David. How dreadful! Are you accusing me of something?"

"Leave it, Dave," said Monty, now stood as a barrier in front of an increasingly agitated Dave, lest his friend should find himself at Her Majesty's pleasure.

All Dave could do was to clench and unclench his fists in succession, before finally prodding a finger in the air in Franks' general direction. "You're lucky Monty's holding me back, Rodney! Otherwise, I'd take your head clean off your shoulders!"

Rodney Franks really was a master at being a pain in the arse. He was like a hyena nipping away at a lion. But, he did know when the time had come to retreat. "Oh, Dave!" shouted Rodney, only when he was a safe distance away. He held his pinkie finger to his mouth, to simulate a phone. "You should have called the TV company to make sure they'd still be coming, dear boy! Such a horrible shame they cancelled!"

Dave kicked at a traffic cone in frustration as Franks took his leave. It helped a little. But only a little. "Why was I so stupid?" he shouted to the heavens. "I know how devious that bastard is, and I only had to call the TV crew yesterday to confirm! *Shiiit!*" Then he turned to Monty. "So. Did the guys at the gate give us a tally?"

"Yeah. We've had a little over two thousand come through in attendance," Monty told him.

"That's good," said Dave, nodding, forefinger curled over his lips like a question mark. "Good, good. That's actually a lot more than we've expected. So that's good."

"It is," Monty agreed. "But that still makes us short, unfortunately."

Dave held his finger to his lips, eyes shifting up and to the left as he ran the figures around his head. "Shit, shit, shit. We're still about forty grand short, aren't we? That's a lot. Rodney Franks has shafted us right over on this one. I mean, if we were to win the race outright, we would keep the prize money. But I can't say it's entirely likely we'd win. Plus I'm not sure how it'd look anyway, collecting prize money for a race we've ourselves organised."

Monty threw an angry glare to Rodney's camp, shooting daggers from his eyes, but to no avail. Of course, it may not have helped that half of the daggers missed.

"We need to ask Frank and Stan to come up with more money on their end, Dave. It's the only way," Monty proposed.

Dave removed his finger from his lips and used his hand to knead his forehead. "Monty, they've sunk a fortune into this already," he said. "This may sound stupid, but I've really enjoyed what we've done getting this whole thing off the ground. Frank and Stan wanted to get professional help... wait, let me rephrase... they wanted to bring in *professionals*, that is. They wanted to bring in professionals to run the day. But I assured them that we could do it, didn't I?"

"You and me," Monty said. "Yeah."

"Right. I told them to trust us with it, and that's just what they've done, haven't they? Monty, this means a lot to me. To *us*. Yeah? And I think I'd rather do this without being bailed out by the two of them. They don't need that. They don't bloody need that. And I want to repay them for what they've done for us. Do you know what I mean?" Dave went on. "I just want to do what I promised," he said. "I just want to do what I promised, yeah?"

Monty smiled. "I know exactly what you mean, Dave," he told his friend, clapping him on the shoulder. "Something will come up, Dave, don't you worry," he said. "Something is sure to come up, just you see."

Dave forced a half-smile out of his face before giving a sudden start, eyes going wide.

"What is it?" Monty asked, concerned.

"It's Lee," Dave answered him. "Why is Lee walking around like he's on his way to join a fox hunt?"

"You could say he *did* find his fox, Dave," Monty explained. "He's just proposed to Stella. Impressive it was, too, from what I could see. Music, a troupe of acrobats, and even a pair of lions. The lions were my favourite part."

"Bloody hell, that must've cost a fortune. That's money that could've gone to... No, I shouldn't think that," Dave said, correcting himself. He thought for a moment. "Real lions?" he asked. But he didn't wait for an answer to that. Because lions, real or no, paled in comparison to... "Lee and Stella. Fucking hell," he observed. "That boy has certainly got his work cut out," he offered, at which point both he and Monty fell silent, pondering this.

"Deserves a medal," suggested Monty after a bit. "Or sainthood," he added, shivering briefly at the thought.

"Or a sainthood," Dave agreed, shuddering as well, and doing back up his coveralls.

The garage of Team Frank & Stan had become the focal point for the local press who'd turned up — the regular, non-paying variety — and an increasing number of autograph hunters, both groups eager to greet Guy Martin on the conclusion of his initial two-hour stint. His racing prowess, as it turned out, extended to four-wheeled machines, evidenced by the fact he'd smashed the lap record several times, leaving the team nestled in overall second place as a result.

Whereas Dave had collapsed from the van like a seasick landsman unaccustomed to a pitching deck, Guy, on the other hand, sprang out from his seat like a Lincolnshire cat, offering Monty, there to greet him, an energetic high-five. "That was seriously good fun! I absolutely loved that! Bloody, bloody brilliant!" he shouted, even though Monty was standing right in front of him. Helmet now in hand, he moved on to his clutch of admirers as fresh as if he'd just woken up from a lovely nap. At which point he began signing autographs with a practised fluidity, pausing only for the occasional fan-requested selfie, with himself of course included in the shot. And speaking of photos...

"Smile!" shouted Molly, who was doing a sterling job as the unofficial team photographer.

"Lindum!" Guy called out, turning with a camera-ready grin.

"Perfect!" Molly returned. Though it was of course impossible to take a bad photograph of Guy Martin, as the camera adored him.

"Dave?" Molly called over, raising her camera up.

"Uh... Double Gloucester?" he said. But the joke wasn't so funny the second time around. Plus, everything just naturally sounded better when Guy Martin said it anyway.

"Perfect," Molly said, somewhat less enthusiastically, but giving Dave a jovial wave.

"Don't forget the camera adds ten pounds!" Dave reminded her, helpfully. "Hey, if you see your father, will you tell he and Stan that Monty's just headed out, and that Guy's got us up to second place?"

Molly moved in for a close-up shot of Dave, seeing as how Guy Martin was currently surrounded and so presently unavailable, and Dave obliged her with his most sincere catalogue pose. She glanced over to Guy, but he was still busy. She lowered her camera.

"They should be over soon, actually," she said to Dave, pointing over to the fairground. "Honestly, they're like two big children. They were playing on that thing where you sit on a big tube and beat each other up with inflatable sticks. I did remind my father that this was perhaps not the most dignified of ideas, nor the safest, for two grown men, but he told me to bugger off! Not in those words of course, but... No, actually, now I think on it, I believe he did use those exact words!" she said, laughing. "I do have some good photos of Stan being sent face-first into the ball pit, though."

"That sounds like something Stan would enjoy," Dave grinned. "Anyway, I'm going to jump in the shower right now because I'm in a bit of a desperate state, as Lee might say. I want to be fresh for my next trip out on the track."

"Or because a certain young lady will be here soon?" Molly teased him.

"You could be right, Molly, you could be right. Or, my attending to personal hygiene could be purely incidental!"

"I'm not buying it, Dave," Molly answered him, laughing.

"Yes well I'll be going for that shower now," he told her. "So I don't want to catch you peering around the corner taking shots of me in the nude, yet again!" He said this last bit loudly, expecting to generate some sort of buzz. But, unfortunately for Dave, it was only Guy Martin anybody was interested in at the present time.

In every direction, Molly's camera was met with smiling faces. She just clicked away, capturing the natural expression of people thoroughly enjoying themselves. She lowered her camera, taking in the joyous, exuberant atmosphere for a moment, her own face smiling along with that of the others. When she'd initially been told about the charity fundraiser event, she'd envisioned nothing more than a glorified go-kart race, with a few men and their dogs turning out to watch a few clapped-out vans pottering around a track on a Sunday morning. She couldn't conceive how the event would in fact turn out, with thousands in attendance and in what, from the looks of things, the enjoyment on people's faces, would likely turn out to be a recurring event. She was proud of her father and Stan. Proud of everyone involved in making it happen.

"Excuse me!" shouted a voice from behind. "Excuse me? Miss?"

Molly turned, finding a man in an orange tabard waving to her, which she took to be a request to have a picture taken. She raised up her camera obligingly but, once in the viewfinder, she saw he hadn't broken into a pose as expected. "Excuse me!" he repeated, waving his arms to get her attention still.

"Yes?" she said, bringing the camera down, shifting her focus.

"I saw you earlier talking to the two fellows with the inflatable sticks, and, well, are you Molly?"

"Oh no," she said. "What sort of mischief have those two gotten themselves into now?"

"No, it's nothing like that," the marshal said, holding his hand out in front of him. "Look, I don't want to panic you, but I need to tell you there's been some sort of an accident."

"What? What kind of accident? How do you mean?" Molly replied, her vague, somewhat-indulgent type of annoyance regarding her father and Stan's shenanigans now shifting to alarm. "What's happened??"

"I didn't see it, I'm afraid. But he's with the ambulance now. I was asked to come and fetch you."

Molly hurried along, accompanied by the helpful marshal. "Ambulance? Is he okay?" she asked. But she didn't wait for a response, having caught a glimpse of the paramedics further up the field. "I tried bloody telling him he should be taking it easier. He's got a condition, you know. He's ill. But my father doesn't listen to anybody," she told the marshal.

"I don't know anything about that, I'm afraid," the marshal told her, unsure what else to say.

"Excuse me," she said, once they'd come up to the ambulance. There was a circle of curious onlookers gathered round, blocking the way. "Excuse me!" she said again, in a rather more forceful tone this time. "Please, let me through!"

And there was her father, head down, slumped up against the ambulance, one arm covering his face, a paramedic attending to him.

"Dad!" shouted Molly, relieved to see him standing, at least. "I told you to take it easy!" she scolded him as she moved in closer. "I *told* him," she repeated, this time to the paramedic, the concern in her voice obvious, as she reached his side.

"You need to be careful," Molly admonished her father dotingly, checking him over from head to toe, from stem to stern, despite the paramedic's available presence. "You're not indestructible, you know," she carried on. "Have you broken anything?" she asked. "Has he broken anything?" she asked, turning to the paramedic, but didn't wait for a response from her, instead continuing directly, saying to her father, "My god, Dad, you gave me a fright," and leaning in and giving him a cuddle. "Dad? Dad, why are you not saying anything? Dad...?"

She pulled away his arm from his face.

The colour was gone from Frank's face, save for his eyes, which were bloodshot, and his ashen cheeks were wet. He opened his mouth, but no words came out.

"Oh my god, Dad, what's happened to you??"

"He's fine, don't worry," the paramedic offered sympathetically. She smiled encouragingly. "All things considered," she added.

"All things...? What does that mean?" Molly said, pressing and prodding on her father, searching for injuries. "I don't understand. What's happened to him?"

The paramedic looked at Frank, placing a comforting hand on his shoulder gently, and then looked back to Molly. "Nothing, physically," she told Molly. "This gentleman is fine, as far as I'm aware. Again, all things considered."

"I don't understand!" shouted Molly. "Why do you keep saying that? What does that mean??"

Frank's jaw was still held open. Somehow words issued forth, from someplace deep within, even though his mouth wasn't moving. His voice was hoarse and dry. "Molly, it's not me," he said. "It's Stan. They think... No, they don't think... they know... he's had a heart attack."

## Chapter
# NINETEEN

The unseasonal warmth that'd so generously provided its blessing that afternoon inevitably yielded to the shortening winter's evening, giving up the ghost. Darkness fell upon the inaugural Isle Le Mans TT, and, like the sun's departing rays, those who'd been there mostly for the Family Fun Day eventually slipped away.

The day's activities, however, were far from over and both the diminishing light and lack of Fun Fair noises brought about a sense of pure racing as the sound of screaming engines were now even more apparent and the headlights illuminating the tarmac rather captivating. The most stalwart amongst the race spectators could be found congregated near to the pit area, since it was a veritable hive of activity, especially as fatigue mixed with lack of daylight were not ingredients for incident-free racing. In fact, a steady stream of vehicles appeared with crash-related damage, with most being treated quickly with, say, a wheel & tyre assembly swopped out and perhaps a wing pulled out of the way to keep a wheel well clear. On occasion, however, a vehicle did not fare so well and had to be taken out of the game entirely.

Team Frank & Stan's VW Transporter van was coping well, and aside from the unwanted advances it'd received earlier in the day from Napier & Thomas' vehicle it had managed to remain relatively dent-free. The constant pressure from the circuit racing, however, was demanding on the tyres and the van had gone through more rubber than a discount prostitute at a rodeo cowboy convention.

♪ *Strangers in the night!* ♪ sang Dave at full velocity, and at full volume as well to keep himself awake. To the spectators, this also served as a strange sort of serenade, if a brief one as Team Frank & Stan's van whizzed by, since Dave had the windows down so the cool evening air against his cheeks could help keep him alert. Having the windows down created a bit of drag on the vehicle, but it was a necessary trade-off.

The stopwatch fastened onto the dashboard counted down from two hours, with thirty-one minutes still remaining for Dave's turn at the wheel. ♪ *Exchanging glances! Wondering in the* ♪ —"Oh, shit!" he screamed, as the tyre wall side barrier appeared before him at once. "Come on Dave, keep your wits about you!" he shouted to himself, steering deftly away from the wall. The track in front, illuminated as it was only by headlights, was disconcerting, and especially so on a fairly circuitous track where the occasional sharp bend would come up somewhat unexpectedly.

Dave's lap time had decreased dramatically under cover of darkness, but so did that of the other teams. Those who'd attempted to carry on at top speed as they had during the daylight hours found themselves coming to rather a bad end, with their vehicles quickly taken out of the action from resulting crashes, and with the drivers and crew joining the ranks of the observers and relegated to mere spectator status thereafter.

Dave struggled with the level of concentration required, and with his most recent near miss with the tyre wall, his lap time decreased even further out of caution. Of the original twenty-five vans on the starting grid, only sixteen remained, which made for a little more room to negotiate, at least. But Dave was beginning to get a bizarre nighttime version of snow blindness, with the track appearing as if he were driving in a long, black, endless tunnel, with only the odd flicker of another van's headlights to break the unchanging effect. Cramps in his back were also becoming more frequent and, despite his best efforts, he felt himself leaning over the steering wheel.

## FRANK & STAN'S BUCKET LIST #3: ISLE 'LE MANS' TT

"Twenty-seven minutes, Dave! You can do this!" he said, shouting to himself again. He eased his head out the window, like a dog taken out for a drive in the family car. The chilled air acted as an alarm clock but the effect was short-lived as he could only hold this pose briefly, it being too difficult to properly pilot the van in this position. Every time Dave passed the pit area on each lap, Monty would, without fail, scream and wave his arms in praise and encouragement. Good ol' Monty.

As for the competition, the BBC-sponsored team were romping away, taking the lead, and The Stig, as it were, their chap in white overalls and helmet, was visibly quicker than anyone else on the track and a real class act. Those racers with an ego bigger than their ability attempting to match his speed, as previously described, led to their premature downfall. Also, and most unfortunately for Team Frank & Stan, Rodney Franks' team were still circulating at a very respectable pace. Their BTCC driver was sublime, in point of fact, with his average lap time showing up at second place on the leaderboard and only a short measure behind The Stig. Happily, Team Frank & Stan's own Guy Martin was a short distance behind, in third. Fortunately, as well, Dave and Monty were the equal of Napier and Thomas, and the result of this was that Team Frank & Stan showed up quite respectably in the top-five overall listings on the leaderboard.

"Twenty-one minutes! Dave, you've got this!" Dave shouted, rallying himself on as before. "C'mon, you can— oh, bugger!" were the last words he uttered, sadly, before the tyre wall he'd so expertly avoided on an earlier lap now captured its prize like a balding rubber harvester of vehicular souls.

There was no concern for his own safety as Dave jumped down from the van and out onto the track area, crouching by the front wing to assess the damage...

"We'll have to get this towed away!" shouted the first marshal to arrive on the scene moments later, and started reaching for his radio, to that end, but Dave protested.

"I can still drive her! She's all right!" he insisted.

The marshal lowered his radio, craning his neck up to look over Dave's shoulder at the damage himself. "I'll give you one chance before I have it towed," he offered. "After that—"

Dave leapt back in the cab, reversed away from the tyre-wall would-be reaper, and spun the van's tyres over the grass runoff area until he gained traction, finding purchase.

"She's absolutely fine!" shouted Dave to the sceptical marshal as he sped the van away, offering a thumbs-up, and quickly returning to the race. "Running like a dream! Right as rain!" he carried on, more to himself now, since the marshal could no longer hear him. Truth be told, though, he was unsure if he'd even make it back the short distance to the pit.

Dave wrestled with the steering wheel, and if he hadn't the good fortune, at least, of being less than a hundred metres from home, it soon became clear that their race would most certainly have been over if that were not the case.

He limped the injured van into the garage, where the team jumped into action. Dave exited the van, looking more wounded — in spirit, at least — than the vehicle. "I'm sorry. I only switched off for a second and then I was in those bloody tyres!" he told Guy and Monty as they rushed towards him. "I've bloody let you down! I've lost the race for us for sure! I'm sorry, lads. I'm so, so sorry."

Guy and Monty immediately set upon him, slapping Dave's back like they were trying to frantically dislodge something stuck in his throat. "Bollocks!" shouted Guy, patting away furiously. "Don't you dare say you've cost us this race! That there could've happened to any of us out there! Any of us! You hear? It's not easy, and if we have to retire from this race then so be it, but it won't be from—"

An object on the periphery had suddenly caught Martin's eye. "Something wicked this way comes," he explained to the others, grimly. Then, turning to the source of the unpleasantness, "Oi!" he shouted, his usually amiable face contorting into a mask of anger. "Bugger off, you!"

Rodney Franks strolled in like he owned the place. Which, unfortunately, he did.

"Now, now, Mr Martin. I only wanted to pop down to see if I could possibly be of assistance in any way. That was quite a smash-up my friend Dave had out there, and —"

"I'm not your friend, *Rodney*..." Dave cut in... "in any way, shape, or form, and you know that full well," he said.

"My goodness, Dave, I hate to say this," Franks continued on, with his same too-familiar form of address. "But that crash seems to have done something horrendous to your face. Do you want me to call the paramedics over? Maybe they could dash you off to a surgeon? Before the damage is irreversible?"

"Piss off, Rodney," growled Dave. "Your concern is touching, but the boys will have the van up and running in no time. And it's only cosmetic damage, so don't you worry. That's the van, I mean. There's nothing wrong with my face, you fecking tw–"

"He's not worth it, Dave," said Guy, holding Dave back to prevent a good pummelling upon Rodney Franks' person.

"Maybe, maybe not," Dave replied. "But there's only one way to find out, isn't there?"

Franks, of course, was there to gauge the severity and extent of the van's damage. But his investigative efforts were stymied by Guy, Monty, and Dave, who together provided a united front against his advances, leaving him little choice but to reluctantly take his leave. "Just let me know if there's any way I can help!" he called back over his shoulder, skipping off to return to whatever dark, fetid hole from whence he came.

Once Rodney was out of sight, Dave looked over his face in the van's side-view mirror, just to make sure Franks wasn't entirely taking the piss, but his face was fine, leading him to exclaim again, "Fecking tw–"

"Sorry, Dave," came the voice of one of the mechanics from under the van. "The suspension's well and truly knackered," he continued, rolling himself out from underneath on a wheeled creeper. "I've not got the spare parts to fix this, so I'm afraid it's game over."

Dave wiped some moisture from his cheek that had collected there, and he closed his eyes. "Well that's it, then." He opened his eyes back up, facing Guy and Monty again. "I'm sorry," he told them once more, and sighed a weary sigh. Guy held up his hand, pivoting it back-and-forth at the wrist, in a *it-can't-be-helped, mate* motion.

For Guy Martin and the rest of the crew, it was a sense of loss from a racing perspective, which was bad enough in itself. But, for Dave and Monty, it was so much more than that. Yes, they were concerned for their jobs. Beyond that, however, and much more significantly, they'd seen how much everyone had put into making the TT Farm a reality. The farm would have been an immensely important part of the community, and a boon for the Isle of Man. And now those hopes were dashed, their dreams torn away, simply as the result of a minute, momentary lapse of attention and a bloody tyre wall got in the way of it all.

Dave and Monty trudged out of the garage, hearts heavy, coming to a rest by a perimeter wall, and joining several other figures there huddled together watching as the remaining vans hurtled by.

A friendly chap with overalls covered in oil leaned in closer to Dave. With the copious oil stains over him, he looked something like a surgeon who'd just lost a trauma patient. "Heya. How's the van, then?" he asked, his sympathetic tone readily apparent. "I saw when you came off the track. You had quite a bump there."

Dave appreciated the camaraderie. "Suspension's buggered and we're out of the race," he commiserated. "We haven't got the parts we need," he told the fellow. "And you?"

"Engine blew. Hence, this," the oil-covered chap replied with a shrug of acceptance, resigned to his fate, and motioning to his saturated uniform. "But there's always next year, yeah?"

Dave raised his right arm up, firmly extending his middle finger as Rodney Franks' van went past. He couldn't see who was driving, Napier, Thomas, or the BTCC fella, but it didn't matter. His hearty salute, childish as it may have been, provided him at least a fleeting reprieve from the grief he felt.

The men lined up were like jilted lovers, dumped by the exes, all with a story of woe to share and joined together by a sense of what could have been. After a bit of quiet contemplation, the oil-covered chap had a few words to say.

"What about our suspension?"

"How's that?" asked Monty half-heartedly, as Dave still had his middle finger extended, but with a far-away look now in his eyes. "Your suspension ruined as well?"

"No, no," the other fellow answered. "Just the opposite."

Dave was suddenly paying attention again. The oil-covered chap continued...

"No, see, the engine in our van is in hundreds of pieces. It's done for, and ain't never comin' back to life. But the suspension's perfect. Not a scratch. And we're driving a VW as well. Not the exact same model, mind you, but the undercarriages of these vehicles often share the same suspension, yeah? No guarantees, now, but you're welcome to see if you can salvage what you—"

But Dave and Monty were already sprinting back to their garage to retrieve their mechanics that were, within seconds, lying under the oily chap's van and picking away at it like tramps on a roasted chicken's carcass.

"Well? How does it look...?" Dave was asking impatiently, after what seemed forever and a day, pacing about like an expectant father.

By this point, Guy was also under the van himself, lending a hand, and muttering to himself incoherently. Eventually, he presented himself to Dave, appearing from under their own van's chassis with a grin. Guy looked back at the other mechanics, and then up to Dave and Monty again. "Yeah," he said. "Yeah, we can do this, I think. This'll work."

"How long?" shouted Monty, hopping on the spot like he was in dire need of a wee.

"Ten more minutes!" answered Guy, already back under the van now. "Get yourself suited up and ready! We're back in the game!"

"You're up, Dave, it's still your turn," Monty said, slapping his friend's arm.

But the crash appeared to have dinted Dave's confidence as well as the van. Dave took in several deep breaths before finally answering.

"I can't do this," he said. "I think I've lost my conviction, Monty. What if I crash her again? Then we're truly done for."

Monty's response was to slap Dave across the face with his racing glove like a trout. "Shut it, you big girl's blouse!" he scolded him lovingly. "You're a bloody TT winner, Dave, or have you forgotten? You know how to handle pressure, you silly sod! Now get yourself suited up and ready, and you get out there and try your best," he told Dave, slapping the glove across Dave's chest now every few words to bring the point home. "Nothing can stop you! You're a beast! Nothing can stand in your way!" he said, hammering away. "Nothing can... oh forfucksake, what does this idiot want again?" groaned Monty, greeted by the vision of Rodney Franks, standing in their way, along with two rather reluctant-looking scrutineers he'd pulled along with him.

Rodney looked at the two officials, and then pointed to the donor suspension van, now sat cannibalised in Team Frank & Stan's garage, and tapping the air in front of him like a manic woodpecker. "They can't do that!" he insisted, with his trademark juvenile petulance. "Their van is out of the race, so that's it, they're disqualified! They can't just go and build another van!"

The officials did not appear to be entirely happy held in the company of Rodney Franks, with one of the two not even attempting to hide the look of open contempt over his face. "We don't have rules covering this," he said. Rodney started to protest, but the official would have none of it, shutting him down instantly. "In case you'd forgotten, this is a charity race, and not the F1 World Championship. And so as to your little throw-your-dummy-out-of-the-pram complaint, you've absolutely no luck there, I'm afraid, and I'm not at all interested. Can't help you. Come on, Derek," he said to his friend. "I'm not paid enough to deal with helmets like this idiot." And he and Derek left, leaving Rodney Franks twisting in the wind.

If Rodney were a cartoon, as young Tyler had suggested — a *bad* cartoon — he would presently have had steam coming out of his ears. A passing policeman, alerted by the commotion, poked his nose into the garage. "Right. What's all this, then? Everything okay in here?" he asked, his expert eyes training in on Franks, knowing a ne'er-do-well when he saw one.

Dave smiled a happy smile as the mechanics, meanwhile, toiled feverishly with the van. "Wonderful here, officer," Dave replied. "Although this chap," he added, nodding his head in Rodney's general direction. "Appears to be lost, as he's in the wrong garage."

"Come on, you!" said the officer to Rodney, obligingly. "Let's move along, shall we?"

With that sorted, an optimistic voice under the van shouted, "Two minutes!"

Monty scurried over to the open laptop on the workbench counter to check the race monitor live timings, but was somewhat disheartened by what greeted him. "We were seven laps ahead of Rodney's team, but with this delay, we're now nine laps down on them," he informed the others.

"At least we've got a chance, Monty!" shouted Guy, fist-bumping his dejected colleague. "Am I right or am I right?"

"You're right," Monty had to admit. And, then, noticing they had new visitors — welcome visitors, of the non-Rodney Franks variety — said, "Heya! There's a welcome sight for a change!!"

Dave was not in disagreement.

"Tyler really wanted to wish you good luck," Rebecca announced to Dave. "And so did I. So, you know... good luck," she said, standing on her tip-toes and placing a kiss on Dave's cheek, resulting in a serious case of blushing on Dave's part.

Ordinarily, Monty would have jumped right in under such circumstances and taken immense delight in pointing out Dave's acute embarrassment. But on this occasion he let it go, offering a warm smile instead. It felt like the right thing to do.

"Good luck, Big Dave!" Tyler chimed in. "Open up the bottle!"

"Throttle, honey!" Rebecca gently corrected her son. "You were supposed to say open up the *throttle!*"

"I like his idea better!" Monty laughed.

"As do I!" Dave agreed, ruffling Tyler's hair.

"It's all yours!" the last mechanic announced, slamming shut the bonnet. "She should be fine now. Just make sure you don't introduce her to that tyre wall again!"

Dave threw on his helmet and jumped into the cab, strapping himself in. Guy and Monty slapped the side of the van as he reversed out of the garage. Then came Dave's rallying cry...

"Right! It's on, chaps!" But then he looked worriedly at Becks, who was quite happily not a chap.

"It's okay!" she shouted. "Just go! Go, go, go!"

*Chapter*
# TWENTY

Frank gripped Jessie's hand as the doctor approached, looking over Stan's patient notes on his clipboard. "I think he's smiling," whispered Jessie. "Hopefully that's positive news?"

"I hope so too," Frank told her, easing out of the moulded plastic chair in the hospital waiting room, and standing to properly greet the physician. Frank cast a quick glance over to Molly, Stella, and Lee, before returning his full attention to the doctor.

"Are you family?" asked the doctor kindly, and directly to Frank, since Frank was the one standing.

"Yes!" Frank answered him. "I'm the, *ehm*, brother," he said, feeling a small white lie wouldn't hurt in the present situation.

"I'm Dr Sampson," the doctor said, offering a firm, friendly handshake. "I've got some great news!" Dr Sampson announced. "Everything went according to plan, and a new little girl has been brought into the world."

Frank's smile evaporated. "I don't understand. Has Stan had sex-reassignment surgery? I thought...?" Frank glanced back to Jessie and the others, but their faces told him that they were just as perplexed as he was. "I don't understand," Frank said again, his worry now muddled with bewilderment.

But before the good doctor could say another word, a colleague had arrived by his side, tapped him on the shoulder, and spoken something discreetly into his ear.

"Ah. Apologies," Dr Sampson came back. "Slight mistake. Only you were the first to stand, and sat here amongst the others, I thought surely... Well. You understand, of course."

Frank didn't understand, but he was starting to. He watched on as Dr Sampson turned to the others in the group waiting. That is, the larger group of people waiting that Frank & Co had sat amidst for lack of other available seating. The larger group, some of which, Frank now noticed, were sporting non-lit cigars out their mouths, while others were clutching a collective raft of festive helium balloons with things like *Congratulations!* and *It's a Girl!* emblazoned across them.

"So, *em*, yes, as I said," Dr Sampson went on, now addressing this larger group. "Mother is doing just fine, as is the brand-new baby girl. Father passed out during delivery, as the only complication, but he's by now recovered and back on his feet. So all's well."

The group thanked the doctor for the news, though the surprise factor had been markedly reduced. "Not so dramatic hearing it the second time around," someone grumbled, and several in the group cast Frank an evil eye.

"Sorry," Frank offered, pleading stupidity. "Apologies. And, *erm*, congratulations," he said, sitting back down.

The second doctor addressed Frank. "I'm Stan's doctor. You're here for Stan, then?" he asked.

"Yes!" answered Frank, desperate for news. But the doctor was looking away, smiling broadly, his attention on the other group and the celebratory balloons.

"Oi! Over here! Out with it!" barked Stella.

"Ah. Sorry about that," said the second doctor, still smiling. "So. Stan is doing just fine," he told them.

"Thank goodness," said Lee.

Frank looked on, brow furrowed, waiting for the doctor to continue. He did not at all appreciate the wide grin on this fellow's face, given the grave circumstances of Stan's arrival to the hospital and the seriousness of his condition. It was wildly inappropriate and terribly unprofessional, Frank thought, and he would most definitely be entering a complaint once this was all said and done.

"So. The patient is conscious," the doctor went on. "We're still conducting some tests, so he's going to be with us for a bit longer, but these are just routine at this point so no cause for concern," he said cheerfully. "Don't worry, he's quite comfortable at the moment. We've given him some morphine for the pain."

Frank was beginning to get fairly angry at the untimely nature of this doctor's unrelentingly sunny demeanour.

Stella gave out a choking sob. "I thought we'd lost the stupid old bugger," she blubbered.

"I'm sorry?" said the doctor, cocking his head, still grinning. "It's not so serious, having one of these. Very common, actually. You'd be surprised how many people come in each with—"

"You bastard!" Frank shouted, rising from his chair again.

At Frank's outburst, a large, thickset guard, great in both height and circumference, appeared from around a corner. "Dr Slughorn?" he asked, before the doctor casually waved him away.

"It's all right, Nigel, but thank you."

Nigel nodded. "Right. Call me if you need me," he said, slipping away again, presumably to eat another side of beef.

"Nigel's the dearest thing," Dr Slughorn remarked, accompanied by an affectionate chuckle, and more to himself than those he was addressing. "Would you like to see your brother now?" he asked abruptly. But nobody responded to the question. "Sir? Your brother? Would you like to see him now?" He was looking directly at Frank as he said this.

Frank blinked. Then he looked behind him, though saw no one there. He turned back around, realisation kicking in. "Oh! Yes! My brother! Yes!" he said. He coughed. "Yes, please," he said, happy to finally dispense with the chatter, and also happy to rid himself of what he saw as Dr Slughorn's smarmy grin.

Just as they were about to be led away to Stan's recovery room, however, Dave and Monty all but took the ward doors off their hinges, arriving on the scene like a corpulent Batman and a plump, ageing Robin.

"We just heard!" a frantic Dave shouted. "How is he?" demanded Dave of the doctor.

"Are you family?" asked the doctor.

Monty glanced at Dave. "His brothers, yes," Monty told the doctor, pointing between the two of them.

"Right. Brothers," Dave confirmed.

The doctor looked to his clipboard, riffling through the notes there. "Stan has a lot of brothers," he said, then shrugged and looked back up to them. "Well. Anyway," he told those assembled, his cheerful grin yet retained. "Your Stan nearly passed—"

"Passed??" echoed Dave.

"Oh my dear lord," said Molly.

"Jayzus," said Lee.

"*Nearly passed?*" Frank said, repeating the doctor's words. "*Then why are you—?*"

"Yes, it was rather a big one he had!" said Dr Slughorn merrily. "Of course others have had much larger, and gotten through it just fine. But for a first-timer, I imagine, it might seem—"

"You bastard!" Frank shouted, for a second time.

"I'm sorry?" Dr Slughorn asked, for a second time. "It's no cause for alarm," he said with a little laugh. "Honestly, we just provide them something for the pain, give them loads of water, and most times they'll pass—"

Stella had, at this point, had quite enough. "Now you listen here, Chuckles!" she said, snatching the clipboard from his hands, and looming over him. "If you laugh one more fucking time, *you're* the one who'll need a doctor!"

Nigel reappeared, and Dr Slughorn held up a hand, indicating he should remain at stand-by. "I say," he remarked to the overly concerned, increasingly agitated group before him. "Surely you're making an awful lot of fuss over a—?"

"Are you certain you're a doctor, Dr Slughorn?" asked Frank incredulously. "Is that even your real name? Who has a name like that?? What kind of outfit are you running here???"

"I have a name like that?" Dr Slughorn suggested. "And I don't run things here...?" As he said this, he was motioning to Nigel, the doctor beginning to realise the gravity of the situation when Stella started curling her hands into fists and cracking her knuckles in anticipation of a smackdown.

Nigel stepped closer just as Stella began to advance menacingly toward the good doctor. But he stopped, uncertain as to how to proceed. Yes, an attack upon the doctor's person by the husky woman did appear imminent. And yet Nigel found himself strangely drawn to the brutish beauty. And so he hesitated.

"Really an awful lot of fuss over a kidney stone," the doctor reiterated, this time managing to complete the observation.

"The... what?" said Stella, halting mid-stride.

"The what?" said Frank.

"The what?" said Dave. "We were told Stan had a heart attack!"

"We came straight away, as soon as we were given the news," added Monty. "Why didn't anyone tell us sooner?"

"A heart attack? Goodness gracious, no," Dr Slughorn said to them all. "May I...?" he asked of Stella, and an apologetic Stella handed him back his clipboard. "Yes," he went on, checking his notes quickly, though he didn't really need to. It was more in an effort to re-establish himself as the doctor in charge. "As I said, really quite common," he went on, holding the clipboard to his breast now. "We see patients come in nearly every day with them. It can certainly be alarming to someone who's never had one before, but ordinarily it's nothing too terribly serious and be sorted out easily enough."

"Oh," Frank told the doctor. "Oh," he told Nigel, who was now simply observing placidly.

Nigel, for his part, found himself considerably relieved. Despite his redoubtable appearance, he actually hated violence and made an effort, whenever possible, to avoid conflict at all costs.

Dr Slughorn continued, "Yes. Now your Mr Sidcup's stone is on the large side, but not so large that he can't pass it naturally. So we're trying for that, and giving him medication to manage the pain in the meantime. We'll have done imaging tests by now, and I'll view the results shortly along with our resident urologist. If Stanley can't pass the stone naturally, there's an option of extracorporeal shock wave lithotripsy, which, don't worry, is not as medieval as it sounds. It's just breaking the stone up with sound waves."

"Oh," said Frank.

"Right," the doctor went on. "And if the lithotripsy method isn't workable, then we just go in and snatch the little blighter out."

"Oh," said Frank.

"Snatch it out?" enquired Lee.

"Yes. We go up through the urethra and grab the little bugger," the doctor explained.

Lee, Monty, and Dave all winced and shuddered at this.

"He wouldn't feel a thing," Dr Slughorn assured them. "He'd be put under for it. Simple, easy procedure. Up the urethra, snatch up the stone, pull it out, and Bob's your uncle. No trouble at all. And the stent is left in the urethra for a few weeks during healing, and then slipped out at that time during a simple office follow-up visit. Easy peasy lemon squeezy!" he said, with a jolly chuckle.

At which point Lee, Monty, and Dave all winced and shuddered once again.

"Oh," said Frank.

There was a moment of silence as the reality of the situation settled in, until Molly spoke up.

"*Haaaannng* on," she said. "Dad," she said, turning to her father. "Didn't you tell me *quite specifically* that Stan'd had a heart attack?"

"Oh," said Frank.

"Quite specifically?" she pressed.

All eyes were now on Frank. Even Nigel, off to the side, still present, raised an eyebrow as if to say, *Well, then?*

"I thought..." Frank began. "I could've sworn that paramedic said... No wait... actually... actually, it was Stan, wasn't it? ... He told me... What did he tell me? ... He told me... he told me he thought he was dying, didn't he? He didn't... I suppose he didn't actually say heart attack specifically, did he? Not specifically. I just assumed..." he said, trailing off.

"Jayzus, Frank," said Lee.

Frank placed his hands over his face, and for a moment looked like he was about to introduce a fit of laughter, but his shoulders heaved. "I thought I'd lost him!" he sobbed. "I thought that stupid bastard had checked out before me!"

Stella pulled a handkerchief from her bosom and handed it to Frank, who readily accepted it, burying his face in it to sop up his tears as he continued to sob.

Nigel, who couldn't bear to see anyone in pain, stepped in to gently pat Frank on the back, sneaking admiring glances at Stella as he did so. To which Lee couldn't but notice, though did not get upset. "Bad luck, fella," Lee leaned over and whispered up into Nigel's ear. "This one's already taken, mate."

The sense of relief, of course, over Stan not dying was shared by all present, all Stan's closest friends, gathered there together to comfort each other in their moment of perceived grief. They had all, every one of them, thought about what Stan meant to them, and the notion of his possible loss had brought them all together in shared compassion. Stella managed to sum it up best...

"A bloody kidney stone!" she said, with a coarse cackle. "That scrawny little get did his best dying swan impression over a smegging kidney stone! Wait till I take the piss out of him over this! What a complete and utter wet lettuce!" To which no one could disagree. "Right, I'm going for a fag," she announced.

Dave looked at his watch. "It's not often I say this, but I'm with Stella this time. Come on, Monty, we need to get back to the race. To think Rodney Franks nearly won his bet over a soddin' kidney stone."

"Now I'm in the mood for steak-and-kidney pie," Monty mused aloud, as they both made their way out.

🏍

Up in the distance, a succession of van headlights flickered into view and then were gone again, like searchlights during the Blitz.

"Get your foot down, Monty! We're almost there!" commanded Dave. "Assuming Guy's still going, the poor bugger is going to be knackered! Why are we slowing down?"

Monty flicked on the car headlights to full beam. "I'm good, Dave, but I can't drive a car through a locked gate now, can I?" he told his anxious partner. "Why the hell are the gates all locked up?"

"*Shiiiiit*, I forgot!" replied Dave. "It was to do with the bloody insurance! The main gates had to be locked after the Fun Day ended, probably to stop people driving onto the ruddy race course by mistake. We'll need to leave the car for now and scale the fence, Monty," he told his mate.

"Do we now?" replied Monty, laughing at the absurdity of Dave's idea. "Seriously? You think we're going to be able to scale that, Dave, the two of us? It's got to be, what..." he said, arching his neck... "Twenty feet high? At least? The only way we'd get over that is if we'd been shot from a catapult."

"But..." Dave began, but he knew Monty was right. Still, it seemed the only way, and he was determined.

"Wait, over there, Dave," Monty told him. "I think I can see someone. Just there. Am I imagining things, or is there...?"

A faint light twirled against the pitch-black backdrop, like a sparkler on Guy Fawkes Night. It moved ever closer, slowly, with the light very gradually becoming increasingly brighter as it danced along. Eventually, a whistling man, slight of build, was revealed, twirling his torch like a baton as he meandered around the perimeter of the carpark. Finally, he came to a stop in front of their car, peering through a gap on the other side of the fence like an inquisitive horse.

"Guys! You can't park there, guys!" he called over, as Monty wound his driver-side window down.

"Let us in!" shouted Monty. "We've got to get in!"

"No, no!" replied the suspiciously slim man, pointing his torch at the car. "You can't park there, guys!"

"I'm not trying to park here, I'm trying to get in! We need to get in!" Monty protested.

"We don't have time for this," said Dave. "Crap, we don't have time for this, seriously."

"Hang on, Dave. Look closer. Is that not our friend Adrian?" said Monty. "Wait, is Adrian our friend?" he asked. "I can never actually remember."

"Adrian?" replied Dave. "That bloody jobsworth we nearly ended up fighting with at the TT? Fucking hell, I think you're right. That boy doesn't half get around, does he? But after our two previous encounters, I don't fancy our chances of getting through, now, with him remaining conscious."

And with that, Dave began reaching around, feeling about for anything that might be used as a form of blunt instrument.

"You can't hit him, Dave," Monty reminded his overzealous comrade-in-arms. "He's only doing his job, doing what he's been paid to do. Plus he's only a kid."

"Best not to take any chances?" Dave offered, but Monty opted for words over physical violence...

"It's Adrian, isn't it? Remember us? Dave and Monty? We're all friends, aren't we?"

Adrian eyed them suspiciously through the darkness. "I'm not so certain," he said. I seem to recall—"

"It looks like you've been working out, Adrian? You look well fit?" Dave offered, stepping out of the car.

"Right, stay back, you!" returned Adrian, waving his torch in an advisory fashion. "And there's no point in trying flattery, sir, as it will have no effect on me, I can assure you. I can't let you in, and that's that. Rules-is-rules."

Dave reached into his back pocket for his wallet, walking up to the fence as he did so.

"Here, no sudden moves!" Adrian shouted. "That's far enough!"

"No, look," Dave explained, counting out notes. "Take this," he told Adrian. "There's seventy pounds I've got here. Seventy pounds, right?"

Adrian stepped up to the fence, allowing Dave to stuff the money into his jacket pocket through the barrier.

"It's our way of making up for the confusion and potential upset from our previous encounters," Dave went on. "Yeah? There you go.

It's all yours. Keep it. It's all yours," he said, slapping Adrian on the chest through the gap in the fence, like sealing an envelope.

"Keep your hands to yourself, sir!" Adrian warned him.

Worried this could all go tits-up very quickly, and that he'd have just wasted seventy pounds, Dave did his best to calm the boy. "No offence meant!" he assured him. "We're all friends here. All friends. Yeah?"

Adrian saluted with his torch. "Very good, sir. Now you best be on your way," he told them. "I've got to return to my patrolling," he said, and he turned as if to commence doing just that.

"What about my seventy pounds!" Dave protested.

"You mean *my* seventy pounds?" Adrian corrected him, patting his now well-padded pocket.

"Look, we need to get in there as we're part of the race," Monty pleaded, attempting to be the voice of reason. "So be a good lad and open up the gates for us? Please? *Please*, Adrian. I know you mean well."

"I'm just doing my job," Adrian answered him, softening up a bit from Monty's gentle, kindly tone.

"I know you are," replied Monty.

"It's not an easy job. Not just anyone can do it," Adrian told him.

"No it's not. And no they can't, can they?" Monty said. His approach seemed to be gaining traction. "Now about this gate...?"

"The thing of it is, sir," Adrian admitted. "Is that I couldn't open this gate even if I wanted to. I don't have the keys for it. It's not within my jurisdiction, I'm afraid."

Monty's shoulders sagged. This appeared to be the end of the road. Until Adrian provided another option...

"Really, all you've got to do is just go through the smaller gate further up, the one for foot traffic. It's just there," he said, pointing.

"The... smaller gate?" Monty said.

"Right. For foot traffic," Adrian explained. "It's only cars that aren't allowed. People on foot can still go straight through."

"Why didn't you say so before??" an angry Dave interjected.

"You didn't ask nicely?" Adrian offered.

"What about the seventy pounds I gave you? That's not asking nicely??" a perturbed Dave asked.

"I didn't like your tone," Adrian elucidated. "But thanks for the seventy pounds," he said, patting his pocket again.

Before Dave could explode in anger, Monty came through, defusing the situation. "Right. Seventy pounds to keep an eye on the car, Adrian? How does that sound?"

"Sure," answered Adrian agreeably. "I still have to make my rounds. But I'll check on it each time I come by."

"Done," agreed Monty.

"Seventy pounds," grumbled Dave between heavy breaths as he and Monty sprinted across the carpark. "Seventy bloody pounds."

"It was well worth it, Dave!" said Monty, huffing and puffing. "We're almost there!"

With the pair of them desperately gasping for air, the racing circuit finally came into view. "There's not many vans left on the track," Dave observed, panting. "I don't think I can see our van out there. Monty? Can you see her...?"

"I can't," Monty came back. "At least not at the moment...?"

The two of them walked through the pit area, towards their garage, where the crew stood outside with mugs of tea in hand. Never had Monty and Dave wanted so much to see a garage empty. But, as they moved closer, they could see the outline of a van parked up within.

Dave fell to his knees, punching the tarmac, howling at the moon like a demonic werewolf. "Bastard!" he screamed, all-the-while continuing his assault on the track. Monty joined him, for he didn't like to see his friend suffer alone, but rather than scream in anger, he placed his head on the ground in abject disappointment. The dream was over.

After much screaming and general disruption, a mechanic by the name of Mike wandered over, standing above Dave and Monty, who were both maintaining a praying-to-Mecca position on the cold surface at present.

"How's your friend Stan getting on?" asked Mike. "Did he turn out all right?" enquired the mechanic, casually nibbling on a wholemeal biscuit.

Dave looked up at Mike the Mechanic, tears filling his eyes, prompting Mike to reach into his sleeve of biscuits and hand Dave a digestive.

A digestive is not what Dave was looking for, but he accepted it anyway. Hell, a biscuit's a biscuit, he thought. "Stan's absolutely fine, as it turns out," replied Dave to Mike. "But I can't promise he will be when I get my hands on him, sending us on a wild goose chase like that."

"At least we got some exercise, there at the end," said Monty, trying to look on the bright side of things.

"Yes, there was that," Dave had to admit.

"Of course it's made me famished, that exercise," Monty remarked, eying the sleeve of digestives in Mike's hand and hoping for a biscuit himself. "Absolutely ravenous?"

"Where's Guy… Is he injured?" Dave asked.

"Where's Guy? How do you mean?" Mike answered him, unsure if Dave had received a bump on the head. "He's out on track. Where else would he be?"

Dave jumped to his feet, grabbing the mechanic by the coveralls and pulling him close. "He's still going? What about the van??"

"Here. Mind my biscuits there," Mike objected, easing away from Dave's grip. "Guy's flying, and the van's holding it together."

"Ah-ha!" Monty shouted, returning to his feet and pointing towards the garage. When Mike the Mechanic looked to the garage to see what Monty was pointing at, Monty stole several biscuits from Mike's digestives sleeve. He was, after all, no fool.

"What? That van?" asked Mike. "Yeah, that's the parts van. Whadja think it was?" He looked back to Monty, but Monty suddenly wasn't speaking anymore, his mouth stuffed with biscuits as it was. Mike reached for another biscuit for himself and found his cache surprisingly lighter. He looked to the ground, thinking he must have dropped some.

"Mike! Details!" Dave urged him.

"Hmm? Oh," said Mike. "Well Guy's due back in about twenty minutes, so whoever's next up should think about getting ready, I expect?"

"And??" Dave pressed.

"Oh," said Mike again, remembering Monty and Dave had missed a good deal of the action. "Right, okay, so we're still within sniffing distance."

"That cannot be right. Can it?" asked Dave, wide-eyed.

"It's right alright," Mike assured him.

Dave turned to Monty. "Monty, my old son, you're up next, if I recall," Dave told him. "And assuming Mike's not having us on, there is no reason we cannot do this!"

Dave raised his eyes to the sky, offering a brief silent prayer. When he returned his eyes earthward, he loudly exclaimed, "Guy Martin, you absolute freakin' legend!"

At which point he and Monty joined hands and danced around in circles, like a game of Ring-a-Ring o' Rosy.

## Chapter
# TWENTY-ONE

*... You're listening to Manx Radio here on the Isle of Man and this is Chris Kinley who is, miraculously, still awake. I've managed to sneak in a few minutes of sleep, but I must admit, I'm starting to feel a little punch-drunk. I felt a little radio silence might be in order, as I think most of our local audience are asleep, but we've had a fantastic reaction from our friends further afield who've been listening in to our updates from the inaugural Isle Le Mans TT and so I'm carrying on...*

*As I walk around the pit area, it really is a party atmosphere exhibited, I can't help but notice. The guys are here to race, obviously, but it's a friendly, congenial sort of sensibility predominant here at the Isle Le Mans TT that you're not often witness to at a similar racing event...*

*I can see campfires burning away on the nearby fields, where family and friends of the competitors have set up camp for the evening, some of whom look like they've perhaps indulged in the beer tent longer than they should have, judging by the chap I can see staggering to a tent! I will confess to indulging in a few hotdogs and a couple of cold beers that were on offer myself. If you didn't manage to get down to the event this year, and there's a repeat of it next year, trust me, you'll want to make it here. It's truly been one of the best days I can remember!*

*... If I can focus my eyes on my watch... Yes, I see it's coming up to about six a.m. on the Isle of Man, and if my sleep-deprived brain can do the maths, we've been going for twenty-one hours. As anticipated, the demands on the drivers and vehicles has been intense, so much so that we're down to only eleven outfits left in the race. If you bear with me... excuse me, step aside, thank you, coming through...*

*Yes, here we go, I'm stood in front of the live timing board. I've got to hand it to the BBC's crew, they've really put the hammer down and are miles ahead of the rest. In second place, and I'm seriously impressed with this, is Peter Hickman's team. We know these guys are quick on two wheels, but they've surpassed themselves and currently sit, as I said, in second. Third place is Thomas and Napier, who you will recall are one of the teams that've opted to enter a sidecar, which they can use for a maximum of two hours, and, interestingly, have not yet taken it out. The only other team yet to use their sidecar is Guy Martin's team, so I suspect they've each got one eye on the other in that regard. I've heard a little whisper on the grapevine that there's no love lost between the two teams...*

*Guy Martin's team are just outside of the top five at the moment, but we should remember they had mechanical problems earlier so fair play for coming back into this. In fact, as I speak, I've just clapped eyes on the very team, or two of the three at least, Dave Quirk and Shaun 'Monty' Montgomery...*

*Now then, boys. Having fun?*

DQ: What's not to love, Chris? Racing and hotdogs, it's the perfect combination!

SM: Hotdogs.

CK: I understand you both had to make an emergency drive to the hospital, but Guy didn't let you down while you were gone, did he? He was flying!

DQ: You know, Chris. You read about people, particularly those considered famous, which Guy is, but I can honestly say he's the most down-to-earth, hardworking chaps we've ever met. You know we're doing all this to raise funds for the TT Farm, and Guy can't do enough to help. In fact he's already threatened to come back over to tune the farm machinery for us! Which we actually wouldn't mind at all. Overall, everyone here has been brilliant. Well, except for one lone idiot. But now's not the time for that, Chris, and I'll refrain from commenting any further on that.

CK: *You've both driven through the early hours, so I imagine you're running on pure adrenalin at this point in the game?*

SM: Not really, Chris, but we're so pumped up that it's keeping us going!

CK: *That's what I just... Nevermind. Guy's on his final stint at present, and then you're right back in this, and dare I say, you may make it onto the podium yet.*

DQ: Where's Napier and Thomas, if you don't mind me asking?

CK: *They're sat in third at the moment, but, like you, they're due out on the sidecar for the final two hours.*

DQ: How many laps are we behind Napier and Thomas?

CK: *About nine at the moment, and for the benefit of those at home, it's not about who crosses the finish line first when that horn sounds after twenty-four hours. It's about which team is quickest overall and has managed to complete the most laps. So slow and steady may be a tactic that doesn't guarantee victory. Presently, the BBC's outfit have extended their lead, with Peter Hickman's team hot on their heels. So, Dave and Monty. Guy's out for a little under an hour still, and then it's over to you for the final two hours, where you'll be finishing up in the sidecar. Excited?*

DQ: I can't wait, Chris, and hopefully the sun will be coming up and it'll be getting a bit lighter as we get to the closing stages. In fact, on that subject, Chris, I need to go and make myself a little bit lighter ahead of our next session. All those hotdogs, if you know what I mean.

CK: *Thanks for the imagery, Dave. We'll be with all the teams right up until the end, so, with that, I'll hand back to the studio.*

---

"Monty, I'm a bit anxious about the set-up of this bike, if I'm being honest," said Dave. "I know Henk's mechanics are the best in the business, but not being hands-on myself from the outset on this rig is doing my head in. It was good to see the McMullan brothers on ours, earlier. But we'd have taken her around quicker than they did, I know we would have. As for this one, Monty, you'll have to push it tighter, yeah? I can see light coming in."

Monty brought together the fairing, as instructed. "That's all we've got, Dave. Any more and it'll crack under the pressure."

"Looks good, mate. How are we doing for time, by the way?"

"We've got about thirty minutes before Guy's due back in."

"Great, because fine-tuning this machine is turning out to be a bigger job than I first imagined. Still, by giving it some proper attention now, it can only help us when we're out on track, am I right?"

"You're right, Dave. But just mind you don't give it too much strain. We don't want anything to rupture at this stage. Can I do anything more to help?"

"No, I've got this on my end," replied Dave, eyes narrowed in concentration. "You just keep doing what you're doing, holding that bit together while I tighten the bolts down, yeah? And this is what teamwork is all about, Monty, me old son!"

"But I'm doing most of the work?"

After a bit more diligence, Dave was satisfied, leaning back and wiping the wrench in his hand with a cloth rag. "There," he said. "I think that's done it, Monty. What do you reckon?"

Monty nodded in agreement, collecting his own tools together. "Looks good to me as well," he confirmed.

"Oh, I saw my mum earlier," mentioned Dave. "Stan's staying in hospital overnight, she tells me. She's brought Frank back, though, but he's having a powernap out in the car. Or at least he was. As for why he's napping in the car, specifically, guess who else couldn't get back into the carpark?"

"*Ha-ha!* They met up with Adrian?"

"The lad was just doing his job, Monty," Dave admonished him with a laugh, wagging his finger. "Dunno why Frank stayed with the car, though. Stubbornness, maybe."

"Dave, I know it turned out to only be a kidney stone," Monty came back, turning serious. "But it put the fear of God into me, I have to confess, when it seemed…"

"I agree about Stan," Dave answered, picking up Monty's trail of thought. "We've only known Frank and Stan for a couple of years but they're like…"

"Fathers?" suggested Monty, finishing Dave's sentence like an old married couple.

"Fathers," replied Dave. "Yes, that's it."

"No, wait," said Monty, reconsidering. How about older brothers? Or what about uncles? Uncles might be better?"

"I think—" Dave started to say, but Monty wasn't finished yet.

"Maybe not uncles. Maybe Scoutmasters? Or carnival barkers? No, I've got it! Spaceship captains! I think that's the one. I think it's spaceship captains." Monty looked to Dave for approval, but was met instead by the bemused sort of expression one might give someone who is…

"Are you high?" asked Dave.

"Just high on life, Dave."

"Oh…kay…?"

"Just trying to provide you with some alternatives to consider, Dave."

"Oh…kay…?"

"Just didn't want to be too hasty, Dave."

I appreciate that Monty. Thank you," Dave told him, hoping to put the subject to bed.

"Not a problem," Monty assured him.

The two of them walked around the pit area, like a commander and his first lieutenant surveying the field before battle. The temporary garages were situated in an L-shaped formation and, sadly, the majority were now occupied — meaning their machinery had returned to home base, likely due to either mechanical failure or driver error. Those involved who didn't make it to the final hurdle were still in attendance, however, with most offering encouragement and assistance to those teams still in the race. It was difficult to not be impressed by the camaraderie on hand, as members of each team in turn offered Dave and Monty their best wishes as the pair composed themselves during their gentle stroll.

They appeared calm enough on the outside, Monty and Dave, but the magnitude of their task ahead was not lost on them. Their future, and that of the farm, would be formed on the next two hours. Dave didn't want to admit it to himself, but felt the nerves more for this race than he did when competing in his winning Isle of Man TT race. This wasn't about personal glory; this was about something bigger. Dave had seen first-hand what the TT farm meant to people. He'd seen Tyler, for instance, a young boy, timid and without much self-confidence, develop into a self-assured, inquisitive child in only a short time, free to express himself in a safe environment. And he'd seen Becks, Tyler's mum, crippled with anxiety, constantly looking over her shoulder, and previously just worried about simply existing and keeping her son safe from harm. Now, she had a future, as well as the chance to learn new skills and make new friends. They both had this, mother and son, thanks to the charity. They both had this thanks to the TT Farm. And although Becks and her son were the first residents, the hope was that there would be many, many more. The thought of the TT Farm being demolished — and by Rodney Franks, no less, to add insult to injury — to make way for a bloody hotel was sickening. And speaking of Franks...

"What a stroke of luck!" Dave exclaimed, but then quickly shushed himself as well as Monty with his finger to his lips. He pointed to the rear of a van near to one of the garages, parked up with its rear doors wide open. He took a step closer, to make certain that what he thought he saw was in fact what he saw, and then he looked to Monty, mischief dancing in his eyes. "Rodney Franks," he whispered. "Must be tired, poor chap, because he's having a little bit of a lie-down."

The outline of a slumbering figure lay stretched out the length of an inflatable mattress in the back of the van, and it certainly couldn't have been the opulent accommodations to which Franks would have been accustomed.

"Should I go and get the septic tank from that port-a-loo we just walked past?" asked Monty. He was being quite serious.

"I like your way of thinking, Monty. I'm tempted to just jump in and start throwing punches, myself," Dave told him. "Hang on. I've just caught sight of DCI Adrian. And that gives me an idea, I think. Hold on a minute," said Dave, holding out a cautionary arm. "Right. He's gone the other way. We're okay. Okay, so here's my idea. Give me your wallet, Monty."

"What...? I don't think I like this idea, Dave," protested Monty. "Why do I have to give you my wallet??"

"No, don't worry, it'll be brilliant, you'll see. Give it here. Quickly," said Dave. "Trust me on this."

"I really don't think I like this idea of yours, Dave," Monty reiterated. "Why does it have to be *my* wallet? Unlike yours, mine still has money in it!"

"Shh, not so loud!" Dave warned him. "And, yes, that's why yours is perfect! Now, c'mon, hand it over before Adrian comes back and it's too late! You don't want to ruin it, do you? Don't ruin it!"

"I don't even know what *it* is. But all's I know is that I don't like it," Monty moaned, reluctantly handing over his oil-stained Daffy Duck-themed wallet. "I want that back," he insisted. "Me and Daffy go back a long way."

"You'll get it back! Don't worry!" Dave said again. And of course the more Dave said *don't worry*, the more Monty worried.

Dave took Monty's wallet, together with his own, once he'd made sure the coast was clear, he moved closer to the van where Sleeping Beauty was, fortunately, still snoring away. Dave carefully placed the two wallets on the airbed, tucked up beside Rodney, and stepped back, admiring his handiwork.

"What the hell are you doing?" asked Monty, incredulous, barely able to speak at his supposed friend's inexplicable actions.

"Shh, you'll see! Come on!" Dave told him, taking Monty by the hand and skipping away with him like a happy primary school girl.

"I don't like this game!" Monty cried, but before he could say anything else, they happened upon Adrian.

Dave tapped Adrian on the shoulder from behind. "Excuse me, Adrian?" he said. "I need your help."

Adrian turned around smartly, clicking his heels together and pleased to be called upon. "Yes, sir? Atcher service," he said. But, then, seeing who it was, "Oh it's you. Look here, that money is already earmarked for weaponry, so I shan't be giving it back."

"No, it's not that at all!" Dave told him, employing a panicked expression over his face. "We need your help! Adrian, some vile, drunken fool, some pure dastardly rogue of ill intent, has been running around the grounds! I didn't see his face, but he ran past our garage when we had our heads buried in our bike, and now we can't find our wallets! Who knows what other sorts of mischief he's perpetrated...?"

There was more bollocks he could come up with, but before Dave had even reached the climax of his delivery, Adrian had already adopted a superhero-style action pose. "Mischief-making, you say?" Not on my watch, sir! No, sir, not on my watch! Now did you by chance see which way this scoundrel was heading??"

Dave shrugged his shoulders, feigning ignorance, cueing Monty and giving him the opportunity to contribute in on the act. Monty was none too pleased at this, but had no choice but to improvise accordingly. "I think he jumped into one of the vans, Adrian. Up there, in fact. Just there," he said, pointing, of course, to the van in which Rodney Franks currently slept.

Adrian nodded in grave acknowledgement. He produced a walkie-talkie from his combat belt, holding it tenderly, like a newborn child. It was clear he'd been desperate to make use of it in a live situation.

With Adrian now engaged, Dave stole a glance at Monty, shooting him a smile, as if all was going accordingly to plan. Monty, quite understandably, remained unconvinced.

Adrian depressed a button on the side of his walkie-talkie with his thumb and cleared his throat. "Percy? We've got a Code Seven," he spoke into the device. "I repeat, we've got a Code Seven, and I require backup." Satisfied with his performance, he did add one thing... "This is not a drill."

And then Adrian turned his attention to Dave and Monty. "You gentlemen did the right thing bringing this to my attention, he told them.

With Percy soon on scene, Adrian and assistant quickly set off to apprehend the identified criminal troublemaker. Dave and Monty didn't hang around for too long, as they had a race, after all, leaving things in Adrian's capable hands.

"Nice work, Dave," said Monty with a slap on Dave's back as they made haste back to their garage. "Bloody good job."

"Thanks!" replied a well-chuffed Dave.

"Just one thing?" Monty offered.

"Yes?"

"When you generate another cunning plan in your brain...?"

"Yes?" asked Dave.

"Can it please not involve taking my wallet from me?"

*Chapter*
# TWENTY-TWO

Dave revved the tuned 600cc engine, keeping one eye on the return lane for Guy to come back in, and one eye on the marshal. He flicked the throttle with rhythmic precision, eager to get the oil flowing and the engine to temperature. Every fibre of his body was telling him to go to bed, as opposed to racing for the next two hours. Instead, he looked back to Monty — who returned an enthusiastic thumb extension — before looking back to the track ahead. Dave rotated his neck, giving his eyes time to adjust to the darkness on tarmac before him, though fortunately the upgraded headlight system he'd installed worked wonders.

Out on the track, Guy hurtled around the final corner before braking for the pit lane speed restriction. Dave took a deep breath as the marshal prepared to slap him on the shoulder. Dave pulled in the clutch and knocked the bike into first gear, ready for the signal, and, with clutch now held in, gave a further flick of the throttle. Guy had done all he could for the team, and his efforts were magnificent. And, presently, with that slap finally coming down on Dave's back, Dave released the sidecar's clutch and he and Monty were off like a shot. He knew it was now down to them.

He darted a quick glance back to Napier and Thomas, who sat waiting for their own slap on the shoulder, and with a fluid motion Dave slammed down the visor on his helmet and returned his attention to the course ahead, opening the throttle and sending Henk's loaned machine hurtling towards the first bend.

The speed differential between a race-tuned sidecar and a virtually standard van was staggering, and the turn was upon him all too soon. With the tyres still relatively cold, the sidecar snaked under braking, and for a heart-stopping moment Dave winced, fearing he was going into the tyre wall before he'd even moved out of first gear. But he wrestled the bike into submission, navigated the turn, unclenched his bum cheeks, and got his head down for the first straight.

Dave hadn't looked at the scoreboard before he and Monty had set off, and insisted nobody tell him where they currently stood on the leaderboard. He knew he needed to give it everything he had for the next two hours, and having that lap tally on his mind would only have distracted him from the task at hand. Whilst he didn't know it, however, Dave would surely have taken comfort from the fact that Team Frank & Stan were presently five laps to the good — thanks to Guy Martin's enduring efforts — over Rodney Franks' outfit of Napier & Thomas. Coming out ahead of Franks was of course their primary concern.

The machinery under Dave and Monty's arses was the equal if not the better to Napier & Thomas' machine. Also, while Dave and Monty may not have had quite as much racing experience as Napier & Thomas, they more than made up for it in passion. The difference between them was that Napier and Thomas were racing merely for a paycheque, and for a complete bellend to boot. Dave and Monty, on the other hand, were racing for their careers, and they were racing for their community. And the lads had spunk. Loads of it.

The gruelling challenge of racing for twenty-four hours had well and truly taken its toll, with only seven outfits remaining in the competition. Two of the seven had sidecars out on the course for this last two-hour leg, and fewer rolling obstacles would make the lap times quicker for these three-wheeled rockets.

Dave had to mentally adjust to the different riding style required between small-scale circuit racing and the Isle of Man TT. For Dave, the TT would always be the ultimate test, but he had to change his mindset as the team of Napier & Thomas were masters on the smaller circuit.

Dave tucked his head down even more than he had before, and lowered his entire bodily stance to make it as streamlined as possible. While he couldn't see them, he knew that Napier and Thomas couldn't be far behind and would be stuck to them like barnacles.

The first three laps of this final segment were completed smartly and in short order. Dave's confidence, like the heat and grip on the bike's tyres, increased steadily. He was ready for this. He could do this. "We can do this thing, mate!" Dave shouted aloud, against the wind, to his partner.

"Beans on toast! Sausages!" Monty shouted back, already sorting out his victory breakfast for after.

The Team Frank & Stan crew took up position behind a wall on the start/finish line, Frank now among them. Frank, a little more refreshed after his nap in the car, looked up the line of heads peering with hope and anticipation at the headlights out on track. They all looked rather dapper, decked out as they were in their matching white polo shirts with *TT FARM* plastered over the front of them. Frank smiled. It wasn't lost on him how this racing they currently watched so keenly had brought his group of precious friends together. Moments like this would stay with him always.

"Excuse me," said Frank to a passing marshal. "Would you be kind enough to take a picture of us?" he asked, with the marshal appearing very happy to comply. "We'll get another with Dave and Monty later," he explained to the others.

Frank extended his arms, allowing Molly and Jessie to tuck inside either wing. Along with the pit crew, Stella and Lee were also present, as were Rebecca and Tyler. Guy Martin was among them, of course. And even a bleary-eyed Henk, who'd just woken up from having one too many beers over the course of the night, had joined them as well.

"Ready?" said the newly-promoted-to-team-photographer marshal, but who was then distracted from the viewfinder. "Is he with you?" the marshal asked, in reference to the madman running straight towards them, arms flailing like an over-excited cephalopod.

"Bloody wait for me!" shouted the bounding figure. "Hold on! I'm coming! I'm coming!"

"A familiar refrain," laughed Stella.

Frank raised one of his arms in a welcoming greeting as Stan joined the crease. "My old friend Stanley," Frank said fondly. "I was just thinking this photo wouldn't be complete without you."

"I wasn't going to miss an opportunity to have my picture taken, Frank, now was I?" Stan announced in reply, taking his finger and rubbing his cosmetically enhanced teeth to remove any possible imperfections in preparation for the shot.

"So how's the... you know... all that?" asked Frank, pointing vaguely in the direction of Stan's nether regions.

"I never thought I'd be sick of men prodding around down there, Frank, but I finally managed to pass the bugger on my own, no surgery required," Stan told him. "That little blighter caused me no end of worry. I thought I was dying! I thought it was the end of poor Stanley Sidcup!"

"Yes, we *know*," said Frank, though not unkindly.

"And for more good news," Stan went on. "I could swear I've just seen Rodney Franks using his cravat to wipe blood from his nose. He was surrounded by security guards, both small and large. What do reckon that's all about?"

Frank grinned. "I'm sure I don't know," he told Stan. "Just good fortune?"

"Smile, everyone!" shouted the marshal-slash-photographer once everyone was back in position.

"Kidney stones!" said Frank.

"Kidney stones!" they all repeated, each of them sporting their broadest of smiles.

## FRANK & STAN'S BUCKET LIST #3: ISLE 'LE MANS' TT

Dave was exceptionally grateful to have seen the sun finally come up over the horizon. Riding in the dark, with no streetlamps to light the course, was like driving through a warp tunnel. It was a nightmare trying to judge braking points, and you'd find yourself on top of vehicles in front of you in an instant if you weren't very careful. But, to be fair to Napier and Thomas, they were running their own race, as it was dangerous enough out there, and the two outfits had seen very little of each other this time around.

The main thing on Dave's mind at present was the petrol tank, or rather, what remained in it. The 40-litre capacity tank would be less generous than usual because of the shorter-type circuit course they were competing on as a result of the constant braking-and-accelerating, braking-and-accelerating cycle inherent to racing on this sort of track. The tactic they'd gone for was one fuel stop just after the hour mark, which would, it was hoped, see them to the conclusion of the race.

And so, with no proper conception of time, Dave was grateful to see his pit team indicating one more lap till they came in for fuel. His body felt like it was shutting down, both physically and mentally. Fortunately, at least, Henk's sidecar hadn't missed a beat.

As soon as their outfit came to a blessed halt after that one remaining lap, Monty gratefully jumped out. Neither of them were what you'd call svelte, and Monty had been performing gymnastic miracles for the whole of the preceding hour, throwing himself around to maximise the grip on the tyres. Thus, the opportunity to take a much-needed stretch during the brief reprieve the filling of the fuel tank offered was most welcome.

"How the bike doing? How's she holding up?" asked Mike the Mechanic, in between distribution of water to the lads.

"Fine," Monty gasped, coming up for air after demolishing the contents of one of the offered bottles. "Running like a dream."

Mike took Monty and Dave's helmets, in order to perform a quick change-over of the visors. As the previous hour had been raced mostly early in the morning and still in darkness, the visors were relatively free from splodged flying critters. Still, there was nothing wrong with having clean, fresh windscreens. He called over to Dave and Monty as he did this. "So do you want to know where you are?" he asked them, conscious of their previous request to remain uninformed.

"We're here? With you?" Monty said, hazarding a guess.

"In the race, you silly sod!" Mike returned, with a laugh.

"Oh, right. Of course," Monty replied. He rubbed his eyes, trying to change his brain over, making the transition, at least for the benefit of the few remaining minutes of the pit stop, from race mode to normal-thinking mode.

Dave arched his neck in Monty's direction and shrugged his shoulders. It was like they were being asked if they wanted to know the sex of their new baby. "Your call, Monty."

"Right, then," decided Monty for the both of them. "Tell us."

"You're six laps ahead!" Mike declared. "They've already been in for their own fuel stop, Napier and Thomas, so you'll maybe drop half a lap." He handed them back their helmets. "Here you go. All sorted," he said. "And thirty seconds till the tank's full," he said, indicating when they'd be needing to resume position on the bike. Monty gave his back one more good stretch before climbing aboard again, offering a similarly re-mounted Dave a slap on the shoulder as he did so.

Once refuelled, Dave raised a hand in salute to their faithful crew as he head out. Though he didn't need any further motivation, it nevertheless presented itself in the form of Rodney Franks' bruised noggin popping up, peering over a tyre wall at them with a recently procured black eye. It was certainly a sight that sent Dave on his travels thinking happy thoughts along the way. He offered a smart salute to Rodney, as well, as he accelerated from the pit lane and roared back out onto the track.

Dave was unsure if the knowledge of their lead was a positive one. Indeed, he now caught himself approaching turns with a degree of caution rather than attacking them aggressively as he'd done before. Yes, six laps sounded significant, but that could all change by overshooting a bend, for instance, or as a result of mechanical failure. And, in fact, for the latter, he always had his ear out for any fluctuation in the engine note. Dave knew their recent fuel stop would have had an impact, but he also knew they must be still well in the lead, at least as compared to Rodney's team.

With the increasing daylight, Dave caught a glimpse of Napier and Thomas a good way ahead on the track. With his competitive instinct kicking in, Dave's natural inclination was to open the throttle and chase them down. Fortunately, his sensible side, such as it was, won out. He knew all he had to do was just to keep them in his sights, and by doing so he and Monty would finish above them. As grand as it would have been, Dave had no interest in topping the leaderboard. His primary concern, first and foremost, was to come out ahead of Rodney Franks' team.

Along with the increasing daylight, the number of spectators also increased commensurately. There were those waking up with a tender head after an evening of camping, and also those early birds who arrived to soak up the finale of the race, with carpark gate finally reopened to that end.

Dave was able to relax and shake himself loose, and with each completed lap, he took immense enjoyment from seeing Rodney shaking furiously and gesticulating wildly at this own team each time they crossed the start line. He'd learned long ago to never count your chips whilst you were still at the table. Still, Dave felt good. He could sense that Napier & Thomas had slackened the pace for some unexplained reason, and the decrease in their lap time was apparently contributing to an increase in Rodney's blood pressure.

On every level, the event had been a roaring success. Thousands of people had turned out to support it, with people travelling huge distances to be there. The TV crew failing to appear had been a kick to the testicles, to be sure, but the framework was there to repeat the event the following year, bigger and better.

Trackside, Frank and Stan were virtually sat on top of each other, counting down the minutes until the end of the race. "Come on, Dave and Monty!" Stan screamed, as he had every time the boys had gone past. "You can do this!" Then, directed towards his best mate, "How long, Frank?" But he knew the answer already, since he was looking at the very same scoreboard.

"Fifteen minutes to go!" replied Stan, in answer to his own question, moments later. "They're five laps in front! How about this, Frank? Does it not make you feel alive??"

Frank placed his arm around Stan. "It makes me feel..." he began, but then trailed off as the very loud sound of a very perturbed Henk cut through, blotting out all else. Rodney Franks' name could be made out, interspersed between volleys of Dutch expletives, likely to do with various diseases, plagues, or other assorted unpleasant and unsanitary conditions with which Rodney was afflicted. Though not spoken in English, the intent was clear, so much so that Rebecca thought it best to discreetly cover Tyler's ears. Frank and Stan were at a loss as to the origin of Henk's ire, aside from it being directed at Rodney Franks, and accompanied by a veritable cornucopia of angry gestures directed up pit lane in Franks' general direction. But then they saw the smile on Henk's face, and realised Henk was hurling abuse at Rodney in delight.

The scoreboard clock ticked past 8:50 a.m., and the team of Napier & Thomas had made no inroads into the lead. In fact, their pace had dropped significantly. They must have known they had no chance of making up the deficit. With a little vigour on its part, it almost looked for a moment, so slackened was Napier & Thomas' pace, as if a van that'd come up behind them was about to overtake Rodney Franks' outfit.

"They're slowing down," remarked Stan. "Guys, they're slowing down." There was slight worry in Stan's voice.

"Napier and Thomas? They're slowing down even more?" asked Frank, but in the time it took him to say this, he could now see what Stan was talking about, noticing it as well. "Oh. Why are they...?"

"They're still slowing down," said Stan, this time turning to the rest of the crew. "Why's Dave slowing down?" he asked to anybody that'd listen. For the first time since daylight broke, Napier & Thomas were now putting a considerable distance between themselves and the machine of Dave & Monty.

"It's fine?" offered Frank. "There's not a chance in hell Napier and Thomas are going to catch up on those laps in, what, nine minutes? No chance," he said. And yet there was an uncertainty in his voice.

Stan rose up and slapped his hands down on the wall that'd been their resting post. "Why are they stopping??" he shouted. "Please tell me they're not stopping!"

But, sadly, Stan's visual acuity was not letting him down. And in fact the rest of the crew now adopted his meerkat-like posture, looking at each other in confusion and alarm.

Dave and Monty's sidecar shuddered to a halt on the opposite side of the track to pit lane.

"Help them!" screamed Stan. "Somebody help them!"

"They must have run out of fuel?" Mike the Mechanic wondered aloud.

"Well get them some!" a hyperventilating Stan demanded hysterically, and not understanding why no one in the crew was taking action. He looked about desperately for a petrol can, but Mike placed his hand on his.

"I'm sorry, Stan," he said. "I'm sorry, guys," he explained to the group at large, for those who didn't already know. "The only way we can refuel is in the pits. I hate to tell you this, but there's nothing we can do for them if they've no fuel left. Not with only a few minutes on the clock remaining."

"Maybe it's a loose wire or something they can fix themselves?" Frank offered up.

But that hope was dashed by the sight of Dave dismounting. He removed his helmet and proceeded to beat the machine with his fist before collapsing on his knees.

"I don't think Dave's confident of getting her going again," observed Mike unhappily.

Frank, Stan and the others were distraught. The lead was four laps, but with Dave and Monty now out of the game, Napier and Thomas could easily regain the lead over them. In fact, in the remaining time, all they needed to do was take it easy and bring her home and their comeback was assured. And this would soon become immediately apparent to them, since they were sure to spot Team Frank & Stan's early retirement in the race as they'd ride past Dave and Monty sobbing on the grass on the next go-round.

"Low-hanging scrotum!" shouted Henk, as Rodney Franks came dancing down pit lane, taking his own delighted turn shouting obscenities at Henk this time.

Mike the Mechanic, while no longer being able to assist on the track, did a magnificent job of intercepting Franks, containing him like an oil spill, and diverting him back to his own camp in a precision armlock before Henk could make Rodney's facial injuries that much more extensive.

Each subsequent completed lap by the team of Napier & Thomas became more agonising than the last for Team Frank & Stan, as it progressively ate into Dave and Monty's lead over them. And the clock, it would seem, would not do Team Frank & Stan any favours as it appeared to be slowing down to a veritable snail's pace the closer the race got to its conclusion.

Meanwhile, from his own vantage point, Rodney Franks continued screaming at Napier and Thomas every time they went past, to an extent that those spectators nearest the madman moved away. Whether he was screaming encouragement or screaming at them for not moving faster was anyone's guess, at this point. Likely a mixture of both.

Napier and Thomas were half a lap away from drawing level with Dave and Monty's completed lap tally, leaving them approximately three minutes to easily complete an additional lap or two that would secure victory, at least over Team Frank & Stan. Dave and Monty had retreated to the rear of the run-off area beside the track, and they could only watch on helplessly as all theirs and Guy's hard work was being undone. However…

With one final corner before taking the lead over Team Frank & Stan, Rodney Franks' sidecar slowed considerably, and then failed to negotiate the bend. It came to a surprisingly gentle halt, kissing the tyre wall.

"What's going on? What happened?" asked Frank. "Is that the end of the race?"

## FRANK & STAN'S BUCKET LIST #3: ISLE 'LE MANS' TT

Stan ran back to catch a view of the nearest scoreboard. "Nope, they've got more than enough time to complete another lap, Frank!" Stan called out.

And yet Napier and Thomas were now out of their machine. And not only that, but they'd made their way back down the track on foot and were presently offering Dave and Monty the most cordial of handshakes.

"We've finished ahead of them!" screamed Frank. "Stan, we've finished ahead of them! They've only gone and done it! Our team have only gone and bloody done it!" he shouted, before a flurry of arms enveloped him.

Henk disappeared at pace. It was fairly evident where he might be headed.

With a final check of his wristwatch, the chief marshal held aloft an air horn, giving it a generous burst, which prompted a modest though still-appreciated firework display, signalling the official conclusion of the inaugural Isle Le Mans TT.

Dave Quirk, Shaun 'Monty' Montgomery, and Guy Martin had only gone and bloody done it. They'd beaten Rodney Franks.

## *Chapter* TWENTY-THREE

"Chuck me a beer, will you Stan?" asked Frank, using his toe to push the swing once again.

Stan reached back into the portable insulated cooler box and tossed Frank a can of lager as requested, then got up and threw another log onto the firepit before them. Stan sat back down and they rocked gently back and forth, the both of them, in the wooden swing seat set up in front of the fire a safe distance away, staring contentedly at the fire, and out over the evening's moonlit field beyond.

"Imagine, Stan. All of this could have been lost to Rodney's hotel. It doesn't bear thinking about." He looked over his shoulder to the farmhouse. He laughed at the mock-up estate agent sign that Dave had painted, with proud words written on it in huge lettering, a statement to anybody driving past unsure of the intentions for this magnificent building:

### SOLD to the TT Farm

Frank sipped his beer, staring into the dancing flames. "I thought I'd lost you yesterday, Stan," he said quietly. "I know it didn't turn out to be that serious—"

"It bloody was!" Stan insisted. "I thought I was dying! I didn't know what was going on, all I knew was that my insides were all wrong!"

"Ah. That would explain the sex-change operation you nearly had," Frank teased him.

"The what, now?" asked Stan, his face going extra pale in the moonlight.

"Your insides being all wrong. See, originally we thought... or, rather, I thought... Right, so there was a mix-up at the hospital and... Well, nevermind. I'll tell you about it another time." Frank slapped his old friend on the leg. "Don't you worry about it for now," he assured him.

"Actually I think I'll just continue worrying about it, thank-you-very-much," Stan replied, casting a worried glance down to his trouser area. "That sounds like something I really ought to be worrying about!"

Frank laughed. "It was all a silly misunderstanding," he told him. "No harm done in the end."

"It's the end I'm particularly worried about!" protested Stan. "I'd hate to see it fashioned into a—"

"Dr Slughorn turned out to be a fine fellow," Frank interrupted, quickly changing the subject away from Stan's bits.

"He had cold hands," Stan considered thoughtfully. "But, yeah, nice fellow. I quite liked him. Of course, I tend to fall in love with anybody who's kind enough to handle my—"

"Can we please stop talking about your *tackle!*" said Frank, taking objection to the current line of discussion.

"You brought it up!" Stan reminded him, returning Frank's playful, affectionate slap on the knee.

They settled back into the wooden bench, the two of them, enjoying the warmth of the fire, rocking gently, and reflecting.

Eventually, it was Stan who broke the comfortable silence...

"You were just worried that I'd be shuffling off this mortal coil before you, and you'd have to arrange my funeral and look after Stella all on your own."

Frank laughed, loudly. Perhaps too loudly for Stan's liking.

"Hold on, it wasn't meant to be *that* funny!"

"Not the bit about you dying, you old drama queen—"

"Dr Slughorn told me it's one of the most painful pains you can have! Right up there with childbirth and gout! Only worse than those, I'm sure!"

"—But the part about looking after Stella. That's Lee's job now!" Frank said, laughing. "Blimey, Stan, what a difference a couple of years makes."

"No time to rest on our laurels now, Frank," Stan answered him, back to business. "We've got to get this place up and running, we've got the TT which will be here before you know, a wedding to prepare for, and we'll need to start thinking about next year's Isle Le Mans TT."

"Stan, I was thinking of doing something, but wouldn't mind running it past you in the mean—" Frank began to say, but he didn't have the opportunity to complete his sentence as there was an interruption. A very lovely interruption.

"Here you are!" said Jessie in a lilting, sing-songy voice. "Room for one more?" she asked.

"Always room for you, Jessie!" said Frank and Stan in perfect unison, both leaning in and placing a kiss on either cheek as she nestled in between them like a rose among thorns.

"Where are the others?" asked Stan, but he was soon to get his answer as...

The idyllic quiet of the Isle of Man countryside was shattered with the chanting of, *"Let's all do the Conga!"* and the arrival of the rest of the gang coming out to join them from the farmhouse. They made their way across the courtyard of the Isle of Man TT Farm in lively, celebratory form, all dancing in line in a roundabout, circuitous route — much like the race that'd finished up earlier that morning.

"I don't know any of that lot are still going," said Frank. "We snoozed the day away, of course, but I'm not sure Dave and Monty got any sleep at all over the course of the race, nor throughout the day today."

"They're fuelled by alcohol today," Stan observed, waving Dave and Monty over.

Dave broke the conga line, but only long enough to offer up a surprise...

"I know it's only November, and so maybe a bit early for this, but, with this place officially becoming ours an everything, we wanted to make it feel a little more homey. We've been at it all day!" he told them, grinning inanely. "Mum knows what I'm talking about!"

"We've not gotten any sleep at all!" Monty called over, with his erratic eye now even more erratic than usual. It did that when he was tired or drunk, so with the present combination of the two factors joined together, the wonky eye was currently spinning like the reels on a slot machine.

"Jessie, what are they on about...?" asked Frank, but Jessie only told him, with a wink, that he'd soon see.

Dave returned to the task at hand, pulling out an electrical extension cord and shouting for Frank and Stan to come see. And so they did, standing at the edge of the courtyard, waiting to see what Dave and the rest had conjured up. Frank stood with Stan on one side of him and Jessie on the other, an arm around Stan's shoulder and the other around Jessie's waist.

The entire crew who'd made it happen were at hand, all stood waiting now on Dave's next move.

"We've been working on this most of the day," Dave announced.

"Yes, yes, just get on with it!" said Stan, squirming like he was in need of a wee.

"Patience!" Dave called out with a laugh. "It needs a proper introduction!"

Stan whimpered, but protested no more.

"Right," Dave continued. "So myself, Monty, Guy, and Tyler have been toiling away at this all day while you two were catching up on your sleep. Tyler? Where are you, Tyler?" he called out, inviting him forward. "Ah! There you are. Tyler, you can have the honours if you'd like?"

Tyler looked to his mum, received an approving nod, and placed his hand on the switch. "Ready, Big Dave?" he asked, looking back to Dave for the signal.

"Ready!" shouted Dave.

## FRANK & STAN'S BUCKET LIST #3: ISLE 'LE MANS' TT

With the flick of a switch, the courtyard lit up like Santa's Grotto. And not just the courtyard. Multicoloured bulbs lit up the entire roofline of the farmhouse, surrounded the windows, and even continuing down to the tree next to the barn and lighting it up in addition.

"Good lad! Now the other!" Dave instructed the wee one.

With the flick of a second switch, the tractor Dave, Monty, and Guy so lovingly refurbished, now parked near to the house for the occasion and strewn about with flashing Christmas lights, burst into brilliant illumination as well.

"Bloody hell!" shouted Frank, with eyes the size of two Scotch eggs. "That looks fantastic!"

"We should phone the airport and warn them. Otherwise, we'll have aircraft landing with all these lights!" joked Stan.

Frank looked on contentedly as the festivities recommenced, watching those he cared most about enjoying themselves. Dave had produced a CD player and put on some music with a proper beat, and it was a joy to watch people dancing around the courtyard of a farm that was weeks away from being demolished. Even Stella was getting in on the act, cutting her finest moves to the music.

"She looks quite happy," remarked Stan, to which Frank couldn't disagree. "Here, Dave. Come over here a moment, will you?" Stan called out.

Dave arrived with a waltzing series of steps, producing a most splendid bow at the conclusion. "You rang?"

Stan looked to Frank, then back up to Dave. "So we've been speaking earlier, Dave, Frank and myself. We're going to make up the shortfall. You know, from what the charity missed out on with the TV company not turning up."

"No need," Dave replied immediately. "Guy!" he shouted. "Oi! Guy! Come over here if you don't mind?"

Guy was a smiler by nature, but even he'd surpassed himself the last twenty-hours. His teeth were in danger of drying out, he'd grinned that much.

"Now then. Right," he said, popping open the beer in his hand. "What a day. I'm so glad I bumped into you couple of lunatics!" he said. "Proper, proper great couple of days."

"You're coming back next year?" asked Frank.

"Just try and stop me, boss," Guy assured him.

"It's been wonderful to have you, Guy," Frank told him. "I mean that sincerely. Without your help, this wouldn't have happened. You're always welcome here, Guy. You're part of Team Frank-and-Stan now. You're one of *us*!"

"I'm welling up here," said Guy, dabbing at his eyes in so theatrical a manner it made Stan proud. "You're a singular bunch of people, you lot. Mad as a box of frogs, mind you. But a right class act, for certain."

"About the shortfall?" Dave reminded them. "Right. So Guy's donated his van."

"What do you mean?" asked Stan.

"Yes, how do you mean?" Frank echoed.

"Just that," explained Dave. "The beauty he used in that TV show, his tricked-out Ford Transit van, the one he just so happened to bring with him over here, he's donated it to the charity. Stella's already got it listed on eBay and we've exceeded what we need to make up the shortfall, and the way it's going it looks like there's going to be loads left over to put towards the building work as well!"

A plume of smoke arrived three seconds before Stella, who looked particularly pleased with herself. "I've just been checking my phone and the auction's flying," she informed them, taking a long, solid draw off her ciggie, sucking on it so hard it made Guy wince. "Guy," she said, turning to him. "For someone so famous, you're actually all right. And I think you should know."

"What is it you think I should know?" Guy innocently asked.

"Well I ain't done telling you yet, am I??" Stella scolded him.

"Sorry," Guy told her. "Continue?"

I've been thinking about this, and now we've become friends, I'm thinking of renaming my dildo."

"Your dildo?" asked a confused Guy.

"Yes, my dildo," explained Stella. "Currently named Guy Martin."

"I see," replied a nonplussed Guy.

"It's all about respect," Stella carried on. "So, from now on, Brad Pitt is going to be joined in the bedside drawer by Benedict Cumberbatch. I quite like the new Holmes."

"Oi!" Jessie objected. "Benedict Cumberbatch's the name of mine, you can't use that!"

"I think I'm going to be sick in my mouth, Mum," Dave told her. "Please tell me you're joking?" he asked desperately.

"Of *course* I'm joking," Jessie told her son. "Mine is called *Martin Freeman*," she offered with a playful wink.

"And on that note, I should tell you I've thrown you into the auction as well," Stella informed Guy. "The winner doesn't just get the van, but they get *you* for a day also. It should go without saying that they can do whatever they want with you."

"They can?" asked an increasingly alarmed Guy Martin.

"Yes," Stella said, as if this should have been painfully obvious. "I've had a few questions from those bidding in that regard, and so naturally I said you were willing to do anything."

"Naturally?" repeated an increasingly apprehensive Guy Martin.

"Naturally," confirmed a completely unconcerned Stella.

Guy's ready smile evaded him for a moment. "I think we may need to review that one, Stella...?" said an increasingly concerned, actually, Guy Martin.

Stella gripped Guy's head, thrusting it into her heaving cleavage. "Don't you worry, Guy. I'm coming with you on the day, and I'll look after you," she explained. "You know. To supervise, and such," she told him, rubbing the back of his neck soothingly. Well, it was soothing to Stella. It likely would have been no comfort to Guy, even if he could hear her. Which he presently couldn't. Because his head was currently buried in her tits.

"Do we know who actually won the race today?" enquired Frank of anyone. "It's really terrible of me, I suppose, but I don't even know. I've been so caught up in our own celebrations..."

"The BBC's team won," Monty answered him. "And it was great to have ol' Dod Spence in attendance to hand over the trophy named after him. He was honestly happy to be involved. I was speaking to him afterwards and that bloke is a true gent of the highest order. He definitely epitomises what the TT is all about, and that's for certain."

"The BBC had a fantastic team, no doubt about that," remarked Guy, coming up for air. He ran his hands through his hair, casually trying to sort himself out, as if he didn't just have his entire head buried in Stella's boom. Even though he did.

"Dave, did you tell them about Napier and Thomas?" Monty added.

"No, I completely forgot!" he said, snapping his fingers. "Right, so we just assumed their early retirement was due to fuel, like us, yeah? Only it wasn't."

"It wasn't?" Stan asked.

"*Ohhhh, noooo,*" Dave went on. "Get this. *They did it on purpose.* And Rodney Franks was going absolutely mental about it, I heard!"

"But why would they do it on purpose?" asked Frank.

Dave rubbed his hands gleefully at the thought of Rodney Franks' vexation. "Okay. So it turns out Napier and Thomas aren't the complete arseholes we thought they were. They'd gotten wind of the bet, see? And they knew that Rodney would take the TT Farm away from us if they won. Apparently, from what I'm told, Napier had problems earlier in his life, and it was a similar charity that got him through a truly difficult time in his youth. So. When they knew they were going to come out ahead of us on that final lap, they *pulled over.*"

"They just...?"

"*They just bloody pulled over!*" Dave repeated. "Those gorgeous lads! They're currently out of a job, mind you. But, with their talent, those boys will find a new team in next to no time."

"Holy shit," said a gobsmacked Stan.

"Holy shit," said a gobsmacked Frank.

"Holy shit," said Rebecca, covering Tyler's ears.

"And that also explains why they didn't seem in any terrible hurry that leg of the race," Stan considered. "I wondered why they weren't going all-out on their sidecar like they should've been."

"Hmm," said Frank, trying to think of a proper tribute to the pair. He rapped the top of his beer can with his ring. "Here's to

Napier and Thomas!" he offered with honest enthusiasm. It was all he could come up with at a moment's notice.

"Here, here!" came the enthusiastic replies.

"Look, while I've got your attention, can I just take a moment of your time?" Frank said to all assembled. "I'm not very good at speeches, so bear with me here. But I just wanted to let you know that I love you all very much, and I'll remember this weekend for the rest of my life. Stan really gave us quite a fright yesterday, and I know it ended up being only a kidney stone—"

"I thought for certain I was dying!" Stan clarified for the sake of those that didn't know. "It was scary!"

Frank smiled and continued. "I'm pleased Stan is feeling better, and that, in the end, he managed to pass the uninvited lodger through his todger. But it did make me realise how quickly things can change. We all know that I'm not in the best of health, but it's being with you and getting involved in all of this..." he said, indicating the farm with a wave of his hand... "That gives me a reason to keep going, and to love every bloody minute of it. For that, I wanted to thank you all for being part of my life. And seeing Stan in hospital yesterday made me realise, more than ever, that life's about living. There's no point putting things off for another day if you can do them today. And, so, on that theme..."

Frank patted Dave and Monty both on the shoulder, each in turn, and then pivoted around to face Jessie. He dropped down onto one knee, and he took her hand in his.

"Frank..." Jessie began, but then decided to let Frank finish, as it really looked like he was about to say something he was very keen on saying.

"Jessie, I've not known you for years, but you've had a wonderful impact on my life. Jessie, you've made me smile when I hadn't smiled for a long time. You made me realise life wasn't about the things you buy to fill it, it's about the people you surround yourself with. It's about being a nice person, and, Jessie, you're one of the nicest people I've ever met. Jessie? I love you. Would you do me the immense honour of being my wife?"

Jessie placed her free hand over her mouth, looking over to Dave, but he was already sobbing. "Oh, bollocks, there goes my bottom lip, Mum," said Dave. "It's gone wobbling on me and I can't stop it!"

"Don't even try," Monty told him. "It can't be done!" he said, his own bottom lip gone wibbly-wobbly. "Just go with it, Dave! Just go with!" he blubbered.

Jessie looked directly into Frank's waiting eyes. "Frank," she said, her voice breaking. "Frank, it would be my distinct pleasure to gratefully become your wife."

"That's my dad!" Molly announced proudly, handing tissues to Dave and Monty, and keeping one for herself as she needed one as well. "And that's his new wife!"

"Not yet," said a beaming Jessie, squeezing Frank's hand. "But soon enough."

"We should have a joint wedding," suggested Stella, taking a swig from her flask she had produced from parts unknown upon her person.

"No drugs!" Frank cautioned her, but then realised what she was on about. "Oh, you meant... of course... sorry. That's actually a wonderful idea, Stella."

"Sure and it is," Lee agreed. "Assuming you'll have us, Frank, of course. We wouldn't want to steal your thunder!"

"Oh!" cried Monty. "Oh, I've got it!" he announced through the happy tears.

"You've got what?" asked Dave, through his own waterworks.

"An idea!" said Monty. "Listen to this!"

"We're listening," said Stan. Frank might have said something, but his lips were busy at the moment.

"Okay. If Jessie is getting married to you," said Monty, pointing to Frank. "Then you pretty much come as a pair, right? Right. So. Here's my idea. We'll have to call Jessie, then..."

Monty trailed off, keeping them all in suspense. Well, keeping himself in suspense, mostly. Still...

"Wait for it..." he said, teasing the moment out.

"We're waiting," said Frank, snogging now on hold.

"We're waiting," said Jessie, snogging also on hold.

"We'll have to call Jessie... we'll have to call her..."
Stan shifted from one foot to the other.
"We'll have to call her the Bride of Frank-and-Stan! Do you get it? Everyone? Do you...?"
"We get it, Monty," Dave answered him, applauding his friend's big moment. "That's pretty good, me old son. It really is."
"It is?" asked Becks, before quickly correcting herself. "I mean, yes, yes it is!"
"Truly it is," said Lee, encouragingly.
Stella just shrugged and took another slug of liquor from her flask.
Molly was still busy applying a tissue to her eyes.
"I don't get it," said Tyler.
"It must be some kind of inside joke," Guy Martin said, kneeling down to whisper to the wee one. "I don't get it either."
Monty accepted the praise, soaking it up. It was a long time coming, he felt. Long overdue, in fact. "Was it as good as the name *Isle Le Mans TT*, Dave?" he asked. "Only that should have been mine. You know that, right? I should've gotten the credit for that. But I'm prepared to let that one go if this one's just as good?"
Dave patted Monty's back, then pulled him in for a hug. "Sure, Monty," he told him. "This is totally better than *Isle Le Mans TT*," he said. But at the same time he said this, he was also shaking his head from side to side. And it became clear why he'd pulled Monty in for a hug. It was so he could mouth the words *'Nowhere near as good'* over Monty's head, so that anyone in range could see. And which was just what he did.
Frank raised a beer aloft in the air, and cleared his throat. "Here's to Team Frank-and-Stan! I love each and every one of you!"

# The End

## J C Williams
Author

authorjcwilliams@gmail.com
@jcwilliamsbooks
@jcwilliamsauthor

If you've enjoyed this volume, have a gander at the other books in the Frank 'n' Stan series! All available on amazon.com in both print and Kindle editions.

You may also enjoy the *Lonely Heart Attack Club* series, and Book One of *The Seaside Detective Agency*, also set in the lovely Isle of Man!

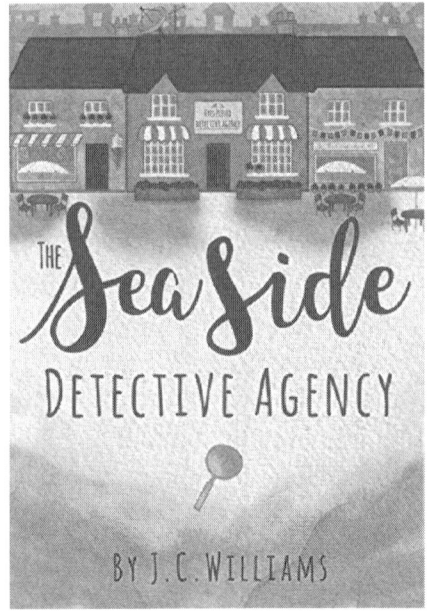

You may also wish to check out *The Flip of a Coin*,
as well as my two books aimed at a younger audience,
*Cabbage von Dagel*, and *Hamish McScabbard*!

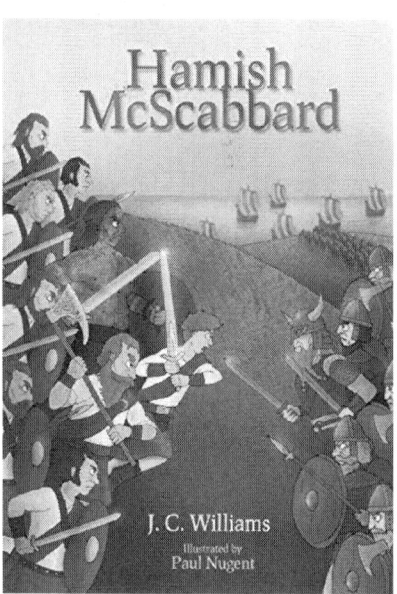

And coming soon...

Coming soon... *Luke 'n' Conor's Hundred-to-One Club!*

Also...

And for the *very* adventurous among you, you may wish to give my hardworking editor's most peculiar book a butcher's! It needs a good seeing-to! Lavishly illustrated by award-winning artist Tony Millionaire of *Maakies* and *Sock Monkey* fame.

Printed in Great Britain
by Amazon